The Lessons

NAOMI ALDERMAN

PENGUIN BOOKS

PENGUIN BOOKS

Published by the Penguin Group
Penguin Books Ltd, 80 Strand, London WC2R ORL, England
Penguin Group (USA), Inc., 375 Hudson Street, New York, New York 10014, USA
Penguin Group (Canada), 90 Eglinton Avenue East, Suite 700, Toronto, Ontario, Canada M4P 2Y3
(a division of Pearson Penguin Canada Inc.)
Penguin Ireland, 25 St Stephen's Green, Dublin 2, Ireland (a division of Penguin Books Ltd)
Penguin Group (Australia), 250 Camberwell Road, Camberwell, Victoria 3124, Australia
(a division of Pearson Australia Group Pty Ltd)
Penguin Books India Pvt Ltd, 11 Community Centre, Panchsheel Park, New Delhi – 110 017, India
Penguin Group (NZ), 67 Apollo Drive, Rosedale, Auckland 0632, New Zealand
(a division of Pearson New Zealand Ltd)
Penguin Books (South Africa) (Pty) Ltd, 24 Sturdee Avenue, Rosebank,
Johannesburg 2196, South Africa

Penguin Books Ltd, Registered Offices: 80 Strand, London WC2R ORL, England

www.penguin.com

First published by Viking 2010
Published in Penguin Books 2011

002

Copyright © N Alderman Ltd, 2010
Epigraph copyright © C. P. Cavafy, reproduced by permission of the Estate of C. P. Cavafy
c/o Rogers, Coleridge and White Ltd, 20 Powis Mews, London W11 1JN

The moral right of the author has been asserted

Printed in Great Britain by Clays Ltd, St Ives plc

A CIP catalogue record for this book is available from the British Library

ISBN: 978-0-141-02596-4

www.greenpenguin.co.uk

MIX
Paper from
responsible sources
FSC
www.fsc.org
FSC™ C018179

Penguin Books is committed to a sustainable
future for our business, our readers and our planet.
This book is made from Forest Stewardship
Council™ certified paper.

ALWAYS LEARNING   **PEARSON**

For my grandmother Lily

Like the beautiful bodies of those who died before they
     had aged,
sadly shut away in a sumptuous mausoleum,
roses by the head, jasmine at the feet –
so appear the longings that have passed
without being satisfied, not one of them granted
a night of sensual pleasure, or one of its radiant mornings.

'Longings' by C. P. Cavafy, translated by Edmund Keeley and
Philip Sherrard

Prologue

When I returned from San Ceterino late in the afternoon, I found that Mark and his friends had thrown half the food in our kitchen into the swimming pool. Through the clear water I could see a panettone dissolving into a shimmer of red and green crystallized fruit, while the poolside tiles were smeared with yolks and broken shell fragments. A sodden pizza lolled lazily on the bottom of the pool, flapping at one edge like a mottled tongue. Jars of artichokes and peppers had spilled an oil slick across the surface of the water. Ripe tomatoes and peaches, two bunches of grapes, a selection of wax-paper-wrapped cheeses and cartons of milk were strewn across the underwater tiles, still intact. A poached salmon had broken into fragments, chunks of it floating by the pool filter. And among the food, various other forms of debris: a plastic garden chair, cigarette ends, a soggy paperback still barely afloat.

A quiche was ground to eggy mush on the tiles; I nudged it with the toe of my plimsoll. I looked around. No one in sight. I'd only been gone since 10 a.m. Mark must have called his friends almost as soon as I left. Faint strains of television chatter drew my attention to the converted stable block behind me. Yes. Deal with the kids first, then find Mark. I walked down the gravel path towards the stable block's lounge. The television was louder here, and I could hear occasional laughter and bursts of Italian conversation.

I pushed open the door. The room was stiflingly hot. Clothing and half-empty bags of snacks were strewn over the floor. A CD had apparently been used as an ashtray. Three nearly naked brown bodies were draped over the sofas – Stephano and Bruno were wearing only shorts, feet dangling over the arms of one sofa. Stephano's sister Magdalena was lying on her back on the other, wearing a pair of jeans and an orange bikini top, a carton of popcorn balanced on her stomach. Three pairs of eyes flicked up at me, then back to the

I

television screen. Wile E. Coyote was attempting to heave a boulder over a cliff, little realizing that Road Runner was right behind him. Road Runner beeped. The coyote dropped the boulder on himself. The three Italians laughed and I found myself momentarily astonished that there should still be people who watched Wile E. Coyote cartoons and laughed out loud. But they're children really. Stephano's the eldest and he can't be more than eighteen.

'Right,' I said, 'party's over. Time for you to be going.'

They looked at me, then back at the screen. Wile E. Coyote had purchased a box of ACME dynamite. Any moment now it was going to explode in his face.

I picked up a handful of clothing and threw it at the boys.

'I *said*, time to be going.'

Stephano pouted at me.

'But Mark said we could stay. Watch TV.'

'I'm sure he did, but now *I'm* telling you to leave.'

Stephano looked at me sullenly, trying to gauge whether I had any power in this situation. Still, he was young and I'd been a teacher for long enough to know how to return the stare. If he'd been a year or two older, he'd have faced me down, sworn at me. But then, if he'd been a year or two older, Mark wouldn't have been interested.

Stephano stood up with an irritated shrug and pulled his T-shirt over his head. Bruno did likewise and they began to gather together their belongings. I noticed Bruno slip a couple of DVDs into his bag as he packed, but said nothing. Magdalena couldn't find her top. I brought her an old T-shirt of mine and she made a moue but accepted the shirt. The three of them headed off down the hill.

After they'd left, I found that I was shaking. In the bathroom, I splashed some cold water on my face and stared at myself in the mirror. I looked older, tired and very white, my stubble showing darkly against my skin.

I walked around the pool to the pine summer house, always so pleasantly fresh even on the hottest days. I smelled the herbal scent of pot. The three kids had probably just smoked a joint, but judging by the state of the pool Mark had taken something a little more potent. The door of the summer house was ajar. Just inside the threshold, clothing was scattered on the rattan mats. I recognized the trousers Mark had been wearing when I'd left for work in the morning, and a T-shirt that was too small to belong to anyone other than Magdalena. The smell was more intense inside the summer house, that telltale thick musky scent. They'd had a party, then. Of course.

The main room was disordered; Mark's remaining clothes were piled in a little heap on the table, they'd thrown cigarette ends into the old music box, the floor was wet and two of the cane armchairs were on their sides. No broken glass though. That was a blessing considering the last time. I found Mark where I expected, in the little bedroom, naked on the sticky sheets. He was lying on his back. I thought he was asleep at first, but when I stepped into the room, intending to cover him with a sheet, he opened his eyes and sat up.

He was drunk of course, but of course not just drunk. His cheeks were flushed, his eyes large, his movements jerky and uncoordinated. He moved his head back and forth, trying to bring me into focus. At last, he smiled.

'Oh, it's you, James, you –' He broke off, looked around him and continued after a moment. 'You've been gone for *days*. We had to hide, in here we had to hide. There was danger outside but it's better here.'

'There's no danger. I've only been gone a few hours. Only since 10. It's 6 now.'

He smiled at me again. A stupid smile. He shook his head.

'No . . . I know. You've been gone for days. That's why we had to make preparations, you see, we had to make everything ready.'

'Ready for what?'

He shook his head and touched one finger clumsily to the side of his nose.

'Mark, what happened to the pool?'

He blinked at me.

'The pool, Mark. It's full of food.'

He looked at me, trying to keep his face solemn, but his mouth kept twitching and he broke into giggles.

'It was *soup*. We made soup! We were hungry, so I said let's make

3

the biggest soup in the world! You haven't eaten it all, have you? Have you?'

'No, I . . .' I rested my thumbs on my temples and massaged my forehead. 'I'm very tired, Mark. You should rest too. We'll talk in the morning, OK?'

He looked at me, suddenly sly.

'Are the boys here? You should send them. I want . . . I want the boys here.'

I felt a tightening around my head, as of a strap being pulled closer and closer.

'I've sent them home. Their parents would be worried otherwise. You remember what happened before, don't you? You shouldn't keep them up here so long.'

He muttered something, too low for me to catch.

I turned to leave.

'I *said*, you want me all to yourself, then!' Mark shouted after me.

I stood with my hand on the door.

'No,' I said, 'I want to call the pool man to get the mess you've made cleared up so I can get to bed before midnight. I have work in the morning.'

'You *do*,' he said. 'You *do* want me to yourself. That's all you've ever wanted. The only reason you're here is that you think one day I'll run out of other people and you'll still be here waiting.'

I felt a blush begin to rise.

'That's enough, Mark.' I sounded, even to my own ears, less certain than I had talking to Stephano.

'It's *not*,' he said. 'What do you go to that job for anyway? Just to pretend that I don't pay the rent and the bills and the housekeeper and the bloody pool man too. This is what you've always wanted, isn't it? Since Oxford all you've ever wanted . . .'

I turned my back on him and walked out of the summer house. He raised his voice as I left but I thought of other things and closed my ears to him.

He was sorry later. I'd known he would be. It's the same every time.

4

I heard him padding around the kitchen in the early hours of the morning. He'd been crying – his eyes and cheeks had that squashed, overripe look – but he doesn't cry in front of me any more. He'd showered – his hair was still damp and falling into his eyes. He blinked at me through his fringe and apologized over and over again until I could hardly bear to hear him keep talking.

I made coffee and we sat in the living room. We talked a little about the house, the trip to the mountains we'd planned but which he kept putting off. It was a peace offering. He wore me down, as he always does. My anger dissipates as soon as we begin to speak, and I remember how he used to be. He knows this.

After we'd talked for a while, he said, 'What I like about having you here, James, is that you remember me. You *know*. No one that we see here knows. To them I'm just some English bloke with too much money who drinks too much and smokes too much and takes too many drugs. But as long as you're here, as long as you remember how I used to be, I'm more than that. Do you see?'

I did see. I'd known all this for a long time. We'd talked about it before.

When the sun began to rise, we took cans of cider into the orchard, disturbing clouds of spindle-legged crane flies as we walked through the grass. There are benches placed at odd intervals – some whim of Mark's from the days he still imagined holding frequent parties here. But he never had the wood properly treated and many of them have already rotted through.

We found one which still had all its struts intact, next to a rusted oil drum in which he'd once hoped to plant creeping violets. It stood empty now, half-filled with rain water, another reminder of Mark's problem – or at least one of Mark's definitions of his problem: that his ambition has never been quite large enough to fill up his money. We sat in silence as the sun came up, taking long pulls on our drinks and listening to the cacophonous cackle of birds awaking in the trees.

Eventually Mark said, 'I want her back. I want Daisy back.'

I said, 'I know.'

He said, 'She's all I want, all the time. Even when I'm . . . all the time.'

I said, 'I know.'

He leaned closer and I put my arm around his shoulder. I kicked my legs against the oil drum. The noise of it was louder than I'd expected – a wild clanging, as though I'd struck a huge brass gong. Above us three geese honked, flying in triangular formation across the blue-white sky.

SECTION I

The Lies

I

First year, November, third week of term

For me, it began with a fall. Not, as Mark might have said, a fall from grace. Nor was it the hopeless, headlong capitulation of love. That came later. It began simply with a tumble on an icy path. I stumbled, I tottered, I teetered, I fell. There's no disgrace in falling. Everyone falls. But I have found that getting up has proved more difficult than I could have anticipated on that icy path in Oxford long ago.

I ran, in the first faint hum of early-morning light, along a quiet path by the river. I ran for pleasure. Night had licked the leaves of the overhanging willow trees with frost. The path was muddy, but the mud had frozen into crackling shards. My breath came in quick gasps, achingly cold, steam-snorting.

I ran in steady, effortless, piston rhythm. A full-body rhythm: my feet on the path, my thighs bunching and loosening, vertebrae and diaphragm, flexors and extensors, all the mechanisms of the human body running smooth and true. The blood thumped in my ears. I was cold but I did not feel it. I ducked my head under a low-hanging branch of ice-prickled hawthorn, moving without thinking. Running emptied me of all thought. This was why I ran. It was three weeks since I'd arrived in Oxford, and things weren't going to plan.

There had been a plan. At least, it seemed to me there had been. My sister Anne, an Oxford graduate, had told me what to do. She had come to our parents' house, my mother had roasted a chicken for dinner, so that she could tell me these things. I was to join societies, I was to participate in activities, I was to work extremely hard. Oh yes, Anne had said, leaning forward to wrench a leg off the chicken carcass, and I was to make friends with the right sort of people. She herself had fallen in with the Labour Club during John Major's

9

premiership, when the Conservative Party lay bloated and dully throbbing, like a dying star. Her boyfriend, Paul, a pale and blinking specimen, worked for the Labour Party. Great things were expected of him. I'd do well, Anne said, to find similarly influential friends. Our parents smiled as we talked. My father poured another half-glass of wine. Anne bit into her chicken leg down to the white bone and gelatinous gristle at the joint. I noticed that I was thinking of Anne. I quickened my running pace a little. My breath became more ragged. I rounded a bend, and thought vanished into a new vista of half-thawed ice-river.

Oxford is beautiful; its beauty is its plumage, its method of pro-creation. The beauty of the dream of Oxford, of spires and quiet learning, of the life of the mind, of effortless superiority, all these had beguiled me. Oxford was a tree decked with presents; all I had to do was reach out my hand and pluck them. I would achieve a first, I would gain a blue, I would make rich, influential, powerful friends. Oxford would paint me with a thin layer of gold.

In my first meeting with my tutors, Dr Strong and Dr Boycott, I had taken down the list of books on the smooth, white page of my notebook in clear fountain-pen strokes. The very thought of it thrilled me: an Oxford reading list in preparation for an Oxford tutorial.

One of the other men in the group – Ivar, a Norwegian – said, 'Isn't this rather a lot? For one week?'

Dr Strong and Dr Boycott exchanged a glance. The rest of the students looked down at the swirling green and gold curlicues of the carpet. We knew that Ivar had shamed us.

'We expect a lot, Mr Guntersen,' said Dr Boycott at last. 'That is why you are here.'

Dr Strong stroked his beard impassively. His legs were stretched out in front of him, feet clad only in sandals although the cold of autumn had already begun to bite.

Dr Boycott broke into a smile. 'I'm sure you'll find yourselves more than capable, with a little application. And if not –' his smile deepened – 'Oxford's not for you. And best to find that out now, eh?'

We seven Gloucester College physicists walked out of Dr Boycott's book-lined study and stood, a little dazed, in the quad. The sun was passing in and out of shadow. The creeping plants covering the walls were dying russet. We looked at each other, half-friendly, half-appraising, and, with smiles, loped towards the library. I remember this as the last moment I believed without question in my intellectual powers. My dreams were there: the influential friends, the first, the running blue. All this was within my grasp. And here I was, running. Surely all must be well?

I rounded the second sharp bend, feet digging into mud and ice to gain traction. The morning mist had not yet dissipated, and as I left the grove of overhanging trees my surroundings blurred and dissolved. I ran on, my feet dislodging small stones and pebbles, and, once or twice, almost sliding from under me. The cold became delicious, my pace was strong. I came to a forking of the ways and chose the longer path.

'Oxford is a race,' Anne had said. 'No more, no less. Remember that.' We all knew it, each of the physics men. We did not discuss our first assignment, did not sit together in the library. Later, when times became more desperate, we pulled each other by the collar over fences and hurdles, copying one another's work in a manner we would have scorned at school. But this first time, we worked as each of us was accustomed to work, each the best in his class, each entirely alone. I chose a seat sheltered on three sides by long walls of books. The sun, shining through stained glass, illuminated motes of dust and cast gules and amethyst on my squared paper. I attempted a question, expecting to find it simple. My work at school had always been simple. But this was not so easy. I made some notes. I looked around at the other students, then back down to my work. I tried again. I was uncertain. In the gallery and in the deep central book well the other students were hard at work. Soon, their industry began to seem oppressive to me. They made notes. They flicked through books. Would none of them ever take a break? Were none of them puzzled, as I was, with a hot itch of incomprehension at the base of my skull?

It was that itch, and my inability to tolerate it, which proved my eventual undoing. I was not undone on that day, or the next, or the next. But the slow increase of days pulled me downward. I have blamed the fall for what happened, but it seems to me that it had begun to happen even before. Even in that first week I began to work in my bare little college room and not in the library. Away from distraction, I said to myself. But also away from the companionship of labour. I slept a little more each day. After the second tutor group meeting, I took a nap in the middle of the day. I wondered if I was sickening for something.

I understand now that I should have drawn comfort from that second meeting. After my days of quiet intense effort, I sat somewhere around the middle of the pack. Not as good as Everard or Panapoulou, but not as lost as Kendall or Daswani.

'Yes,' said Dr Strong as he handed me back my work, 'keep at it.'

These were words of encouragement. I see that now. At the time, I tasted ashes. Like every student in Oxford, I had only ever been the best. To be average, to be 'normal', seemed beyond humiliation to me. The true star of the group was Guntersen. He alone received the plaudits of Dr Strong. He alone had solved the eleventh question. In the quad, a tall willowy woman was waiting for him. She greeted him in Spanish and he spoke to her in the same language. As they embraced I caught a hint of her perfume: cinnamon and cloves. They walked towards the lodge arm in arm, her hair dark and curly, his blond and straight.

'To the winner –' Kendall leaned in uncomfortably close. I could smell old cups of tea on his breath – 'go the spoils.'

I slept that afternoon until it was dark outside and the college bell was ringing to summon us for dinner. I looked at the next tutorial sheet on my desk, pristine and unconquered. I wondered if Guntersen was already hard at work in the library. In the corridor, I heard the sound of girls laughing and wondered, with a pang, who they were, what they were talking about. I thought of Guntersen's Spanish girl-friend, of the easy way he rested his arm around her shoulders. A run, I thought, to clear my head.

I ran then without any firm idea of destination or direction. I rounded Hertford, under the Bridge of Sighs, headed towards the University Parks. It was only after a week of exploration that I had found my favourite route. A long quiet trail through the open country to the south of Oxford. I could guarantee to be almost alone if I came out early enough in the morning. On that day, I had set out at 6.30 a.m., just before dawn. The path would not be in heavy use for two hours yet. This thought pleased me. I ran between two saplings, breaking a spider's web strung between them. A memory tickled. Wasn't there a parable of an inspirational spider, representing diligence or resilience?

I should have been more resilient, I thought. I should have been more diligent. I had worked hard, certainly, but had I worked hard enough? Guntersen had worked harder. He was probably working even now. If he wasn't in bed with that Spanish woman.

I had found myself thinking of this woman more frequently than was sensible. It was not that no other opportunities presented themselves to me. Two girls on my staircase, Judy and Hannah, had separately made drunken attempts at conversation. Judy had found me in the Gloucester College bar, spent twenty minutes telling me about her parents' divorce, then put her hand on my knee, at which point I made my excuses. Hannah I encountered in the corridor outside my room on the way to get milk from the fridge. She was pretty, in a tousled and bleary way, but stank of cider and cigarettes.

'James!' she said. 'James, James gorgeous James, Mr James Stieff.'

'Yes,' I said.

The corridor was narrow. She put her hand on my chest and pushed me back towards the wall.

'Mysterious James,' she said, 'prettiest boy on staircase eight, no doubt about it.'

She pressed her body against me. She smelled faintly of vomit.

'Lots of girls would like to get to know you, Mr James Stieff. We all talk about you because you are so very . . .' She wriggled slightly, a stale odour of sweat and smoke in her hair. 'Just so very . . .' She reached her hand down to my crotch. 'Are you stiff, Mr Stieff?'

I wasn't. Not by any means. I pushed her away from me.

'You should go to bed,' I said, and I think she said, 'With you?' but by then I was letting myself back into my room and closing the door behind me.

A few days later the Gloucester College gossip sheet, pinned up in every lavatory in the college, named me '5th hottest male fresher', said that I had indulged in a 'four-in-a-bed sex romp' with Judy, Hannah and a girl I had never met called Elaine, and that the next JCR Meeting would vote on whether I had won the crown of College Slag from someone called Mick. I pulled down the sheets whenever I saw them and did not attend the JCR Meeting.

But Guntersen's Spanish woman obsessed me. Her name, I had learned from Kendall, who made it his business to know such things, was Emmanuella. She was from Madrid, studying law at St Catherine's. How had Guntersen met her? This Kendall did not know and I dared not press him to find out.

'Foreign students,' Kendall had said, 'they stick together.'

'Rich students you mean,' said Daswani.

I did not quite know how it had come about that I spent so much time in the college bar with these two. I did not like them. I felt myself their intellectual superior; this both repelled me from them and drew me to them.

'Same thing,' said Kendall. 'Massive fees for foreign students, only the rich ones can pay them.'

Daswani nodded sagely into his beer.

Can this be it, I thought? Is this all Oxford has to offer? For all the promises of glamour and glory, is this it? Passes from drunken stale-smelling girls? To be mediocre, sitting in a damp-walled bar on a Wednesday night with other mediocrities, tracing shapes in beer with my finger on a scratched table? I could not accept it. Guntersen and his girlfriend spoke of other possibilities.

I talked to her, once. It was early in the morning, I was returning from my run as she and Guntersen were kissing at the gates to the college library. They kissed with intent, his hand sliding down her back, grasping her leg at the top of her thigh, her arms encircling his waist, reaching up under his cable-knit sweater. I stopped to stretch my calves on the low stone wall next to the library gates. They didn't notice me. As the 8 a.m. bell rang, the great curved wooden doors to the building opened from the inside. Guntersen pulled away, returned, kissed her again, his hand in her hair, and then was gone, into the library to do battle on the plains of physics.

Emmanuella noticed me then. I was bending over, stretching my hamstrings, a deeply undignified position. Her face was still pillow-creased, her hair dishevelled. I caught her eye and she smiled.

'You are in Ivar's tutor group, yes? James?'

'Yes.'

'He says you are quite good.'

It was the 'quite' that destroyed me.

'Aha?'

'Oh,' she laughed softly, reached out and touched my arm. Her fingertips were warm and brown against my goose-prickled white. 'That means he thinks you're very clever. Don't be offended. He's not . . .' She broke off and looked at me. 'You run?'

'Only for . . . yes. Yes, I run.'

'Of course. Don't race Ivar. He likes to win.'

I smiled.

'Perhaps if we raced, I would win.'

She smiled back.

'Perhaps.'

And she turned and walked towards Broad Street.

When I ran I thought of her, and of him. I thought of them entwined together, pressed up against the iron curls of the library gate. I thought of them, and of Guntersen's hard work and Kendall's tea-breath and of the work that still awaited me in my room. I thought of the Oxford life that, it seemed to me, was always happening somewhere else.

I rounded another bend, a sharp one, and began the downhill part of the run. My breath was coming in quick clear gasps, I was not yet tired. I ran along the edge of a water meadow. I thought of the work I had left to do that day. I had reached number five out of twelve on the question sheet. Tomorrow was tutorial day. I could perhaps finish another question today. I let the thought go. The birdsong was louder here. I wondered if Guntersen ever came this way, if he ever heard these birds sing. My feet hit the hard dry earth, one-two, one-two, and I thought of Guntersen and Emmanuella and wondered if they ever came here together, in the early morning, she putting her arms around his neck and he leaning her against a rough-barked tree. I closed my eyes for a moment, imagining it and, and. And this was enough.

My right foot came down not on hard earth but slid across ice. It turned right, and then round, and, with a wrenching tearing twist, further round and away. I tumbled and, as I fell, the leg twisted further, buckling under my weight, and there was a sick sensation in the joint and in my stomach and I found I was thinking of my sister Anne, again, and of her twisting the drumstick off the chicken, revealing the inner white of bone and string-like sinews and the gristle of the joint. And then there was violent, loud, aggressive pain, drowning out everything else, and then there was nothing at all.

2

First year, November, fifth week of term

When I woke, it was to pain again. And to a confusion so intense and overpowering that my senses became muddled and mingled. A dizzying panoply of vomit and earth, of the sound of jagged sinews and the taste of cold, and a sound like the iron tongue of pain on my leg. Confusion and then silence. Another burst of noise and light and stench and pain and metal. And then silence.

There was a dream, or perhaps a vision, in which a girl with long dark curly hair came to sit at my bedside. She pressed against my knee and the pain was holy and progressive. Later, there was a doctor, who grasped my heel and the back of my calf and said, 'This may hurt a little,' and the pain was not sacred but frantic bubbling agony.

I still dream of this, and sometimes in my dreams I imagine that I already knew Mark at this moment. He is there by my bed, his head tilted to one side, saying, 'Pain, James, is the answer not the question.' It's because of his Catholicism, which I took so long to understand, and his insistence that a life without pain has no meaning. I suppose in a way I wish I had known him then, and this is why he appears in my dreams. Perhaps his respect for suffering might have kept me from such self-pity.

But I had yet to meet Mark. There was no one to rescue me but my parents and they had little to say. The hospital gave me medication for the pain, a fibreglass brace for my leg, and a pair of crutches. The college moved me to a ground-floor room.

My mother said, 'Are you sure, darling? You don't want to come home?'

My father stared out of the window, on to Turl Street, where girls in long woollen scarves were loitering by lamp posts.

'Yes,' I said. 'Yes, quite sure.'

My father said, at last, 'No sense in missing more work.'

Pain was the repeated refrain of my days, punctuating them with clear and resonant chimes. I began to learn how to make it sound and how to silence it. Pain when I twist suddenly to the left, but not the right. When I descend a staircase but not when I ascend. When I roll to the right in my sleep. The doctors had given me exercises, had told me that my injury was serious but that it would improve. They had said the discomfort would decrease. But would it disappear entirely? On that, they frowned and sighed and said, 'Perhaps.' Perhaps it would always hurt? They wrung their hands before they muttered, 'Yes.'

I had missed a week by the time I was well enough to return to physics. I composed a note to Dr Boycott and, by return of pigeon post, he asked me to come to his rooms. At 4.30 he opened the door in response to my knock with every appearance of astonishment.

'Ah, Mr, er . . .?'

He looked at me hopefully, waiting for assistance.

'Stieff. James Stieff. I'm a first year.'

A pause.

'I sent you a note, Dr Boycott. You replied.'

He blinked. 'Ah, you are the student who has hurt your . . . hurt your . . .' He stared at the thick case around my knee. 'Your leg?'

He showed me into his office. It was large with a deep-piled leaf-green carpet and mahogany bookcases. He motioned me to sit in an armchair next to the fireplace. I lowered myself into it with difficulty, keeping my leg as straight as possible. I could not prevent a moment of ice-sharp pain, the separation of flesh. I gasped. Dr Boycott looked at me.

'Yes, the problem is, Dr Boycott, that I missed last week's work. And now I can't seem to –' I laughed, trying to indicate that this was a minor problem, one which must be easily rectified. 'Well, this week's work seems pretty much impossible to me.'

Dr Boycott observed me through his half-moon glasses.

'I see. It is unfortunate. Last week's work was crucial. Yes, I can't see how you can carry on without having understood that.'

He chuckled, amused by the idea of such a hare-brained plan.

'Well then,' I said with relief, 'obviously I'll be a week behind for the rest of term. You won't mind my taking my tutorials a week later?'

'Oh,' he said. 'Oh no, I'm afraid not. I work to a strict schedule. All work must be marked together. I can hardly –' he laughed again, hands clasped over his stomach, amused beyond measure – 'hardly arrange special tutorials just for you.'

'But,' I said, 'Dr Boycott, you just said yourself that I couldn't hope to understand the next worksheet without –'

There was a knock at the door.

'Come in!' called Dr Boycott.

A man entered, one of Dr Boycott's graduate students.

'Ah, Trevor, just in time. I'll make tea. Mr Stieff was just leaving, weren't you, Mr Stieff?'

'But I –'

'Very good. I'm sure you'll work it out. Yes, yes.'

And I found that I was standing at the top of the winding stair outside Dr Boycott's office, the white-panelled door with its battered brass doorknob closed firmly behind me. Gingerly, step by awkward step, I made my way down the stairs.

In the group tutorial the following morning Dr Boycott called on me again and again for answers that he must have known I could not possess.

'Mr Stieff, did you find problem eight particularly tricky?'

'Well, Dr Boycott, I . . .'

I squirmed in my seat. There was a lick of pain at my knee, a pointed tongue of it.

'Come, Mr Stieff, why not attempt it now? What about problem three? You must at least see that those two are practically identical.'

'But, Dr Boycott, I told you that –'

'It was your knee you bashed, wasn't it, Mr Stieff, and not your head?'

The other students laughed. Dr Boycott looked around contentedly, a classroom comedian satisfied with his reward. I felt the blush slowly rising up my face, creeping from the concealment of my collar to the burning-red tips of my ears.

Guntersen said, 'Actually, Dr Boycott, I used a different methodology for problem eight.'

Dr Boycott turned his attention to Guntersen, leaving me still red-faced and ashamed.

After the tutorial, two women were waiting for Guntersen in the quad: Emmanuella and someone I had not seen before – she was shortish, well proportioned, with long straight brown hair. She wore a red sweater over a crisp white shirt and a pair of dark grey woollen trousers. She was a member of my college, I knew – in my year – but I had no idea of her name. Guntersen kissed first Emmanuella and then this woman on the cheek.

'We've been at Mark's,' I heard her say. A slight, yet discernible look of irritation flickered across Guntersen's face. I considered this look long after they had left the quad.

As term drove on, my weekly telephone calls to my parents became ever more brief. Yes, I told them, the knee was healing well. It wasn't. The thing the doctors had feared had come to pass. I could walk on it reasonably much of the time, but any attempt to run brought back the glacial, nauseating pain. And they had shaken their heads further, to tell me that although I might expect a little more improvement I would not, no, I would not run again. Yes, I told my parents, I had mostly caught up with the work I had missed; I might just have to stay up a little longer than planned at Christmas to finish things off. I hadn't caught up; each week that went past, I slipped lower in the class rankings. And yes, I said again, I was making friends. I wasn't. My injury had isolated me. Or, it would be more accurate to say, my injury hastened the isolation I myself had encouraged.

For this is the heart of the matter: disasters occur where accidents meet character.

Here's the truth: two inexplicable things occurred, one outside me and the other within. My knee was shattered, my work disrupted, my understanding fractured. No action of mine could have prevented this. But then. Well. Let me be very clear. I could have worked, as I'd told my parents I would. I could have buckled down, pulled up my socks, rolled up my sleeves and made all the other sartorial adjustments that indicate determination of mind. I could have regained my place somewhere in the middle of the physics pack. I say I 'could' in the certain knowledge that this action wasn't beyond me. And yet . . . it was beyond me.

Term came to an end and I remained in Oxford. I told myself every morning, 'Today I must work,' and sat at my desk or took my books to the library. And did not work, but stared at the page with a mist in front of my eyes, unable to concentrate for fear of not being able to concentrate, hating myself so intensely that I was forced to twist my right leg out violently, to be erased by the all-engulfing, stereoscopic, clean white pain. Sometimes I sat in the stale JCR, staring at the television. At other times, I told myself I needed a quick nap, and woke hours later, groggy and confused, a headache pulsing in my eyeballs. I did not understand why I behaved as I did.

Things would have been different, I told myself, if Guntersen had gone home along with the other students. In fact, I was waiting only for him to leave and then I would begin work. But he sat day after day in the almost-empty library, remorselessly working. I became paranoid. Guntersen had clearly only stayed in Oxford because he knew I was waiting for him to leave, to stop me working. Emmanuella began to accompany him to the library. They sat in the central well, clearly visible from the gallery, where I took my position. They were side by side, heads bent over their books, breaking off occasionally for a variety of kisses, which I began to categorize. The quick affectionate peck as if to say 'here I am', the triumphant hug-and-kiss at the end of a section of work, the long voluptuous embrace which was often followed by an hour's absence from the library and a shower-damp, flushed return.

At times, they were joined by friends. Guntersen's friends: other members of the college rowing team. Or Emmanuella's friends: the woman in the red sweater, her long straight hair brushing her music notation paper as she hunched over it; another woman, short and large-bosomed with corkscrewing spirals of curly hair and a pair of serious black glasses.

21

Emmanuella's friends passed notes to one another on slips of paper torn from their notebooks, read them, smiled and returned to work. Once, they left one of these tiny notes on the table. After I was sure they would not return, I walked stiffly down to the lower level and picked up the scrap of squared paper. On it were written two sentences. The first, in Emmanuella's flowing hand, said, 'Mark doesn't think he is.' The second, in staccato, spiky handwriting, said, 'Well then, it must be true.' I kept it, between the pages of my own unused notebook.

So there was no escape. Either Guntersen and Emmanuella were with friends, or they were alone. If alone, either they were kissing, or they were working. Either I was in the library, watching them, or in my room, drowsily coming to rest over my work, head swimming. I tried walking but could not go for any distance before the pain returned, at first soggy – a filmy mist of discomfort – and then, if I went on, whip-sharp, teeth and claws. I tried sitting in other locations around the library, but then I simply imagined what they were doing, picking up on tiny sounds and suggestions to weave a writhing erotic tableau.

It was three weeks to Christmas and then two weeks, and soon it would be absolutely time to leave and my work was vile to me. I found more and more that I could not even think of it, that my mind glanced off as I tried to approach it. I would, I knew, have to go home soon. My parents would insist on my 'resting'. And no work would be done as no work had been done and then, and then . . . But I could see no further than this, the terror was too immense.

It was Sunday, two weeks before Christmas. At 4 p.m. the sky was already darkening over Gloucester College, dark-painted clouds on an ink-wash sky. The lamps had been lit around Chapel Quad, pools of weak yellow against the ancient stones. My knee was hurting again, a gnawing pain that faded in and out of my conscious mind, grasping the joint in its strong jaws, relaxing the pressure and then applying it again. I had thought I would use the telephone in Chapel Quad to call my parents, to tell them I was ready to come home. Instead, I sat on one of the benches and wrapped my fleece around me. White-cold wind set the pain in my knee thrumming like a metal cord. If I didn't call now, then what? And then what? I couldn't see. The future had shrunk away from me, days contracting to hours, hours to minutes. The fingers of my hands were very white, the nail beds pale blue-purple.

I wanted . . . I wanted . . . But I did not know what to want. I wanted to be a child again, for my own desires to be unimportant, to be taken up into greater arms than mine and not need to think. Was it then that the music struck up? Can it really have been just then? Or was it that I only noticed it then? Notes splashed on my inner ear, bursting in fat droplets. And I noticed that the chapel lights were on. A service was in progress, some part of Advent. Notes rising and falling and a choir singing and all the memory of Christmas carol services leapt upon my heart. I stood up and limped into the chapel.

The choir sang 'Jesu Joy of Man's Desiring'. I took an empty seat at the end of one of the rows and listened with the kind of intensity I had never before known for music. The two simple lines of melody conversed with each other, a simplicity of constant joy beneath the rising and falling of speech. Each note, each leaping phrase, was addressed to me only – a message of hope, an acknowledgement of despair. It was a pulse, soft and sustained; it was a word of consolation for the echoes of existence. It was the beauty that might contain truth.

And then it was over, and there was silence and a shuffling of prayer books and a muttering as a new reader walked to the lectern, ready to deliver one of the Advent lessons. I found I could not bear this. The music might have contained truth, but these lessons never would, for me, and so it was all revealed a lie. And my knee hurt and my fear rose, and nothing had been resolved.

'Hello,' whispered a woman's voice next to me.

I looked, and saw that I had sat down next to that girl, the friend of Emmanuella's, the girl who seemed always to be wearing a red sweater. Her eyes were clear blue-grey, and she looked at me directly.

This, this was the chance I'd waited for. Here, if I said the right things, I could enfold her into my life, and wrap myself in hers, in the Oxford life I had somehow missed. Fear and panic engulfed me again, that I would not find those right words. Before I could reply, she spoke again.

'I've seen you. In the library. You're one of Ivar's friends, aren't you? Aren't you James? I'm Jess.'

And, to my own surprise and horror, I began to cry.

3

First year, December, tenth week of term

The service was soon over, with a collective mutter and closing of prayer books. The tears that rolled silently down my cheeks had ceased, for the moment, and I scrubbed at my face with my sweater sleeve. Jess, looking at me kindly, said, 'Hey, do you want to come back to my room? For a cup of tea?' and I knew it was pity, though the Kendall in me winked and nudged me in the ribs. I felt raw from the bone-heart to the skin. I had not known I was lonely; it had been so all-engulfing as to be invisible.

Jess's room was smaller than mine but warmer. The quality of the light was different, yellow not blue. A half-full suitcase was on her floor, her wardrobe open for the packing. She busied herself boiling the kettle, finding tea bags, running to the communal fridge in the hall for milk. I sat on her desk chair, sniffed and wept some more and hated myself and apologized and she said, 'Don't apologize,' and I apologized again.

I said, 'I don't usually do this, I never, never, I . . .'

She placed a warm mug into my hands and said, 'It's fine. Tell me what's up.'

And, in gulps and gasps, I told her.

There was a relief in it, pouring out everything, from the shame of the tutorial to the humiliation of Anne's instructions, from Kendall's tea-breath to the girl I had seen but could not possess. I did not tell Jess who that unpossessable girl was, this was my one privacy, a tinfoil shield over the centre of my heart. But Jess smiled when I mentioned her and I knew that she had guessed.

I did not know I had so much to say, so many words stored up. As I spoke, she folded her clothes and slowly filled her suitcase. Nothing I said seemed to shock her. There was a pleasing precision to her movements. When she sat, she crossed one ankle over the other, or tucked one leg under her. When she walked, it was concise and purposeful. I liked this. I liked watching her move.

At one point she said, 'I have a friend who says that Oxford is hell. Perfect hell without redemption. But the people make it heaven.' She tipped her head to one side as if easing stiff muscles in her neck.

I looked around her room. It did not seem to me the room of a person whose experience of Oxford was hell. She had a teapot decorated with multicoloured polka dots, pictures of her friends and postcards were stuck in the frame of the mirror, Christmas cards were arrayed on her bookshelves, a violin case sat on a chair by her music stand, there were neatly labelled lever-arch files stacked by her desk and various fliers for concerts and theatre productions pinned to the board. It looked to me to be a full life, and an ordered one, a purposeful one. An Oxford life, as I had imagined it.

She began to take the books from the shelves.

'I think I'll leave the stuff on the walls till last. It's horrible seeing naked walls, isn't it?'

I thought of my own bare room, the tangle of unwashed laundry, the half-pint of soured milk by the bedside, the work which chattered and muttered at me from the desk.

She said, 'We all have blue days. I have them too.'

I imagined her blue days. Days when she might need to talk to a friend, or read a novel, or treat herself to a chocolate. Blue, I wanted to say, is a different colour to black. But already I was a little afraid of frightening her off.

She knelt on the ground and leaned forward, rolling a poster into a tight tube. Her jumper rode up, exposing a slice of freckled back. I could not help staring. They were real, those freckles. This girl seemed more real to me than anything in the world. More real than my terror, more real than my ambition, more real than my fantasies of Emmanuella. I remembered how it felt to want something real. Something that might be within my grasp.

At 1 a.m. her packing was done. Files were tidily stacked in plastic bags, the wardrobe was empty, the bookcases cleared. Only her bedclothes and toothbrush remained.

'Thank you,' she said, 'for keeping me company. I'm really grateful, you know! I only stayed up for the Christmas concert; everyone else went home yesterday.'

I looked at her, aware I should say something, unable to find anything more to say.

'Still, time for bed now.'

I nodded and went to scurry away, and she smiled and said, 'Come back here a moment.'

And I thought, this is fast, too fast, but my heart was thumping and I thought, yes, just take me with you wherever you are going, I don't need my life any more, I will take yours. I bent towards her, expecting an embrace, uncertain what might happen next, waiting for her lead. She kissed me chastely on the cheek.

'Listen,' she said, 'are you busy over the break? After Christmas, I mean?'

'No.' One or two friends from school had written to me, hoping to meet up. I hoped fervently never to see any of them again.

'Only a few of us . . . well, one or two of us, well. It's nothing exciting, we're just getting together in someone's house, in Oxford. And I thought you might like to. Well.'

Some look must have passed over my face. A shadow of something uncontrollable.

'Oh, don't worry, it's nothing strenuous, not with your –' She motioned to my knee but then grimaced. 'Now I've said the wrong thing.'

'No, no, it's not. Not at all. I'm free, I'd love to.'

'Oh *good*.' She grinned again. 'Emmanuella said she thought you were nice and look how . . .'

'Oh.' I gulped and swallowed and said, 'Is Emmanuella coming too?'

'Sadly not.' Jess smiled. 'She's in Spain for the break.'

'And . . . Guntersen?'

Jess laughed.

'God, no. Mark can't stand him. To be honest –' Jess lowered her voice – 'I think Emmanuella's starting to be of the same opinion. Sorry, I know he's your friend, but –'

'No,' I said quickly, 'he's not my friend.'

'Oh.' A pause, and then, 'So there's nothing to worry about.'

We exchanged home addresses and phone numbers before we parted, written in blue ballpoint on torn-off corners of paper from her notebook. I held hers in my hand and stared at it, admiring the curl of her rounded letters: the fat s, the jaunty j. She smiled and yawned and stretched.

'Go on,' she said. 'We'll talk next week.'

I stood dazed at the top of her staircase. The stairs swam before my vision, my eyes defocusing uncontrollably. I prepared to wince my way down the staircase, sighed and gasped and waited for redemption and realized it had already come to pass.

In the morning, my pain came in dull twinges, like a blurred telegraph signal nagging and then falling silent and nagging again. I woke early and sat in bed, with the blankets tented over my one good knee, the other a thickened mound by its side, as the dawn slowly revealed the room. At 8 a.m., without thinking too hard or for too long, I limped down the staircase and into Chapel Quad. The quad was deserted, the flagstones mossed up with frost. I placed the foot of my crutch with care, glad I had brought it, and thought again, with an echoing flutter in the centre of my being, that I would always be afraid of falling now.

It was early to call but my parents are early risers.

'It's time to come home,' I said. 'Can you pick me up tomorrow? Or Wednesday?'

'Oh!' said my mother, a half-mocking half-laugh behind her words, 'you're not staying there for Christmas after all?'

I said nothing.

'Have you finished your work?'

'Yes,' I said, 'I think I'm finished.'

I wondered and worried over when might be the right moment to call her. Not too soon, for fear of being too demanding. But not too late, for fear of seeming uninterested. But she telephoned me first. It was Boxing Day and there had been dinner the day before with

Anne and Paul and talk of Major and Heseltine and the threat from the Liberal Democrats. Anne had asked searchingly about my work, the societies I had joined, and seemed only partially mollified by my mother's explanation about my knee.

'Next term,' she said. 'Hilary term is when it all kicks off. You have to be ready.'

Later that evening, the telephone rang.

'Hello,' she said, 'it's Jess. Do you remember me?'

'Yes, of course I . . .'

There was laughter in the background, a man's voice.

'Listen,' she said. 'I'm driving to Oxford the day after tomorrow, almost past you. It'd be no trouble. Do you want to be rescued?'

'Yes,' I whispered into the telephone. 'Yes, I do.'

She picked me up in an elderly estate car. My parents, grateful to see me with a friend, a girl, had been over-enthusiastic, winking and smiling. We bundled my bag into the car and left as soon as we could.

'I'm sorry about them,' I said.

'If we're going to get on,' she said, 'you'll have to stop apologizing.'

'Oh, I –'

'Don't do it.' She was smiling, still looking at the road. Her lips were pressed together hard and I could see a dimple in her left cheek.

'I . . . what?'

'Don't apologize for apologizing.'

'I . . . um . . .'

'What?'

I furrowed my brow. The conversation seemed to have escaped from me rather more quickly than I'd hoped.

'I'm just, well. I don't know what to say now.'

She grinned. We were nearing a red traffic light. As the car came to a halt she leaned towards me and kissed my right cheek, then turned back to her driving.

'I'll tell you what. Why don't you tell me how your Christmas was? How were the dreaded Anne and the leech-like Paul? Did you get any good presents? Any good arguments?'

And so I did.

I noticed something on that drive that continued to be true for as long as I knew Jess. Her presence calmed me, like a soothing hand in the centre of my chest bringing quiet to every muscle fibre and threaded sinew. Infatuation cannot last, and even love may be less certain than I'd once hoped, but this essential quiet, the stillness she brought to me, that lasted. Mark said to me once, 'She's like God to you: she inexplicably calms inexplicable fears.' And in this, as in so much, he is irritatingly right.

We arrived in Oxford at 3 p.m., when the sun was low on the horizon. We drove north, through the city centre and up into Jericho, a maze-like Oxford district, its tangled streets lined with Victorian labourers' cottages. It had been a cold, bright day but now the clouds had begun to gather and a few spots of rain burst on the windscreen.

'Is it Mark's house we're going to?' I said.

'Yes,' said Jess, 'it's his house. He's . . . yes.'

'Is he a second year? Living out?'

'No, he's a first year like us but he's . . .' She breathed out a long breath. 'Well, he's rich. You'll see. He's good fun though. A bit . . . unexpected at times, that's all.'

We turned a corner on to another terraced Jericho street and saw that it was a dead end. The end of the street was a high wall.

'Is it one of these terraced houses?' I said.

She smiled and shook her head. 'I don't think so. Not Mark.'

We parked the car and walked to the end of the road. It was only as I levered myself from the car and felt a sudden thrust of pain in my knee that I realized I had forgotten about it all this time. I eyed my stick, half-hidden by my suitcase on the back seat of the car, but could not bear to take it with me. I wanted so much to appear normal to this girl. Ahead, Jess was already striding towards a battered green door set into the dead-end wall at the end of the road. The wall was high, almost as high as the houses, and the top was covered with rusty barbed wire. Jess pulled a key out of her pocket, raised her eyebrows, fitted the key into the lock in the green door and turned. She opened the door and we walked through.

*

Beyond was a garden, or what might once have been a garden.

It was large and dark and dense. So large, in fact, that it was impossible to gain any sense of its size from where we stood. Trees, perhaps once planted in ornamental fans, had broken through the rusted metal staples holding them back and grown together to form a tight mass of branches. To our left and right, we could make out the traces of paved paths heading through the undergrowth, but these were too densely thicketed to admit us.

Ahead, though, someone had clearly recently hacked a way through. Swathes of the thickly massed branches had been cut, and a winding path led away from the door. Jess grinned at me and walked boldly forward. I, regretting my stick, glanced back and saw a crest embossed high on the wall. It was a shield containing a small circle with, engraved beneath, partially obscured by bird droppings, the two words 'Annulet House'. I turned back and followed Jess.

Overhanging branches and overgrown bushes blocked our way; the path was moss-sodden and squelched as we walked. All around us climbing vines trailed down and brambles caught our clothes. But among the devastation we could see traces of the place's former order. Through the leaves and moss, I spotted a mosaic pavement ten feet square, cracked and discoloured. At one point, rounding a corner, we were suddenly faced by a massive statue of the god Pan, goat-legged, pipes to his mouth, his face and body pockmarked and lichen-streaked. I thought I glimpsed a sundial in a clearing to our left, unreachable by sun.

At last we came through the tangle and out on to a stone-flagged area with two curved sets of stairs leading up to a crumbling Georgian house. It was enormous – the main section was three storeys tall, with seven windows along each floor, and its façade had faded into mottled beauty. The paint peeling in crackled strips from the shutters on the ground-floor windows had scattered green and white shards across the paving stones.

'How can this possibly be here?' I said. 'How can it be here and not in the guidebooks, and no one knows?'

Jess said, '*We* know, don't we?'

'Yes, but . . .'

'Oxford's full of secrets. It's tradition.'

She put her arm companionably around my waist and drew me with her to peer in through the window at the top of the door. We were at the back of the house and through the rippled bottle-bottom glass I could see a large red-flagged kitchen. There was a black range, an oak table that could comfortably seat twelve, and piles of packing cases.

Jess opened the kitchen door and we went in. The house was cold and silent. I looked into the open crates. In one, a bust of a bearded man poking his tongue out nestled among shreds of newspaper written in the Cyrillic alphabet. In another were a dozen blue crystal balls; in a third, a set of extremely impractical-looking massive cast-iron saucepans, each big enough to cook a meal for thirty.

'But whose house is this?' I said. 'I mean, really? It can't be . . . This Mark's a student, isn't he?'

'Is someone,' said a voice from behind us, 'taking my name in vain?'

I turned. A previously unnoticed door next to the larder had opened, giving a glimpse of a small sitting room beyond. A man was leaning in the doorway, with blond hair that flopped into his eyes, wearing a pair of low-slung jeans with a loose banker's shirt: blue striped, with white collars and cuffs. The outfit and his demeanour, half-amused half-wary, made him ageless: he could have been a boyish don or a precocious twelve-year-old.

'Mark!' said Jess.

'Ah,' he said, 'this must be the *paramour*. Quite as beautiful as you said, Jessica. Yes. It's our house.'

'No,' she said, smiling, 'it's yours.'

'It's the same thing,' said Mark, and reached out his arms to embrace her.

4

I did not like Mark; that much became immediately clear. I did not like his word 'paramour'. I did not like the way he spoke.

'Darling,' he said, 'you mustn't take it like that. Any friend of Jess's is a friend of mine. You are deliciously welcome.'

I did not like the way he looked at me, a tilt of the head, a mocking raised eyebrow, and particularly not the way he looked at Jess. I was territorial already, defensive. I wanted to read a special interest into her behaviour towards me and so I did not like how he touched her, the way she sat so close to him, her knees crossed towards him, his hand resting casually on her thigh. I did not like that at all.

We were the first to arrive, but it became clear from Mark's enumeration of the guest list that there would be others – many, many others.

'Sounds like you've invited half of Oxford,' said Jess.

'Only the best people,' said Mark, shaking his head. 'Like the two of you, my dears.' He squeezed Jess's thigh and ruffled my hair. I stiffened and sat back.

The short curly-haired woman I'd seen before in the library arrived as Mark was showing us the garden. She was Jess's friend from school – it was she who had introduced Jess to Mark – and had an air of solidity and good humour. She wore a green velvet jacket and a pair of glasses over which she looked at me and said, to Jess, 'And who's this?'

'This is James,' said Jess. 'He's . . . a physicist.'

She stuck out her hand. Her handshake was firm, her smile sardonic.

'Well, how do you do, James-the-physicist? I'm Franny.'

'Hello,' I said. 'Did you have a good Christmas?'

'Oh, you know,' she said, watching Mark greet a group of three blonde girls. 'Same old. Drinking the blood of Christian children, cursing the name of Jesus.'

She bent towards me and gave a wry half-smile, unblinking.

'*Jewish*.'

'Oh!' I said. 'I'm sorry.'

'No need to be sorry,' she said, examining a crumbling bird-bath with apparent disdain. 'Runs in the family.'

Blond, broad-shouldered Simon arrived shortly after Franny.

'How long have you been together?' I asked after he'd greeted her with a lingering kiss.

'Oh, we're not,' she replied. 'We're just there for each other in times of horniness.'

I rapidly began to lose track of the new arrivals. There were five Norwegian girls, three blonde and two brunette, all of whom seemed to be named Ulla or variations thereof. There were eight members of the Balliol football team, all wearing Balliol jerseys, who set upon the bottles of brandy they found in the kitchen with a great deal of enthusiasm. There were various ex-public schoolboys with names like Rory and Sheridan, each of whom arrived with a matching girl named Tommy or Georgie or, in the case of one particularly svelte girl, Lumpy.

Mark greeted every new arrival with histrionic enthusiasm, clutching and gasping and exclaiming over the magnificence and delightfulness of each of his friends. He could not sit still. He decided he must show us the house, the whole thing, at once.

The place made no sense: one could see its antecedents, but it had been so touched with madness that it no longer cohered at all. There were, we found when we later attempted to count them, somewhere between thirty-nine and forty-two rooms; no counting ever quite reached the same number. The oldest part of the house was Elizabethan: small panelled rooms at the centre of the ground floor. But generations had accreted layers of plaster and brick around stone. The Georgians had concealed it behind a false front. The Victorians were responsible for the broken greenhouses and the pointed extension at the back of the house. The Edwardians had added the tennis court and rockeries and then the place had ceased at the start of the Second World War.

'Oh yes,' said Mark, explaining this to us. 'It belonged to my father's great-aunt Clytemnestra. No one's bothered to go over it since she died. So they gave it to me.'

'They *gave* it to you?' I said.

I realized as soon as I'd said it that I should have remained silent. No one else seemed to think this point was worth commenting on. The rest of the group looked at me inquisitively. Only Jess seemed unconcerned; she smiled and winked.

'Oh yes, well, they were so delighted I'd finally decided to come to heel,' said Mark. He raised his eyebrows. 'I believe they planned it all along, you know, although they'd never admit it.'

'That's . . . nice of them?' I didn't know who 'they' were, but this seemed a safe response to the news that someone had given Mark a house.

He screwed up his nose.

'Not really,' he said. 'I had to nag them and nag them for it even so. All the uncles and cousins seem to think it's vulgar to own a house. But my father saw it my way. None of *them* want the place at all is the thing, because it's a bit rough around the edges. But –' he smiled suddenly, pirouetting on the spot, arms outstretched as if to embrace the blue and gold study we were standing in – 'so am I. I love it! So fuck 'em.'

'Yes,' I said.

Jess squeezed my arm.

Later, we unpacked our things in the Chinese-papered bedrooms Mark had allotted to us. They were two adjoining rooms, with a warped communicating door which was swollen with damp and would not shut though we tugged and pushed at it. The half-open door felt curiously intimate, as though we had been given just one room.

'I don't understand,' I said, 'how it is that if Mark's so rich... he is rich, isn't he?'

Jess nodded.

'And his family are rich. So why is this house in such a state of decay? I mean . . . where are the marble bathrooms and luxury yachts?'

She frowned. We were in Jess's room. I sitting in a broken split-cane chair, she on the bed.

'I think . . . really rich people, not new rich but generations of richness . . . don't think about *things* in the same way the rest of us do. Maybe because they don't have to. Mark doesn't, anyway. He's really funny about money. But he's so generous. You'll see. Look how he's got this place ready for us.'

I opened the doors of the walnut wardrobe, its veneers curling with damp. At least, I tried to open them. One handle came off in my hand. Jess snorted, and tried to hide the laugh in her sleeve.

'In what sense,' I said, 'is this house ready?'

'Only in the sense that a very rich man with no idea about normal life might think it's ready. But don't be like that. It's lovely really. An adventure!' She threw herself back on to the bed and spread her arms and legs into a wide X shape. 'And in any case, there are clean sheets on the beds, empty drawers and a stuffed . . . Actually, what is that on the mantelpiece? A skunk? I don't like the way it's looking at me.'

She leapt up, stalked over to the fireplace and picked up the glass-eyed animal by its stiff brush tail. She looked around the room for a suitable place to deposit it.

'Bathroom?' I suggested.

'God, no. Wouldn't want to come face to face with *that* at 4 a.m.'

'Under the bed?'

'Might come to life. Feels like that sort of house, don't you think?'

Jess surveyed the view out of the window. An enormous privet hedge was beneath, grown wildly out of shape. She grinned, ran round behind me and pushed me towards the window, the touch of her hands on my back both firm and thrilling. One-handed, she pushed up the sash, leaned out of the window holding the stuffed skunk by its tail and dropped it gently into the centre of the privet.

'There,' she said. 'Released back to its natural habitat.'

In the evening, the party began in earnest. Three men in rugby shirts had run cables through the house, stuck down with rug-shredding gaffer tape. A few hours after dark, with pizza boxes already littering several of the living rooms, and groups of people making fires in the unswept grates, a sudden thunderclap of music struck across the house. The bass was insistent, distorting through the walls and ceilings. And more people arrived.

Jess said, 'Come downstairs with me. It'll be fun.'

I said, 'Not yet. In a few minutes. Promise.'

She tipped her head and looked at me, a little puzzled.

And I thought, and I could see she thought, who is this man? Who have I brought here?

She left and went downstairs.

After ten minutes, I went to stand on the balconied landing. I looked down through the banisters to the hall three floors below. There were blonde girls in pink cocktail dresses and fur-collared coats laughing, and a pile of coats and handbags and shoes spilling across the marble-chequered floor.

In the hall below, a girl said, 'How high is it? How far up does it go?'

She tipped her head back, a blue and silver scarf tied around her neck, and said, 'Oh! There's someone up there.'

Mark's head came into view in the oval of floor space.

'It is the gloriously good-looking James,' he said. 'Jess found him first, though, so hands off. Why are you loitering up there, James? Get down here and let us ogle you!'

And, while in my mind I dithered and wondered, somehow his command had set me free. I went downstairs.

'And what are you?' said a man whose name was Llewellyn, or Montgomery, or Noel, or St John or Stephan or Bobo or Kit.

'This is James,' said Mark, and took my arm. 'He's at college with Grunter – you know Grunter?'

'What, that Norwegian bloke? I met him at Rhodes House drinks. Emmanuella brought him. Friends with him, are you?'

Before I could respond, Mark said, 'Certainly not. Grunter is the most boring man in Oxford and you know I've had that statistically confirmed. I couldn't possibly have any friend of his at my party. You think he's boring too, don't you, James? Never talks about anything but work, barely talks to anyone but Manny.'

'I, um, yes,' and suddenly I saw that yes, Guntersen was boring. He was. Boring. Yes.

'I've told Manny time and time and time again,' Mark continued, 'but does she listen? No. Tall blond men with broad shoulders, she can't see past them. Whereas –' he looked me up and down appraisingly – 'yes . . . What she needs is a nice pretty English boy like you, don't you agree?'

'I . . . um,' I said.

'Don't you worry,' said Mark. 'I'm going to convince her sooner or later that Grunter is too boring for anyone to bear. So if Jess turns you down, we'll fix you up with Manny.'

Something must have shown in my face then. A flash of desire, a momentary indication that, my God, for someone to fix me up with Emmanuella was all I had hoped for in life. I tried to hide it but, looking back, I think it must have shown in my face.

I was unwilling to wander from this theme, but the conversation moved on. A girl in a black beaded choker lit a cigarette and blew smoke rings.

Mark put his arms around two of the women nearest to him and said, 'Come along. If you're good I'll show you my gazebo.'

He laughed and walked the girls towards the back of the house. I wanted to follow but did not wish to appear pathetic.

The air was soupy, thick with conversation, smoke and perfume. I wondered where Jess was, then jabbed at myself for wondering. I mustn't be following her around all evening. It was a party, after all. It couldn't be so very hard to talk to people.

I recognized Franny and stood next to her for a few minutes.

'Mum and Dad insist that I have to find a husband who is of the blood pure,' she said, holding Simon's arm tightly.

'What's Si,' said a girl, 'too mongrel?'

'Oh no,' said Franny, 'just mongrel enough.'

In a sitting room by a side door to the garden a young man was drawing on a hookah, while another lay sprawled on the rose-patterned carpet next to him.

'Don't bother Dev,' the first man said, 'he's mashed. Fancy a draw?'

He extended the pipe to me. A thin line of spittle hung between it and his lip for a moment before collapsing.

'No thank you,' I said.

In a black and white tiled room, a couple was having sex on a mildewed sofa. They seemed oblivious of the people passing by the open doorway. His chest was bare. She was dressed as a 1920s flapper with black feathers in her hair and a beaded cocktail dress that shook as she moved on top of him. Her fishnet tights were ripped between her thighs. His head was back, staring unseeing at the ceiling. Hers was down, looking at her red-nailed hands on his chest. They were making no noise at all, and I wondered whether they were a couple, and this public display was something they always did or whether they had met here, perhaps only minutes before, and each was participating for their own private reasons.

In a green-papered room looking out on the statues, a group was engaged in conversation.

'I think I'm drunk.'

'Obviously you're not, or you wouldn't be able to think it.'

'Isn't that *madness*, not drunkenness?'

'Why, do you think you're mad?'

A wing-backed armchair was free. I sat in it and listened to the strangeness. On a table was an array of produce from Fortnum & Mason nestled in duck-egg-blue paper: a wheel of cheese, a tower of chocolate fairy cakes and brightly coloured jellies in vodka glasses. Several small jars containing caviar had been thrust into a fire bucket filled with ice.

'Is that caviar?' someone said.

'Of course,' said someone else.

'I wonder what would happen if you snorted it.'

'I'd pay £50 to see you try.'

The lighting in the room was dim and unsettling. Around the walls were photographs of film stars. Some I recognized and some I did not; some were signed and some unsigned. I squinted at them for a little while, challenging myself to name them, but the chatter soon became soporific. My eyelids grew heavy. I was on the edge of a dream when a loud sound alerted me that, across the room, something was going on.

I opened my eyes.

Mark had entered, accompanied by a crowd. He gestured at the pictures in one corner of the room, a group of five shots of the same delicate-featured woman. In one arty black and white photograph she was wearing dark glasses, with a cigarette holder clamped between her teeth. In another she was lying back on a chaise longue, wearing a beaded evening gown that was slit all along the leg. Her left leg was raised and her arms spread wide.

Mark leaned towards the woman standing next to him and whispered something in her ear. The other guests smiled and muttered. The woman turned her head and I saw that it was Jess. I must have made a sound of some sort, for Mark swung round quickly, pirouetting on the ball of one foot.

'James!' he crowed. 'You are quite the man I was looking for, a man of taste, a man of refinement. Tell me, what do you think of this group of pictures?'

'Hmmm?' I said.

'These pictures. This woman. What do you think of them?'

'Mark,' said Jess. There was a warning in her tone, a hint of something. She walked towards me and perched on the arm of my chair, taking my hand in hers.

'Come on, James,' said Mark, 'what do you think of the pictures?'

Something else was going on. I didn't know what it was, but I knew that. Next to me Jess stiffened. I felt her hand close around mine.

'Don't, Mark,' she said.

Mark tipped his head to one side, flicked a quick look at me, then looked at Jess.

'I'm only asking.'

Jess pursed her lips. After a moment, she said, 'Ask. Someone. Else.'

Mark met her gaze. I saw him move his tongue inside his closed mouth, licking his top front teeth, pushing his lips out.

'Fine,' he said, then, all smiles, turned to a man staggering unsteadily across the room.

'Rob,' he said, 'what do you think of my pictures?'

Rob collapsed on to a sofa and looked around him with exaggerated concentration.

'Do you like them, Rob?'

All at once, no one else in the room seemed to be talking.

Rob peered at the walls. Spotting the one closest to him, the woman nude, draped with multicoloured art silk, he broke into a grin.

'Dirty pictures, is it?'

Mark grinned.

'Yeah, that sort of thing,' he said. 'What do you think of her?'

Rob looked at another picture in which the woman was dressed in diaphanous silk, her naked breasts clearly visible through the fabric. Rob blinked and pulled his head back a little, having some difficulty focusing.

'She's fucking *gorgeous*,' he said at last.

Mark lit a cigarette, took a deep drag and blew the smoke out slowly, in a steady stream. He held the cigarette just a little away from his mouth and said, 'She's fantastic, isn't she? Would you, you know, do her?'

Rob squinted at the picture. He smiled drunkenly. 'Fuck, yeah. Who is she? Your girlfriend or something?'

Mark took another long, slow pull on his cigarette, then said, 'That's my mother.'

It is at this point that my memory begins to blur. Although nothing had yet passed my lips I find that in my recollection the ferns and trees had already started to creep from the wallpaper to spread their tendrils through the room. Everything felt dangerous and confused.

The music grew louder. Mark was dancing and talking and running his hand through his blond hair and squeezing my shoulder. Jess got up to dance and said, 'Come on, come on,' but I remained seated. Someone gave me a cake and I ate it. It tasted a little dry. I chewed it more thoroughly. Time dilated and contracted and across the room Jess was dancing and laughing and talking, tossing her hair back from her shoulders and touching another man, a man who was not me, on the arm.

Time passed again. It seemed to be doing so more slowly. I thought I saw all sorts of wonders. A woman I had never met took off her beaded top and bra and danced. Simon threw Franny over his shoulder and carried her through the room, like a caveman with his trophy. I seemed to see Mark dancing with another man, hip to hip and chest to chest, sinuous and strong. My head felt heavy I wanted to rest it and Jess was there in her gold dress with sequins all over and I was wearing jeans but nonetheless I walked to her and laid my head in her lap.

'Very affectionate,' someone said. And this seemed to me the funniest thing in the world, the funniest thing I had ever heard, and I laughed and laughed with Jess's hand on the back of my neck.

'Did you . . .?' said Jess to someone.

'No, not me, I don't share,' someone said.

'Then which one of you?' said Jess.

Mark said, 'It was me.'

'Oh, God, what did you give him?'

'Just some weed.'

'How much, for fuck's sake?'

The room was triangulated, its dimensions folding in, the vanishing point closer than it should have been, and I stood up because I needed a better vantage place to see and be seen.

'For fuck's sake,' someone was saying, 'without telling him?'

'I thought it would help him relax. He just seemed a bit . . . you know.'

In my head a siren went off. It was distant at first, but growing closer and with a line into my heart and the beating that grew more and more intense with every thrashing crashing chastening word. My body is eating itself, I thought.

'Mark,' said Jess, and her hand was on his chest and she was saying further words but I could not hear them at all.

I saw how this worked. I was here to be the moon, reflecting Mark's glory because Jess was in love with him and they were playing a long and intricate game. And my wanting of her, and my need and my desire were only trophies she had brought to offer him. I would have run, but the teeth in my knee began to gnaw, so I crawled down the corridor papered with velvet bees and if she called after me I did not notice.

Outside in the garden the air was cool and still. I stood up and walked slowly. The music throbbed from the lighted windows of the house, pulsing to the beat of the blood in my eyeballs, but the cool muted it, turning it leafy and distant. Though my shirt was thin and the rain had wet the grass, I walked through the garden further and further from the people and the tumult of destruction.

In the early-morning light Jess found me. I was sitting on the lawn with my back resting against the sundial, staring at my hands, seeing the fat beneath the skin and the blood beneath the fat and the muscle beneath the blood and the bones beneath the muscle and on and on until the colours of my skin parsed into atoms and parts of atoms, the tiniest parts of reflecting light beneath which all of us are made of nothing.

I said, 'I can't stay here, I can't.'

And she held my head and pressed my cheek very close to her breasts.

'It'll get better,' she said. 'You'll see.'

She sat down next to me and slipped her arm around my waist, resting my head on her shoulder.

'Are you . . .' I said, 'are you in love with Mark?'

She blinked and blushed, and I thought – yes, yes you are. And she said, 'Don't be an idiot. Mark's *gay*.'

I thought for a moment. I brought to mind the half-remembered image of Mark dancing with a taller man the previous night. I felt entirely a fool.

43

'What are you . . .? Why did you even bring me here?'

She turned her head towards me, pursed her lips into a smile, eyes dancing.

'Because I fancy you, obviously.'

And she kissed me as though there had never been any question we would do otherwise.

We did not have sex that morning, or in the several nights and mornings that followed; it would be two or three delicious weeks before we progressed through the slow removal of clothes above the duvet to the things that might happen beneath it.

That morning, we lay on her bed together. She brought me a large glass of water and I sipped it slowly. She made me lean back on the bed.

'I'd follow you anywhere,' I said.

'I know,' she said.

'What are we going to do now?' I said.

'Now? You are going to sleep and I –' she leaned forward and retrieved a book from her bedside table – 'am going to read *Hetherington's Theory of Composition* while you do.'

'And then?'

'We'll talk about that when you wake up. I can take you home if you like. But sleep first.'

When I woke, it was late afternoon and the sun was already red-gold and low in the sky. My head hurt and my mouth was dry. I opened my eyes, then quickly closed them again. Someone was sitting in a chair next to the bed.

'Oh,' they said, 'you're awake. Do you want some water? I can make breakfast – we've got good sausages. Or I do an excellent bacon sandwich. You'd like my bacon sandwich.'

I opened my eyes again, more slowly.

It was Mark, standing by the bed, holding a glass of water close to my lips.

I jerked my head back. Pain shot like an icicle down my neck and into my spine.

'Yeah,' he said, 'I thought of that. Here's a bottle.'

He passed me a glass bottle of Perrier. I looked at him, then examined the seal. Digging the metal cap into the palm of my hand, I cracked opened the bottle and drank deeply, directly from it.

Mark watched me gravely.

'Where's Jess?' I said at last.

'She went out for a walk. She'll be back soon.'

My head felt heavy and old, layers of rust accreted round a thick iron sphere. My right leg was dead. I wiggled my toes to move the blood around and waited for the prickles in my thigh and calf, and the slower dull ache in my knee.

'Do you . . .' Mark stood awkwardly. 'Do you remember much about last night?'

'I remember what you did.'

'Yeah. Look.' I thought he was about to excuse himself, to tell me it had been a mistake or an accident.

'It's not that I want you to like me,' he said.

'Good,' I said, 'I don't.'

He blinked at me, cocking his head to one side.

'Listen,' he said, 'what do you want?'

'Want?' My voice was flat.

'You make it sound so . . .' He frowned. 'It's not payment, not like that. Just, what do you want? That I can help with? I owe you one. That's all. Because I'm sorry.'

My head crackled and bled with white static humming. I licked my lips. I tasted blood.

I took another sip of water, feeling the bubbles bursting on my tongue as a gentle agony.

'I don't want anything from you, Mark.'

He stood up and moved close to my bed. His thighs were pressed against the mattress. He bent down smiling, the way one might lean over to tuck a child into bed.

'Yes,' he said, 'I think you do. I think I know how to make it up to you.'

*

Jess returned as the sun was setting. Her hair was loose, windswept from her walk. She embraced me so naturally, and when we kissed she tasted of autumn berries, tart and sweet. She put my hesitant hand on her breast and I felt the nipple, small and hard beneath her sweater.

She said, 'I'm sorry, really sorry about last night. I didn't think he'd . . .'

But my heart was pounding and my skin was electric, and my thumb was on the point of her breast.

'It doesn't matter,' I said. 'It's fine. Let's not talk about him now.'

And after a minute or two all thought faded away.

5

Kendall jostled me as we crowded into the library.

'You've had a busy vac, eh?'

I supposed he had seen Jess and me kissing before we parted into subject groups, she downstairs to sit with the rest of the music students, I up in the gallery with the physicists.

'Mmm,' I said.

There was a bustling of rulers and special pencils and lucky protractors. A few words whispered as we found our places in the ancient library. I was accustomed to a more utilitarian exam setting: the school gym, underneath the basketball hoops, with rubberized floors that squeaked when we shuffled our chairs. But Oxford is defined by its superfluity of beauty, by its application of beauty to the mundane. The morning light filtered through the library windows, splashing crimson on the pale floor tiles. The gold-tooled volumes of the College Record gleamed. Each of us had our own wooden inkwell, lined with indigo glass, in case we should care to write our answers with a dip-pen.

'Quickly, please!' called the librarian.

'Fast work,' said Kendall, winking. 'Nice one.'

I smiled. 'Yeah.'

'Why do you think they call them collections?' He was speaking quite loudly, even though the library was becoming hushed. 'Why collections? Why not exams? Or tests? What are they collecting?'

I made an indeterminate noise. It might have been a 'hmph', or perhaps an 'ahm'.

'At least we're in it together, right, Stieff? None of us will do well, not except . . .' He jerked his head towards the next table, where Guntersen was laying out pencils, eraser and calculator at right angles. I thought, Mark is right, he is boring. Terribly, terribly boring. The thought pleased me.

'Did you notice that Spanish girl wasn't with him today? No good-luck kisses?'

I had noticed.

'She's probably got exams now too,' I said. I took out my clear pencil case.

'What do you think they'd do if we failed though?' Kendall whispered. 'What do you think they'd . . .'

Kendall's voice trailed off. I looked at him squarely. He had a soft face: squashy nose, thick lips, ears with long lobes, a round schoolboy haircut. He was sweating and he looked unwell, with a yellow tinge to his face. I suddenly felt pity for Kendall. I had Jess at least, now. We'd spoken daily since the party; at first I'd called her from the phone box at the end of my parents' road, and then we'd come up early together to Oxford, excited to be near each other. What did Kendall have?

'It'll be fine,' I said. 'What's the worst that can happen? They won't send us down after one term.'

'Quiet now!' said the librarian.

The whispered conversations died away. The second hand of the great ornamental clock swooped around. The minute hand ticked: 9.30 a.m.

'You may turn over your papers and begin now.'

Jess and I had come back to Oxford just after New Year, almost two weeks before the start of term. It had been her suggestion and I, longing to escape the suffocating environment of my parents' house, eager to see her again, had agreed enthusiastically. We'd holed ourselves up in her bedroom and worked. It was only ten days of effort, but there was a calm, methodical manner to it that had given me hope.

'I know nothing,' I'd said. 'There's no way I'll pass.'

'First thing,' she said, 'what's the mark scheme?'

We pored over past papers, as I remembered the less bright boys at my school had been forced to do. We worked out where answering a question would gain most marks, which marks could be got most easily.

'Look at it this way,' said Jess. 'You could learn all four topics a bit, and you wouldn't do as well as if you learned one very thoroughly and skipped the rest. Which is your favourite?'

I had never prepared to fail before.

'Don't think of it like that,' said Jess. 'You're doing what needs to be done.'

There's a sense of mastery that comes in examinations. It's an experience that is rare in the outside world. The number of questions, the different ways they can be presented: these things are limited, and each can be explored, studied, perfected. No wonder we spend our adult lives feeling we're simply pretending to know what we're doing. After sixteen years spent doing exams, where the lessons we've received perfectly fit the challenges we're faced with, our preparation for the unpredictable events of normal life will always seem shoddy and haphazard.

Even in the half-baked way we had planned, there was a kind of mastery in my performance that day. I knew where to go and what to do. I read through the questions, found the one I understood and worked through it calmly. While it continued it was all-engaging. For an hour I lived in the rule of the squared paper, the sinusoid, the curves tending to infinity.

After an hour I looked up. I had been dimly aware of a noise to my right, a fidgeting and sighing. Kendall was still sweating, gnawing at the end of his pencil, sinking toothmarks into the wood. By some instinct he knew I was looking at him and grasped my glance.

Clowning, he rolled his eyes, motioned to the paper, shook his head, let out a theatrical sigh. I felt suddenly irritated by him. Did he think we were the same, he and I? Did he think I was also so hopeless that I had to treat all of this as a joke? I may have let out a little tut, and returned to my paper, looking for the questions on which we'd decided I could score at least half-marks.

But Kendall was harder to ignore now that he had perceived me. He tapped his fingers. He shifted in place. He breathed heavily. After a few minutes I looked over again. He was not looking at me.

His head was bowed over the exam paper. His eyes were red and wet. As I watched, his shoulders shook in a silent sob.

If I were Jess, I thought, I'd put my arm around him. That's what a good person does. If I were good like that, I'd stop writing the exam and ask if he was OK. Or I'd pass him a note. But then, if I were caught, my exam paper would be voided. Dr Boycott might accuse me of cheating. Do good people never think of themselves?

Kendall's shoulders heaved again. He gulped. I should at least offer him a tissue. Did I even have a tissue? I felt in my pockets. No. Hadn't anyone else noticed he was crying? I looked around the library. Most of the other people were concealed by the bookshelves and carrel partitions. All the people in our section – Guntersen and Daswani, Everard and Panapoulou and Glick – were looking down at their work, writing furiously. Kendall wiped his nose with the back of his hand, gulped and looked at the exam paper again. He picked up his pencil. He glanced at me and gave a resigned shrug, as if to say, 'Well, back to it.' I made a little grimace, as if to say, 'No other choice,' and continued. I found a question that I thought I might get three-quarters of the way through. I tried to ignore all other thoughts.

At ninety minutes into the exam, and without warning, Kendall made an unnerving noise. It was, perhaps, the beginning of a bellow. The first strangulated note of a roar, cut off before it reached full strength. It was loud, though, loud enough that one or two of the others looked up and the invigilating librarian turned her head sharply to us.

Kendall, aware of the attention, seemed to shrink into himself, wishing our gazes away, then sprang out, jumping up from his chair, giving another of the same anguished half-howls. He stood, mouth open, gazing at the student body of Gloucester College. Like an animal turning to flee, he threw pencils, exam paper and work to the floor and ran from the library.

Guntersen looked at me, shrugged and returned to his writing.

'I like to think,' said Mark, pouring himself another glass of red, 'that he was overcome with a sense of his own deep and abiding unattractiveness. Perhaps he caught a glimpse of himself in a particularly shiny set square – do you still use set squares? – and understood with a terrifying finality that no one will ever sleep with him. I like to think that's what it was.'

'Shhhh, Mark,' said Jess, tapping him on the knee. 'You didn't hear that noise he made. It echoed all over the library. Down in the lower level we thought someone must have hurt themselves. Poor thing, we don't even know where he's gone.'

'Home, probably,' said Franny. 'If you can't even deal with a college collection . . .' She let the thought drift into silence.

We were in the kitchen of Mark's house in Jericho. I had not been here since the day after the party, and the place looked different now. The packing cases were gone, the Aga gave the room a mellow warmth, there was a plate of ripe and runny cheese and crusty bread on the table, along with several bottles of good red wine. Mark had summoned us here with handwritten notes: 'Post-collection celebration, 3 p.m., Annulet House. Do come. Mark.' This had irritated me when I found the envelope in my pigeonhole. It had irritated me further when I saw that Jess's identical card contained the postscript 'Do bring J. the pretty paramour. Drag him if you must.'

'Who does he think he is?' I said.

'He's just trying to be funny,' said Jess. 'Come on. You can always leave if you don't like it.'

Franny and Simon were already there when we arrived and shortly afterwards there was a tap at the kitchen door.

'Ah!' said Mark. 'At last!'

He pulled the door open with a flourish. It was Emmanuella, more tanned than I remembered her, in a grey wool dress and black calf-length boots with a large iron brooch pinned to her shoulder. She embraced Mark, pulling him to her. Her scent wafted across the room, full of heat and light. I stared at her, and hated myself for staring, and hated myself for finding Jess fleetingly a little colourless by comparison.

Mark made a play of looking around and behind her. 'Manny . . .' he said.

Emmanuella frowned.

'Do not please call me Manny.'

'Where's Grunter?'

'Who?'

'Grunter.'

'Who?' She placed emphasis on the syllable.

'Fine, then. Where's Gunther Snoreson?'

'We have decided to part. I have come from telling him. I did not think it was –'

My stomach gave a little leap at this, a little involuntary shudder.

'Yes, yes,' said Mark, interrupting her. 'That's all I wanted to know. I'm just glad I've finally convinced you to see sense. Can't put up with another moment of his droning voice . . . Now,' he said, leading Emmanuella to the table, 'I've got a proposition for you all.'

'I've told you a million times,' said Franny. 'No orgies unless I'm really, really drunk.'

Mark grinned and tipped his head to one side. 'That can be arranged, darling, but not tonight. Listen.' He dropped his voice lower. 'This house is mine now. Properly mine. The trustees have agreed to it. And I can do what I like here. So. Would you come and live with me? Here?' There was a pause, a silence. 'For free, I mean,' he said. 'I don't need to charge you rent.' And for a moment he seemed excruciatingly vulnerable, as he always did when talking about money – as if, paradoxically, it were a conversation about something he didn't have, could never have, had never even seen. Always afraid he would refer to it incorrectly and reveal his ignorance.

'Wow,' said Simon.

'Goodness,' said Jess.

'I'm in,' said Franny.

This was a complicated offer, more complicated even than we could have known then. Only Emmanuella seemed entirely unperturbed by it, and she was rich; rich enough to know that this was a kindness she could afford to repay if necessary, that she would not be acquiring an ongoing debt.

Nonetheless, and despite all misgivings, we got drunk that afternoon as if it were all settled. The red wine dwindled and Mark replaced it with brandy. As the darkness descended, he lit lamps around the room and produced from the Aga a roast haunch of venison, studded with garlic and rosemary.

'Will it be like this every night, darling?' said Franny. She was affectionately drunk, her arms draped around Simon's shoulders.

'Oh, every every night,' said Mark. 'Come live with me and be my loves and we shall all the pleasures keep.'

'S'not "loves", it's *love*,' said Jess. Her arms were folded on the table, her head laid on them. Until she spoke, I'd assumed she was asleep. 'Can't have more than one love, thass not how it works.'

'You've clearly been going to entirely the wrong parties, my darling,' he said.

'Mmmmm . . .' she said. 'I don' think . . .' She lapsed into silence.

Mark walked around the table to Jess and rubbed her back gently between the shoulder blades.

'C'mon, darling, time for bed. James, why don't you take her upstairs?'

I stroked the side of Jess's face, where the freckles met the hairline, by her ear.

'Jess,' I said, 'Jess, it's time for bed now.'

She turned a smiling face to me and kissed me squarely on the lips. There was no reaction from the others. I felt a strange sensation, a combination of delight and concern. Mark had made up a bed for us both, apparently anticipating that we would only want one. We did only want one, but this was a new development, so new that I was a little surprised Jess had told Mark. Were we together now, decidedly together? What did that mean?

I supported her up the stairs to our room. She lay on the bed and was instantly asleep. I covered her with a blanket and sat by her for a minute or two.

She muttered something. I leaned closer.

'What's that?'

She sighed and said again, 'You're so beautiful.'

She rolled over and wrapped her arm across my leg. I sat perfectly still and after a few minutes her breathing became steady and even.

Downstairs, the party was winding to its conclusion. Emmanuella was lying on the sofa in the yellow salon, her dress bunched up around her thighs. Mark was on the floor by her side, singing a French song, a children's lullaby, softly.

Simon was sitting in the large red leather armchair, feet up on the coffee table, puffing thoughtfully at a cigar.

'Had to carry Franny up to bed,' he said. 'Completely overcome by the alcohol. Of course, it hasno effect onme, nonewhassoever.'

Mark smiled, then broke off singing to say, 'He did carry her, you know. Quite astonishing.'

'Always happy to help a lady. 'Cept if she's being sick. I remember once, she spewed up so much that . . .'

Emmanuella sat up abruptly.

'If it has reached the time for the vomit tales, I also must go to bed.'

'Quite right,' said Mark, 'quite right. No sort of stories for a lady.'

'I wonder, James,' said Emmanuella, 'whether you would be kind and escort me to bed?' She exchanged a look with Mark, a look I could not quite understand. A meeting of eyes, like the sealing of an agreement.

She took my arm. Her perfume had mellowed over the evening, combining with the wine to become an amber glowing scent, rich and honey-dropped. I found myself wondering, without intending to do so, whether she smelled like this inside her clothes. Whether it was perfume at all, or just the warm brown scent of her skin.

She led me slowly to her room on the first floor. I went to leave her at the door but she tugged on my arm and said, 'No, no, I will fall without you. Take me to the bed.'

There were fresh flowers in her room, jugs of white roses. Above the bed was a crucifix, the blood painted a wet red but the face serene. I looked away from it and noticed a small holdall by the bed and a book on the nightstand. She had known already that she would be staying, then. How much thought had gone into this apparently artless afternoon?

Emmanuella sat down on the bed, took off her boots and stretched her stockinged toes. The counterpane was very smooth and white. She patted it, inviting me to sit by her. I sat down. She rested her head on my shoulder and ran her arm around my waist. I could feel the outline of her breast against my side.

'Do you like me?' she said, so low that I had to incline my head towards her to catch the words.

'I . . . yes. Yes, I like you,' I said.

She snuggled closer.

'I like you too. You are very handsome,' she said.

She raised her head, brought it close to mine and, very softly, breathed into my ear. A thrill of pleasure went through me. I risked a mistake and moved my hand across her legs, squeezing her knee gently. She sighed.

'Mark has told me so many good things about you,' she said.

Mark. Was it possible that this had been *planned*? Had he guessed I liked her? Had he told her?

Emmanuella bit my earlobe very gently. The sensation was exhilarating.

'Close the door,' she whispered.

I stood up, walked to the door. Outside in the corridor the light was still on. To my surprise, at the far end of the passage, I could see the door to Simon's room half ajar. Inside, Mark and Simon were sprawled on the gigantic four-poster bed, giggling. I looked back to Emmanuella. Her eyes were half-closed, her head nodding forwards. Is it to my credit or discredit that this alone convinced me?

I walked back into the room, leaving the door open. I brushed the hair out of her eyes and pushed her back gently on to the bed. She sighed happily. I leaned forward and whispered, 'Time for you to sleep.'

She nodded, and wrapped her arms around the pillow, clutching it like a child with a teddy bear.

Out in the corridor I closed the door and stood for a moment, resting my back on it. It was then that I saw Mark at the other end of the passage. He pushed open the door to Simon's room, carrying something in his hand. Simon lay sprawled still on the bed, his shirt open to the waist. Mark turned, saw me watching him and winked, then went into Simon's room and closed the door behind him.

Upstairs Jess was still asleep, snoring softly. I sat on the sofa and looked out of the window at the dark garden shifting in the wind. I wondered what I would do with this invitation – at once sensible and ludicrous. If I took it, then what? I would have a group of friends ready-made, a way out of the misery of college life. I had longed, since arriving in Oxford, to move away – my whole trajectory seemed to me an attempt to run away from the place, to take up residence somewhere smaller.

And if I did not take it, then what? Back to college, and to struggle, and to the life I had hated so much last term. And what could I say to Jess to make her understand? 'I think perhaps he invited us all here, and plied us with alcohol, to give me the chance to sleep with Emmanuella if I wanted'? She would go on with this life and I would have to return to mine. No. It was this that drove me, in the end. Not a running-to, but a running-from. I did not want to end like Kendall, bolting from an exam hall, with nowhere to go.

I saw Kendall a few days later in Chapel Quad. He was lying on a bench by the ivy-covered wall, his head resting on his rucksack. I thought he was asleep, but as I walked past he lifted his head and called to me.

'Stieff!' he said. 'Off to Boycott?'

'Yup,' I said. It was my ten-minute slot with the tutor to receive the results of my collections. I could not delay.

'Good luck,' he said. 'Hope it goes well. I suppose . . .' He frowned. 'I might not see you again.'

I stared at him, puzzled.

'I'm . . . er, well, I'm leaving Oxford. Talked it through with Boycott. It's all for the best, probably. It only gets harder from here and, you know, if it hasn't been good so far . . .'

I was aware of the seconds ticking by. Dr Boycott would be caustic if I was late. Nonetheless.

'But where are you going?'

He wrinkled his nose. 'Manchester. My UCCA reserve. Jumped to take me when I called.'

'Oh,' I said. 'Um.' I did not know what to say. It was as if Kendall had told me he had been diagnosed with a chronic and painful disease. I do not defend this; this is how we thought.

'It'll be good,' I said at last. 'Better than here. Big fish, small pond – be nice not to be running to catch up all the time.'

'Yeah,' said Kendall. 'Not so many bloody tutorials, away from Boycott and all this . . .'

He stopped and looked around. The quad was peaceful in its

medieval splendour, with ivy-covered walls, clipped grass and stone arches. Beauty is a lie, but it is so hard to spot.

'Yeah,' I said, 'good to get away from all this. But sorry, I have to run. Good luck with everything!'

I started to walk away.

'No problem,' said Kendall. 'I might catch you later, yeah?'

'Yeah,' I said. 'Sure.'

'I need not tell you, Mr Stieff,' said Dr Boycott, 'that these are disappointing results.'

Dr Strong, sitting by his side, nodded silently.

My knee ached – I had forced it upstairs at a sprint to reach the office on time. It was displeased with this treatment and produced short, stabbing pains, enough to make me gasp.

'We had such high hopes of you, but you seem to have –' Dr Boycott paused – 'fallen far below them this term.'

'I'm sorry Dr Boycott, but I –'

Dr Boycott interrupted me.

'Nonetheless!' he flourished the exam paper. 'Your answer to the question on Lagrangian dynamics was good. Thus, I think we may say,' and he looked to the right and left, as though speaking to a large and attentive audience rather than merely to myself and the taciturn Dr Strong, 'that we have hope! Put your back into it, Mr Stieff. We need a sprint from you this term, a sprint!'

'Yes, Dr Boycott,' I said. I found I was a little overwhelmed by having been told that a single answer of mine was good.

'Run along, then,' said Dr Boycott. 'More effort is what you need this term. More effort.'

I hobbled from the room, strangely elated. I would go and see Kendall again, I thought, put my arm around his shoulders and commiserate with him properly. I walked back as fast as I could manage, my knee spitting embers in the cold, but when I reached Chapel Quad Kendall was gone.

6

First year, April, first week of term

We took up Mark's offer. Of course we did. Jess discussed the matter with her eminently reasonable parents, who, having assured themselves that the house was adequate and the friends not intolerable, took the view that this was a natural stage in their daughter's fledging and if she wanted to live with her friends she should not be prevented.

My parents were suspicious and wondered not unnaturally – though at the time it seemed wholly unreasonable – whether after my bad first term I should be changing my living arrangements. Strangely, it was Anne's intervention that swayed them in the end. She had been at college with a third cousin of Mark's – on his father's side, which contained a lot of House of Lords relations of whom Mark was entirely dismissive – and convinced my parents that I was finally 'mixing with the right people' and that rent-free living arrangements were common among this group.

The Junior Dean of Gloucester College initially frowned upon the idea, saying, 'We are keen to integrate all members into college life, at least in their first year.' There it was Jess who argued the point, drawing attention to her membership of the college choir, attendance at chapel and excellent reports from her tutors. Little was expected of me, perhaps because I was known in college primarily for my injury. The arrangement was grudgingly allowed, although – it was made clear – we could not expect any reimbursement of rent and other fees paid in advance.

Jess and I became closer over that term, partly because of the joint battles with college authorities but also quite naturally. I wanted her and was surprised to find that she liked me too. She seemed quite as content in my company as I was in hers, and I found I did not really need other friends in college. We would spend the days at lectures or in the library, and then in the evenings we ate dinner together in hall and Jess – if she did not have orchestra rehearsals – would practise her violin while I read. It was, for Oxford, a very settled time. Franny joked that we already seemed to have been going out for years and this pleased me. After a few weeks of this life I wondered if we needed to move into Mark's house at all, or whether we could continue just as we had been.

But the wheels were already in motion. We moved into the house in March, towards the end of Hilary term, and began to get to know one another's habits and routines. I learned, for example, that Mark suffered from insomnia and frequently read his theology set books in the music room at 3 a.m., listening to 1930s dance records, and that for all her apparent nonchalance Franny worked harder than anyone I'd ever known – even Jess or Guntersen. Simon already harboured ambitions – he read, with intense seriousness, a multi-volume biography of Winston Churchill and Tony Benn's diaries, and I once walked into his room to find him addressing an empty armchair with the words 'Now really, Prime Minister . . .'. Emmanuella, despite her privilege, was an excellent cook, and the house was frequently filled with the aromas of Spanish cuisine.

One morning in April, Jess and I knew instantly from the insistent staccato of the knock at the door that the person trying to wake us up was Franny and no other.

Jess opened the door. Wordlessly, Franny marched into the room and slammed the door behind her. She was in her long white night-dress, her hair frizzy and wild.

'Have you *seen* who's in the kitchen?' she said at last.

We shook our heads.

'We've only just woken up,' I said.

'You'll never guess who he's bloody brought home this time.'

At least twice a week, Mark brought a young man home – often a 'townie' rather than another undergraduate. Once there had been a boy from sixth-form college. All of these had been agreeable if taciturn – a succession of crop-headed young men shovelling down cornflakes and leaving with a brisk 'cheers'. There was the slight matter of illegality to detain us, but as Mark himself was officially below the age of consent for gay sex at that time the whole thing seemed so uncertain as to be better ignored.

'It's only bloody Rufus McGowan!' said Franny.

We looked blank.

'Junior Dean of St Thomas's? Wrote *Thinking the State*? Gave the Stimfield lectures in political thought?' More blank looks. 'He was my *tutor* last term?'

'Oh, Good Lord,' said Jess.

'Too bloody right. I *heard* them last night. Heard them, Jess! At it! The author of *Thinking the State*.'

She breathed in and out slowly. 'I walked into the kitchen, saw him, he looked at me, I looked at him, and I turned and ran. Actually ran.'

'Perhaps Mark didn't know he was your tutor when he, um, found him?' I ventured.

'Oh yes, I'm sure of that,' spat Franny. 'I'm sure he didn't walk up to him at the urinals and go, "Fancy coming back to mine for a shag? By the way, did you ever teach British political history to any of the following people? I just ask because it might be awkward at breakfast?"'

We went down to breakfast together, to face off against Rufus McGowan en masse. He was the oldest person Mark had ever brought to the breakfast table by at least fifteen years, serious-faced, with a deep furrow in his brow and an untidy mop of curly red-brown hair. When we entered the kitchen, he was reading *The Times* and wearing a pair of pyjamas evidently intended for a much larger man – the striped top billowed around him and the trousers flopped over his feet. But for all his absurd appearance, it was unquestionably like having breakfast with a tutor. He rattled his paper, harrumphed and poured himself a cup of tea without offering any of us a drop. Mark himself sat contentedly at the other end of the table, munching his toast and reading a novel, apparently unaware of all that was going on around him.

Having become accustomed to Mark's night-time conquests needing to be put at ease, Jess wished Dr McGowan a good morning. He peered at her, nodded without saying a word and returned to his reading. The experience was miserably reminiscent of attending a tutorial, at least in my case: the tutors had very little to say in response to whatever I happened to offer them.

After a few moments Dr McGowan said, 'I see an UNPROFOR force has been ambushed in Bosnia. A clear example that rules of engagement are worthless. They can never anticipate battlefield conditions. Don't you agree, Miss Roth?'

Franny blanched and paused halfway through taking a piece of toast.

'Um,' she said. 'I, um . . .'

'And can you tell me who drafted the rules of engagement in Bosnia?'

'Um. General Cot?'

'Hmmm.' I had the distinct impression that Dr McGowan would rather Franny had got the answer wrong. 'He's been recalled by the UN, of course.'

Jess, noticing that Franny was attempting to back out of the room, grabbed her arm, squeezed it and drew her to the far side of the kitchen to make tea with us in abject silence.

Emmanuella came down next. She was in the house for only about half of each week and I'd been trying to stay out of her way. The drunken moment that first night hadn't been repeated; in fact she'd been a little cold with me. I couldn't tell if she was offended that I'd turned her down or annoyed that I'd gone as far as I had without stopping. In any case, she'd taken up with another Scandinavian athlete – this time Lars, a fencer from Oriel. I found unexpectedly that my jealousy was tinged with relief.

Lars was not with her this morning, however, and, expecting to see another of Mark's charming young boys, she leaned across the table and rattled the paper playfully. Her expression when it was put down and she saw not an eighteen-year-old but a man of mature years was one of undisguised horror.

'Oh!' she said. Then, recovering herself slightly and evidently thinking she must have misunderstood the situation, she put out her hand and said, 'I am Emmanuella. You are . . . a relative –' she looked around the table with confusion – 'a relative of Mark?'

'Come now, darling,' said Mark, looking up from his novel at last, 'you know better than that.' He looked at Emmanuella meaningfully, until she blushed, said, 'Oh!' and blushed still deeper.

Dr McGowan shook her hand, which she appeared to have forgotten she'd left in a position to be shaken, nodded and returned once more to the paper.

Simon, arriving in the kitchen at just the moment that this exchange took place, could do little more than stand at the doorway and gasp – he too had attended Dr McGowan's lectures, though more sporadically than Franny. Eventually, seeming to take the view that what he didn't acknowledge couldn't see him, he marched into the kitchen and busied himself at once making bacon and eggs. This flushed Dr McGowan. He had apparently been quite willing to appear oblivious of us, as long as we did not appear oblivious of *him*.

Observing Simon's back, he put down his paper with a great rustling and said in a low rumble, 'Good morning. I am Dr Rufus McGowan. And you are?'

Simon appeared to lose about ten years instantly, becoming a frightened schoolboy confronted with an angry master.

He said, 'Er, Simon . . .'

Dr McGowan looked at him. Simon went red.

'Studying?'

'Um . . . PPE.'

'Ah.' Dr McGowan leaned back in his chair, arms folded in front of him. Even in oversized pyjamas, the authority of an Oxford tutor was absolute. 'And what did you make of the assassination of the presidents of Rwanda and Burundi and the aftermath?'

Simon's eyes bulged.

'Um. I . . . um. It's disappointing?'

Dr McGowan stared at him for longer than was humane.

'What college are you at?' The word 'boy' seemed to hang inaudibly at the end of the sentence.

'Um . . . Keble.'

Dr McGowan snorted and returned to his paper as if *this* explained the evident dimness of Simon.

*

'What were you *thinking*?' asked Franny after Dr McGowan had left.

Mark shrugged his shoulders defensively.

'He's certainly different from your usual type,' said Jess. 'Where did you find him?'

Franny rolled her eyes.

'Martyrs' Memorial,' he said.

There was a little silence while we stared at Mark, thinking it through. Emmanuella, however, did not understand.

'You met him at the Memorial? But there is nothing there. Only the statues and a public bathroom.'

Mark nodded and grinned.

'What did you talk about?'

Mark leaned forward, his voice a low rumble, and said, 'There wasn't much talking involved.'

'But how . . .'

'Darling Manny,' he said. 'The lavatories under the Martyrs' Memorial are a place where gentlemen can find other gentlemen to give one another relief for the urges of the flesh. Dr McGowan and I have obliged one another there on several occasions. This time I suggested we repair somewhere more . . . congenial, and he agreed.'

'Oh!' said Emmanuella, her eyes widening. Then she frowned. 'I do not think this is very respectful to the martyrs, Mark, even if they were not Catholics.'

He frowned at her, then beamed. 'Yes,' he said, 'how right you are. I shall have to mention it at confession.'

'An interview with a divine,' said Dr Snippet. 'Doesn't it strike you that way, Mr Stieff?'

'I beg your pardon?'

Dr Snippet sighed and blew his nose.

'It is the root of all we do here, Mr Stieff. If you'll forgive me for going off on a tangent for a moment.'

It was by no means unusual for Dr Snippet to go off on a tangent. My one-on-one tutorials with him were a special benefit, conferred without warning by the college presumably in recognition of my lacklustre academic attainments. But the man never stuck to the subject at hand. When I'd asked whether his musings were relevant for the exams, he'd tutted and said, 'Mr Stieff, if all you cared about was examination results, you could have gone to –' he coughed, as if about to say a rude word – 'Keele. You are here not for a degree but for an education.'

'I mean to say, Mr Stieff,' said Dr Snippet, 'that is how we began. The tutorial. Five hundred years ago, when this college was founded, I would have been a priest and you a young nobleman. We would all have been Catholics then, and the private confession of one's sins would have been familiar to us. Much as – aheh-aheh-aheh – you come now to confess your sins of incomprehension.

'Psychotherapeutic practice, of course,' he continued, 'draws from quite the same wellspring. The monasteries may have been dissolved, Mr Stieff, but their ways are all around us! Of course, there would have been no *women* in the colleges then. Still, times change and we change with them.' He blew his nose so loudly that I was unable to decide if I had really heard him say, 'More's the pity.'

When I returned to Annulet House that afternoon, the phone was ringing in the side passage by the kitchen. I ran in to answer it.

'Hello?' I said. 'Hello?' I was breathless and the line was crackly.

'Marco!' called a woman's voice, followed by a babble of Italian.

'Stop, stop,' I said, catching my breath. 'Do you speak English? *Inglese?*'

There was a pause.

'I wish to speak to Mark. Is he there, please?' said the woman in accented tones.

'Um,' I said. 'He's not in.'

'Who is this, please?'

'It's, um, it's James. A friend of Mark's. I live here too.'

'Ahhhhh, he told me this. Some friends, to keep him company. *Bene.* Now James, this is Isabella. I am Mark's mother.'

She paused, as if knowing that I would need a moment to gather my thoughts. I thought with horror of the photographs in the study of a woman in diaphanous silk, and of the things Mark had told me about his parents.

Mark's father, Sir Mewan Winters, had ploughed the family money into industry in the 1950s and 1960s, turned his moderate fortune into a vast one and then, in the early 1970s, just after his fiftieth birthday and long a confirmed bachelor – with various cousins and nephews eagerly anticipating the inheritance that would one day be theirs – made a sudden match with Isabella, an actress who had appeared in a few mildly erotic Italian movies and was almost thirty years his junior. Mark had been their only child, and the marriage hadn't lasted. His mother had been too unstable, his father too distant. Mark was packed off to boarding school at seven, only for Isabella to remove him on a sudden whim at thirteen. According to Mark, she led a rackety life and had dragged him with her through much of it: several husbands, with one not always quite given up when the next was acquired, constant travel and now a great deal of time spent in California with a much younger lover, a weekly colonic irrigation, a personal vegan chef and a psychic counsellor on Tuesdays and Thursdays.

'Oh,' I said, 'er, hello.'

I think I expected she would suddenly start chanting at me.

'James,' she said, in a perfectly sensible voice, 'can you give to Mark a message from me? Tell him I will be in Oxford at the end of next week, yes? You will all like to meet me? You are not too busy?'

'Oh,' I said, trying desperately to stop remembering that I had seen a photograph of her naked breasts, 'yes I'd love to meet you. Er, that is, um, no, we're not too busy.'

She made a curt 'mm' sound, then said, 'I am glad. You will tell Mark that we spoke about this? You will not forget?'

'I won't forget.' I certainly wouldn't.

'You will give him the message as soon as you see him?'

'I'll even leave it for him, in case I'm out.'

She laughed. 'Good! Very responsible young man, James! Make sure he understands, James. At the end of next week. Friday.'

She gave me a number in Paris where she could be reached and hung up.

I stood in the passage holding the note I'd written. I looked around. Where could I put it that Mark would be sure to find it? The kitchen was cluttered with several days' worth of breakfast things. Mark employed a cleaner to come in twice a week to tidy up after us. Was today one of her days? Might she throw away this scrap of paper? An obvious solution came to mind.

Upstairs, I pushed open the door to Mark's bedroom with a jangle of nerves. It felt unexpectedly intimate to be here without his knowledge or permission. The room was large with, at one end, an enormous curved bay window. The bed was huge too – a cream-curtained four-poster. Mark's clothes were scattered across the floor, heaped in piles and bundled into black rubbish bags.

Books, mostly theology with titles like *Blood of Crucifixion* and *The Annotated Doctrine of Atonement*, were stacked neatly at one side of the little walnut desk, and pages of notes were arranged in a half-circle on the floor around the chair. I picked one up idly and read the essay title 'A God Who Does Not Suffer Cannot Save: Discuss'.

After a few moments I put the essay down, slightly bewildered. I'd known Mark was studying theology, but hadn't thought anyone could take it seriously. I was not religious. My parents were somewhere between agnostic and the woolliest Church of England. They'd married in a church, Anne and I had been baptized, and that had been that. Anne was a positive and committed atheist, asserting that 'the whole thing's rubbish. Not just rubbish. Pernicious rubbish'.

I put the note on his desk. As I stepped back, I noticed the edge of a brown figure hanging on the wall, mostly concealed behind the sweep of the curtains. I walked over to it and gingerly pulled back the edge of the curtain to find, as I'd half-known I would, a dark brown wooden crucifix, the length of my forearm, polished to a burnished gleam. The figure on the cross was emaciated, each rib showing clearly through the skin, a deep hollow between chest and pelvis. The figure's mouth was open in a grimace of agony, the flesh of the hands was ripped and battered around the nails.

It would have been better if it had been openly on display. That way I might have said to myself that it was a piece of art, appreciated for its skill and technique. But this hidden figure was something else.

An object for prayer, for belief. A private ritual. I felt revolted by the image, by its implicit praise for suffering and for humiliation and for pain. I wanted to hold up my wretched grinding knee and say, 'This? Is there glory in this?'

After a few dizzy and uncertain moments, I pulled the curtain back and limped from the room.

Mark did not return home until past midnight, by which time I had forgotten about the note. Franny had found a box of hats in the cellar labelled 'Maud, 1936' and was going through it. We particularly liked the fez decorated with two stuffed pheasants lolling uneasily on wires. Our first-year university exams were only a few weeks away now, and we longed for distractions.

'What do you think?' said Franny, sweeping her head from side to side to make the long tail feathers shake. 'Am I fit to be seen at Ascot?'

'Absolutely not,' said Simon, making a grab for the hat. 'You'd frighten the horses.'

Franny laughed and made to grab it back. There was a brief, noisy tussle.

'What's all this?' came a voice from the other side of the door.

It was Mark. I hadn't heard him come in; none of us had. We eyed each other nervously. We were still uncertain how free we could be with the things we found in the house.

Mark pushed open the door. He held up his hand. He was shaking.

'Who . . .' he began, but could not continue. He breathed in and out twice, then started again. 'Who left this bloody note for me?'

We looked at each other. For just a second, I felt as bewildered as the rest. I had left a note, but surely he must mean some other note, some more offensive missive?

His voice was almost a whisper. 'Who left this note in my room?'

I cleared my throat.

'Erm. I did? Sorry. I mean, sorry, I didn't mean to go into your room without permission. I just couldn't think of where else to leave it and your mother seemed so insistent that . . .'

He stared at me, as if I was an enemy he'd underestimated.

'You? You spoke to my mother?'

The others were staring at me. I couldn't imagine what they thought I'd written to Mark. I began to wonder if I'd had some sort of psychotic break and instead of 'Mark, your mum called, she's coming to visit next week' I'd written 'Mark, your mum called, she's a filthy whore', and smeared it with excrement.

'The phone was ringing,' I said. 'When I got in the phone was ringing so I answered it and –' I looked around – 'all it says is that Mark's mum is coming to visit.'

'Oh,' said Jess mechanically. 'That's lovely news, isn't it, Mark?'

'Ahm,' said Mark, and dropped the hand holding the note to his side. A few drops of blood rolled stickily down his hand and splashed on to the pale green carpet. They made perfect round circles. Mark looked down at his hand and then at all of us. His eyes were afraid, dumb and desperate.

'Oh!' said Emmanuella. 'Mark, you have hurt yourself!'

Mark did nothing. He stood in place and the blood rolled down his arm, dripping on to the carpet.

It was Jess, at last, who stood up and took him by the hand to the bathroom. It was Jess who cleaned his arm and dressed his wounds, not commenting on the five perfectly regular lateral scores across the inside of his upper arm. It was Jess who, afterwards, when he was quiet and peaceful, pulled back the sheets and put him to bed and gave me the razor to put in with my shaving kit until we came to some decision. It was Jess who did these things: the things a good person does.

7

First year, June, seventh week of term

It is striking to me now that it did not occur to any of us to telephone Isabella and persuade her to put off her visit. These days, if she were to call the house in San Ceterino, Mark would be cool and formal. He insists on speaking English with her, claiming that his Italian is too rusty to understand the rapid shower of her syllables. This is a lie; his Italian is perfect, far better than mine. But English slows her, brings her into a world of politeness, where she cannot quite bring off certain of her particular effects.

We did not think of our parents in this way though, not then: not as problems to be managed or contained, not even as entities quite separate from us.

So she arrived, as she had said she would, wearing a cream trouser suit and a wide-brimmed hat and carrying two turquoise suitcases. The wicker bag slung over her left arm, which appeared at first glance to contain a teddy bear, turned out on closer inspection to be a dog-carrier with the head of a little terrier puppy peeping incongruously out, like a gruesome experiment in dog-bag hybridization. She was still recognizable as the woman from the photographs – older, of course, the skin creased around her eyes, her hands beginning to mottle with liver spots – but nonetheless this was the woman whose half-naked form was displayed in a variety of poses on the walls of one of the small sitting rooms. I was reminded, suddenly, of Franny's horror at having heard Dr Rufus McGowan in bed with Mark. For all that we were here to learn, it was possible to have too much knowledge.

'Ooooof!' She mimed wiping the sweat from her brow. 'It is so hot. And not a drop of water for me to drink.'

'You should have called from the station, Mamma,' said Mark.

'I would have come to get you.' He spread out his arms to embrace her.

'*Momento*,' she said, hoisting her bag. 'I must let Colonel Felipe out of his bag. Poor he, he has been so good.' She swung the bag round, released a hidden clasp and lifted the dog out. His legs waggled as she held him up. She deposited him on the terrace and he swayed slightly, before skittering off towards the rose bushes.

'I named him Colonel Felipe after my great-grandfather,' she said. 'He was a colonel in the army of Pavia. Seven hundred men were lost owing directly to his order to advance to the left, facing right. He meant to say, "To the right, facing left". Or –' she waved a hand uncertainly – 'perhaps it was the other way. The poor man felt such shame he attempted suicide but owing to a defective pistol was unable to finish the task. He shot his right ear off instead. Is it not terribly sad?'

'Mamma . . .' began Mark.

'Marco, do not stand there doing nothing. Bring some water please in a bowl for Colonel Felipe. He is thirsty.'

Mark backed away a pace or two, then turned and hurried through to the kitchen. While he was gone, Isabella introduced herself to us all. We tried to call her 'Signora Ranelli' – or, in my case, 'Mrs Winters', momentarily forgetting that Mark's parents had been divorced for many years – but she brushed off these attempts at formality.

'Isabella, please. Call me only Isabella. No Mrs,' she continued, 'no Signora. Isabella. Like one of your friends.'

As Mark returned from the house, carrying a deep pudding basin of water for the dog, Isabella frowned at him.

'No, no. Can you not see that this is too deep for poor Colonel Felipe? He will not be able to reach with his little head! Or he will drown! Bring a smaller bowl.'

Throwing a look of loathing at the dog that made me suspect he rather hoped to drown it, Mark went back into the house. We stood awkwardly in silence on the terrace until he returned a few moments later with a soup plate of water.

Isabella looked at him suspiciously.

'You do not look well, Marco. You do not speak. Do you sleep? Has he slept well?'

She looked around at all of us, frowning. We nodded eagerly, although it wasn't true: he hadn't slept well for days before her arrival.

'Good. You must learn to take care of yourself, Marco. Now give Colonel Felipe his water please.'

Mark, moving clumsily, put down the dog's water. It took a few eager sips, then stopped, its head cocked to one side, waiting. Isabella looked at it fondly and as if this, only this, had reminded her, she spread out her arms to Mark.

'Marrrrco, how good it is, how good to see you.'

She wrapped her glittering ring-coated fingers around his shoulders and pulled his face down to hers. She planted kisses on his cheeks, one two, one two. Then, quickly, she muttered something in Italian, too low and too fast for me to catch even if I had been able to understand it. Mark flinched. He took two rapid steps backwards.

'Now, my darlings,' she said, 'you will forgive me. I am so tired and it has been such a long way. Do you, perhaps, in all of this big house, have a chair?'

'Mamma . . .' murmured Mark, but Emmanuella was already leading Isabella through the open French doors to the garden room. Isabella swung back and laced her arm through Jess's, who allowed herself to be taken through. Simon shrugged, picked up the turquoise cases and followed.

On the terrace, Colonel Felipe had finished his water and relieved himself on the terrace, and was now attacking a small privet bush, snarling and making little runs at it.

Franny reached out a tentative arm and touched Mark between the shoulder blades. He did not shrug her off.

She said, 'Are you all right?'

Mark smiled. 'God, yeah. She's a pain, though, isn't she?'

'Totally. Yeah, totally. D'you think we should bring the Colonel in?'

We stared in silence at Colonel Felipe. He had a branch of privet between his teeth and was shaking it about, yipping and pulling his lips back to bare his pink and black gums.

'I'm not going anywhere near the little rat.' He drew his foot back thoughtfully, balancing on one leg, as if about to aim a swift hard kick at the Colonel. For a moment, I thought he'd do it. But as he got close enough almost to brush the dog's fur, he pulled back, wheeled around and marched into the house.

'. . . and all this doing was for nothing, for the villa fell from the cliff into the ocean!' Isabella finished as we walked through the French doors.

Simon guffawed appreciatively. In those few minutes, one of Isabella's suitcases had been opened. It was full of tissue-paper wrappings: pink and gold and green and white and blue. Isabella had taken Jess and Emmanuella to sit on either side of her and was patting their hands.

'Marco,' she said, 'you remember Ginella? We saw her that summer in Las Palmas?'

Mark nodded warily.

'I have been telling your friends about when . . .' She looked at him, suddenly uncertain. 'Ah, it does not matter. Marco, I must hear all about your studies. Have you been working hard? Come here, come and sit by me.'

She patted the half-inch of space on the sofa between her and Jess. Mark, ignoring her, sat sullenly in a chair a little way off.

He indicated the tissue paper. 'So what's all this, Ma? Did you buy up half of Paris?'

'Oh!' said Isabella. 'Only a few things, some little things. For your friends.'

She bent over the suitcases and pulled out various gifts: a pair of leather driving gloves for Simon, a blank calfskin book for me, some bath salts and perfume in intricate glass bottles and silk scarves for the girls.

I felt uncomfortable. I was not accustomed to receiving expensive gifts, let alone from a friend's mother. Only Emmanuella knew the proper form. She swooped down on Isabella, kissed her, then wound her scarf around her neck, trying out different knots in the mirror. Simon, noticing how well this reception looked, put his gloves on too, but the effect was not the same.

From the bottom of the case Isabella pulled a large gift box covered in white suede.

'Can you guess what it is I have brought for you, Marco?'

Mark assumed a satirical expression.

'Why no, Mamma. Is it Enrico's wig collection?'

'Marco!' Isabella rapped him on the knee, but she smiled. 'Enrico was my second husband, after Marco's father,' she confided. 'He was a pig, a tyrant, not even half as much money as he said. I divorced him after five months. And, for a joke, Marco and I stole all his toupees and made a bonfire of them. But they were plastic! They did not burn, they melted all into the grass and the gardener had to dig them out. The smell was beyond description.' She flared her nostrils as if the scent had again invaded her nose. 'No, no, Marco. I have brought you something wonderful. Open, open.'

Mark pulled at the gold ribbons tying down the lid and opened the box. He stared at the contents for a second or two completely impassively. He looked at his mother with suspicion.

'Really?' he said.

'Certainly, why not?'

Slowly, Mark lifted out an object of gold and glass and placed it on the coffee table.

It was a shining confection, an ornate glass box covered with gold scrollwork, with six curved gold feet like eagle's talons holding on to orbs. There was a white velvet-lined central compartment and a mechanism of notched cylinders and metal combs.

Mark felt underneath the box, turned an unseen key – we heard the strained cranking – then opened the lid. A metallic note sounding out a childhood tune: 'Au Clair de la Lune'. It was a music box. We listened in silence as the melody played out three times and the box wound down, the final notes coming in a syrupy slow dragging drip.

'Of course,' Mark said when the tune was finished, 'it's a very gaudy thing.'

'You loved it when you were a boy, Marco, do you remember?' Before giving him a chance to reply Isabella barrelled on. 'It was my mother's. It is precious. It was made for her family 150 years ago, very rare. This box, Marco could not hear it enough. He used to ask for it in the night when he was frightened and she would put it on the little table by his bed and start it to play. She left the door so he could see the light from the hallway. Do you remember, Marco? In the night?'

Mark's expression was hooded, his eyes half-closed.

'I remember,' he said at last. 'I loved it.'

'You should thank your mamma for bringing this beautiful thing for you all the way from California.'

And he murmured, 'Thank you, Mamma.'

The following day, Isabella invited a monk for tea. Franny told me once that Mark's father – who was the source of Mark's money but was mostly absent from his life – had made a vast donation to his own old college to secure their agreement for Mark to study philosophy and theology, even though they did not officially offer this subject. He had likewise arranged, through some arcane connection, that Mark should take half his tutorials among the monks of St Benet's Hall.

Father Hugh was, I believe, a fairly senior figure at the college. It was impossible to take him seriously, though. First, because of Mark's nickname for him, 'Hugh the Huge Hunky Monk', and with his strong jaw, rough mop of brown curls and muscular physique, I could see what Mark meant. He had a way of crossing his legs and hurling himself against the sofa at moments of animation which suggested that his cassock was about to open, laying bare all that ought to remain concealed. He had brought with him an oiled olive-wood rosary as a gift for Isabella – I guessed that Mark's family had exhibited their generosity to Benet's too – and two people he described as 'young Christians'. They were Rosemary – a girl with a nose made for dripping and a shapeless outfit of pale blue – and Eoin, who, despite his name, was thoroughly English and wore the Oriel College rowing jersey.

I wasn't invited to the tea party and all the others were out. But as I crossed the hall, Mark called to me through the open door to the long salon. He was hunched over, on a chair between the two sofas, one occupied by his mother and Rosemary, the other by Father Hugh and Eoin. He looked like a tethered dog.

'James!' he said. 'James! Come and have tea with us!'

Isabella frowned. The monk and his two young friends looked at me with shining-eyed interest. I almost said no. But then Mark caught my gaze again. He put the tips of his fingers together into an almost-praying gesture and mouthed 'Please'. So I came in and sat down.

Eoin had just returned from the Himalayas, as he was pleased to inform us after introductions had been made. He pronounced the word with extraordinary stress on the second syllable, gulping all his sentences from the back of his throat.

'Yuh,' he said, 'eight days climbing. Failed to summit because Callan Gosset – do you know Callan?'

This, startlingly, was directed at me. On further reflection, I supposed that he had every right to assume that I came from his social group: he had found me living in this house, after all. I shook my head.

'No? Shame. Top man, Callan. Absolutely barking mad, been digging wells in Namibia with Icthus Relief?'

I shook my head again.

'No? Never mind. The thing was, Callan's fingers froze. Tried to thaw them out, all five of us pissed on them. Sorry.' This was to Isabella with a rueful smile. 'But nothing for it. Gangrene set in, had to get back to base camp. Missed the summit by 120 feet.'

Father Hugh kicked his sandalled feet out, billowing his cassock dangerously.

'It was all for Christian Aid, wasn't it, Eoin? Wonderful cause, I always say.'

'Oh, yuh,' said Eoin, through a mouthful of cake. 'Tremendous thing, sponsored, raised £15,000. Thereabouts.'

Isabella nodded appreciatively. 'Isn't that lovely, Marco? All the money for charity.'

Mark muttered something under his breath. I thought I might have heard the words 'sponsored silence', but it was too low for me to catch.

'What was that, Mark?' boomed Father Hugh.

'Oh, I was just thinking, Eoin, that you should try other sponsored activities. Maybe an ascent of the Eiger?'

Eoin took another sandwich from the pile on the table in front of him and bit down happily.

'Yuh,' he said, 'this summer, kayaking along the Amazon. For the Glaucoma Trust.'

'Marvellous,' murmured Isabella.

'Still a few places if you want to come,' Eoin said to me and Mark, wolfing another sandwich. 'Have to register, get vaccinations. Three weeks in a canoe, Amazon river, chance of a lifetime.'

I shook my head. Mark turned smoothly in his seat.

'What about you, Rosemary?' he said. 'Got any summer plans you can't cancel?'

Rosemary sniffed away a non-existent drip and spoke so quietly that we all instinctively leaned forward.

'I'll be in Rome,' she whispered.

'Oh!' Isabella leaned even further forward, full of excitement. 'Roma! The most beautiful city in the world! Where do you stay? What do you see?'

Rosemary sniffed again and cleared her throat. If possible, she spoke even more softly.

'The Sisters of Holy Charity have kindly given me board,' she said. 'I am studying manuscripts held in the Vatican.' She lowered her voice a touch. 'For my PhD.'

Father Hugh smiled a toothy but engaging smile.

'Rosemary's quite a star of the Theology Department. She's at All Souls, you know.'

Even I could not fail to look at Rosemary with increased respect at this news. All Souls College is one of Oxford's legends, the kind of anachronism that surely could not have survived until the present day, and yet it stands. It is a college with no students, giving fellowships to those who – having naturally gained a first – are bright enough to impress the other fellows in its examinations, one of which consists of writing for three hours on a single word.

Isabella, confused about the meaning of the words 'All Souls', nonetheless registered the admiration on my face and Mark's.

'You see, Marco,' she said, 'it is not only duddy-fuddies in the Catholic Society, is it, Father?'

'No indeed,' he said, 'and we don't demand any particular commitment. Although naturally –' he shifted his legs again in that disturbing way – 'I always say that the more you put in, the more you get out. Are *you* a Catholic, James?'

'I? Oh, er, no,' I said. I decided to be bold. 'I'm not a Christian, actually. I'm an agnostic if anything, I suppose.'

Father Hugh laughed three bellowing guffaws.

'You're not even sure about that, eh? Well, we're not prejudiced. Come along to the Catholic Society in any case for wine and my atrocious home-made shepherd's pie. Bring Mark.'

'Oh no, I don't think I –'

'You should go, Marco,' chimed in Isabella. 'It is good for you to have Catholic friends. This is what I want for you. It would keep you from . . . I . . .' She trailed off, looked at me and said, 'I do not mean to be offence, James, but I would like Marco to have more Catholic friends. Not so many a-nose-stick. A nice group of Catholic friends would help him with his . . .' She frowned as if reaching for a word, then finished, 'It would help him.'

Even Eoin and Rosemary shifted a little in their seats at this. Mark became very still, very quiet.

'Now, of course, we don't want to tell anyone who to be friends with, do we?' Father Hugh rearranged himself and chuckled. 'I always say that a wide social circle provides the furniture for a mental –'

'But,' said Isabella, cutting across him, 'excuse me, do you not think that a circle can be too wide, Father? Not every friend is suitable.'

'Ah yes, that's certainly true,' said Father Hugh, 'but nonetheless I think we can allow some –'

'And the right group helps a person to follow a good path.' She turned her anxious frown on Mark. 'Like the Lord, Marco, and His disciples.'

'You think I should get myself some disciples, Ma?' He seemed curiously detached. Quiet still and slow. 'Twelve people to follow me about and do what I tell them? Sounds good to me.'

'Do not be silly, Marco!' She slapped her hand vigorously on his forearm in agitation, alarming Colonel Felipe, who bounded across the room to cower underneath an armchair. 'You are always so, always you try not to understand, always you . . .'

She broke suddenly into a stream of Italian, too rapid for me to catch even a word or two. Her hands were balled into angry fists. She pointed first at me, then at Rosemary and Eoin, speaking emphatically. There were little squeaks of rage. I should not have cared to have this speech directed at me.

Mark stiffened under the assault. At last, when the flow of her words ceased, he said, 'So you still don't trust me, is what you're saying? It's not enough for Father Hugh to keep an eye on me.' Father Hugh stirred but did not attempt a denial. 'You want me on a leash. Perhaps you want to carry me in your handbag too, like your bloody dog?'

Father Hugh, raising his hand in a benedictory fashion, said, 'I'm sure your mother only wants what's best for you, Mark. I'm sure we all do.' He beamed at the group. 'Family discussions can become so heated, and I always say –'

Isabella spoke over him again, but more quietly, her fury spent. 'I do trust you. That is why I brought you the box. I know you can be trusted now. I know you are different now. But the Catholic Society . . .'

'I don't care about the fucking music box. Take it back for all I care. I don't want anything from you. And I don't want anything from the fucking Catholic Society either.'

Mark spoke very low and very quickly, and then there was silence. Eoin was still holding a sandwich mid-bite. Rosemary had folded her hands neatly in her lap and was staring at them.

Father Hugh stirred again, refolded his legs and said, 'Families know just how to needle each other, I always say. But it's good to air grievances and to move on. Now, Mark, I'm sure your mother simply means that you might enjoy from time to time the company of delightful energetic young people like Eoin here, or Rosemary.'

The two sat stock still, appearing neither delightful nor energetic.

'No one wants you to give up your other friends, of course not, but –'

'You don't know what she wants,' said Mark. He stood up. 'I apologize, Father Hugh, but I have to go now.' He lurched out of the room and slammed the door behind him.

At the noise, Colonel Felipe began to yap loudly, baring his little pointed teeth and shaking his head. Isabella rushed over to the armchair, gathered the Colonel to her and petted him, cooing in soft Italian until he calmed.

'Oh, Father Hugh, Father Hugh. I am so sorry for this . . . all this anger, I am so sorry.'

It seemed like a good moment for me to excuse myself. Father Hugh shook my one hand between his two, shaking his head and grinning winningly as he muttered, 'Agnostic . . .'

He, Isabella and Colonel Felipe headed out through the back of the house towards the garden, while I climbed the stairs slowly to the first floor. My knee was hurting a great deal, as it often does in hot weather even now. I took the stairs one at a time, keeping my injured leg stiff and bending only the good knee.

At the top of the stairs I paused. Should I go after Mark? Perhaps he would be grateful for the company. I stepped heavily along the corridor when I heard a crash, a loud exasperated growl and several short bangs coming from his room.

'Mark?' I called, and the noise ceased.

'Mark?' I said again.

'I'm fine!' he called out. 'It's nothing.' His voice was thick.

I stood for a little while in the corridor.

'Sure?' I said at last.

'Yup, yeah. It's nothing. I'm fine.'

I stood a while longer, then turned and walked back towards my room.

The next morning, Sunday, Isabella made ready to leave. She repacked her suitcases, with Colonel Felipe yapping and snarling among the Bodleian-branded carrier bags and the Oxford University sweaters. I hid in my bedroom, hoping to remain out of sight. It was then that Mark came to ask me for the return of his razor.

I hesitated.

'For God's sake,' he said, holding out his hand. 'If I wanted to again, don't you think I could just get something from the kitchen?'

He waited patiently while I went through my bag. The razor was old, horn-handled, a pleasant thing to hold in one's palm. I passed it to him without comment.

It was only when he turned to go that I found myself saying, 'What did she say to you yesterday? What happened?'

He cocked his head to the side.

'Ancient history, my friend, ancient history.'

'But what?' I persisted, surprised at myself. I found I wanted to know very much. 'What history? That is –' I could not help the hedge – 'if you don't mind saying.'

'Oh . . .' He thrust his hands deep into his pockets. 'We were alone together for a long time, Ma and me. She has notions. About my soul, you know. I think she secretly hopes I'll become a monk. Keep me safe.'

'Because you're gay?'

His eye was mocking and sharp.

'Lord, no. She doesn't care about that. No, no.'

He smiled faintly, a strange-angled smile.

'So what, then? What's she afraid of?'

He thinned his lips and said, very quickly, 'Look, I had a breakdown once, OK? It's not serious. It never was. She panicked a bit.' Then, blinking, looking for a moment quite different from the man I'd known up to now, younger and more serious, he said, 'Don't tell the others. I'd rather they didn't know.'

He turned and walked swiftly downstairs.

Mark went out that afternoon unexpectedly. He had said goodbye to his mother, but she would not leave without bidding him farewell again on the doorstep. So we waited and waited for his return. When he finally reappeared at 6.30 in the evening, Isabella was irritable and Colonel Felipe was unapproachable, growling and chewing an anti-macassar to pieces.

'We have been waiting, Marco. Where have you been? I have been ready to leave for hours and we have been waiting for you.'

'I don't see why you had to wait for me,' said Mark. 'You could have left when you were ready. *I* wouldn't have minded.'

Isabella frowned deeply.

'It's nicer this way, though,' Jess said quickly. 'We can all say good-bye together, can't we?'

This appeal brought a general nodding agreement. Isabella, though, glanced sidelong at Jess. I wondered how we all appeared to her. A gathering of heathens, trying to draw her son from the true path? Could she really think that Jess, of all people, would do harm?

'No, Marco,' said Isabella, 'I could not have left. I need something from you. I have decided to take the music box home with me. My mamma's box. It is too valuable to leave in this house without proper locks. We will keep it in California, where we are insured.'

Mark blanched.

'You can't,' he said dully.

'I think I must, Marco,' said Isabella. 'Bring it to me, please.'

'I can't,' said Mark. 'I . . . I don't know where it is.'

Isabella frowned.

'But, what do you mean, Marco? Where did you put it? Have you lost it?'

'I don't know,' said Mark. He was looking at the floor. A flush was slowly travelling up his neck.

Despite myself, I felt heat rising in my own cheeks in sympathy.

'Marco,' said Isabella, 'bring the box now, please.'

'I told you,' he said through gritted teeth, 'I. Don't. Know. Where. It. Is.' He breathed in and out once, a choked and grating breath, then gabbled, 'I went to look for it in my room last night but it was gone and I don't know where it is someone must have come into the house and taken it.'

'Taken . . .' Isabella brought a freckled hand to her face.

The rest of us looked furtively at one another. That one of us could have stolen the music box was unthinkable.

'It must have been a thief,' supplied Mark, 'who sneaked in some time.'

'And this thief knew where to find your music box, Marco? In all this great house?' Her arms were folded across her chest now.

'I . . .' Mark hesitated then, with casual bravado, 'Well, you did wrap it rather gaudily, Mother.'

Isabella drew breath. We waited. If the box had been stolen, if one of us were suspected as dishonest, this house was over.

'Wait,' said Simon, standing up. 'I think I might have seen it . . . Wait here.'

He sprinted up the staircase. We heard him thump along the corridor on the first floor and throw open a door at the far end of the hall.

'I've found it!' Simon shouted.

He dashed down the stairs, taking them two at a time, holding the white suede box.

'I've found it!' he said again. 'It was in the storeroom. Spotted it this morning when I went to look for towels. You put it there by mistake, didn't you? Last night?'

Mark nodded slowly. 'Yes, by mistake. That sounds . . . yes. Stupid of me.'

His speech was thick and drawn out.

'Come on, Mamma,' he said. 'Now you have the box, let me drive you to the station.'

Isabella took the box from Simon's hands and opened the lid. Half a syllable escaped from Mark's lips, an unintelligible noise, and Isabella said, 'Oh.' She put it on the table and I saw what was inside.

The music box was broken. The glass panes were cracked, the lid unhinged, one of the legs twisted. The mechanism had become unhoused and was rattling around inside the box. The ornate surface of the box was shattered, as if it had been thrown, hard, against a wall.

'How did this happen?' said Isabella.

'I . . .' said Mark, 'I don't know, I don't know.' He was twisting, his entire body writhing awkwardly in a gesture of such self-disgust that we all knew at once what had happened.

'I don't know,' he said again, more softly.

Later, when we were alone, Jess asked why I'd done what I did, and I could not explain except by shrugging and saying, 'It wasn't so hard.' I could not explain that I'd thought about the word 'break-down', looked at the shattered box and understood what Mark was afraid of. It wasn't just that Mark's family could take the house away from him – away from us – though that was bad enough. It was that whatever independence he had won, in his dependent life, could be revealed as a sham. He needed us, I realized. The mythical group of friends who are closer than family, who replace family. It is a lie, of course. Friends are friends and family is family. But it is a neces-sary lie.

I thought he needed to be saved and that it was for me to do. In that moment I was lost.

'It was me,' I said.

Isabella turned astonished eyes to me.

'*You*, James? But why? Why would you do this?'

'I, er, it was an accident,' I said. 'I, um, I dropped it.'

There was no going back now, only plunging onward.

'I, er, well, I dropped it from the attic. Yes,' I said, warming to my theme, 'I often go there to, you know, get away from everything. I took it there yesterday afternoon. I just wanted to play with it but I was really stupid and I was hanging out of the window and fiddling with the box and, bang, dropped it. Four storeys. And then I, um . . . well, it bounced off the flagstones and fell into the under-growth, and I had to go trampling around to find it, and I think I must have trodden on it a few times. When I found it . . .' I trailed off, gazing at the broken thing.

Isabella stared at me, then back at the box, then back to my face.

'But,' she said, 'but why did you not tell me? Why did you put it back into the box?'

'I was embarrassed,' I said. 'I didn't want to tell you I'd done some-thing so stupid. I thought I could confess to Mark after you left. I'm . . . I'm really sorry. Mark, I'm so, so sorry. I know it meant a lot to you, your grandmother . . .' I looked into his eyes.

'Mark?' I said. 'Mark, can you forgive me?'

He blinked. He became, again, Mark. Cool in repose, elegant in outline.

'Oh, James,' he said, and his voice was warm, 'of course I forgive you. Of course, of course, it was only a silly, silly mistake, wasn't it? Wasn't it, Mamma?'

Isabella could scarcely fail to concur.

'Oh yes, James, you are forgiven.'

Mark stretched out his arms and welcomed me into his embrace.

8

First year, Preliminary Examinations and the Long Vacation

Mark talks a great deal about sacrifice. It's one of his themes, although at times he places himself in the martyr's role and at times in the place of the one for whom sacrifices are made, depending on his mood. After debating the matter with himself – my own ideas do not figure in his theology – he comes to the conclusion that both partners in a sacrifice are one. Like God and His son, the one who demands the sacrifice and the one who is sacrificed are the same.

Mark enjoys these paradoxes. He sometimes returns to the music-box episode in his entanglements but is always careful to point out that it was not a true sacrifice, because I had nothing to lose. At the worst, Isabella would have asked me to pay for the box and Mark would have given me the money. He says it was a piece of theatre. 'You've always been the more dramatic of the two of us, you know. You're just quieter about it.'

In a sense, he is right. At his moments of high drama he is silent, acting without debate or announcement. I think of him poised like a half-folded penknife on the edge of the water, or of his face like a stone at the funeral. It's only when there's nothing worth saying that he can't stop talking.

'One slice or two?' asked Mark, poised bread in hand at the toaster. 'I don't know why I say one or two, actually. It could easily be three or four or five or a whole toasted loaf. Or, for that matter, a half a slice, a quarter, an eighth, a sixteenth. James, you understand maths, so maybe you can continue?'

'A thirty-second,' I said, looking over my notes again, and munching my Weetabix. 'A sixty-fourth, a one-hundred-and-twenty-eighth, a two-hundred-and-fifty-sixth, a five-hundred-and-twelfth. I think,'

I said, looking up, 'that to all practical purposes that'd surely be a crumb of toast. Do I need to go on into atoms?'

'Certainly not,' said Jess. 'You'd never find the atomic marmalade to have with it. Two please. Slices, not atoms. Why don't *you* sit down and have some breakfast?'

Mark bounced on the balls of his feet, fiddled with the glass jars of pasta and rice, almost dropped one of the lids, recovered, spun on his heel, replaced the lid and jumped back to attention when the toaster popped.

'I think better on an empty stomach.' He frowned. 'Or is that sex?'

'You'd better work it out before you start the exam,' said Jess, 'or you'll confuse the invigilators.'

'Confuse or delight,' said Mark. 'Don't you know you're allowed to take off anything you like once you're inside Exam Schools?'

We knew. We knew all such ridiculous, beautiful tales and traditions. We were dressed in subfusc: black trousers, white shirts, black ties, academic gowns and mortarboards – the compulsory attire for university examinations. Franny, who had already started the reading for next year's sociology paper, called it 'a typical assertion of financial and intellectual superiority by a potlatch-like act: Oxford students demonstrate that they're so rich they can afford special exam clothes and so clever they can be brilliant even when uncomfortable'.

But Franny and Simon had finished their exams the day before and were still in bed, and I rather enjoyed the ceremonial. The previous afternoon I'd purchased red carnations, which showed that this was our last day of exams.

Jess finished her toast, took a swig of tea and said, 'Flower me.'

I pinned the carnation carefully to her gown.

Mark leaned forward to watch and when I was finished said, 'Now do me,' and puffed out his chest towards me.

I pinned a flower to him willingly. Things had changed between us since the music box. Not drastically, not violently, but the change was clear to me. I felt warmer towards him.

Jess leaned up on tiptoes for a kiss and Mark hugged me.

'Champagne on the lawn at 6, all right?' he said.

'Good luck,' I said.

'See you on the other side,' he said.

Exams were over just before the longest day in the year, when the light of the evening lasted until past 10 p.m., and the night was gentle. We lay in the sun on the lawn that afternoon, our bodies extended like spokes around the sundial, warmed and drowsy. Mark rolled a joint and passed it round.

Franny lay with her head in Simon's lap as they compared choices, rubric by rubric.

She said, 'You did the one on de Gaulle? It didn't look like it offered much opportunity to be clever.'

Simon patted her curls gently. 'I'm not as clever as you though, so it doesn't matter.'

Franny made a 'come come' noise, but I could tell this remark had pleased her.

Emmanuella smoked a long white cigarette from a packet with a Scandinavian name, leaned back and streamed the smoke into the air. She was wearing a loose orange halter dress, her hair pouring down her bare back.

She said, 'I was not surprised by any question. Not at all.'

Simon leaned forward, pulled her hair and said, 'Stop showing off.'

Emmanuella pinked and pouted and took some more champagne.

The bottle passed around again. We brought out food and wound the radio cord through the grass to play Fox FM, tinny and distorted. When 'Boys and Girls' came on, with its creaking, insistent beat, Mark and Franny danced on the lawn. The sky turned from pale blue to a deeper, more magnanimous hue. It became a glorious, silk-black evening filled with glow-worms, a plethora of tiny lights winking and flashing from the bushes, like the stars which were that night almost musically bright.

At midnight, Simon yawned and said, 'Mates, I've got to get to bed.'

After the general protest had died down he said, 'Got to. Start work on Thursday, Dad's coming tomorrow at 8 and I haven't started packing yet.'

There was more argument. The champagne bottle lolled on the blue velvet grass and the stars swam, and eventually it was Mark who said, 'He's got work. He has to.'

And Simon said, 'I'll see you all in a couple of weeks anyway, right?'

'At your parents', yeah,' said Jess.

'Not me,' said Emmanuella. 'I must be in Madrid all summer.'

And Simon let out a roar and charged at Emmanuella. She screamed as he lifted her up to the stars and crunched a martini glass under his sandal, letting out all the glitter and bubbles. He spun her around, the orange dress streaming out behind her like underwater seaweed, and crushed her to him in a hug and set her down giggling and gasping on to the grass.

He looked around.

'Anyone else?'

We shook our heads.

'Right then,' and he beat his chest at the sky and he and Franny went to bed.

Not long after that Lars arrived for Emmanuella. He crashed through the garden to reach us, and when he emerged, he appeared downcast and serious, even though he had arrived so late, and so clumsily and with such an obvious purpose. Emmanuella allowed him to help her to her feet and I thought, I never understood her at all, never knew a particle of who she was. She wished us goodnight graciously and the orange dress swirled in the grass and I could tell that Lars was impatient to his fingers' ends to be touching her. I found I felt amused, with only the tiniest flicker of smoky jealousy at the edge of my thoughts.

And then we were three. We sat among the remnants of the picnic, eating an olive or quail's egg from time to time. We lit several of the storm-lantern candles dotted around the edges of the lawn and they cast a gentle light. We drank a little more, peering into the bottles' ends to see whether every drop had gone, and buoyed by our own lightness we stayed up a little longer and a little longer.

It was 3 a.m. and Jess had already fallen asleep several times for a moment or two in my arms when she whispered that she was so tired she had to go to bed. Through her starched pale pink shirt, her breasts pushed against my chest as she kissed me goodnight. I placed my hand between her shoulder blades and pulled her down for a kiss: wet, open-mouthed, her body resting on mine, pushing down into me. Her left leg was between mine. I could feel the pressure of her pelvis on my stomach, the slight friction. Mark, lying on his back next to me, heel to head, sat up and said, 'Oh, just go and fuck already.' Jess's eyes were half-closing with sleep and she smiled and shook her head a little. She lay for a while along my body, and then gently disentangled herself and went to bed.

'It's nearly dawn,' said Mark. 'We should be facing east at a time like this.'

I looked and saw that at the edge of the world a thin line of blue had cracked open the black and glittering sky. One or two birds had noticed this too; a bubbling warble came from the holly hedge. So we repaired, with the final bottle of champagne, to the huge swing chair suspended from a low-hanging oak branch and sat in silence for a while watching the crack of light widen and day enter the world again. I found myself thinking, perhaps this will be the last time, perhaps I'll be sent down after those exams, perhaps this is all I was ever going to get.

And without quite meaning to I said aloud, 'I'm afraid I'll never get to come here again.'

Mark was lying back in the swing chair, one foot trailing near the ground. He gave it a push and we rocked gently.

'I'm not going to throw you out, am I?' he said.

'I know,' I said. 'It's not that.'

'You can come here whenever you like.'

I took a breath and spoke. 'I might fail,' I said. 'I might be sent down. I really might.'

I hadn't said it to Jess, not like this. She believed in thinking positively, in not allowing doubts to enter one's mind.

'Yeah,' said Mark. 'I might too, but it doesn't really matter, does it?'

'I'd have to go back home.'

'Don't see why. If you get sent down you can carry on living here, can't you?'

'Really?'

'Of course. You could go to Brookes or something if you wanted. There's no reason . . .' He toed the grass thoughtfully. 'There's no reason we all can't go on living here forever, you know.'

'Forever?'

Mark dug his heel into the ground and set the swing going again.

'Why not? Why not forever? The house is big enough, and we could make it as we liked it, and change it when we wanted. Why should it ever end?'

'I should think we'll want to get jobs, won't we? Simon wants to be Prime Minister.'

Mark wrinkled his nose. 'Oh, jobs. Well, he can be Prime Minister from here, can't he?'

He sat up and jabbed at the ground with both heels, sending the swing arcing back, his legs held stiff in front of him.

'Yes, if you just rename the house Chequers, I expect that'd sort it.'

Mark laughed.

'See? It's not so hard. But really, you've got nothing to worry about. You're welcome here. Especially after . . .'

He looked at me and then at his feet. The swing had come to a halt again, and he kicked gently at the dandelion clouds among the grass.

'It was OK. She couldn't be as angry with me as she could with you, you know? It was fine.'

'It was good,' said Mark. 'You were good. It was more than I deserved. Do you know,' he spoke quickly, 'do you know I mentioned you in confession? What I did to you the first night, I am sorry for it, with the hash cake. I am sorry. I had a penance for it particularly. And all the other clumsy things. I am so often stupid, but I am sorry. Do you think we can be friends?'

He said this with the simple sincerity of a child and I found that I could not help responding in the same way.

'Yes, I hope so,' I said.

He hugged me then, briefly, one arm thrown around my shoulders, and I hugged him back.

Afterwards, we sat for a while in silence beneath the vast, lightening skyful of stars. While some cover of darkness still remained, he started to talk, quite slowly and precisely, about his mother. He told me about her four marriages 'so far' and her lovers and her strange oeuvre of 1960s movies and her exotically aristocratic relatives and her house in California with the macrobiotic chef.

'For a long time we only had each other,' he said at one point.

Then later, after he had told the story of how his mother set one of his father's Jaguars on fire during their divorce, he said, 'It doesn't sound quite normal, does it?'

And I said, 'She's not like my mother. But I don't think normal's so great either.'

He said, 'I'm so fucking embarrassed, you know? That you all had to put up with her and her weirdness and Father Hugh and . . . I'm just so fucking embarrassed.'

And I said, 'You don't have anything to be embarrassed about. She's horrible to you, but she was charming to us.'

He looked at me gratefully. A long, careful look.

He put one foot on the ground to steady himself, leaned forward, rested his hand on my upper arm and pressed his lips to mine. There was a moment's pause. He closed his eyes, then opened them again. Neither of us moved. He blinked. I put a hand between us, resting it in the centre of his chest, and pushed him off.

I said, 'Mark, you know that I don't, you know. I'm just not attracted to men.'

'Jesus, James, I'm sorry. Must be the drink. Fuck. I didn't mean anything by it. It was just, you know . . .'

'It's fine, Mark. Really. It's fine.'

We sat for a few moments in silence, until the loud, fluid song of the blackbird began. All at once, the dawn chorus rose up like jungle chattering, wild and insistent, without any possibility of comprehension. We staggered into the house and wished each other goodnight.

* * *

'Apparently we'll see it as we come over the hill,' said Franny, looking down at her notes. 'The road bends to the left and it's in the crook of the river to our right.'

Jess slowed down as we reached the crest of the hill, on the bend where the overhanging trees fell away. We looked obediently down to the right. We saw an eiderdown landscape, soft and billowing, polygons of green and shocking rapeseed yellow like pieces of paper cut by a child. At the bottom of the hill, where the cut pieces met in a knot of trees and the river sparkled, we saw a white-painted house.

'I see it!' said Jess. 'Oh, look at Dorset, it's so pretty.' And, as we pulled away, 'Why is it that we can't make towns that are as pretty as the countryside?'

'Oh,' said Franny, 'it's a proof of the existence of God, didn't you know? Nature is made by God and so is perfect, whereas towns are only made by boring old man, so they're rubbish. Apparently that's what Nicola thinks, anyway.'

'No, is she really so po-faced about it?' asked Jess.

'S'what Simon says. Evangelical vicar has nabbed her for Christ.'

Jess consulted the map and made a right turn, taking us through a stony village, its little cottages crammed together.

'She'll grow out of it,' said Jess. 'She's probably just got a crush on the vicar.'

This remark irritated me, as Jess did more when she was with Franny than when we were alone. Franny's world-weary demeanour brought out a falsely adult edge in Jess, a set of pat statements that made her sound like someone's mother. It was part of the grown-up persona which had first attracted me, but it came with a hardness that I found tiring.

'Nicola's the oldest sister, is that right?' I asked.

'Yup,' said Franny, 'oldest after Simon. She's thirteen. Then there's Eloise, who's eight, and Leo, who's four.'

'Four!' I said. It was faintly scandalous to imagine that anyone of my parents' age could have a four-year-old child. The implication that they were still having sex was impossible to ignore.

'I *know*,' said Franny. 'Simon says he used to take Leo out in his pushchair and old women berated him for being a teenage dad.'

She rolled down the window, lit a cigarette and puffed on it briefly, five or six drags, before flicking it on to the road.

'There it is,' she said. 'Park Farm, there, see the green sign? Turn in there.'

*

The Wedmores were variations on a theme of pink and cream. Next to Simon's ruddy skin and straw-coloured hair, one could see how they all fitted together. Nicola, the evangelical thirteen-year-old, had bright blonde hair and cream-coloured skin, rising to pink in the apples of her cheeks. She wore a wooden cross on a leather thong. Eloise, eight years old and bookish, was all pale, even to her eyelashes, wearing a dark blue print dress that made her look paler still. She complained, as soon as we arrived, that she had a headache and knew it must be sunstroke, while the others laughed and rolled their eyes because Eloise was a known hypochondriac. Rebecca, their mother, was sunburned, rosy, short-cropped hair a thick dark yellow, dressed in rolled-up dungarees and leading Leo, all golden-headed and curious, by the hand. Only David, the father, was dark-haired, but his shoulders and his blunt nose were Simon's too.

One could also see where Simon's personality had grown. There was his father in his stolidity and good humour. When his mother made a little gesture, flattening her lips and cradling her jaw in her hand as she thought, I caught Jess's eye and we smiled, because Simon had this precise gesture, exactly the same. And in the dynamics of the family too, in the shouting for attention at the table and Nicola saying, 'Eloise, for the last time put that book down and pass the potatoes,' and Eloise sticking her tongue out and pouting, and Rebecca frowning and chiding but smiling at the same time, and David calmly reaching behind and passing the potatoes, in all of these things Simon was clearly visible.

The family went to bed at 10 p.m. or so, and Rebecca said, 'Don't stay up too late. And remember to put everything in the dishwasher when you've finished.'

And these last words reminded me of the old rusty tap in the kitchen at Annulet House that had to be opened and closed with a pair of pliers. I thought that being wealthy was not the same thing as being grown up and it was startling to me that I had never thought so before.

We stayed up late, of course, as we always did. We opened another bottle of wine, and Nicola stayed downstairs to talk. She was coming into spots with a shiny face, a little awkward in the floral dress which accentuated her already-large bosom. She spoke earnestly about her church and the vicar, while Franny shot Jess a knowing glance. Nicola was interested in Franny, curious but wary.

She said, 'So, Si, is Franny your *girlfriend*? You never say properly.'

And Simon looked at Franny and Franny looked at Simon.

'I wouldn't say *girlfriend*,' said Franny.

'Fiancée?' said Simon.

Nicola's eyes opened very wide.

'Don't tease the girl, Simon. We're not so much boyfriend-and-girlfriend,' Franny began, 'we don't so much go out as . . .'

'You don't so much go out as stay in,' said Mark.

Nicola looked a little puzzled by this.

'Modern life is so complicated,' said Jess. 'They're very lovely friends is all.'

'And do you have a boyfriend, Nicola?' said Franny, looking at her over her glasses. 'Or a girlfriend, don't want to make assumptions.'

Nicola blushed. 'Oh no,' she said, 'I'm too young. Our vicar says that . . .'

Mark rolled his eyes at us.

'She's been like this all day, you know. Our vicar this, our vicar that. I want to meet this vicar if he's got a thirteen-year-old-girl so interested in him.'

Nicola's flush crept up her neck, pink and prickled.

'It's not like that,' she said. 'He tells us a lot of true things, that's all, things that . . .'

Mark interrupted again. 'Well, if he tells you you're too young for a boyfriend at thirteen he's not telling you anything true at all. Even *I* had a boyfriend at thirteen.'

Nicola blinked, tried to laugh as if to prove that this must be a joke, then stopped. I noticed that Jess met her eyes and smiled kindly.

'I don't understand . . .' said Nicola, then stopped, looked at us and said, 'Are you *gay*?'

Mark said, 'Not only gay, my darling, but positively ecstatic.'

'Oh,' she said. She looked crestfallen.

Mark had arrived at the house a few hours before us; he and

Nicola had spent the afternoon chatting together in the orchard. I thought how impressive he would appear to a thirteen-year-old girl.

She frowned, then said, 'Our vicar says there's no such thing as gay, just misguided.'

Franny drew in her breath sharply.

'Now come on, Nic . . .' said Simon.

'That's what he says.' She nodded. 'He's not so horrible as you think, Si. He says gay people deserve our sympathy and compassion, but their desires are sinful.'

'Oh yes,' muttered Franny, 'I wonder what he makes of Jews.'

Nicola drew breath to speak, got as far as saying, 'Well,' when Simon said swiftly, 'That's enough, Nicola,' and then, apologetically, to us, 'She's only repeating what she's heard.'

'Don't talk about me like I'm five years old.'

'Stop talking nonsense and I will,' and to us, 'I'm really sorry about this.'

'Don't be sorry,' said Mark, pouring himself another glass of wine. 'It's not nonsense. It's faith, that's all. I'm a religious man myself, you know, Nicola. More wine?'

Nicola accepted the glass of red wine and sipped it slowly.

'Now,' said Mark, 'tell us what your vicar says about gay people and we can have a proper conversation about it.'

Franny said, 'But if you start telling me what he says about Jews, I'm going to bed.'

Mark tutted. 'I'm sure that, like me, he thinks Jews are perfectly splendid, doesn't he, Nicola?'

Nicola said, 'Well, he . . .'

'Go on,' Franny drawled.

Nicola fiddled with her napkin.

'Maybe it really is time for bed now,' said Jess.

'Yes, I . . .' began Simon.

'He thinks Jews would be happier if they accepted Christ,' said Nicola quickly. 'And he says that gay people deserve our compassion, but they ought to try to not be gay because that's what God wants.'

'Ah, a progressive,' said Franny. 'At least he doesn't want us all burned, Mark.'

'Maybe he's right,' said Mark. 'How do you know, my darling Fran, that you wouldn't be happier if you accepted Christ?'

'Since I have a hard enough time accepting the tenets of my own religion,' said Franny, pointedly picking up a piece of Parma ham from the cheeseboard, showing it round the table before popping it into her mouth, 'I hardly think taking on a new one is going to bring me joy.'

'But Nicola's vicar – he does sound like a brave man – might tell you about the Gospel, the Good News, my love. Your religion with all its prejudices against the flesh of the pig is no more. Only believe in Christ and your troubles will be at an end.'

'And you?' said Franny, more jovial now, 'I suppose you'd be happiest as a celibate, would you?'

'I shouldn't think so,' said Mark contentedly, 'but who knows what miracles the power of God might bring about in my life.'

'Do you really believe that, Mark?' I ventured.

'Really?' He popped an olive into his mouth. 'Yes. Yes, I think I really do. He died for my sins, and for yours, Nicola, and perhaps for yours, Jess and James and Simon. But not for yours, Franny, you wicked heretic.'

He picked up her hand from the table and kissed the back of it, and I could not tell how much of what he said was a joke.

'But as for me, Nicola, the spirit may be willing but the flesh is weak and I do rather like men, I'm afraid to tell you.'

Nicola nodded, dipped her head down and then, thinking again, said, 'But have you *ever* kissed a girl?'

Mark tipped his head to one side and raised his eyebrows. I was intrigued to know the answer to this question.

Evidently Franny was too. After a few moments, she said, 'Go on, Mark, have you?'

'Yes,' he said. 'Quite a few actually, specially when I was younger. I don't mind it at all, but then girls' mouths are the same as boys', aren't they?'

'So,' Nicola pursued, 'maybe you'd like it if you . . . Well, you don't really know, do you, what you'd like to do with girls?'

'Nicola,' said Jess gently, 'perhaps none of us know what might happen in the future, but he knows how he feels now.'

Nicola looked uncertainly around the table.

'I suppose people can change though,' she said at last.

It had become late again, and then early once more. We said good-night at 5 a.m., shaking our heads and watching the stars wink out in the sky. Nicola hugged us, one after the other, even as her eyelids drooped and I wondered if we had done right by her, but I was too tired to make sense of it.

The next day, we took a picnic to the river. Simon and I carried the basket on the walk down, while Jess and Franny carried large tartan blankets rolled up and tied with string. Leo rode on Mark's shoulders, singing out like a little bird and pointing at trees and flowers whose names he knew, shouting them joyfully. When three or four white butterflies circled his head he swung and tried to grab at them, and almost fell. After that Nicola walked alongside Mark, holding Leo's hand and reminding him of the stories of the place: where the swing used to be, where Eloise got frightened by the cow, where they'd come in the autumn to cut logs for the fire.

We chose a spot by the river, under the shade of an alder tree. Nicola brought out hunks of cheese and bread, hard-boiled eggs, ham, apples and bars of chocolate. We feasted, splashed at the river a little – dangling our legs in but too tired to swim – then spread out one of the blankets, tramping down the grass to make it flat and comfortable.

'You can't sleep!' said Leo, as first Franny and then Jess lay down on the blanket.

'Yes, we can,' said Franny. 'We're tired.'

'But I'm boooored.' Leo directed this at Mark, who was already settling himself against the tree trunk, eyes closed.

'We'll play with you later,' said Mark.

Leo came uncertainly and tugged on my shirt.

'Can we play a game now?'

'Sorry, kiddo.' I found I felt comfortably grown up in this position, replying to the request in the same way my parents had to me on long summer days. 'You'll have to play by yourself for a bit, OK?'

Leo wasn't happy with this.

'I'm booooooored,' he roared again. He kicked at the tree trunk.

I tried, afterwards, to remember who first suggested that Leo should be a monkey, hiding in the branches of the tree. We were tired of him, exhausted by the constant demands of a small child, hungover from the night before, and it could have been any of us. I think perhaps it was Franny but I cannot be sure. In any case, the idea was eagerly adopted. We could watch him play and lie very still in one place at the same time.

Leo said, 'Yes, yes. I can go "ook ook" like a monkey and throw nuts on you.'

Simon lifted him up into the branches of the tree that hung over the bank out into the river.

He clung happily to a branch, advancing hand over foot. I lay on my back and watched him wander through the branches. There are few things as beautiful as the sky observed through the leaves of a tree. The constant small movements, as if the leaves were alive and wriggling, the dapples of light and shade, patches of light opening up and closing again, the places where leaf over leaf produces a rich saturation of colour, or where the sunshine creates translucency. Like the layered frills of a petticoat or the delicate fanned ceiling of Christ Church Cathedral, so much of what we make in art is an attempt to recreate the simple beauty of a tree.

Leo grabbed a chunk of leaves, ripped them off and scattered them down on us.

'I'm a monkey!' he said. 'Ook ook!'

'Hey!' said Franny, sitting up. 'Don't do that. You nearly got me in the eye.'

Leo stretched out his arms, T-shirt riding up, and hauled himself a little higher in the tree.

'I'm a monkey,' he said again. 'You can't catch me!'

He threw another handful of leaves and twigs. A few of the pieces were quite large and heavy. They scattered drily on the baked earth.

'Don't do that, Leo,' said Jess. 'You really might hurt someone.'

'Time to come down now, Leo,' said Nicola.

He had climbed up higher than we realized, higher than any of us could reach without climbing ourselves.

Leo threw down another heavy handful of leaves and twigs and bark.

'Ook ook!' he said. 'Ook ook! I'm the monkey and you're all the other animals in the jungle and the monkey is the naughty one!'

He was bouncing up and down, obviously excited to be out of our reach.

He threw more leaves. Two handfuls this time, and as he hurled them, palms splayed open like starfish, he lost his balance, rocked backward on the branch, seemed about to fall, then clutched at the branch above and steadied himself.

He was unafraid, but we became quiet.

'Come on,' said Nicola, making her voice serious. 'Enough of this game. Come down, Leo. Come down now, please.'

'Yes,' said Simon, shading his eyes from the sun with his forearm, 'come down or I'll come up there and get you myself.'

Leo squirmed and wriggled further out along the branch.

'Oh, come on, Leo,' said Simon. 'Or we'll just have to shake you out of the tree.'

Leo squeaked indignantly and climbed another few inches along the branch, out over the river.

'For goodness' sake, Leo,' said Nicola. 'You're going to have to –'

And there was a sudden crack. The bough did not break, but bent like a spring and Leo jolted forward and reached his arms out to steady himself and as he reached the branch sprang again, past the stronger supporting branches it had rested on and, head over foot, arms outstretched, spinning like an acrobat, Leo fell.

While he tumbled it was comical. His little mouth was as round as an o, his eyebrows raised, his hands still reaching out. For that brief flash of time it was the funniest thing I'd ever seen. And then he hit the water and screamed, and sound and colour returned to the world. His head went down under the surface. I couldn't see him. I looked at the place he had vanished for the space of a heartbeat, two, three, and then he reappeared, struggling, gasping, several feet away from the bank. Much further out than he'd fallen in.

He was facing towards us, but moving with the current of the river downstream. And suddenly his head vanished. Just under, then back. And I was still smiling, but only because my body was unable to stop. He went under again and then came back, his arms thrashing helplessly in the water, coughing and coughing. He was near enough that we could see the fear in his face, but too far away for us to be able to reach him.

At once we were all action, each of us doing something different, loudly, at the same time.

'Throw him a rope,' shouted Simon, though we didn't have a rope.

'Break off a branch!' shouted Franny, and tried to do so.

Jess started to wade towards Leo but he was moving too quickly, away, downstream. And while we were dithering, wondering how to fetch help, whether we should take a boat and row out, Mark said nothing. I looked for him and saw him on the bank, tiptoe, hinged over like a half-open penknife. He stood poised like that for a moment, balanced, his toes gripping the bank, his head down. He pushed off cleanly, dropped into the water without a sound and surfaced a few yards downstream, towards Leo.

Leo's head went down. It did not re-emerge. The seconds elongated while Mark receded, slicing through the water faster than the current. He was a good swimmer; summers spent in the sea by his mother's Italian house had left him with the compact, muscular shoulders and torso of a strong front crawl. He dived, but came up empty-handed. He looked around, struggling against the current. He dived again and came up cupping a small white head, his arm underneath the chin. We stood on the bank and watched, unable to move or speak.

Mark ran through the shallows and back to the bank with Leo's small body resting on his shoulder. We ran to him. We couldn't see whether Leo was moving.

Nicola said, 'Is he all right? Mark, is he all right?'

Mark laid the boy on the grass. Leo was a ghastly, ghostly grey; no sign of life came from him. Mark put his face close to Leo's mouth, listening. Then he tipped the boy's head back and breathed deeply into his lungs. One breath. Another. And suddenly Leo was coughing, choking. He turned to the side and vomited out a great lungful of greenish water, and Nicola said, 'Oh!' and dropped to her knees beside Leo, rubbing his chest with her hands and the corners of her skirt.

Mark looked up. His shirt clung to his chest, his trousers were gone, lost somewhere in the river. Blood was pouring from a cut on his temple, near the hairline; he must have struck something underneath the water when he dived.

Franny said, 'Mark, you're bleeding. You should . . .'

He spoke over her. 'Someone run to get help, for God's sake! Nicola, fetch the picnic blanket. We need to get him warm.'

Simon ran back towards the main road and the farmhouse, not even stopping to put his shoes back on. Mark stripped Leo out of his clothes, wrapped him in the picnic blanket and hugged him close to his body, rocking him gently, muttering under his breath. All I could think was how shocking it was to see Leo's nakedness, suddenly, in the midst of a summer picnic, and how pale to the point of blueness his body had been. Nicola knelt beside Mark, rubbing Leo's hair and holding him with one arm while his teeth chattered and he shook and shuddered.

'Come here,' said Mark. 'Hug him with me, to keep him warm.' He pulled her across, so that the two of them had Leo's small body sandwiched between them as they sat face to face. 'Not too close!' Mark said. 'We mustn't hurt him. Let him breathe.'

Nicola moved back fractionally. Her eyes remained on Mark, wide and frightened. He smiled at her, suddenly – an old Mark smile as if he'd just thought of a wicked joke to tell – and interlaced his fingers with hers. They sat like that, rubbing Leo's arms and legs, until we heard the siren of the ambulance approaching.

The interview with Rebecca, after we had left Nicola, Mark and David at the hospital, was the most painful of all. The ambulance men had tutted at us, and Simon had shaken while he telephoned his parents from the hospital, but we had not heard their voices, and when they arrived all they wanted was to see Leo and then, when they knew, to thank Mark and thank him again, and tell him again how grateful they were. Nicola would not let Mark go, would not cease holding him though the danger was long gone, and he stayed with her and she stayed by Leo's bed.

The rest of us had nothing to say to Rebecca. We stood awkwardly in her kitchen while she asked again and again, 'What were you thinking? What were you thinking, letting a little boy like that climb a tree over the river? Not watching him? Not holding him? What were you thinking?'

She seemed both distraught and genuinely puzzled. But we had no answer for her. We did not know what we'd been thinking and it seemed best to leave.

Jess and I arrived at my parents' house early in the morning, before either of them was awake. It was 4.30 a.m. and the sky was opalescent, pearl-blue feathered with grey. We kissed in the car for a long time, my hands roving under her sweater and tangled in her hair. She smelled a little sour from lack of sleep and I felt a thread of disgust and reminded myself that I must smell the same.

At last I said goodbye to her and let myself into the silent house. The hallway and the stairs were smaller than I remembered and drained of colour. I had not remembered that the walls of the kitchen were so beige, or that the paper orrery in my bedroom had become so faded and dusty over the years. I could hear my father's slow snores through the door to my parents' bedroom. I went to wash my hands and splash water on my face in the bathroom and noticed, for the first time, that there was a dark line of mildew where the basin met the tiles.

My parents had placed a neat white pile of post on my pillow. I took off my shoes and lay down, fully clothed, opening the letters one by one and hoping for sleep to take me at last. There were bank statements, a magazine, a couple of postcards and then a white envelope with an Oxford postmark. I opened it with a sense of exhausted detachment. 'Mr James Stieff,' it said, 'has satisfied the examiners.' My Prelims result. I had passed. Just barely: one of the marks was a lower second and the others thirds. I stared at the paper. Here, in this room, where I had slaved for my four A-grades at A-level, it seemed like a joke. Sleep was coming on me though in waves of broken images and nonsense thoughts. It washed against my shores, lapping insistently, dissolving me. Still clutching the letter, I let it take me down.

9

Second year, October, two weeks before the start of term

'Your problem, James,' said Anne, 'is that you have no focus.'

Paul, whose face reminded me more of a frog every time I saw him, nodded in silent agreement. He and Anne had driven up from London with a pile of Labour Party posters in the back seat. Paul's amphibian features looked out sternly from a stack of leaflets headed 'Paul Probert: Tough on Crime'. I wasn't sure what good they thought my parents could do with these leaflets, 100 miles from his prospective constituency.

'I'm sure he's doing his best,' ventured my mother.

'I'm sure he's not,' said Anne. 'He's wasted his first year at Oxford, totally wasted it, and I'm sorry, James, but you'll thank me in the end for telling you this. I knew people like you at Wadham. Lazy people. With no ambition.'

Anne had no trouble at all demonstrating her own ambition. She rarely had trouble talking about herself. She'd proudly shown us her Home Office access pass, and her mention in Hansard for excellent work on the regulation of cod-liver oil. Within the year, it appeared, she might be promoted to the giddy heights of Assistant Deputy Vice-Chair of an important committee tasked with investigating soya beans. Fixing me with the beady eye of an Assistant Deputy Vice-Chair addressing a recalcitrant minister, she barked, 'James! Have you ever even been to the Union?'

'No, I . . .'

Anne nodded silently and turned to my parents with a raised eyebrow. I found myself imagining how Mark might react to Anne.

'We paid a lot of money for that membership, James,' rumbled my father.

'I know you did, Dad. I . . .'

'Don't forget, darling, he was very ill,' said my mother, but Anne had found her stride and was not to be deflected from it.

'He wasn't ill, he hurt his leg, and I don't see what that has to do with anything else. Fine, he's out for a blue. But it shouldn't have stopped him working. That's just giving in.'

Paul coughed and interjected, 'I had German measles once. German measles quite serious, you know, for an adult.' He paused, apparently waiting for us all to commiserate with him on this grave misfortune. As we remained silent, he continued, 'It was when I was up for an OUSU election. OUSU, important stepping stone. Career-wise, vital.'

Anne nodded vehemently, as if to a committee meeting. I wondered if she'd type up and circulate some minutes of the conversation.

'And what did you do, Paul?'

Paul blinked, 'Well, I went to hustings, you know. Important to make the effort. That's what you do.'

Anne began, 'And you see, that's exactly what I'm –'

'I don't see what this has got to do with you, Paul,' I snapped, 'or Anne, for that matter. You're not my mum and dad.'

Anne paused for a moment, mildly startled, I thought, by my answering her at all. 'I'm sure Mum and Dad agree with me, don't you?'

'Your sister did very well at Oxford . . .' began my mother.

'She made use of the opportunity, is what she's saying,' said my father.

'I'm not telling you any of this for the good of my health,' said Anne.

Later, I called Jess from the phone box at the end of our road, feeding it with 20p pieces as I listened to her calming voice. She had achieved a first in each of her Prelim exams and had received a crisp white letter informing her that she was to be awarded a scholarship of £500 a year.

'That's brilliant,' I said flatly. 'You deserve it. I just wish . . . I wish I had your focus.'

'It's over now,' she said. 'Second year. You can make a fresh start. You passed, didn't you? That's all that matters.'

'Do you know how the others did?'

She did. Franny had also averaged a first, Emmanuella and Simon upper seconds and Mark . . . Well, all he'd admit was that he'd got through 'by the skin, my darling, the very epidermis of my molars'.

The whole thing was so ridiculously haphazard. At school, if a student like me or like Mark – recognized as bright and capable – had barely scraped their way through an important exam, there would have been concerned meetings, offers of extra help, a determination to find out what had gone wrong. Someone would have noticed.

'Do you think I should take up . . . extracurricular activities?'

'Are you asking me if I want you to start shagging someone else?' Jess said, chuckling.

'You know what I mean.'

'I suppose so. If you want to. It might give you something to do while I'm rehearsing for the concert.'

I thought of the crowds I'd walked through at Freshers' Fair, of the different lives that had been on offer there: the Marxist Society, the Experimental Theatre Club, the Wine Society, the Doctor Who Society, the Angling Club, the Archery League. I had signed up for a few of these organizations, still received twice-termly mailings from the Film Society and the Debating Club, but they reminded me too intensely of my depression of the previous winter.

'I think I'll just concentrate on my work,' I said.

Guntersen, naturally, had received a scholarship and with it the long-sleeved gown that demonstrated his intellectual superiority. He wore it to every available formal hall and, without any requirement, to the first tutor-group meeting of term in Dr Boycott's office.

Panapoulou too, a strangely remote and tic-ridden student, was sporting the long sleeves, although in his case I suspected he'd simply forgotten to take his gown off after the previous night's dinner. His constant fidgeting made him seem to wrestle with the fabric, hoisting it back and then tugging it forward. He was kind though, if distant, and had helped me several times when I was in the library struggling with an impossible question sheet. He smiled at me before Boycott began to speak. We had all made sure to discover how the others had done. I was the very worst of all. Had I been at a more competitive college, I might have been thrown out, culled for the sake of the league tables. I was fortunate that Gloucester College did not, at that time, adopt such draconian measures, but my social standing had fallen with this calamity. Everard and Glick would not meet my eyes.

'Gentlemen,' said Dr Boycott, 'another year begins, and with it greater challenges, greater expectation. We are still quorate, I am happy to note. Some of you,' he nodded to Guntersen and Panapoulou, 'have fulfilled your early promise admirably, while others –' he inclined his head fractionally towards Daswani and me – 'have, shall we say, yet to prove yourselves. However! We begin afresh with high hopes and expectations.'

Dr Strong nodded happily. His front pair of glasses swung and clattered against the back pair.

'From the very best to the very worst of you –' and here, or was it my imagination, he seemed to nod towards me again – 'your talents are undisputed. But let us now put our shoulders to the wheel, let us stride forth, let us climb ever higher towards the peaks we are capable of ascending, let us spread forth our wings and, reaching our hands towards the prize and unfurling our sails, let us take flight!'

He paused, seeming exhausted after this encomium of educational ecstasy, scratched his chin thoughtfully and gave out the term's tutorial lists.

When I think of that term now, it is the music that returns to me. The music and the image of Jess practising in the early mornings, in the ice-skimmed conservatory at the side of the house so as not to wake anyone, two pairs of socks on her feet, tracksuit pulled over her pyjamas, leaning into the melody again and again, warming her fingers on her mug of coffee to soften the ligaments and then trying once more, and once more.

Although she had explained to me, quite clearly, that the orchestra would need more of her time this term, I hadn't imagined her absence would be so wide. She had won the prestigious position of soloist for a performance by one the university orchestras. The piece was Sibelius's Violin Concerto in D Minor; it has a metallic, alien sound, an emotional slipknot at the throat. The emotion of it is so unlike Jess that, the first time she played the CD to me, I could not imagine that she could channel it. At times, the mood is almost cheerful, even romantic, and then within moments it becomes frantic again, broken-hearted, filled with despair. It is a manic-depressive episode in half-hour miniature. Sometimes I sat in the conservatory, trying to work as she played, but it often became unbearable as she repeated the same musical phrase twenty or thirty or forty times, searching for an intonation that pleased her. She claimed not to mind – or even notice – whether I was there or not, and so I frequently left her to play alone.

On occasion Randolph, another violinist, would come to practise with her. His face was red and bull-like, his demeanour unsettlingly aggressive. He listened to Jess with a frown, and corrected her, his hand on her shoulder blades as she played, his fingers dancing with hers on the neck of the instrument. He greeted me curtly and took, without invitation, to calling me 'Jim'.

With Jess's own academic work still pressing, she was often out of the house until 11 p.m. or midnight, waking up at 6 a.m. to begin practice again. She reserved Sunday afternoons and evenings to spend with me, but I could not help feeling that I had been scheduled like a visit to the dentist or some weekly chore. Still, I told myself, it would not last long.

'The problem,' said Mark, 'your problem, is that you don't understand about love.'

We were quite drunk. There had been a number of us in the Old Fire Station bar, several of Mark's friends and Simon and some of his OUSU cronies, and we had drunk quite a large amount and quite a quantity of it had been champagne, for no other reason, Mark said, than that it was Wednesday.

I stared at Mark. He, perhaps, was not quite as drunk as I.

'Whajoo mean?'

'The nature,' he said, rolling his glass in his hand, 'the nature of love. You don't understand it. Not at all. You don't understand it at all.'

'Me?!' I said. 'I'm the one wither girlfriend.'

'Yes,' said Mark, 'but you're not a Christian, thass your trouble. You don't understand that love is sacrifice.'

I thought on this, a little confusedly.

'I thought love was supposed to be fun,' I said, 'fun fun fun. Like in pop songs.'

Mark shook his head violently but then stopped, looking queasy.

'Nonono. Sacrifice. Don't you understand?' He spoke very earnestly. 'Sorry, sorry, I know I go on about it too much, I know I do, but Jesus . . .' He sang a few bars. '"Little children all should be, kind obedient good as he." Point is . . . point is . . . The Imitation of Christ. Loving selflessly. Not putting yourself first, not asking for anything, only looking what you can do for them.'

I thought about this, turning it over.

'But then what d'you get out of it?'

He smiled. 'Satisfaction. Alllllso, they should be sacrificing themselves for you. So it all works out! But most important, think of them not of you.'

'S'that why you never date then, Mark? All that sacrifice too much for you?'

He stared at me, his eyes defocusing, then, snapping his head up sharply, he said clearly, so clearly that I would have half believed he was stone-cold sober, 'Who do you think pays for everything, James? The house, the food, the parties? Who's paying for the drink this evening? Believe me, I understand about doing things for other people.' His head lolled forward again and his speech was slurred. 'Sacrifice. Thass what I'm talking about.'

I knew that he was drunk and I was drunk, but I was stung. I had been spending more time with Mark over the past few weeks, while Jess was so busy. And it was true that he had paid my way in bars and restaurants more often than I had. But he was always insistent that I shouldn't concern myself with such trifles, that he could well afford it, that he would barely feel the cost. I did not like to have this thrown in my face now.

'Fine,' I said, scarcely thinking of what I was doing. 'Barmaid!'

A bored-looking woman slouched over to our table.

'I'd like the bill, please,' I said, 'for the whole table. I'll pay it.'

'No,' said Mark, 'no, no. Thass not what I . . . I didn't . . .'

'It's fine,' I said to Mark, 'my treat. Sacrifice.'

There had been ten of us at the table, until Simon and his friends had gone to a Student Union party. We had drunk a great deal. The woman returned with the bill. The figure on it seemed to have a decimal point one place further to the right than I had expected, but nonetheless I pulled from my wallet the credit card my parents had given me 'for textbooks and emergencies'.

'Put it on that,' I said.

I began to feel queasy before we left the bar, with a thumping, throbbing sensation in my arms and legs. We were on Little Clarendon Street, working our way up towards Jericho, when the roiling in my stomach became too much to bear. I think it was the sight of the George & Davis' ice-cream café and unavoidable thoughts of rich, thick, sugary, buttery fat that finally convinced my complaining gut to offload its cargo. I vomited, long draughts of alcoholic liquid, my head pounding, stumbled and ended up kneeling in my own beery effluvia. I had hit the ground hard going down and a bloom of pain burst in my fragile knee. I vomited again.

Mark supported me the rest of the way home, arm around my waist, my arm around his neck. I felt exhausted, unwell, needing a bath and a sleep. We stumbled into the kitchen to get water and there was Jess. She was drinking a mug of the camomile tea she liked so much, listening to Fox FM playing quietly, reading a textbook, one knee pulled up, foot resting on the edge of the chair. Her nose wrinkled as we crashed through the kitchen door. I remember I was giggling. The room distorted and Jess was staring at me with unconcealed revulsion.

'Whassamatter?' I said. 'Whassamatter? We're jus' getting some water.'

She smiled a little, and I remembered how much I loved her. Like apple daisies, like moonshine calves, like waterfall rainboxes and blue-crystal electricity spaceships.

'Nothing's the matter. I'm tired, that's all.'

I tried to communicate the love, how I loved her smile, like it was the battery that kept my heart beating, and how her little brown ponytail and her tipped-up nose made me want to grab her and bend her over the table and fuck her like crazy because of all the love for every part of her sweet and beautiful body, but all I managed to say was, 'I love yooooooou.'

'I love you too. But please have a shower before you come to bed, OK?'

'Ohhhh, Jess,' I said, and tried to nuzzle my face against hers, 'I love you, love you, love you.'

She thrust a protesting hand at me and I grabbed it and pulled her up.

'Come and dance with me, lovely Jess, sweet Jess, I'm a mess, full of stress, but you're the best, yeah I confess, I . . . ummm . . .' I ran out of rhyme, but pulled her into a dancing embrace, in time to the soft music from the radio.

She tried to move away, still laughing a little.

'I confess,' she said, 'I like you less, when your excess has placed a stress on your finesse.'

'Oh, very good,' said Mark, and I loved her ten thousand times more.

She pulled away again, but I caught her by the arm and I wanted her so dearly that I ignored her saying, 'James, stop it now,' and pulled her towards me, tugging hard on her right wrist, twisting the narrow bones more than I intended. I felt the tendons on the back of her hand crunch and roll under my fingers. Her thumb turned outwards. She inhaled sharply and pulled her hand out of my grasp, nursing it close to her, wincing.

'For fuck's sake, James,' she said, probing the wrist gingerly, 'for fuck's sake.'

Remorse drenched me.

'What? Did I hurt you? I'm so sorry, I'm sorry, lemme see, can I help? Ice?'

She looked at me with pure disgust.

'I'm going to sleep in one of the spare rooms tonight. Just . . . sleep it off. I'll see you in the morning.'

'But Jess, sweet Jess in your dress . . .'

She gathered up her score with her left hand.

'I'm wearing jeans, you idiot.'

I tried to follow her, but Mark pulled me back.

The next evening her arm was held stiffly in a blue plastic brace, strapped against her chest. She was drinking tea in the kitchen with Franny and Simon, though at the instant I entered the room they made some muttering 'time to work' noises and bustled out. My pulse thundered in my ears.

'What did . . .' I began.

'They think it's going to be fine,' said Jess, looking at her tea and not at me at all. 'Just bruised, needs rest and then I can get back to practice.'

'Oh, well that's . . .'

'No,' she said, 'it's not. I'm going to lose a week of practice, maybe more. I can't afford that.'

'Jess,' I said, making my voice soft and soothing, 'Jess, it'll be OK. It'll heal.'

'You don't know that,' she said quietly.

'Well, no. But it'll probably be fine, totally fine.'

I put my hands on her shoulders, where she liked me to massage her. She stood up.

'I'm sorry but I can't . . . I can't do this with you right now.'

'But . . . it was an accident.'

'I'm sorry, James, I just can't. Not now.'

Even once the brace had come off and she was practising again, she did not return to our bedroom. Sometimes I watched her practising in the conservatory from the side of the house, my view half-obscured by the Virginia creeper. Several times, Randolph came to help her practise and his arm around her waist and his swaying hips next to hers forced me to walk through the conservatory absent-mindedly, as if I'd forgotten a book.

'For God's sake, James,' she said, 'I wish you'd stop lurking here with that hangdog expression,' and Randolph laughed, a low rumbling chuckle.

After five or six days of this, I cornered her in the kitchen and spoke without preamble the question which was at the very top of my thoughts: 'Have we broken up?'

She was carrying a jar of jam, a packet of croissants, a plate, a knife, all in her left hand.

'Um,' she said, 'do you want to break up?'

'No. No. I don't I . . . I love you.'

'Then we haven't broken up.'

'But what . . . why are you still sleeping upstairs?'

'I just need a bit of time, James. Just a little time.'

'How long?'

She exhaled sharply through her nose, a bull-snort of impatience.

'I can't tell you how long. But you'll make it longer if you keep badgering me.'

I stared at her, speechless.

'Look,' her voice softened, 'we will talk about it, OK? But I've lost a lot of time. I can't make time for all this now. That's your problem, James. You need something other than me to think about. Just . . . do something else. Take your mind off it.'

She stepped around me and back to the conservatory.

The next morning I stood in the hall, sorting the post. It had become a comforting ritual, now that Jess and I no longer had tea in bed together each morning. There was a letter from my parents – I recognized my mother's handwriting – one for Jess from her sister, several each for Franny – she had schoolfriends at different universities who wrote to each other ceaselessly – and for Emmanuella, in the distinctive continental handwriting. And for Mark, a parcel from California – these came at least weekly and had contained everything from a jar of cactus jam to a long fur coat – and a letter from Dorset. I didn't notice him standing on the stairs above me until he snatched the letter out of my hands.

I looked at him quizzically. He frowned, raising an eyebrow and said, 'It's from Nicola. You remember, Simon's sister. She writes to me sometimes.'

I laughed. 'What, mad Christian Nicola?'

'I wish you wouldn't say "mad" and "Christian" as if they went together.'

'Fine. I meant to say, "What, Nicola with the massive boobs?"'

He beamed and said, 'Happily I wouldn't notice such things. Our friendship is on a more spiritual level.'

'You're not going to show me, then?'

'Certainly not. Letters are private. What about yours, anyway?'

'Oh,' I said, 'it'll just be my mother's usual letter: a list of all the things Anne's done, how proud she's made them, how happy they are to have her as a daughter and what a disappointment I am by comparison.'

I crumpled the letter up and thrust it into my pocket.

I only came to read it just before bed, after yet another evening spent fruitlessly trying to understand my latest question sheet and – equally fruitlessly – to avoid watching Jess practise. And when I looked it was not the usual screed at all.

The letter was in my mother's rounded handwriting:

> *Dear James,*
>
> *Daddy and I are very unhappy about your credit card bill. £270 in a bar! It's too much, James. Anne thinks, and we agree, that paying this bill will just encourage you to do it again. You need to learn to be responsible with your money. We don't want you to waste the opportunity of Oxford, especially after your results.*
>
> *So, we've decided we won't be paying any more of your bills from now on. Daddy has changed the address so the bills will come to Annulet House. We hope this will help you to concentrate on your studies and not your social life.*
>
> *Love*
> *Mummy*

At the bottom, my father had added a postscript:

> *Learn to live according to your means. It'll serve you well in life. Dad*

This was something of a blow. It was probably true that my charges to that card had grown in the past year. In my first term I had purchased only the absolutely required texts, and those I had sought out in the second-hand department at Blackwell's. But then in my first term I'd been almost suicidally depressed, had had no friends, had not wanted to go anywhere or do anything. Since then, although Mark had provided most necessities, we'd had dinners out at pleasant Oxford restaurants and evening trips to the London theatre, and I'd thought that, after all his generosity, it was only fair for me to buy the odd bottle of wine to contribute. I felt rather angry with my parents. The cost of purchasing that happiness seemed so ridiculously small that I could not believe they wouldn't see it my way if I phoned the next day and spoke to them directly.

They did not see it my way. I talked first with my mother, who, in pleading tones, asked me not to upset my father. 'He was very angry when he saw that bill,' she said, 'very very angry.' My heart quailed somewhat at this news. 'You must remember,' and there was iron in her voice, and I knew to whom she had been speaking, 'that we never had to pay Anne's way like this.'

'Maybe Anne didn't have so many expenses?' I chanced.

'Maybe she didn't associate with such high-living friends,' my mother said peevishly.

I heard my father rumble in the background, 'Is that James on the phone? Tell him I'd like a word with him, if you'd be so good.'

'Your father wants to speak to you.'

I felt tears starting in my eyes. Actual hot, aching, terrified tears, as if I were a young child again and had been caught scribbling on the living-room curtains.

'Fine,' I yelped, 'fine. I don't know what else he can say though.'

There was a clattering as the phone changed hands.

'James, it's your father. Your mother and I are very unhappy with you. We're not prepared to continue to underwrite this frivolous lifestyle. This house nonsense,' he harrumphed, 'it's no good for you. Look what's happened to your work.'

There was a pause. I imagined the way that he would be turning to my mother and she would be nodding and giving him encouragement.

'We'd like you to move back into college,' he said, 'but until then we can't keep paying these bills.'

'What? Any of my bills?'

In the background, my mother said, 'How many bills does he have?' She must have had her ear pressed to the back of the receiver.

'Yes,' said my father, 'how many bills do you have, James? You're living in that house rent-free, your tuition is free, the libraries are free. So, you need a bit for books and a bit for food. We'll give you . . . £50 a month, all right?'

'A month! No, £50 is not all right! Not all right! That's nothing . . .'

'If we see your results improve, we'll think again. It's for your own good, James.'

'But I . . .'

'That's our final decision, James.'

'But . . .'

'We'll talk to you soon, darling.' This was my mother again. 'Work hard. You'll thank us for this later, dear.'

I slumped on the sofa and covered my face with my hands. What would this mean? An end to the casual London jaunts and restaurant meals; an end to being able to pay my way at all.

There was a noise in the sitting room. I lifted my face and saw that Mark was standing a few feet away, hands in his pockets, head tilted quizzically to one side.

'Parents?' he said.

'Yup.'

'May God take all parents and drop them into the sea.'

'Yup,' I said. I was trying to keep the hot tears behind my eyelids from leaking out.

Mark reached into his back pocket, pulled out his wallet, slid out eight unwrinkled £50 notes and held them out to me. He crumpled them slightly as he held them, as if they were napkins or a sheet of notepaper.

'Oh no,' I said, 'I can't. I couldn't. Thanks, but I really can't.'

'Yes, you can,' he said. He pulled my right wrist towards him and pressed the money into my palm, closing my hand over the crackling paper.

'I really can't. I don't know when I'd ever pay you back.'

He shrugged. 'So don't pay me back. I owe you anyway. Services rendered.'

'What, you're paying me?' I said, suddenly disgusted.

He wriggled his shoulders uncomfortably and held his hands up as if to ward me off.

'Don't look at it like that, all right?' he said. 'It's not like that. Look, mate.' He ran his hands through his hair and began to speak very quickly in the slight cockney accent he sometimes took on when embarrassed. 'I've got enough, more than enough, too much maybe, and if I can make your life easier like this, then it's fine, OK? It's no worries. It's . . .' He twisted uncomfortably again and the cockney fell away. 'It's not that much to me, OK?'

I looked at the crumpled notes in my hand. They represented freedom from my parents at that moment. Freedom from having to confess to them that I did not have enough money left to last me the term. Freedom from having to ask them for more.

'OK,' I said. 'Thanks.'

Jess and I made it up. We were always going to. I was hardly likely to treat Jess's hands roughly in future, nor was it hard to understand that her ambitions had their demands.

A few days before the concert, she suggested that I come with her as she shopped for a suitable evening gown. And when she found one which wouldn't chafe her neck as she played, or interfere with her arm movements – a crimson silk dress with a high neckline – she put it on for me once more in our bedroom. And I undid the dress and we made love in the waning afternoon sunlight.

'Do you forgive me?' I said later, when we lay among the tumbled sheets, moisture cooling from our bodies.

She kissed the bridge of my nose, and my forehead, and the lids of my eyes.

'There,' she said, 'absolution. Satisfied?'

She rolled over on to her back, one hand loosely ruffled in my hair.

'It's good we got used to this now, though,' she said, 'because it's never going to be that different. Rehearsals and concerts, I mean.

When I join an orchestra, it's not going to be so different.'

This is a quality of Jess too. She has no self-doubt where it is not warranted. She has never had difficulty in understanding her own capabilities or in failing to believe the indicators of her talent. Sometimes I think that it is this quality – the self-determining spirit, the knowledge of her own purpose – that I have envied the most in her.

At around 5 p.m. on the day of the concert, she began to get ready. Emmanuella helped her, putting on her make-up and pinning her hair back into a bun-style knot, fastened with two long pins. She checked and rechecked her violin, placing it finally into its case with the gentle attention of a mother for a newborn. She flexed her fingers and stretched her limbs. She did not look at the score again, but as we sat in the hallway in our evening wear her hands were practising fingering.

Mark had ordered a taxi and the six of us rode down together, squashed up on the slippery seats, in silence for the most part. At the cathedral, Jess disappeared immediately to one of the back rooms and the rest of us took our places several rows from the front.

As the people began to gather I started to understand quite how important this day was. Many of the attendees were extremely eminent: I spotted the Vice-Chancellor, the Bishop of Oxford and a couple of famous 'telly-dons'. The cathedral was not full – it would take a mighty crowd to fill that grand medieval space – but the nave was certainly well populated. By the time the lights dimmed, at least 250 people were there.

Before she even appeared, while the orchestra were still tuning their instruments, aligning them in an enormous buzzing thrum, I found that my heart was beating faster, that I was, in my mind, with Jess in her dressing room, watching her flex her fingers, tune her violin, twist her neck from side to side as she always did before beginning to play.

Franny batted me on the shoulder with her programme, leaned over and whispered, 'She'll be fine.'

I nodded. The audience grew quiet. Jess walked out. The thing began.

She was calm and still, her face reflective. She smiled in recognition of the applause, exchanged a few words with the conductor and then, almost without warning, they began.

I could not take my eyes from her, not even to scan the orchestra, to see which faces I recognized. Emotions I had never seen before on her flickered across her features: from grotesque revulsion to icy anger to majestic calm. I noted, though, that as she played, tossing her head from side to side, the intricate hair-knot Emmanuella had constructed for her began to slip. I saw her glance to the side and twist her head, trying to shift her hair, to keep it up. It was no use. She pursed her lips. I wondered, for a breath-catching instant, whether she would stop playing entirely in order to rearrange her hair. No. She knew the music too well for that. She waited for a pause of, perhaps, three or four seconds, reached around and, in one motion, swept out the long pins holding up her hair, dropped them on the floor and took up her bow to begin playing again. Liquid, her hair poured down her back, but she was oblivious. She was within the music again, impervious to mere physical considerations.

I could barely wait to get her home that night. Through the applause, the encores, the mulled wine drunk afterwards in a draughty side chapel, the suggestion that we all go out for dinner – vetoed by Jess on the grounds of exhaustion – through all of that I was thinking of the moment when the door would be closed between us and the world. As we sipped our wine, as she was congratulated, I thought of standing behind her, slipping the dress down her shoulder to expose the bare, freckled joint. I imagined myself holding her, arm around her waist, pulling her close to me, placing kisses on her shoulder and the side of her neck, unzipping her, taking her from her dress as carefully and reverently as she removed her violin from its case. As we walked home, a messy crowd spilling from the pavement on to the road, I caught her hand. I thought of the rise of her breasts, which none of these would have shared, of the unexpected darkness of her nipples. I knew I was clutching at straws.

I persuaded her into sex that night. Not forced, never that, but persuaded, seduced. I wanted to be sure I could still do the things I had done before, that I could still hear her soft sighing in the dark and know that I had been responsible for it. She agreed with patience, as ever, and took me to her shoulder and her breast; they were hers to give, of course, not mine to take. She sighed and gasped, but I did not find what I had come for. I could not put my fingers through her skin. I could not hold her in my hand.

10

Second year, January, first week of term

'I think,' said Dr Boycott, 'that for you, Mr Stieff, we must begin to use the stick, in addition to the carrot, wouldn't you agree, Dr Strong?'

Dr Strong nodded his stern confirmation.

'It pains us to do this, of course,' said Dr Boycott, 'but I cannot see that you have left us much choice. These results –' he waved his hand at my collection papers on the table in front of him – 'what have you been doing with your time, Mr Stieff? What? Did you spend the whole of Michaelmas term in a daze?'

I had, in fact, spent most of the previous term in a state of confusion, panic about money and sexual jealousy, but I couldn't see that telling Boycott this would do any good.

'We cannot allow this to continue, you must understand. You risk exposing the good name of Gloucester College physics to ridicule. Yours is the accusing finger which wields the dagger thrusting at our soft underbelly to stab us in the back!'

'I'm sorry, Dr Boycott, I . . . I'm sorry, I had a bad term.'

'You did indeed, Mr Stieff. And if you repeat this performance in your examinations you will take a bad degree, if any degree at all. Tell me, are you thinking of continuing to the fourth year?'

Almost everyone took the optional fourth year to get the MSc in physics. I'd intended to take it when I began the course. But now the idea of staying on in Oxford after Mark, Jess and the others had left did not entice me. I hadn't discussed this with my parents; in fact I'd spent most of the Christmas break either in Annulet House or with Jess's family.

'I . . .' I paused. The circle of my little universe halted too. The plans my parents and I had made together were clear; with a single word I could commit myself to them. Give me a single word and I can move the earth. 'I think . . . not,' I said. 'It wouldn't be a good use of my time. My girlfriend and I are planning to move to London when she finishes her degree – she's a musician.'

Dr Boycott looked bored. It occurred to me that my personal plans mattered not at all to him and this realization, instead of cowing me, made me unafraid.

'Yes, you see, Dr Strong,' I continued, 'you see, my girlfriend and I plan to move in together in London. I'm going to teach. Secondary school, that is, probably maths. The hours will combine well with her career.'

We had not, in fact, firmly committed to this plan but every day made me surer that I did not want to take Simon's route, of milk-round jobs or a City career, and I was unsuited to Jess's vocation or Franny's academic path. It seemed as good a time as any to take a stand.

'A . . . secondary school teacher. That's certainly –' Dr Boycott gave a lizard-like blink – 'commendable. Nonetheless, you will be fit for nothing at all if you cannot achieve a degree. You will take penal collections in four weeks' time on last term's work. You understand, Mr Stieff? You must repeat the examinations which you have just failed so abominably. If you do not pass them on your second attempt, we will be forced to consider your place here.'

It was Mark's twenty-first birthday in the third week of that term. He was a year older than most of us, though he did not advertise this fact, nor did he have any exotic stories of housebuilding in rural Ghana or backpacking across south-east Asia like those who had taken a formal gap year. When asked about the missing year, Mark sometimes said that, with the variety of tutors and stop-gap education he'd had after his parents divorced and his mother took him out of Ampleforth, he'd simply fallen a year behind, and sometimes that he had been ill. I wondered if those few words he'd spoken to me regarding his 'breakdown' were the answer to his missing year, but I had not asked.

In any case, he didn't mark his birthday with any particularly debauched revelry. The most noteworthy event was that Mark received a gift from his father. It startles me now to realize that I never exchanged a word in person with Mark's father. Mark spent the summers at his father's house in the north or travelling when he could not bear to see his mother, but his father never came to Annulet House to see us, only ever arriving when Mark was alone. If it were not for the newspaper profiles of the elderly Sir Mewan Winters, of Winters Industrial, or the eventual obituaries, or the car, one might have suspected he had never existed at all. He was old, and had been old when Mark was born. He sent occasional cards with clipped greetings, he never telephoned and he died a year after we finished Oxford. But on that one occasion – his son's twenty-first birthday – he sent him a car.

It was by far the glossiest vehicle I'd ever seen, sleek red lines and fluidity of composition, like a Vorticist painting. Mark had a battered Citroën which he kept for countryside driving but this was something else. A Ferrari Dino. A classic.

'Bloody nice car,' said Simon. 'Time for a test-drive, I reckon.'

Mark shrugged.

'Tell you what –' he tossed the keys to Simon – 'you take it out for me, tell me what you think.'

Simon's smile was large and incredulous. He weighed the keys in his hand, sat down gravely in the front seat of the car, curling his fingers around the steering wheel with slow intensity. He revved the engine twice, grinned at us and then roared towards the city centre.

'He'll love you forever for that,' said Franny. Then, after a few moments, 'Don't you want to drive it?'

Mark smiled. 'It's all of ours. All of ours, all together. You should all use it whenever you want. It's all of ours.'

Later that evening, Mark put in his usual telephone call to have food and wine sent over for a birthday feast. Meanwhile, we pulled out stacks of board games. Simon and I were making a ham-fisted attempt at a serious chess game when the doorbell rang downstairs.

'I think that must be Maison Blanc,' said Mark. Then, casually, 'James, would you do me a favour and give them their money?'

He drew a few notes from his wallet and passed them to me.

'That ought to cover it,' and, as I walked out, he called behind me, 'Let me know if it's not enough!'

Downstairs, the delivery men carried the boxes through to the kitchen, loading some into the refrigerator. I looked at the notes Mark had given me. It was almost double the cost of the food. I paid the men, giving them an extra £10 each for their trouble.

Upstairs, Jess and Emmanuella were playing Scrabble. Mark suggested they might find it interesting to make this strip Scrabble.

Quietly, I said, 'Mark, your change.'

He frowned at me and at my closed fist, bunched around the money.

'Don't worry about that,' he said. 'Keep it, or throw it in the lake. I don't care.'

None of the others showed any interest in this exchange. I felt my hand bunch around the money, the £50 notes stiff in my palm.

'But Mark, it's . . .' I extended my arm minutely towards him.

'I *said* don't worry about it.'

I thrust my hand into my pocket, feeling the notes and coins tumble around my keys and my packet of chewing gum. Feeling the power of the transaction.

I took my penal collections in the fifth week in a small study next to Dr Strong's rooms. He left the door open between the two rooms and, as I struggled through questions on heat exchange and Onsager reciprocal relations, I could hear Dr Strong making little noises as he worked. For a man so strangely silent in company, he was fairly vocal when alone. He made a bipping, questioning sound when reading, with an occasional long hmmmm, along with a variety of hums, whistles, stampings and puffings. I looked out of the window into Garden Quad, where first years whose names I didn't know were eating lunch, then, with a force of will, drew my attention back to the question paper. I had worked to the point of exhaustion for this exam. I had skipped lectures and arrived at tutorials with an even more dismal level of preparation than usual. I had stayed up late and woken early and studied and striven and blotted out all thoughts other than 'If I fail this exam, they'll send me down.' And, to my surprise, I found that the questions were clearer than I'd thought and ways of approaching them came more readily to my mind.

Time passed. At 3 p.m. Dr Strong knocked on the door, half-smiled and held out his hand for my script. As I stood to leave, he cleared his throat.

'How is your, ahem?' he said.

'My . . .'

He motioned to my leg.

'How is it these days?'

'Oh!' I was startled that Dr Strong had taken any notice of me. 'It's, um, it's sort of settled down. I sometimes have to use my stick, but often it's all right. At least it doesn't hurt all the time any more. Only if I knock it.'

'Ahhh-aa,' said Dr Strong.

He beamed at me and we stood in silence for a few moments. I was unsure whether I was meant to respond any further or leave quietly.

At last I said, 'Well, I should be off.'

Dr Strong nodded.

'Mind out with your, ahm, your, ahm, mind out on the stairs. They're steep,' he said.

Downstairs, still slightly dazed from the exam, I went to the lodge to check my pigeonhole. Next to the glass-panelled room where the porters sat doing their crosswords was the tiled antechamber lined from floor to ceiling with dark-wood pigeonholes. The room smelled, for some reason, unpleasantly of sweat. I riffled through the Sr–St section, pulling out the few letters addressed to me. Among them was a pale green envelope with the St Benet's crest. It was a note from Father Hugh.

Dear James,

I have a small matter I hope to discuss with you. Nothing that need be in the least alarming. Do pop by for a sherry – I should be in any weekday from 4 p.m. to 6 p.m.

My very best wishes,

Fr Hugh

I had nothing else to do so I walked over. Father Hugh appeared entirely delighted with my presence, gave me sherry and offered me a seat. I sat. I drank. The sherry was very good. Father Hugh sat down, spreading his legs a little wider than I was entirely comfortable with, although nothing untoward was visible.

'I'm so glad you could come,' he said. 'How are things?'

'Oh,' I said, 'not too bad.'

I suddenly wondered if he was going to make a pass at me. One did hear things, even then, about Catholic priests.

'My girlfriend,' I continued swiftly, 'is in the University Orchestra. She was rehearsing a lot last term, but . . .' I struggled to think of a way to finish this sentence that didn't alert Father Hugh to my having had no reason to start it, 'not so much this term,' I concluded.

'Mmm, girlfriend,' said Father Hugh, 'I sometimes wonder if you students settle down too early, but I suppose –' he took a sip of sherry – 'better too early than too late.'

'Yes, I suppose so,' I said.

'Well, James,' said Father Hugh, 'I wonder how you think things are with our mutual friend.'

I pushed my lips out noncommittally.

'I suppose you should ask him that,' I said.

'Yes, yes, quite,' said Father Hugh, leaning forward, 'but you know I always say: one gets the best reflection from still water.'

'Is it Mark's mother who wants to know?' I said. I did not like this way of handling things.

Father Hugh steepled his fingertips.

'We're all concerned about Mark, James. All of us here at Benet's, Mark's family . . . I sometimes think . . . well –' he leaned forward confidentially – 'I sometimes think it was a mistake to take him out of Ampleforth. I met him several times when he was a young boy, you know. Such a happy child, and of course his family have so many friends. You know it was my predecessor, Father Anthony, who arranged his parents' annulment. So sad. It affected Mark, of course it would. But I wonder if he would have been better left where he was instead of being dragged off across the world. He needs stability, James.'

'He has stability,' I said. 'We're stable. We're his friends.'

'Ah yes, friends,' said Father Hugh, 'but you can't, forgive me, live in that house with him forever, can you? And then where will he go?'

I shrugged. The question seemed ridiculous to me. Where would any of us go? We'd get jobs and rent flats and hope that we could find someone to love us forever and raise a family or at least pursue our careers. Nothing was certain, everything was possible.

'I shouldn't think Mark would ever have trouble making friends,' I said.

Father Hugh drank a little more sherry.

'Yes, I suspect you are correct there, James. He is a very charming young man. He has certainly made an impression here at Benet's. I suppose you know, though, that he is not quite stable?'

He spoke the last words quickly, fixing me with his gaze to give me to understand that they were not lightly spoken. It was certainly more than I'd ever heard anyone else in Mark's life say.

I looked around the room. Over the cold marble fireplace hung another of those graphic and discomfiting figures of the dying Jesus. The limbs were tortured, straining to get away from the nails, the mangled hands curled around the wounds. Again and again, this same loving attention to the lineaments of suffering and the life lived, the death attained, only for others.

Father Hugh stirred in his chair. I could feign ignorance and probably be met with pretended ignorance in return. But what, I thought, if it would be better for Mark if I were to know more than he was willing to tell me? What then?

'Yes,' I said, 'he told me a little about that.'

Father Hugh leaned back in his chair, magnanimous.

'Ah, I am pleased to hear,' he said, 'pleased indeed to hear that he is sharing his worries. No one, of course, would want him to return to the care of a clinic, but for his own protection we must know if his behaviour becomes truly erratic. You understand? High spirits are one thing, but several years ago he became . . .' Father Hugh paused, staring past me out of the window to the leaf-blown quad beyond, 'he became violent, aggressive. We feared he would do damage to himself. And his behaviour was often . . . inappropriate. Do you understand?'

I said nothing.

'Can I trust you to be a friend to Mark, James?'

'I am his friend,' I said.

'Good,' said Father Hugh, 'then we can pass to the second order of business. Isabella has sent me a gift for you.'

He leapt to his feet, bounded over to the bookcase and retrieved a large brown-paper-wrapped parcel which he deposited in my lap.

'Oh!' I said. 'Shall I . . .?'

'Yes, yes, go on. Open it. I understand you had a rather clumsy incident last year, but the damage has been fully repaired. Isabella has decided to make you a gift of it.'

I tore open the brown paper, already half knowing what was inside. It was the music box, gold and glass and glint, restored to pristine working order. There was a small white card inside with Isabella's name, her address and her numbers in Rome and Los Angeles.

'I can't take this,' I said.

'Oh, but you must,' said Father Hugh. 'After all, you're a friend of Mark's, just as we said.'

At home, in the privacy of my bedroom, I opened the music box and heard it play again the familiar twanging chords of 'Au Clair de la Lune'. The little gears turned, the tiny raised bumps pulled up the metal teeth and let them fall back. I shut the lid, quieting the sound. It seemed miraculous that the thing could have been made whole. It must have taken months of work to repair it. I removed the card and put it into my desk drawer.

I knocked on the door of Mark's room. He was in, sleeping off a hangover. He answered the door in pyjama bottoms, topless. I held out the parcel to him.

'Father Hugh gave me this,' I said. 'It's from your mother. I think it's meant for you – a late birthday present, I expect.'

He looked at the music box. I don't know what I'd expected. A histrionic outburst perhaps, a repetition. Instead his lip curled.

'Just like a bad penny,' he said. 'A priceless antique bad penny. Typical. Thanks, James.'

And went back to bed.

I passed my penals. I passed them well, in fact. Well enough for Dr Strong to give a little bip of excitement as Dr Boycott informed me that, if I continued like this, I 'might prove a credit to this college, Mr Stieff'. I wondered what I'd done differently, and if I could reproduce it in the future. I noted also, with gloomy realism, that the effort I'd put into revising thermodynamics meant that my current work had suffered. Oxford is like this; there is no time for rest.

By the end of term I was struggling again, my head sinking under the water and rising and sinking once more. Kind, lovable Panapoulou – how could I ever have considered him odd? – walked me through several questions on our recent sheets. I had learned that there was little to expect from the tutors in additional support, and it seemed to me that if I could just drag myself, or allow the others to carry me, to the end of term I could spend the vacation trying to learn this new work.

Mark, too, was under threat of penal collections. His college had suddenly deemed his previous term's essays – as crumpled and perfunctory as ever – unsatisfactory in light of their high standards. He, on the other hand, through means of persuasion not available to me, had been granted a reprieve on the condition that he should produce two essays which his tutors considered of adequate quality.

On Sunday morning at the start of ninth week, with the certainty of spring coaxing the garden into green, Emmanuella suggested that we all walk over the Port Meadow to have lunch at the Trout. Quite apart from the work whose demands crowded in on me as soon as term was over, such a walk was beyond me; my knee had flared up again. Mark said he'd run us both over in the Dino. It was only big enough for two anyway.

When his work was finished, we went out to the car.

Mark grinned. 'You know what,' he said, 'let's not go straight to the Trout. We've got time. Let's drive somewhere, how about that? It's Sunday, it's sunny, let's go somewhere beautiful.'

He was all manic energy, bouncing in his seat as we drove up through Summertown and out into the countryside. Instead of taking the most direct route, he turned the car towards the east, choosing the smaller country roads rather than the main highways.

It was beautiful. For a time I stared out of the passenger window at the countryside waking from its winter slumber, the trees budding green, their tiny branches surrounding them like an untidy cloud of hair. This part of the country is galleried, almost stepped, so that tree builds on tree, hill on hill, giving the effect of mistiness even on clear days. I lapsed into a sort of day-dreaming on the landscape, so that I did not notice at first that we were driving too fast.

My warning came with a series of sharp tumbling raps on the side of the car. We had driven – too fast, much too fast, past an overhanging branch which had run its knuckles along the side of the car. I sat up and looked forward. The road was narrow and winding; we would not be able to see any car coming in the opposite direction in time to slow down safely. We rounded the corners faster and faster, the car swerving almost into the ditches at each side. Mark was smiling, just a little, at the corners of his mouth.

We turned sharply around another bend and I saw a car ahead, travelling in the same direction as us, but much more slowly. The road was only one lane wide. I was relieved; he would have to slow down now. But he didn't slow down. Instead, he revved the accelerator and moved closer and closer to the car ahead. He didn't hoot or flash his lights. He even decreased his speed a little. But he was too close. The car in front, a green Volvo with two small children visible in the back, accelerated to try to put some space between us. Mark allowed them to do so, fell back a few feet, but then, after some seconds had passed, began to accelerate again.

I spoke, trying to keep my voice calm and measured.

'You're driving too fast, Mark. And you're too close to the car in front.'

He turned his head towards me, away from the road.

'You know, James,' he began.

'Watch the road, Mark!'

He smiled, raised his eyebrows, looked briefly at the road and accelerated a little. He turned his head back to me.

'You know, James, you worry too much.'

I didn't answer. I was staring at the road in front of us, casting momentary glances towards him – just enough to know that *he* still wasn't looking ahead. I began to breathe faster. What should I do? Wrench the wheel out of his hands, pull hard on the handbrake? Would that be more dangerous?

'Fucking hell, Mark, just look at the road, for Christ's sake!'

He rolled his eyes and turned his head back to the road. I relaxed a little, but we were still accelerating, getting dangerously close to the Volvo.

'You see, James, worry will only give you ulcers.'

I looked at the speedometer. We were doing 85. 'You're going too fast, Mark.'

'Me, I'll never get an ulcer, because I know how to have fun.'

On that last word, fun, he pushed the accelerator down hard, so that our bumper almost touched the back of the Volvo. I saw two white, panicked faces turn round to stare at us.

Mark laughed, then pulled his foot off the accelerator so that the car in front was able to escape a little; it must have been doing 90 at least. The Volvo hooted three or four times and flashed its hazard lights.

Mark wrinkled his mouth and looked at me. 'Do you think they're trying to tell us something?'

He stepped on the accelerator again, the car ludicrously responsive, roaring as if in sight of prey. The Volvo tried to accelerate away, but it did not have the power. We approached inch by inch until, again, we were almost touching. If the car in front had to stop, if there were a car coming the other way, we would plough straight through the back of it, straight across the back seat where the two children were sitting.

'See,' said Mark, though his voice was very distant to me, 'you need to learn how to take some risks, James.'

We pushed forward again. Our bumper touched that of the car in front; I felt the judder. The Volvo glanced suddenly sideways, then righted itself. Mark accelerated again.

I became very calm suddenly. It was as though time elongated; I felt I had minutes in which to decide, very carefully, what to do. Could I wrest the steering wheel from him? No, we would hit one of the banks and die. Could I persuade him to stop?

I said, 'Mark. You must stop. Now.'

He laughed.

I said, 'If you don't slow this car down right now, I swear to you I'll pull the handbrake. We'll do a 360-spin, skid all over the road and bury ourselves in one of those trees. I swear to you I'll do it.'

He opened his mouth, still smiling, then closed it again. He bit his lower lip. I noticed that his forehead was beaded with perspiration.

I knew then that he might kill us both. That he himself did not know why.

'Right now, Mark.'

He took his foot off the accelerator pedal. The speedometer needle wound backwards: 90, 80, 70. As we got to 70, we finally passed a lay-by and the Volvo pulled off the road. As we drove past, I saw the mother turn round to comfort her children. Both were tearful. The boy had been sick.

We drove the remaining ten miles at a slower pace. Mark became thoughtful as we went and, after fifteen minutes or so had passed, he said, 'You know, James, I've noticed that when you drive, you always leave a big space between you and the car in front. And as you drive, you let the space get bigger and bigger. If they slow down, you slow down more. If they speed up, you don't speed up quite so much. Why do you think that is?'

'It's called road safety, Mark. You should try it.'

'No,' he said, 'I don't think that's it.'

'OK, Mark, you tell me. Why?'

He pursed his lips.

'I think,' he said, 'I think it's because you like to let people get away from you. You know. You don't like *being* chased, you like to be the one who pursues. But you can't pursue too hard, or they'll realize you're interested. So you're always tagging along behind people, slowly letting them get away.'

My voice became very level, very tight. I said, 'I have never heard anything so incredibly, pathetically *stupid*. Do you honestly think that you can derive some cod-psychological truths about me from the way that I drive? And after the performance you have just given, which *fucking* one of us do you really think has the problem, Mark? How can you think you have any right to lecture *me* about *my* personality?'

He looked at me, smiling. 'It's true though, isn't it? I expect that's what Father Hugh wanted to tell you too.' He looked back at the road, spun the wheel in his hands and turned the Dino into the pub car park.

II

Second year, May, fifth week of term

When did I begin to be afraid to answer the telephone? Here in San Ceterino we have an answerphone set so that the phones barely ring before Mark's recorded voice requests, drily, that a message be left. When Mark isn't at home I hover by the machine, listening to the call, my hands by my sides, gauging my own response to the idea of speaking to them. Often it's a friend of Mark's from the village, less often a member of his family or one of their financial representatives, least often my parents or Anne telling me a piece of family news in their small, bitter voices. I listen to the recording being made; I stand waiting until the person hangs up. I allow the messages to accumulate, then I delete them. Mark is different: he either picks up the phone impulsively, surprised if the person on the other end isn't entirely delightful, or fails to listen to the messages at all. But then, it's not Mark who's had to receive the calls about him and the things he has done over the years. It's not Mark who's had to decide what to do about them.

There is this to be said for Mark: he never, despite all his wealth and connections, showed the slightest interest in joining the ranks to which that wealth and those connections would have given him instant access. He never cared to attend drinks with the Master of his college, although he was invited with great frequency. He never took sherry with Bill Clinton at Rhodes House, though he received an embossed invitation, hand-delivered. He certainly never belonged to one of those exclusive all-male dining societies which still blight the face of Oxford, although he did once list for us in alphabetical order all the members of the Bullingdon Club he'd ever shagged or snogged. And when Franny angrily informed us that some male members of the Jewish Society, in a depressing attempt to introduce the same misogynist practices as the rest of Oxford to that institution, had formed an all-male dining society, Mark's only comment was, 'My darling, I guarantee you that each and every one of them will meet a bad end. I shall personally see to it if you like.'

It was in that light that he was critical of Father Hugh. The monk was a visitor to the house two or three times in the summer of our second year, always on the pretext that he had 'happened past' and never staying for too long. He never gave the slightest indication that he and I had spoken privately except that, when he made his goodbyes his handshake with me might have lingered a little longer, and his invitation, 'I do hope to see you at the hall,' might have been made to me with a more fixed gaze.

'He's a horrible snob,' said Mark to us after one of these visits. 'He's only interested in bringing on the boys from the good families. He loves nothing better than getting invited to the House of Lords. As if I spoke to any of those people.'

Father Hugh did not attempt to contact me again that term. It was left to me to contact him and I did not, at first, think I would have any reason to do so.

The notorious 'fifth week blues' had struck; the day was cold, grey and melancholy. Jess was working and Emmanuella was still in bed – she often stayed in bed all day if the weather was cold, huddled up in a fur coat, reading and sipping hot chocolate.

I was in the kitchen, the warmest part of the house, flicking through the paper and putting off minute by minute the moment when I would have to return to my work, when the telephone rang. I answered it.

'James?' It was Mark. 'James,' he said, 'you have to come. I've been arrested.'

'What?' I said. 'I mean, why? What have you done? What's happened?' And I thought the worst, it must be the very worst, after all he had done. When he did not answer, I said, 'Is someone hurt, Mark? Have you . . . is someone hurt?'

He breathed in and breathed out and said airily, 'Oh, James. You do make a performance out of a drama. It's just cottaging. Come down and bring me a change of clothes. I've been here all night. Hurry up please, they only gave me 20p.'

I can't say why I did what I did next. Only perhaps that I was afraid, or felt that something was promised. I pulled Isabella's card from my wallet. I turned it over. On the back, Father Hugh had written his private Oxford number. After a little consideration, I dialled.

'Benet's?' said the voice on the other end.

'Oh,' I said, 'I was hoping to speak to Father Hugh.'

The porter sighed and I heard the sound of papers turning.

'He's out,' the porter said at last.

'Can I leave a message?'

Another sigh.

'Could you tell him that James rang? James Stieff? It's about Mark. He's at the police station because . . .' I stopped. What was I going to say to this porter? I couldn't tell him the whole business, ridiculous. 'Actually,' I said, 'never mind. Don't worry about it. I'll speak to him another time. Sorry to trouble you.'

A final lingering sigh.

'That's it then?' said the porter.

'Yes,' I said, 'thanks.'

It was by no means as bad as it could have been. By the time Jess, Emmanuella and I arrived at the police station most of the formalities had already been dealt with. Mark had been questioned but not charged. Police bail was to be arranged.

We met him in a waiting room. He looked dishevelled and exhausted. I handed him the carrier bag of clothes I'd taken from his bedroom. He nodded and attempted a half-smile. This was not the bravado I'd heard in his voice when he called. This Mark, saddened if not chastened, was surprising to me.

I was even more startled when Emmanuella asked, in a cool voice, 'Did you use condoms?'

Mark nodded. Jess and I exchanged a quick look. We had expected more naivety from her, and more judgement.

Emmanuella looked at him, then pulled out a cigarette and offered him one too. 'Still,' she said, 'you must be tested for . . . SIDA – how do you say that?'

'AIDS,' said Mark. 'And I don't have it. I was tested a couple of months ago.'

I stared at the floor. It seemed impossible, but there was graffiti there – someone had drawn a penis pointing towards the table in indelible black marker. I found that I profoundly did not want to be contemplating Mark's sex life. It wasn't that I was disgusted by it, although I had never found the idea in any way alluring, but I found this image sordid. Anonymous encounters and prison cells and AIDS tests. I thought of the comfort and companionship of my life with Jess, of our cosy bed with its clean white sheets and patchwork counterpane. I felt a shred of sympathy for Father Hugh's opinion. Where were all Mark's lovers now?

He seemed to think something along the same lines, for he took up Jess's hand suddenly and rested his cheek on it.

'Thank you for coming for me,' he said. 'I knew you would. You always would, wouldn't you?'

Jess put her arm around his shoulders.

He looked up at us from his seat. 'Let's go home.'

Later that evening the rest of us had a conversation – the kind of conversation we seemed to have a great deal in our final eighteen months at Oxford and subsequently – around the question of what could be done about Mark.

Simon, his legs up on the elephant-foot stool, was unconcerned.

'It's just normal, isn't it?' he said. 'That's just the way Mark is, and it's not as if he's done anything dangerous, is it?'

I had not mentioned his driving to any of them but Jess.

'If you ask me,' said Franny, 'it's the normal response of any bloke who went to a public school. They all come out mad. Either totally repressed or totally unable to control themselves.'

'Hmmm,' said Jess, 'but he wasn't at public school for long, was he? It's more down to his mother, I think. Hyper-critical, hyper-indulgent. No wonder he's confused.'

I wondered about all of this. There seemed to be more to Mark's personality to me than could be easily explained away by reference to his upbringing. Some urge towards self-destruction that was more primal than that. I thought of the figure on the crucifix, and of the ease of Mark's circumstances, and of a phrase I had seen written in one of Mark's essays: 'A pain-free life is unbearable.'

I wanted to explain this but all I could come up with was, 'I don't think he can change. Not by himself.'

The group nodded and became quiet.

'Do you not think,' said Emmanuella after a while, 'that we must save him? For his own good, rescue him?'

'That'd be fine,' said Simon amicably, 'if it were, you know, not completely impossible.'

Emmanuella was silent.

'I don't know, Manny,' said Franny, popping a grape into her mouth from the fruit bowl on the table, 'isn't salvation something only your God can offer?'

I had come to know Father Hugh's notes by their envelopes, by the curlicued hand and the slight cigar whiff of them. And the next morning, when one arrived at Annulet House, I knew that something had gone wrong with my calculations.

> *James,*
>   *Written in haste. I received a garbled message yesterday afternoon from you regarding our young friend. Called at the house this evening, no answer. I am concerned, as I am sure you can imagine. Please call me at once; I am in contact with Rome.*
>   *Yours sincerely,*
>   *Fr Hugh*

This note threw me into a panic. It was 9 a.m. and Mark might be awake or asleep, there was no way of knowing. The reference to Rome was ominous. Had Father Hugh consulted with Isabella or with the Vatican? Was Mark's mother on her way here at this very moment? I telephoned at once.

'James.' Father Hugh's voice was calm and even. 'I'm so glad you've called. Tell me precisely what's happened, please.'

'Um,' I said, 'it was nothing, Father Hugh, nothing really. It's been sorted out now. I didn't mean to leave you a message. I thought I'd told the porter not to.'

'I'm glad to hear it's been sorted out, James, but what actually happened?'

'Oh, it was nothing, not really.'

'George mentioned a police station, James.'

I wondered suddenly what Father Hugh could do if he suspected I was lying to him. Could he call my college? Report me to the university?

'I . . . made a mistake.'

'A mistake?'

'Yes, I, it was just a joke, just one of Mark's jokes.'

Father Hugh was silent for a moment.

'George said you sounded quite alarmed,' he said.

'Oh, I . . . Well, yes, I was taken in by it myself.'

'What sort of a joke,' said Father Hugh, 'was he making?'

'Umm . . .' I said, 'nothing. He didn't say anything. I made a mistake.'

'James,' said Father Hugh, 'I think I understand. You should come and see me in my office, where we can talk privately. Without any chance of being *overheard*. Come this afternoon, James.'

And I thought again of my college and of Father Hugh's influential friends and of the fact that Mark might come down at any moment.

'Yes, Father Hugh,' I said.

Mark was up early that morning. He was subdued and restive, moving from room to room, making himself cups of coffee and leaving them to get cold. I told him, in as few words as possible, about my blunder with Father Hugh. When I'd finished he took a deep breath in and let it out slowly.

'It doesn't matter,' he said, lighting a cigarette with trembling hands. 'Tell him. What does it matter?'

'Seriously?'

He drew deeply on his cigarette. His fingernails were tobacco-stained.

'What's the worst they can do? Only take the house away and send me to some horrible clinic somewhere.'

'Really?' It was so hard to know which of the things he said were real and which imagined.

He smoked his cigarette down to the quick and began another.

'Listen, James,' he said, 'I'm only telling you this because my family seem to want to get their claws into you. They think you're my friend. I don't know why. Probably because you took the blame for the music box. It doesn't matter.' He sighed. 'You remember I told you that I had a breakdown? It was after my parents split up, when my mother was dragging me round Europe with the idea of giving me an education. It wasn't anything serious. I took too many drugs and got into a few fights. But you know how religious people are. My mother sent me to live with a bunch of monks.' He smiled. 'As if she thought there was no such thing as a gay monk. Anyway, it's all over now. I've been better for years. But I'm trying not to give them an excuse to tell the trustees to stop my money, OK? That could make it difficult.'

'Right,' I said.

'That's all though. Just temporarily difficult.'

'Yes,' I said.

He lit another cigarette.

Father Hugh was waiting again with sherry and beaming smiles.

'James,' he said, 'how marvellous of you to come. Now we can have a *proper* chat.'

'Yes,' I said, accepting the sherry and seating myself on the sofa.

'I was glad that you telephoned, James. I entirely understand that one can't always be as direct as one might wish about such things. Especially not in a shared house, shared spaces. But now, tell me what happened.'

'Nothing happened, Father Hugh.'

Father Hugh's smile cracked a little.

'Nothing? Come, come. There's no need to prevaricate now.'

'Nothing happened,' I said.

I sipped a little more sherry. Father Hugh frowned.

'It is quite clear to me that something happened, James. Mark was taken to the police station. It is imperative that you tell me precisely what occurred.'

'Nothing, Father Hugh,' I said, 'nothing happened at all.'

'Now look here,' he began angrily, then, calming himself, said, 'James, perhaps you don't understand the severity of what we're discussing here.'

'We're not discussing anything, Father Hugh.'

Father Hugh leaned back in his chair, kicking out his cassock again in that disturbing fashion.

'James, our friend Mark is a very disturbed young man. Has he told you what happened in Italy six years ago?'

I looked at him innocently over the brim of my glass.

'No, I can see that he has not. Well then, I am forced to tell you in order that you should understand the severity of the situation. Six years ago our friend Mark suffered a mental breakdown. It took the form of wild and erratic behaviour. We are not talking of mere high spirits, James. He became physically violent to his mother on several occasions. And more than that, he behaved to her in ways that were entirely inappropriate.

'He stole. He smashed furniture. Eventually he stole a car and crashed it, only avoiding injuring himself by the most merciful act of God. He was arrested. It was only by the strongest representations made at the very highest level, the *very highest*, James, that Mark was able to avoid a stay in a juvenile detention facility and was instead released into the care of the monks of Santa Albante. Do you understand?'

I gulped and nodded.

'The family were pleased to see him apply himself to the Oxford entrance exam. We, his friends at Benet's and at Ampleforth, are delighted that he is interested in achieving a degree. We are not unhappy that he has found himself a group of friends. But James, we must know if his behaviour has begun to become erratic again. Do you understand?'

I nodded again. I considered whether Mark's cottaging was erratic behaviour. It would probably seem so to Father Hugh. But it had been in fact a very steadfast and reliable behaviour. I thought of the incident in the car. There was that, of course. But it hadn't been repeated: he'd seemed perfectly calm as soon as we entered the pub. But perhaps I should mention it.

Before I could reply, Father Hugh said, 'It goes without saying, James, that Isabella and the family will be very grateful for your assistance. If Mark is unwell again, he will need someone to help him. A companion. I'm sure we could arrange for you to receive signing power for one of his bank accounts.'

I must have shown something in my face at this.

'Of course –' he held up his hands – 'all of this is for Mark's own good.'

I looked at him. How did he see this in me, Father Hugh? He was right. But I did not want to see it in myself.

'I'm sorry, Father Hugh,' I said, 'I don't know what to tell you. Nothing happened. It was all a silly joke.'

Father Hugh sighed.

'Very well, you may go. I may come to visit Mark later today.'

I waited the rest of the day for Father Hugh to arrive, anxiously scanning the road for his long, lean figure. But he did not come. Nor did he come the next day, or the day after. And I had no more notes from him.

12

Third year, October, first week of term

Mark rarely tries to explain himself. He has not the knack for self-examination. Once, after the funeral, I or his mother or Father Hugh or some combination suggested that he should see a counsellor. And he agreed, and went, and sat quite peacefully through several hour-long sessions with the woman, but it made him no better and no worse. And when I said, 'What did she say?' he said, 'I am that I am.'

And so he has never, I think, been able to attribute unknown motives to his actions. Never been able to say, 'Ah, I did so thinking I knew why, but I had hidden myself from myself.'

I have my ideas about why he did certain things, about why he suggested the ball so soon after Father Hugh's attempts to win me over, about what he was planning. Jess suggested it to me a long time ago when, in another of those endless conversations about what was to be done for Mark she said, 'He wanted to save himself, I think, with Nicola. He thought he could put himself out of the reach of temptation.'

But perhaps I am imputing too much complicated thought to him. Perhaps it was all simply an accident, every part of it.

'Now, my dears,' said Mark, 'if you call me a fairy godmother I shall kill you but –' he reached under his plate and pulled out four blue cardboard oblongs – 'you shall go to the ball.'

Franny squealed and grabbed his hand to examine the tickets.

'Ohhhh, very nice. Gloucester College Winter Ball. What excellent taste you do have.'

He did. He had welcomed us back from the long vacation with good wine and roast beef, and dismissed our enquiries about his summer with an airy 'spent it with Dad's family. Mass in the morning,

143

parties in the evening. Dreary beyond belief,' and when dinner was concluded presented us with these tickets. Each was marked with its price: £220. I had not previously been able to afford to go to my college's ball.

'Is it going to be good?' said Mark. This was directed at Jess and me. 'Tell me they put on a good show at Gloucester.'

'I think so,' said Jess hesitantly. We had rather withdrawn from college life.

Simon looked at the tickets with their silver writing. He frowned.

'You've bought four double tickets, though. There are only six of us.'

Mark beamed.

'An extra one for Emmanuella. You'll want to bring Kristian, won't you, Manny?'

Kristian was her new boyfriend; interchangeable, as far as I could tell, with the last. Emmanuella nodded graciously and leaned over the table to kiss Mark on each cheek.

Franny said, 'But doesn't that still leave an extra place?'

And Mark paused, drew breath and said, 'Yes, I suppose so. I rather thought I'd invite Nicola.'

Simon laughed. 'Nic? She'll be a bit out of place at an Oxford ball, won't she?'

Mark's mouth made an odd curl, a half-disappointed sideways curve.

'I think she'll be fine.'

'She's only fifteen, Mark,' said Franny.

'I think she'll be fine,' Mark said again.

Simon cracked open another beer and leaned back in his chair.

'Well,' he said, 'on your head be it.'

Nicola arrived on the morning of the ball by train. She had grown three or four inches and was less awkward and more worldly than when we'd first met her. She was wearing jeans and carrying a copy of *Just Seventeen* and I wondered whether she still doted on the vicar she'd been so fond of quoting last time I'd seen her.

Simon ushered her into the green salon, saying, 'Just don't mess anything up, all right?'

Nicola looked around the room, its antique furniture covered in cigarette burns, the remnants of dinner from last night and the night before still strewn across the floor. She shrugged her shoulders and said, 'If I messed it up any more I'd be tidying.'

She half-smirked at Simon, waiting to see if he'd respond, then turned to us and muttered, 'Hello, James. Hello, Jess.'

But Mark, as if he had detected the sound of her voice with dog-like hearing, suddenly hurled himself through the French doors at the far end of the room. He dashed along the central hall and fell to his knees before Nicola's armchair, shouting, 'Nicolaaaaaaaaaaaaaaa!'

She let out a little scream and threw her arms around his neck, a different girl now. He grabbed her hands and kissed the back of each of them and she wriggled in her seat with pleasure and discomfort.

Sitting at her feet, he said in confidential tones, 'Now tell me about Laura, is she still the biggest bitch in the world?'

Nicola laughed. 'Don't call her that! But, yeah, kind of. On Thursday, when Mr Malone was giving back homework, he gave her Sophie's book instead. And she went, "Ew, I'm not touching this. Tell her to come and get it herself."'

'Oh, dear God. So what happened then?'

'Mr Malone tried to put his foot down, except he's, you know, not the greatest with discipline. In the end Hannah just got up and gave it back to her. Hannah's aces. And Mr Malone went, "You could learn something from Hannah's example," but when he turned his back Laura went –' Nicola stuck her tongue between her bottom lip and her teeth and made a 'nnnn' noise – 'only Mr Malone turned round and caught her.' Nicola paused, and looked around at us all – she had evidently surprised herself by her own lack of reserve – 'I know we're supposed to have Christian charity for everyone, but I really hope she gets expelled.'

'Quite right too. It's no more than she descrves, the little minx.'

'Did I tell you what happened when we went to the cinema two weeks ago? And we were all wearing jeans? Except Sophie came in a proper flowery dress and Laura went, "Did your mum make that?" and Sophie went, "Yes"? Hannah and me were going, "Leave her alone," and she did in the end, but –' Nicola rolled her eyes – 'she's just so horrible, Mark!'

'What a bitch,' said Mark, 'she'll come to a bad end, you mark my words. Now what about your family, how's everyone?'

As Nicola began to explain how Eloise was the most annoying person ever, while Leo was still a pet and her parents were . . . I watched Mark's face. He was rapt, even his habitual tic-like flicking of his hair or fiddling with a cigarette had all but vanished. Nicola bloomed visibly under this attention. Her neck grew longer, her back straighter. As Mark asked in fine-grained detail about her family, her schoolfriends, her work, she was half-child half-adult with him, sometimes flirtatiously playing with her hair or touching his arm, at other moments becoming over-conscious of her actions and backing away. When he stood up and walked around the room her eyes followed him. When he walked into the kitchen to fetch tea and cake she followed him half in a daze.

Franny, observing all this from the far end of the room, looked up from her book as they walked out and said, 'I hope he knows a dog is for life, not just for Christmas.'

'Franny!' said Jess.

Franny rolled her eyes and went back to her book.

'What's this?' said Nicola.

I walked into the kitchen and saw that she was examining the gold and glass music box. Mark had left it carelessly on one of the shelves, apparently hoping that it might walk away of its own volition. It had become a little sticky and looked less than its glittering self.

'Oh, that?' said Mark. 'Just a music box. See, there's a key underneath you turn to make it play.'

'It's amazing,' said Nicola, lifting it up to wind the key. 'So pretty!' She opened the lid and the twinkling notes spilled out.

'Do you like it?'

'It's beautiful,' said Nicola.

'Then it's yours,' he said. 'Take it.'

'Oh no, I can't.' She ran her fingers along the gold rim of the lid, touched the curved legs where the claws held the golden balls. 'I can't.'

'Of course you can. I don't want it. You can have it.'

She looked at him, thoughtful, with the earnestness of a teenager.

'No,' she said, 'I'll just enjoy it while I'm here.'

'Then you must come more often!' said Mark, and spun her a little waltz around the room as the box played to its end.

In the late afternoon, just as it was getting dark, we started to get ready. Dinner jackets and white shirts. Mark left his bow tie undone, starting, he said, as he meant to go on. We drank champagne on the landing while the girls rustled and giggled in Emmanuella's room.

'I hope you're not trying to peek!' called Franny, already two glasses of wine down, 'because I'm totally naked in here.'

'Oh,' said Jess, 'Franny, don't tease them. She's lying.'

'S'true, s'true,' said Franny, 'totally naked except for my bowler hat.'

And at last they stepped out. Jess in her indigo high-necked dress, Emmanuella in her caramel silk, Franny in her dark red velvet and finally Nicola, who had brought her dress in several black rubbish bags taped together, with the hanger hooks poking out of the top. She looked older, perhaps as much as five years older now. Her smattering of acne was covered with make-up, her hair pinned back in a pleat. Her dress was a sea-green confection, 1950s-style, with a nipped-in waist and layers of petticoats under the skirt so that it swung like a bell when she walked.

'My God,' said Mark, 'Nic, what fabulous tits!'

'That's my sister, mate,' said Simon, half-joking.

'Oh, sorry,' said Mark. 'I mean, "Nicola, what magnificent breasts."'

And we went to the ball.

Ostensibly, the ball's 'theme' was Christmas. Laser images of trees, stars and angels were projected on to the ancient walls and mottled drifts of fake snow were piled in the corners of the quads. But, in a cheerful exuberance of mixed messages, there was also a mariachi band in Front Quad and a stall selling tortillas. In Garden Quad a string quartet was gamely performing next to a troupe of wandering jugglers, while in Chapel Quad students in full evening dress were jumping up and down to a techno beat on a plywood dance floor.

'Look! Look!' said Nicola, leafing through her glossy programme, 'they've got a hypnotist and a graphologist and a fortune-teller and a masseur and an ABBA tribute band!'

She jumped up and down in excitement, careless of her high heels, and Mark joined in, the two of them holding hands and jumping in circles. In the corner of the quad, a young man was already vomiting, but the night had barely begun.

We walked through Front Quad, where the mariachis were playing a set the programme called 'Latin rhythms'.

'Come on,' said Mark. 'Come and dance.'

Nicola blushed and stared at him, as if uncertain whether he could really mean it.

'Come on,' he said again, tugging at her hand. 'It doesn't matter if you're rubbish. I'm a fantastic dancer.'

She raised her eyebrows and grinned.

'I'm not rubbish. I bet you're more rubbish than me.'

'Oh, is that so?'

Holding hands, they raced to the edge of the dance floor, where Mark placed Nicola facing us, resting his head momentarily on her shoulder to give us a broad wink. She, seeing our faces, looked round to find him gurning and half-pushed him off.

He slipped his arm around her waist, pressed his stomach against the small of her back and began to sway gently. She giggled and reached her arm down as if to pull his away, but his fingers caught hers and, rolling her eyes and laughing, she too began to circle her hips loosely. He nudged her forward and she spun lightly, away from him and then back, their hands together at her waist, a smile on her lips, a frown of concentration at his brow. He spun her away again and then, as he pulled her back, caught her other hand and arranged her into a ball-room stance, her hand resting on his shoulder. He whispered something into her ear and then they were moving slowly towards the centre of the dance floor. His hips were swaying and he pulled her closer and she laughed sweetly and leaned in to him. He was a good dancer, it was clear; he encouraged her, nudged her into position, moved her without bullying. Two couples passed in front of them and when they parted again I saw that her eyes were closed, her head on his chest.

Simon, I noticed, was watching them with a frown.

'D'you fancy a dance, Si?' said Franny.

He looked thoughtfully at the dance floor and then at Franny.

'Maybe later,' he said. 'Anyone want some punch?'

We shook our heads.

'Back in a minute, then.'

After he had moved away, Franny said quietly, 'We are utterly sure Nicola knows Mark's gay, aren't we?'

'You were there,' said Jess. 'She knows.'

'Then I suppose,' said Franny, 'we just wonder whether Mark knows.'

And she moved off, following Simon.

By the candyfloss stand in Garden Quad, my shoulder was shaken by a man whose face I had to take a moment to resolve into recognition.

'James!' he said. 'How the hell are you? Well? This is my girlfriend, Denise. Denise, this is James Stieff – fucking awesome physicist, top bloke.'

It was Kendall. He looked so much happier than when I had last seen him that he seemed entirely changed. Gone was the pallid, sickly air. Gone was the tea-scent. He seemed to have grown as well, put another inch or two on to himself, or perhaps it was simply that he stood more firmly. His girlfriend was lusciously plump and beautiful, poured into her dress to the point of appetizing overflow.

'What are you doing here?'

'Hars got us a ticket, Hars Daswani?' he said, as music started to play on the stage behind us. 'Thought I'd come back and see how the old place's doing. How are you, mate?'

'I'm . . . yeah, I'm good. How's Manchester?'

'Oh yeah, God . . .' Did I imagine a catch in his voice? 'Yeah, it's great. It's not –' he looked around the quad at the thousands of silver fairy lights winking like stars among the ivy – 'it's not all this, you know. But it's good.'

He sounded momentarily unconvinced. Denise caught my eye and beamed.

'Come on.' She wrapped herself around his arm. 'It's too bloody cold when we're not dancing!'

Kendall smiled at me apologetically. I watched them go and wondered if he knew what he'd escaped, or if he still pined for the quads and rooms lined with ancient books.

We always value things that are hard to get, regardless of their intrinsic worth.

Jess and I walked through the ball mostly arm in arm. I danced a little, but could not continue for long; the cold made my knee ache. She understood. We tried to get in to see the graphologist but the queues were too long, and the hypnotist forgot his patter halfway through when his victims started giggling. The booze was plentiful, though. At one point I thought I spotted Mark and Nicola in the crowds around the fortune-teller's tent, but could not reach them.

At 5.30 a.m. the sun had not yet risen but the breakfast muffins and steaming dishes of scrambled eggs and trays of smoked salmon began to emerge from the kitchens and we called ourselves 'survivors'.

At the trestle tables, Jess and I found Franny, her hair wild, her dress slightly askew.

'Have you seen Mark?' she said, struggling to manage plate and champagne glass and cigarette at once. 'Si's been looking for Nic for an hour.'

Jess and I shook our heads.

'They can't have left, can they?' said Jess, and I thought nervously of where Mark might have taken her, of what escapades he might have suggested.

'I expect they'll turn up,' I said, helping myself to a ladleful of buttery eggs.

*

When the sun was fully up, we went to look for them. We looked in the massage room, where a girl was crying noisily. We looked in the fortune-teller's booth, where a man was slumped by a neat puddle of vomit. We looked in the long dining hall, where Ball Committee members were already patrolling with black rubbish bags and weary expressions. We found them at last beneath one of the arched alcoves in the undercroft, where the noise from the last remaining dance floor above was muffled to a fuzzy pulse of sound, a rapid muted heartbeat. They were nestled close together, Nicola's head resting on Mark's lap, using his folded jacket as a pillow. Her legs were curled under her, the millefeuille layers of her white petticoats surrounding her like sea-foam. He was leaning back against the interior wall of the alcove, one hand protectively around her shoulders, the other stroking her hair. She was asleep and looked so young, so much younger than when awake, her profile as calm as a child's. She was breathing softly and Mark's head was tipped back. But as we approached, Mark looked up, smiled and raised one finger to his lips. And although we knew it was time to leave, we stood back, for a moment, and were silent.

13

Third Year

Soon after that, Oxford was over. It was the work that did it, first of all. The growling chasm of finals towards which we were being swept. Mark, probably driven by a dread of what his family would say if he failed, began spending up to ten hours a day in the library. Jess resigned from the orchestra and Franny became so obsessive in her work timetable that she even started noting down how long she'd spent in the bathroom and added that on to the end of her working day. This is Oxford: it need not be all or nothing, but it lends itself to that way of thinking.

And we began to spiral apart, slowly at first so we did not have to acknowledge what was happening. Franny took to spending part of her week back in college. Simon spent several weekends on recruitment retreats in Surrey or Hampshire, where he participated in group exercises, was interviewed and tested and asked to build a kayak using only three car tyres and a selection of rubber bands. Soon he triumphantly presented us with a letter confirming that, from the end of August, he would be employed by a well-known firm of management consultants. Jess and I spent a similarly fraught few days in London. She auditioned and was offered a position with a prestigious orchestra. I, less grandly, was accepted on to a PGCE course. One night over dinner at the house Emmanuella announced that she would be working as a TV-journalist in Madrid from the autumn, and we all toasted our success in good red wine.

All this news was merely the backdrop to finals, though. They were punishing; the insistent, inescapable mental pressure of Oxford condensed into a single, migraine-like week. Exam after exam after exam, a test of nerve and stamina rather than education or intellect. My exams were earlier than the others', at the end of

March. When I came out of each one, someone in the house would make me tea or soup and say, 'How was it?' Meaning 'Tell us the secret. What is this thing, finals? How is it to be conquered?'

And I did not know how to tell them that it was simply an exam. Like a hundred other exams. Like collections, like penals, like A-levels, like GCSEs, like mocks. For ten days I sat in Exam Schools. I raised my hand if I wanted to go to the bathroom, I tied my papers together using green cord tags with silver ends, I wrote legibly, I showed my workings. The only difference was in the show of the thing: the subfusc and the marble floors and the regulations concerning the holstering of swords.

This external show is meant to impress and terrify, but knowledge acquired at Oxford is no different from knowledge acquired anywhere else. And when the others began their finals, they knew this too.

But finals, for all their hugeness, lasted barely a moment. They were over as soon as they had begun, and then there was only waiting for results, lying in the sun and packing up belongings. We greeted each other with flowers and champagne, and threw flour or glitter on each other's heads. But the end of finals meant the end of other things as well, and this became increasingly clear.

Jess and I put a deposit down on a rented one-bedroom flat in London. Simon, using money saved from his lucrative summer jobs, got a mortgage and *bought* a small flat in London, which seemed to us to be the most grown-up thing we'd ever heard of. Mark's owning a house was one thing; Simon's persuading a bank to lend him money to buy one was quite another. Franny was accepted to read for a PhD at Cambridge and would be moving into graduate accommodation there. By our last night in the house, we had already reached the point where it took some effort to gather the six of us together.

The last night was a week after our results were announced. There were some surprises – Emmanuella received a lower second, while Simon got an upper second, and none of us could ever account for this except that it seemed often to be how things happened between men and women at Oxford, the men appearing to be marked with slightly surprising leniency, the women with surprising strictness. Franny got her first though, as did Jess. Mark received a bare third but redeemed himself ridiculously by winning a prize for his paper on 'Religions and Mythology of the Ancient Near East'. There was even a prize-giving where, according to him, he was presented with a leather-bound copy of *Cory's Ancient Fragments* by seventeen senior dons, each with a long beard and tattered gown. I got a lower second and was pleasantly surprised my mark was no worse. Other than that, I barely felt anything: no disappointment, no anger. Relief, mostly. Relief that it was over. Anne had been right: Oxford is a race and my race was run. I was no longer limping along behind the pack. It was done.

And after these things, we decided that we would have to have one last night of raucous celebration. We called it 'the last good night' later, because although there were other nights when the six of us spent the evening eating and drinking and talking and laughing, they were never quite like that again. I think we knew that this might be the case. That was why Emmanuella told whatever tall, taciturn blond was following her around just then that she had to have the evening off. That was why Franny blew off a night at high table, and Simon rescheduled a meeting with his management consultants, and Mark stayed home from roving.

And it was a good night. Mark ordered in hampers from Fortnum & Mason which Emmanuella scoffed at and made ham hock with split peas without reference to the contents of the hamper. We broke open a bottle of ancient port from the cellars and a wheel of creamy, gooey Stilton. We played card games and Cluedo – which Simon won in the most irritating fashion imaginable, not only guessing the murderer correctly but also telling us what cards we each had in our hands, like some sort of autistic savant. We drank more, we ate more. We played Twister and fell over on top of each other. Mark rolled a spliff and passed it round. Our jokes became funnier, our mood more expansive. I was filled with an immensity of love the like of which I had never felt before – love for the people giggling around the table, for the house with its many rooms which had been so daunting when we first arrived but which had welcomed us so warmly. I looked at the faces of my friends and saw that they were all astonishingly beautiful, and I found myself filled with simple gratitude that I had been allowed to share this time with them and a maudlin sadness too, a nostalgia for the present moment.

What is Oxford? It is like a magician, dazzling viewers with bustle and glitter, misdirecting our attention. What was it for me? Indifferent tuition, uncomfortable accommodation, uninterested pastoral care. It has style: the gowns, cobbled streets, domed libraries and sixteenth-century portraits. It is old and it is beautiful and it is grand. And it is unfair and it is narrow and it is cold. Walking in Oxford, one catches a glimpse through each college doorway, a flash of tended green lawn and ancient courtyards. But the doorways are guarded and the guardians are suspicious and hostile. For people like Mark, everywhere is Oxford: beautiful and ancient. For such people, life is an endless round of Oxfords: the quads and panelled rooms of Eton give way to those of Oxford, then the rooms of the Inner Temple and finally the Lords. For the rest of us, Oxford is an afternoon tour around a stately home: a place of wealth and beauty which, by its velvet ropes and querulous attendants, insists on reminding us that we do not belong. For me, Mark always held the promise that the ropes could be pulled back, that I could gain admittance. The question of how I would then leave did not, at that time, occur to me.

By 5.30 a.m. Emmanuella and Jess were asleep, curled up on Mark's massive bed. We covered them with a blanket. Simon and Franny claimed they were going to play cards in Simon's bedroom, although we knew full well what that meant because it was late, and they had been kissing copiously, and Simon's hand was quite unashamedly stuck down the back of Franny's jeans. Which left Mark and me on the landing.

He said, 'D'you fancy a bacon sandwich?'

I couldn't think of anything I wanted more.

In the kitchen, Mark cut four thick slices off the loaf and set two each on two plates next to the hob. He pulled down a frying pan from the shelf above the sink and set it to warm. I knew better than to offer to help; he had his system.

As he reached for the bacon at the back of the fridge, he said, 'Do you think we should just kill ourselves?'

'What?'

'No, really. I mean, don't you think we should just get it over with now?' He was smiling as he crossed the kitchen, bacon in hand. He took a long knife from the drawer and toyed with it, twisting its point on the tip of one finger. 'We could, you know, hara-kiri, right here in the kitchen.'

He turned the knife towards his chest and mimed the sudden jab in and upward thrust.

'Why would we do that?'

He sighed. He laid the strips of bacon into the pan; immediately, they began to crackle and their smoky odour made my mouth water. It was so late that I had begun to feel the hunger which replaces tiredness: sharp and biting.

'Because our lives are over, James. This is it. The end. We will never have a time like this again.'

I thought of the little flat Jess and I had signed for two weeks earlier, of waking in the morning to make her coffee before work. I thought of living with her, and only her.

'We'll have other times. Different, wonderful times.'

He pushed the bacon around the pan; tiny sizzles rose and hissed away.

'I feel sure,' he said, 'completely sure, that I'll never really be myself again. Not after this. This was it for me. I've had my golden time. All the rest will be silver and brass.'

I rolled my eyes. This was what Jess called his obsessive over-dramatization.

'There'll be other times, Mark. We're not going to become suddenly different, are we? We'll have great times, all together in London.'

He sighed and ran his hand through his hair.

'It's all right for the rest of you. You've got things to go on to – careers. Franny's got her PhD, Simon's got his job, Emmanuella's got her life in Madrid, you and Jess have got each other. What have I got?'

'How about 150 million quid in a trust fund?'

He looked at me as though I'd assayed a very low blow indeed. As if I'd reminded him about some distasteful aspect of his past, or his own mortality. He forked the bacon and flipped it over. There was a low sizzle and the scent of smoke and frying. He pushed the bacon around the pan for a few more seconds, then quickly fished it out, on to the plates. He wiped each slice of bread round the pan, to take up the grease, and put the sandwiches together. He licked his fingers and, with his back towards me, stared at the plates for a moment.

I say to myself now, didn't I know really? Wasn't that why I was fascinated by Mark? Wasn't it why I was in that house to begin with? And I think the answer is no. I didn't know, not really. It did not even feel like a self-deceiving lie. I had concealed the knowledge from myself so well that no act of will could have retrieved it.

He turned round, but instead of holding the two plates his hands were empty and he reached forward, pulled my face towards him and kissed me. I jumped, but didn't pull away. He tasted of cigarettes, of that mint chewing gum he liked. He shifted position. All I can remember is the thought circling around and around in my head: 'I am kissing Mark. Mark is kissing me. I am kissing Mark.' Like a catechism or a times-table; a thought, a true thought, but utterly without meaning or emotion.

After a minute or so, he leaned back, taking his mouth from mine but leaving his hand at the nape of my neck, stroking the hair there softly. His look was questioning, almost nervous. It's funny, but that was what did it; I'd never seen him nervous before, not during finals, not in a roomful of strangers or a dodgy pub. It made him look younger than he was.

I didn't think about anything. I hooked two fingers into his belt loop and tugged him towards me. I could smell the scent of his skin: cigarettes, pot, but underneath that a clean scent, like hay or grass.

He manoeuvred his right leg between mine as we kissed. I could feel his erection pressing hard against my thigh.

'God, James,' he said, 'I've been thinking about this for months. Years.'

I kissed him again, speaking into his mouth. 'Yes,' I said, 'me too. Years.' I hadn't known it until that moment, but it was true.

He fumbled with my belt buckle. All at once, I could feel each of his fingertips, the solid expertise of his palm, the rhythm of his arm. I gasped and leaned into him.

'Now now,' he murmured, 'not yet, not yet. Be patient.'

He moved slowly, holding me tightly, urging me on and restraining me both at once. I felt a flush begin to spread across my stomach and up towards my chest. He pulled off my sweater – more carefully than I would have imagined, with gentle attention – and then took his off quickly, quickly returning to me, pressing against me. The expanse of his skin against mine was almost more than I could bear. His attentions became a little more urgent. Only a little.

He shifted position slightly, a new motion. My mind went blank.

'Yes?' he said, his breath hot in my ear.

'Yes.'

He moved faster. The room became as small as the table we were leaning on, as the places where our bodies touched, as the pressure of his thumb. I pulled the heel of my hand down the small of his back and up again, relishing the ripple of his spine and the transition from downy skin to rough denim, pushing him towards me, increasing contact. I kissed him again, sinking my tongue deep into his mouth. I realized I was shaking. One of his hands was at the nape of my neck, comforting, as he whispered, 'Slowly, slowly,' while the other hand continued its necessary work. I could not go slowly. I touched my lips to the curve of neck and shoulder and his scent was cut grass and his taste was salt. His voice in my ear was sudden, intense.

'Are you sure, James? Are you sure this is what you want?'

I didn't hesitate. 'Yes,' I said. 'Yes, I'm sure.'

He pressed himself into me, liquid and smooth. He kissed me again.

'Yeah,' he said, 'I thought so.'

He moved away slightly. I reached out to pull him towards me and he moved back a pace. There was a moment's pause. I still didn't understand. He looked at me, slightly amused. He bent down, gathered his sweater from the floor and pulled it over his head.

'What,' I said, 'what?'

'James,' he said, pushing first one arm, then the other through the sleeves of his sweater, 'I'm ashamed of you. You're practically a married man.'

I couldn't speak. Blood was pounding, roaring in my brain. I think I opened and closed my mouth a few times. He licked the crook of his thumb and forefinger, raised his eyebrows and smirked.

He bent towards me and kissed me lightly on the lips.

'Don't take it personally. I just wanted to know, that's all.' He smiled. 'I'll be off now. Got to see a man about, well, you know. You can have the sandwiches.'

He raised an eyebrow, turned and walked from the room. After a moment or two I heard the front door slam. On the plates, by the Aga, two bacon sandwiches were congealing.

We were always better at nights than we were at mornings.

I'd managed to get myself showered and tidied before the others woke up. As the water trickled over my skin I thought about Mark, of course, about the feel of his skin and the sensation of him moving beneath my hand. I imagined a consummation. I wondered who he was with at that very moment, and hated myself for wondering. It took a while before I began to think about Jess, and even then my thoughts didn't amount to anything, just a sudden image of, for some reason, her freckled shoulders and the points of her collarbone, along with a feeling of guilt. Not remorse. Different thing.

Mark returned four hours later, skin flushed, eyes bright, as we were waiting for Emmanuella's taxi.

'Making an entrance as usual?' said Franny.

He circled his arms around her waist and spun her round.

'A boy's got to find his pleasure somewhere, you know. But I can't stay away from you, my darling.' He kissed her lightly on the lips. The others watched, amused.

The taxi arrived and Emmanuella kissed us all goodbye, leaving a trail of perfume in the air that lingered after she had gone. We stood in the front garden once her taxi had passed out of sight, none of us wanting to speak.

Simon broke the silence at last, glancing at his watch, saying, 'Bloody hell, look at the time. Better be making tracks.'

'Yes,' I said. 'Yes, we ought to go too.'

I looked at Mark. He looked at me. I waited for him to say something.

Surely he would ask me to stay, or say he needed a private word with me.

He said, 'Yes, you don't want to be late.'

So we packed up the car and left. The daylight was flat, the sky paper-white and undifferentiated. The whole day was exhausted, with a sense that some vital noise had been turned off. Perhaps it was just me and my confusion, but I don't think so. The day was simply inexplicable.

Mark hugged Jess chastely, kissing her cheek and whispering into her ear. Somehow, as he came to hug me, he managed to turn me away from the others, so they couldn't see the subtle pressure of his hip against me. I jumped to attention, as though I was fifteen again. I had to hide myself from Jess with a newspaper as we got into the car and drove away.

SECTION 2
The Trappings

14

About a year later someone – I think it was Franny – made telephone calls and said, 'Let's get the gang back together. I can't believe it's been so long.' And we all said yes, we couldn't believe it either. So long and what with one thing and another we'd barely seen each other, not the whole gang together. Astonishing.

So we arranged to meet in a pub near Simon's office. Jess had a night off. Franny got the train down from Cambridge. Emmanuella was in London working on a travel piece. And Mark, I tried to ask casually, what about Mark? Oh yes, said Jess, Franny had arranged it with him. He was with Simon's family in Dorset, wasn't that funny, and he'd drive up. I thought, can I say no? I thought, can I pretend to be ill? I thought, for God's sake, pull yourself together. So I went.

We arrived first at the bar, Jess and I. It was a Monday night at the start of summer, the place wasn't crowded. We sipped our beers and talked about nothing: my coursework and her practice and our plans for a break.

Franny was the next to arrive, only twenty minutes later, flustered, her hair twisted in a bun at the nape of her neck, fastened with a pencil.

'I'm sorry, I'm sorry,' she said as she kissed us, 'the bus was late, traffic.'

And we said, it's fine, no problem, Simon said he'd be late anyway.

And the whole thing jarred, and was wrong, but I said nothing.

Franny said, 'Simon's coming? He said so? Is he bringing that girl with him, that new girl he's seeing?'

And she said it with such brightness I thought she'd crack every glass in the room.

Jess said, 'He didn't say anything about a girl.'

And Franny said, 'They work together,' and bought another round.

After forty-five minutes Emmanuella came, perfumed and delicious as ever and always. She'd cut her hair short, that was the first thing, and we admired it, the curl and the lustrous shine. She showed us a ring too, bought for her by her new boyfriend – not an *engagement* ring, she laughed at the thought. But a gift, a token. He was a Bourbon, or some kind of royalty, and she thought this a good sign and we thought so too.

'A Bourbon,' said Franny, a little tipsy already, 'like the biscuit. Do you dunk him, Manny? Do you give him a liddle dip?'

And she winked and snorted, but Emmanuella frowned and said nothing and ordered more wine.

At 7.45 there was Simon, at last, after phone calls and messages. He'd been delayed, it was unavoidable, but bloody hell he was sorry and how the fuck were we and what were we drinking and he'd get the round. He bought bottles of expensive wine and talked about markets and explained that next year he'd be working in Chile. Or maybe in Mexico, possibly Greece. He joked, as he spoke about bull and bear markets and emerging sectors for growth, and I looked at Jess and I wondered how I had ever been friends with this man.

By 9 we were hungry. Even Franny and Simon, who'd been jousting with each other all evening. Little digs, little mentions of the past they had shared. She brought up the new girl, what was her name, Xena? Xenia, he said, and how now was Rob? Eventually, starving, I mentioned pizza, and Franny, dismayed, said, 'But how will Mark find us?'

And Jess said, 'It's 9 now. Surely he's a no-show?'

And this led to grumbling, which we did with gusto, because at least this was a topic we shared. It had only been twelve months but already it was obvious that we no longer had much to say to each other. There was affection, certainly, and memories of kindness, but not much of substance except about Mark.

At 9.30, a message, much delayed and much regretted, but Mark would not come. Stuck in Dorblish, he said, with Si's family. And we sighed and said how like Mark, how typical. Except perhaps I saw a flicker of annoyance cross Simon's face, but he ordered another bottle and more crisps and more nuts.

The conversation lulled and grew stiff. There were awkward

pauses. Franny smoked cigarette after cigarette and Emmanuella stole from her pack, and when she said, 'These are not as good as Mark's cigarettes,' Franny said, 'Then why don't you . . .' and then paused and said, 'Bloody Mark. Getting us all here and not showing up.' And we agreed and muttered that it was all Mark's fault.

We drifted away from the bar just after 10. The last few minutes had been better, brighter, after I'd said I needed an early night – school teaching, you know – and I knew that the others had been thankful to get away too. We promised to stay in touch, to see each other more often, but without Mark I could not imagine how it would work. He had been the centre, the one who bound us together, because beside him we seemed more similar to each other. Without him, Emmanuella was too rich, and Franny too opinionated, and Simon too shallow. Without him, we were just a scattering of people.

Jess and I went home together, and I felt so relieved and so full of gratitude that of all these people she was the one I could go home with. I held her hand as we walked to the station, and I thought, if I had to choose again, right now, from the beginning, I would still choose her.

I suppose that some men might have broken with Jess after what happened with Mark. Those men might have joyfully explored the possibilities now laid before them without shame or hesitation. But I had never been such a man – so open to myself, so tolerant of my own person, so optimistic that life was bound to bring me joy. There are other men, more like me I think, who would have confessed all to Jess, put themselves in her hands, begged for forgiveness and under-standing. I have more difficulty in explaining why I did not do this. I think the meagre truth is that I was too frightened to tell her. I couldn't imagine how she'd react. And, more than that, I was fright-ened by the idea of who I might be without her. She was the very centre and focus of my life, she was my rudder. I feared leaving her as I might have feared travelling without possessions or money to a distant land where I knew neither any living soul nor a single word of the native language, with no passage home.

This is not wise. To hang one's life so completely on another person is not sensible. But it's a line written in my character, like a vein of metal scribbled through a stone. I cannot love in any other way than this, so it is for me to choose whom I love with care. Or can one choose at all? But Jess is a good person; she never hurt me intentionally, and this is quite a thing to say about another human being.

In any case, I had not spent my time miserably. Jess and I both had new jobs. Teaching kept me busy most of the time. Jess's work with the orchestra kept her out late, and occasionally travelling, so that we were constantly experiencing joyful reunion. We had our little flat to decorate and domestic life to arrange. And we had each other finally, alone at last. Any fear in me that my desire for Jess might have evaporated was utterly dissipated within a day of moving into our new flat. We made love in our own home, under our own sheets, with our belongings still half in bags and boxes around the bedroom and in the hall. My desire for her was still as strong as ever, my pleasure in her body as intense. And so it continued from then on.

Only sometimes I would think about that night in the kitchen with Mark and a kind of longing would overcome me so that I thought I might fall to my knees. It was a longing filled with self-loathing, with desperation and embarrassment and fear. Like a whiff of solvents, it stunned for a moment and then evaporated. Or sometimes I would hide in the toilet and just *think* around those events, breathing, feeling them, until the thoughts overwhelmed me. I didn't know what to do with these feelings, so I cut them off from the rest of my life. It's an easy trick to master.

So perhaps it was down to me as much as any of us that 'the gang' didn't get together. I didn't want to see Mark, didn't want to be reminded.

It was Jess who arranged such reunions as there were. Franny was our most frequent visitor; she often came down from Cambridge to sleep on our sofa, eat mushroom pie in front of the telly, drink red wine and tell tall tales of Cambridge dons. Emmanuella we saw nothing of. She sent us a videotape of the arts and culture programme she presented, but, as it was in Spanish, we could do no more than verify her identity.

Simon was always sending apologies. We didn't want to see him and Franny together, not any more, so Jess suggested dinners in town, evenings out, a play or two – although plays and dinners and evenings out were always contaminated by the memory of Mark's money. With new friends, we didn't feel ashamed to suggest supermarket pizza and a video. With Simon or with Franny or with Emmanuella, we all wondered why it could not be a Maison Blanc supper or the stalls at an opening night.

Simon, in any case, rarely turned up. Dinners would be cancelled because he had to fly to Aarhus, weekend pub lunches postponed because he was needed in Berlin. There was one stilted and awkward evening of drinks with Simon and his latest girlfriend, Frieda. She had hair like Franny, corkscrew curls with a centre parting, and had similarly angular, dark-framed glasses. She wasn't Franny, though. She didn't understand our jokes, declared herself completely uninterested in politics, and was faintly amused by Simon's protestations that 'everything's politics'. Their relationship didn't last long. The next time we heard from him, he cheerfully told us she'd buggered off back to Switzerland and he wouldn't mind except he knew he'd never get his skis back.

As for Mark, for a long time there was silence. After Oxford, after graduation, nothing. We learned, via an obituary in the paper, that he had lost his father and thus come into more money than he could hope to spend in a dozen lifetimes. We tried to contact him, to express our sorrow, but our phone calls and letters went unanswered. Eventually, though, there were postcards. First, after the failed pub trip, a picture of a bull, horns down, from Seville. He was sorry, so sorry he'd let us down. He'd shut up Annulet House, was travelling, but he'd see us soon, he promised, soon. I hoped he was wrong and said nothing. A few months later, Franny reported a postcard from Argentina, telling how he had made special friends with a gaucho. Later, Emmanuella said she'd had a letter from him postmarked Stockholm, but describing some adventure at the races in Hong Kong. A few months after that, Jess and I had another postcard. It was from Venice, a picture of a line of the key-like structures on the prows of gondolas. On the back was written:

Darlings –
  Can't see a gondola without thinking of you both. Punting, strawberries, champagne etc. Young love. Writing this, I want to be with you now,

snuggled between you in a punt, like three bugs in a bed. Missing you
both. Especially Jess. And especially James.

   Best love,
   M.

Jess laughed when she read this, and stuck the card into the frame of the mirror in our hallway. A few days later, when she was out, I took it down. I turned it over in my hands, reading the words again, tracing the curves of the letter M with my fingertip. I ripped it up and threw it in the outside bin. When Jess wondered what had happened to it, I shrugged and said nothing and thought, if I stay very still, perhaps life will ignore me.

Jess and I found new friends in any case. I was by this time working as a maths teacher at a private school for boys in west London. Some of the other teachers were pleasant company. One, Ajit, reminded me of Simon with his constant talk of 'going on the pull'. He used to say, 'You and your missus, it's like you've been married twenty years,' and this pleased me. Jess's friends from her orchestra often found their way back to our flat after rehearsals, and we settled into a habit of hosting boisterous Sunday night suppers. Because she was often out late, I learned to cook, and found that I enjoyed it. The role-reversal pleased me, the surprise of being the one to pull a whole ham, fragrant and juicy, or a massive glistening lasagne from the oven to feed a tribe of musicians. I came to enjoy the girls' sighs of, 'James, if you weren't taken, I'd marry you myself,' as they dug their spoons through the glittering sugar crust of an apple pie or ladled out piping-hot servings of creamy rice pudding, aromatic with cinnamon and raisins.

They spoke a secret language to which I did not have access, these musicians. They burst into impromptu song, discussed conductors and techniques I'd never heard of, demonstrated bowing techniques using a loaf of French bread and a butter knife. But it was fine. At night after they left and when Jess and I were lying in bed together, she would curl up under my arm and enquire, into my chest, whether I had minded their noise, how late they had stayed. And I would shake my head and tell her that, no, I had enjoyed myself, would be happy to cook for them again next week. And she would snuggle closer.

And this was my life; it was perfectly satisfactory within the limits of what was possible.

I don't know whether I would ever have changed anything of my own volition. I suspect not. I was two years out of university but my pleasant life still felt so tenuous to me, and so fragile, that I could not imagine disturbing it by choice. Better to walk a narrow path, to enjoy what was offered, not to seek for more. I might have remained like that forever, I think, if allowed to do so. But even if we wish to remain stationary, the world around us turns and so we move too. And thus, one Sunday afternoon, as I was waiting for Jess and her friends to return from rehearsals I had a phone call. A leg of lamb was roasting in the oven, the smell of caramelized onions and tenderizing meat beginning to pervade the house with mellow savouriness. I picked up the receiver. I expected it was Jess, calling to say they'd be late.

'James? Is that you?'

It was Mark. My stomach dipped and swirled. I thought, how ridiculous, how utterly absurd, that I should still be afraid now at the sound of his voice.

'James,' he said. 'James?'

I made my voice cold and hard.

'Yes, Mark, how are you?'

'James,' he said, 'mate, congratulate me. I'm getting married.'

I said, 'Married?'

He laughed, a little chuckle in the back of his throat, and all at once I could *see* him, as I had not seen him all these years.

'I know,' he said, 'it's wild. *I'm* getting married. Guess who to?'

'Who?'

He paused, and I knew that he was smirking, as he always did before saying something shocking.

'Nicola,' he said.

'Nicola?' I said. 'Nicola who?'

He made a mock-sigh.

'*Nicola*,' he said. 'Simon's sister Nicola.'

15

'Simon's hopping mad. Absolutely bloody hopping mad.' Franny nodded, agreeing with herself, poured another glass of wine and went on, 'He's every right to be. Mark's done a real number on his parents.'

'Mark can be very impressive if he tries,' Jess said evenly.

'Too bloody right,' said Franny. 'Too bloody right. All those houses and money, very impressive. I mean, what the hell is he playing at?'

The anger in her was tight-coiled, as if Mark had done her some personal injustice.

'You think he's definitely serious?' asked Jess.

Franny picked at her casserole and took a swig of wine.

'Simon thinks he is. Simon's *parents* think he is. Bloody hell, more importantly Nicola thinks he is.'

'It's not some kind of joke, is it?'

'What, playing a joke on Nicola? God, even Mark couldn't be that cruel, surely?'

She lit a cigarette without asking our permission. I surreptitiously pushed a window open as I carried the plates through into the kitchen.

When I came back out, Franny was sitting on the sofa, one foot curled under her, saying, 'He can't get back from Chile for two weeks. He's trying to talk some sense into his parents in the meantime, but they're not listening.'

Jess said, 'Has Simon mentioned that Mark's *gay*? Surely that's the clincher.'

Franny tutted and sighed.

'Well, that's the thing. *He* says he's changed. And they're old enough to go, "Oh, yes, that's how it works. Everyone's a bit gay when they're young and then they grow out of it."'

She shrugged and stubbed her cigarette out in the earth of a pot plant.

I breathed in and out, controlling the slight flutter in the pit of my stomach.

I said, 'Couldn't he have? Changed?'

'*Changed*? Can you really see *Mark* ever changing? You know what he's like. It'll be marriage this year and then next year, I don't know, water polo. God, how can Simon's family possibly buy it?'

We sat for a minute or two in silence. I contemplated how differently Franny felt about Mark now, compared to our time at university, when she had been his staunchest ally. I wondered what he could have done to her. Perhaps it was simply what he had done to everyone – ignored us, fallen out of contact, moved on with his life of wealth and privilege.

After a little while, Jess said, 'Don't forget about Leo. I'm sure they still remember.'

We fell silent again. It was so easy to forget that about Mark, now that he no longer went about reminding us. He had once, actually, saved someone's life.

Franny poured another glass of wine.

'Yes,' she said, 'yes, they'd believe anything he said, wouldn't they?'

I brought in dessert, a pavlova, and cut it into large wedges, the strawberries bleeding into the meringue and cream. We picked at it. None of us had much of an appetite.

Jess said, 'What does Emmanuella think? Do you know?'

Franny nodded, swallowing.

'Spoke to her yesterday. She doesn't believe it, thinks it's some kind of wheeze of Mark's. She laughed when I told her. She thought it was that English humour she doesn't understand.'

'Is she coming back? For the wedding?'

Franny raised an eyebrow. 'Oh, *what* wedding? There can't really be a wedding. She's seventeen, for fuck's sake. She was supposed to go to college next year but now she's saying that, no, she'll go and keep house with him.'

Jess, becoming more mild as Franny became more ferocious, said, 'She's quite religious, after all. They believe in that sort of thing.'

'Oh yes, that's another bloody thing. Now she's suddenly converting. Roman Catholicism. So yes, I'm sure they won't use contraception and then there'll be a whole brood before long. That's if he doesn't get distracted and jilt her for some bloke.'

As she lit another cigarette, I noticed that her hands were shaking.

Later, after we'd finished the meal, Franny returned to the question again, this time pushing it from another direction. She was more drunk, more calm.

'Perhaps it is a joke. Maybe they're both in on it: she's just about smitten enough to participate in any tease with him. He's probably terribly amused to imagine us all having anxious conversations like this about him.'

There was a long pause while we contemplated how like Mark it would be: something to have us all talking about him.

Franny was lying on her back on the carpet now, staring at the ceiling, balancing her wine glass with one hand on her chest. There was an expression of dissatisfaction on her face, a twist of the mouth as if she had tasted something which disgusted her.

She said, 'It's not a joke. I know it's not, not really.'

She spoke so quietly that it was difficult to hear her, as if she herself did not want to hear her own words.

'It's not a joke,' she said again. 'This is what he's always wanted and he's found a way to get it.'

She sat up and leaned against the wall, her knees pulled up to her chest. She dug the fingers of one hand deep into the pile of the carpet. Her hands were quite pale and her face set. She looked up at the ceiling.

She said, 'This is what he's been looking for, you know? You remember how much he loved being on the farm with Simon's family, how much he wanted to be part of that kind of *Englishness*? That wholesome, salt-of-the-earth, country lifestyle? Like the bloody *Hay Wain*. Well, he's found a way to step into the painting. He'll marry Nicola, they'll be blissfully happy, he'll supply the money, she'll supply the homeliness, it'll be perfect.'

She took another swig from her glass.

'I'm only surprised he never thought of marrying you, Jess. Only I expect you wouldn't have gone for it.'

Jess, speaking softly, said, 'Surely . . . I mean, he's never even slept with a girl, has he?'

Franny ran her finger round the wine glass. She swirled the dregs, staining the bowl of the glass.

'I slept with him.' She drained the glass. 'More than once actually. It was quite good – very vigorous, if you know what I mean – so he can't be completely, well not exclusively. I mean, he seemed to enjoy it, it wasn't as if there was any coercion involved.'

She tipped back her head and gave a short barking laugh then, hiccuping, began to cry.

'I'm sorry,' she said, in heaving gasps. 'I'm sorry, I didn't mean . . . I'm sorry.'

Jess knelt down on the carpet next to Franny and put her arm around her shoulders.

'Shhh,' she said, 'shhh. It's OK, it's OK.'

Jess stroked her hair and after a while Franny gulped and brought her tears to an ebb.

We helped her to the spare room, drunk and staggering as she was, and at the doorpost she wished us goodnight. Leaning against the jamb, she said, 'It's not that I thought it would be me, you know. I was never so stupid as that.'

Jess smiled. 'We know.'

And Franny went to bed.

In the kitchen, washing up, we said little. I stood at the sink, washing and rinsing mechanically, handing the plates to Jess to be dried, thinking all the time of how little I had known of Franny in the past few years. We had shared a house, I had known the little intimate details of her daily life: that at times of stress she could eat a whole jar of Nutella with a spoon, that she and Simon used condoms not the Pill, that she suffered from a day a month of agonizing period pain. I had known all this, but not this thing we shared. Or might have shared. Or would have shared if he had wanted me as he'd evidently wanted her. As I washed and scraped and soaked, I imagined Franny and Mark together. I did not want to imagine this but, once I had thought of it, I found myself unable to turn my inner eyes away.

'How long do you think this has been going on with her?' said Jess.

I started, then shrugged.

'Don't know. I had no idea. Didn't she mention anything to you?'

Jess shook her head.

'Not a word. I suppose she was embarrassed.'

'Mmm,' I said.

'Poor Fran,' said Jess. 'What a painful person Mark must be to love.'

16

I picked the receiver up. I put it down again. I sat down. I stood up. I breathed deeply. I rehearsed the different ways of saying, 'Hi, it's James.' I picked the receiver up. I dialled the number. In the heartbeat before it began to ring, I put it down again. I drummed my fingers on the table. I looked at the clock: 6 p.m. An hour or so before Jess would be home. I poured a whisky. I took a gulp. I drank too quickly, choked and spluttered. I drank more slowly. After twenty minutes a slight mellowness began to prickle me. Now, I thought, now. I picked up the receiver. I dialled the number. I listened to it ring and to the click of the receiver on the other end being picked up and to Mark – oh God, Mark – saying, 'Hello.'

'Hi,' I said, 'it's James.'

'Hi, James!' he said, and there was a smile in his voice. 'How the fuck are you?'

I resisted the urge to slam the phone down.

'Fine,' I said, 'I'm fine. Listen. Do you want to meet up? Have a beer? Something? Would be good to talk.'

'Oh, sure,' he said, 'that'd be great. This evening?'

And my pulse pounded and throbbed in my throat, because that wasn't in my plan.

'Um,' I said, 'not tonight.'

'You free tomorrow? I'm all time, you know. Ain't got nothing but time, baby.'

Jesus.

'Um. Yeah. OK. Tomorrow afternoon? I finish school at . . .' I tried to calculate: how long, how short, how much time did I need to prepare for it? 'I could be in Islington at 5 p.m. That's where you are, right, Islington?'

'Your spies are everywhere, Mr Stieff.'

I said nothing. My heart was crashing in my chest.

'But yeah,' he said, 'that'd be fine. Wanna come to the flat?'

'No,' I said, a little too quickly. 'That is, nah, let's go for a beer.'

He named a pub off Upper Street. 'At 5 tomorrow. Cool. Looking forward to it, mate.'

And it was done. The adrenalin coursing through my system left me shaking when I put the phone down.

He was waiting for me when I arrived. It had been raining and his hair was damp, his fringe plastered to his forehead. He didn't see me at first and I had a few seconds to look him over before he noticed my presence. He looked older. Partly it was his clothing. A camel-coloured coat, an indigo suit with winkle-picker boots and a white shirt. Not a serious suit, but I'd never seen him wear a suit at all before. There was a new stillness to his body. I hadn't realized until then that, in the past, he'd always been a little jittery. Playing with matchbooks and cigarettes, or jiggling one knee. Now he was still.

He looked up and a smile, uncalculated and uncomplicated, broke over his face.

'James!' he said. 'Brilliant!'

He stood up and reached out to hug me, but I stepped awkwardly to the side, my hands up. He looked puzzled, but said again, 'Brilliant!' and we sat down. I was silent for too long. I had various things in my mind to say, had stored them up, but none of them were opening lines, and none of them seemed promising here, on a Wednesday afternoon in a half-empty gastropub. They were, I realized, things that were more suitable for shouting, in a kitchen in Oxford, two years earlier.

After a long moment, Mark drew in breath, exhaled – and I remembered his breath hot on my neck, I couldn't help myself, and I thought, oh God, is this madness? – and he said, 'So. Right. What are you drinking?'

Mark went to the bar, giving me time to think, to settle, to stop my leg from twitching, to place my hand on my knee and remind myself that nothing was going to happen here. And when we were sitting back in the armchairs with our beers he said, 'Mate, how the fuck have you been? I'm a bloody idiot not to have been in touch sooner. How is everything? How's Jess?'

I told him about my work at the school. I described Jess's burgeon-ing career, her concerts, her friends, her small reviews in the papers. I told him the amusing stories from her tour. I explained that she was much in demand. He nodded and looked interested, normal. He was sane. Suddenly, startlingly sane. Was this Nicola? Had she taken all the madness from him?

Mark said, 'Are you and Jess planning to get married?'

I shook my head.

'No,' I said. 'We don't believe in it.'

Mark looked at me. He raised his eyebrows and I noticed that, when he did so, fine lines became visible across his forehead. He took another swallow of beer.

'I suppose you think that I'm doing something very stupid indeed.'

I realized that, because I had been unable to do so, he had brought the conversation around to the point.

He took a swig and continued, 'Franny came to see me over the weekend, you know. Utterly lashed. Do you think she's turning into a drunk? Anyway. Yes. She accused me of terrible things, leading Nicola on, lying to her family, taking advantage of Simon. And Manny called me yesterday, wanted to know if it's all a joke. So I hope you're not here to give me the same bloody speech, James, because I'm not interested in hearing it again.'

'No,' I said, 'I'm not.' And it was true; I wasn't.

He frowned at me, then broke into a grin.

'Yeah, I knew you wouldn't. You can understand it, can't you? It's like you and Jess. I do love her.'

I stared at him. He and Nicola were like me and Jess? Was it an accusation or an attempt at comfort?

'I love the whole family . . . even Simon, though he's not being especially pleasant to me right now. And Nicola's so perfect, you see, so simple and sane. Just, normal. Sweet and loving and normal. She's exactly what I need, James. And of course my mother and Father Hugh are delighted. An end to all the old trouble at last.'

A spurt of hot madness erupted in my head. I wanted to throw the glasses to the floor, to shout and overturn tables, as I should have done two years earlier. None of this was what I'd expected. Not this sanity, not this calmness, not this normality. The idea that Mark and I should be talking like this, when I knew the truth of him, when I still thought of him and the memory of his fingers and his palm could still glow hot on my flesh.

'But Mark, you're gay. Aren't you? I mean, aren't you? Really? You're really gay and being with Nicola . . . aren't you going to . . . You're just going to end up hurting her.'

Mark sat back in his chair with a huff, folded his arms across his chest, looked at me for a few moments.

'But you understand this, don't you? What are any of us really, James? What is *really*? Why do we have to decide this when we're sixteen and then stick with it forever? Why can't it be like food? When I was a kid I liked strawberry milkshakes but now I don't. I like dark chocolate instead. Have I perverted my natural desire for strawberry milkshakes into an unnatural desire for dark chocolate? Or was my desire for milkshakes wrong and now I've come to my senses? No. People change. Our tastes develop. I used to like sleeping with boys and now I like sleeping with Nicola. My tastes have changed, that's all. I mean, you must know. It's the same with you.'

I stared at him.

I said slowly, 'It's the same with me. Yes.' And for the first time I thought this might be the truth.

There were words I'd come here to say. They began with 'Mark, what happened between us . . .' and went on I knew not where. A declaration? A rejection? I had hoped that he would at least provide an answer for me. To explain what had happened between us, to explain myself to me.

I had been stupid, had put too much weight on something that would carry no weight at all. For him, it had been a silly game. He had, as he said, simply wanted to know; and he had known and that was the end of that. And what had he known? That for one moment, one late-night last-day-of-Oxford insanity, I had wanted him. It meant nothing more than that. I felt suddenly, joyfully, relieved. Perhaps I need never think of any of it again.

It was the past; a dream. Here we were, in the present, two happily partnered men, old friends from university, catching up on news. It was as wholesome as Nicola's family picnics, as simple as Enid Blyton, as natural as a walk in the country.

After a few moments, Mark said, 'Come on, mate. My flat's only ten minutes away. Let me show you it.'

He edged his hand along the tabletop and nudged my knuckles with his. It was the first time he had touched me in two years.

'All right,' I said.

Even if he hadn't told me so already, I would have known at once that Mark's flat was 'one of the family's places'. It consisted of five large rooms above a bookshop in Islington, along with a kitchen and bathroom. It had that same air of expensive shabbiness that Mark's house in Oxford had possessed. The rooms were linked together by archways and doorless doorframes off a hallway – it was impossible to say which was bedroom, which living room, which dining room or study. An enormous oak table with eight legs was in the same room as the divan bed with curled velvet-covered bolsters at each end. In another room, the walls were covered with bookshelves, up to the ceiling, with three chaise longues tucked under the wall-mounted shelves; the books were antique hardbacks. A third room was half stacked with paintings. Throughout, the atmosphere was heavy with the smell of those French cigarettes Mark liked, and cloisonné saucers full of butts were strewn through the rooms. The place looked as if a rake of the 1890s had shut up his home as the century ended and Mark had moved in 100 years later, smoked a large number of cigarettes but otherwise left everything untouched.

'Nicola says she's going to smarten the place up,' he remarked, throwing his coat down on to a pile of washing.

'Oh yes?' I said. 'What does she want to do with it?'

Mark grinned. 'Burn it to the ground, I think. She anticipates I might do that by myself anyway. But –' he waved a hand at the bookshelves, the window with its view of an Islington side street – 'we're not likely to spend much time in London anyway, so maybe I'll keep it as a pied-à-terre. We've bought a bigger place in Dorset, near her parents.'

Ah yes. The money. The relentless, unstoppable tide of money.

The money that made all things possible and thus left nothing to be simply desirable.

'And my mother's letting me have one of her places in Italy,' he continued. 'San Ceterino. Nice to have a winter getaway. Although Nicola says we mustn't spend Christmas there. They believe in family Christmases.' He threw himself on to an overstuffed chaise longue next to the window. 'Oh, how marvellous to have a family Christmas!'

I sat on a chair near to the window and looked out at the red-painted restaurant across the way. Inside couples, families, single people were eating or chatting to each other. Mark was still talking, something about how Nicola had a plan to 'get rid of all the silly books', but I wasn't listening. I had become entranced, as occasionally happens to me, by the idea of other people's lives. Each one of those people in that restaurant had their own life. There, a father wiping sauce off his small daughter's chin. There, a woman with short steel-grey hair, eating alone. There, a couple chatting, waiting for their food.

I found myself wondering how it would be to have these people's lives instead of my own, to go back to their homes, let myself in with their keys, understand all the objects they owned. What faint traces keep us harnessed to our own lives, unable to wander off and inhabit the lives of others.

Mark said, 'Don't you think so, James?'

I said, 'What?'

'Don't you think that we should just all get married to each other?'

I stared at him.

'I mean, you get married to Jess, obviously, and Franny can marry Simon, Emmanuella can marry Franny's older brother – what's his name? – Miles. He's tall and blond. And I'll marry Nicola. And we should all live together in a big house in, let's say, Tuscany. Or Provence. Or Oxford.'

He stretched out on the chaise longue, showing a slice of hairless stomach as he did so.

'Don't you think so, James? I mean, really, don't you think so? We should all be together. It's so silly that we're not. Together, all the time. I could do it. I'll buy a house, a huge one so we can all have separate kitchens and living rooms: you and me and Franny and Jess and Emmanuella and Simon. All together like in Oxford.'

'We can't, Mark. That's just not the way things work.'

He sat up, cross-legged.

'I know,' he said, 'but why not? Doesn't everyone want this? To stay together with their university friends forever? For things to stay just as they were at college?'

'Well, perhaps,' I said. It was like talking to a child. 'But it can't be like that, can it? We have to go out, get jobs, make a living.'

'Oh, a living. I can take care of all of that. Really, I can. It's no problem.'

I sighed. 'I know you can, Mark. But we don't want you to.'

'I don't see why. I mean, I'm marrying Nicola now and so it's OK for me to pay for things for her. Why can't I just pay for things for all of us? Why can't I, sort of, marry all of you? You don't have to stop doing things. You don't even need to be there all the time. Franny can write her books on economics, and Simon can live there when he's not travelling around the world, and Jess can play her music and you can, oh, I don't know, just lie around all day in a pair of swimming trunks.'

He smiled his wolfish grin and I thought again with surprise, oh, it can be like this, then. We can talk like this and it needn't mean anything at all.

And Mark is so persuasive; his vision for a moment seemed reasonable to me. We could live like children forever: in freedom and unknowing, dependent on the good graces of others. Even Mark's dependence was absolute, for his money had come to him as a gift and if he were ever to reach the bottom of it, he would have no way to replace it. Isn't this the paradise that the religious always imagine themselves to be in? Dependent forever on the beneficence of Almighty God and forever grateful for His bounty?

He yawned, suddenly, as cats do – a yawn that looked as though it might dislocate his jaw.

'Sorry,' he said, stifling another yawn, 'I'm awfully tired. I've been driving back and forth to Dorset a lot and it's making me sleepy.'

He rolled on to his stomach and pulled a rug over himself. I stood up to leave, but he caught me by the cuff.

'No,' he said, 'stay. Until I go to sleep. Like we used to do in Oxford.'

I couldn't remember having done such a thing for him in Oxford. I wanted to remember it, though. He made me want to remember it.

I sat down.

I looked out of the window at the restaurant with its little busy lives. I looked at Mark, his fair hair fallen across his eyes like a schoolboy. I waited. When his breath became deep and regular, I put on my jacket. I pulled the blind down and lit one of the smaller electric lamps. It cast a slight orange glow across the room. I pulled the door closed quietly behind me and walked down the passage to the front door.

I felt something then, as I let myself out of his flat. I didn't know what it was. I thought of him lying there asleep and how easy, how terribly easy that conversation had been. And his flat, the smell of cigarettes around the walls, the discarded clothes among the first editions. The squalor of it and yet the beauty. I stood with his front door open, staring at the green wallpaper of his hallway for a long time.

17

Mark and Nicola married in May, in an open-air ceremony in the grounds of a house near to the Wedmore family home. The day was sunny, the venue picturesque, the flowers eloquent in their simplicity. Nicola carried a bouquet of Michaelmas daisies, Mark wore a yolk-yellow tie, and the guests kept their doubts in check even at the moment of 'speak now or forever hold your peace'.

I was an usher, but my duties were soon over. I had handed out Orders of Service and directed honoured relatives to front-row seats, but after the service began there was nothing for me to do other than listen to the words of God and hold Jess's hand. The thing was stiff, it seemed to me. Formal and so strictly ordained that Mark and Nicola were like characters in a play and we the audience. Mass, a sermon and words from the Bible, Simon bravely working his way through 'love is not jealous, it does not boast' with seeming conviction, although half the people there knew that, even until the previous day, he had been suggesting with increasing force that the wedding should be postponed.

But Mark and Nicola had continued doggedly through all protestations and concerns. 'Love is patient, love is kind.' I would not have thought Mark had such persistence in him; he had never shown it before. 'Love is not rude, it is not self-seeking.' They had simply made their plans, booked the venue, talked to caterers, decided on colour schemes, while all around them shells of anxiety and anger burst and left them unscathed. 'Love always trusts, always hopes, always per—severes.' Was this love? Nicola, seventeen years old and shining-eyed, thought so. Mark, delivered from dilettantism, thought so. Franny said, 'It won't last a year,' and even Jess said, 'They do seem to be hurrying it rather.' 'But where there are prophecies, they will cease. Where there are tongues, they will be stilled.' They made telephone calls, they filed important papers in ring binders, they invited

Mark's mother with all due graciousness. They held each other's hands throughout. And they came to their reward. This very moment: 'What God has joined together, let no man put asunder,' and an eruption of applause.

As we watched Nicola's aunt apply powder to her bosom before the photographs were taken, Jess leaned in to me and whispered in my ear, 'Promise me we'll never have to do this.'

I said, 'I promise.'

'What are you two up to?' said Franny from behind us. 'Planning your own announcement?'

She was a little drunk already and of course it was a wedding, but I wondered when I had last seen her without a drink, or spent an evening with her which she had not ended tottering and staggering. I felt for her, though, remembering what had gone before.

I said, 'You needn't worry about us. We'll never do it. Jess wants to be free to have affairs and ditch me at a moment's notice, don't you?'

And Jess smiled and said nothing.

There were speeches later; Mark was less entertaining than he could be, but irreverent and self-mocking. He said, 'Now that I've found Nicola, I'm delighted to announce that no one can accuse me any more of having more money than sense,' and raucous laughter and scattered applause followed. I was astonished; he had never joked about money before. He made his new bride a little presentation: a gift from his childhood. I knew what it was before she had the box open: the music box, glittering glass and gold, finally finding a suitable home. Nicola and Simon's father, David, gave a rambling, slightly choked speech, remembering Nicola when she was a little girl and saying how quickly this day had come. I was almost certain I heard someone whisper, 'A damn sight too quickly, if you ask me.' Mark gave gifts to the little flower-girls, hoisting them up towards the tiered canopy in his arms, pretending to drop them as they screamed and giggled. He hugged them and planted kisses on their foreheads and Franny, sitting next to me, muttered, 'Yeah, yeah, Mark, we get it.'

I had not realized how much of a wedding is show until I saw this one. No one ever wants to look beyond the trimmings on a wedding day, to see the doubts and the insecurities, the compromises and the fears that lie beneath. It is a parade, a theatrical performance in which all lines have been learned in advance. It is a necessary fiction; without our beguiling fictions how would we ever dream grandly or live boldly? We need the trappings as much as the substance.

I watched Mark's face during his first dance with Nicola, looking for signs of discomfort or pleasure. There was nothing, though, but a smooth confidence which was so new that I could not help but stare at his face. And I saw as he flicked his eyes from the surrounding tables back to his bride – his wife, how astonishing – and turned the full power of his smile on her. And she, excited, smiled back and moved her head a little towards him, and he moved in towards her. And they kissed. I could not help watching; this was what we had all come to see, after all.

The dancing turned, soon enough, from sedate and ceremonial to fast and energetic. They played the Macarena and all Nicola's friends charged forwards, with Mark at their head, to dance, clapping and shimmying and jumping and placing their hands on their hips and swaying. A few of the older relatives began to make their way home. This was not their time any more, after all. Jess knew better than to suggest I'd want to dance; my knee could not bear it. But I sat comfortably while she and Franny joined in with the jumping, staccato throng. Sweat gleamed on Mark's forehead. Nicola rotated her hips and leapt.

A short while later, at our table, Franny became definitively drunk. She had found a man, one of Simon's schoolfriends, and was engaging him in vehement, incomprehensible conversation until she noticed me. She wheeled around in her seat and said, 'James! At last. I need . . . you are the one I need to talk to.'

She had a glass of whisky in one hand and a lit cigarette in the other, and fiddled with her hair so indiscriminately, not caring which hand she put up to it, that she was in constant danger of setting herself alight.

'Oh yes?' I said.

'Yes,' she said, and leaned towards me.

Her dress, a loose wrap of black silk which clung to the curves of her body, had fallen a little too low, so that when she leaned forward her nipples popped over the top. I tried not to look, but my eyes were drawn inexorably back down as they disappeared, reappeared.

'So,' she said, 'honestly, honestly now, how long d'you think it'll last?'

She gestured towards Mark and Nicola with her whisky glass, slopping a few heavy drops over the side. I looked at Mark and Nicola. They were exchanging goodbyes with Nicola's grandparents: tears and hugs.

'Oh, I don't know,' I said. 'It could last a lifetime. It does sometimes happen.'

Franny gave her short bark of a laugh. Her breasts wobbled and one nipple poked over the top of her dress and stayed there.

'A lifetime! Two years, tops. Maybe a bit more if Nicola pops a sprog.' She leered at me. 'But he'll be back in the cottages within a year, I say.'

I smiled and said that I could see Jess calling me from the other side of the room.

On my way across the room, I was caught by Isabella. She was older now, her age was beginning to be unconcealable, her bosom in her sequinned dress was growing crêpey and she herself was strangely vacant. I wondered if she'd taken a tranquillizer to get through the day, as Mark said had often been her habit.

'James!' she said. 'Do you remember me?'

'Of course,' I said. 'Congratulations. You must be very happy.'

She nodded complacently. 'It is what I always wished for him.'

'Yes,' I said. 'Nicola's a lovely girl.'

'After his terrible *trouble*,' she said, and looked at me intently, beetling her brows.

'Mmmm.' I was only half paying attention.

'There was one time,' she said, plucking at my sleeve, 'I thought he would surely kill me! Or worse! We consulted an exorcist, you know, in case there was a demon in him. But it was long ago now.'

'Really?' I said, suddenly intrigued.

'He is safe now,' she said, 'safe from all of that.' And she would not be drawn further on the subject.

I found Emmanuella sitting at a table, calm and smiling, an undrunk glass of champagne by her elbow and her hand resting on the knee of her dark-skinned, blond-haired boyfriend. She smiled when she saw me, tipping her head to one side and allowing a curtain of hair to fall like water.

'*Ola*, James,' she said. 'Have you met Alfonso?'

The boyfriend stood up smartly – almost, but not quite, clicking his heels together – and shook my hand. So this was His Excellency Alfonso Urdangarín y de Borbón – a name Jess and I had sniggered at when we spotted it on the table plan.

'Charming,' said Alfonso. 'Tell me, is this the house where Mark and Nicola intend to live when they are married?'

I laughed. This was a country house rented for the occasion by Mark because Nicola had wanted the wedding to be near her family and he had wanted it to be far away from his.

'No, no,' I said. 'People often rent houses for the day for their wedding.'

Alfonso frowned. 'But I thought . . .' He turned to Emmanuella and they exchanged a few short sentences in Spanish. He turned back to me and bowed gravely. 'I apologize, you are entirely correct.'

I wondered what would happen if I refused to accept his apology. Rapiers at dawn did not seem out of the question.

'No problem,' I said. And then, because I could not think of anything else, I said, 'So . . . what do you do?'

He frowned at me and said, 'Do?'

'Ah,' I nodded. 'Right, yes, OK.'

I made my excuses and moved on.

I found Jess again, talking to Simon. Or standing next to Simon while he watched the dance floor balefully. I slipped beside her and took her hand. Simon said, 'Hi,' and went back to staring at his sister, who was now dancing a vigorous jive with Mark.

Simon had not brought a girl to the wedding. Instead he was

flanked by two tall broad-shouldered farming men, friends from schooldays with dark tans from outdoor work.

'Hello,' said one, 'I'm Dick.'

'I'm Richard,' said the other.

We shook hands.

'I'll get the beers in,' said Richard. Or it might have been Dick.

'Top man,' said Simon, 'I'm too bloody sober.'

Mark and Nicola had taken swing lessons. They were dancing together, eyes wide, mouths open with excitement, feet kicking out to the sides. Mark pulled at Nicola's hand and spun her energetically three, four, five times.

Simon said, low and several times, 'Fuck it. Fuck it. Fuck it.'

I nodded, unsure what to respond.

Dick, or it might have been Richard, said, 'Too true, mate, too true,' and the other came back with the beers.

They were all three leaning back in their chairs, tilting as far as they could without falling over. They began to talk while tilting, taking swigs of beer, like commentators at a cricket match.

'I see Amanda is on the pull tonight,' said one, nodding at a blonde woman in her thirties wearing a short purple dress and matching heels.

'She'll be after you if you don't mind,' said another, and they laughed – deep, humourless laughs.

My final memory of Mark from that day is of the minutes before their going-away, when he came racing up to me, conspiratorial, pulling on my hand to bring me close to his lips as he whispered, 'Did you *hear*? Franny's thrown up all down the front steps!'

I looked at him. He was very close to me – so close that I could smell the sharp scent of his cologne and the musky scent of his sweat. His face was that of an excited schoolboy, flushed and delighted. He raised his eyebrows, grinned, and raced off again.

Jess had to go then, to see to Franny, to help her wash her face, to find a place for her to rest, to get a cab to take her to the hotel. I tried to help too, but Franny was sobbing and swearing, and Jess shook her head at me and mouthed, 'I'll come and find you.'

I thought of her saying, 'What a painful person Mark must be to love,' and I nodded and walked away.

In the main marquee, several teenage couples were kissing each other hungrily on the dance floor, hands under clothes, inside dresses and dress shirts. On the tables, brandy-snap baskets of ice cream were melting into puddles of sticky, milky foam. I took my jacket from the back of my chair, pulled it on and walked out into the cool night air.

The night was cloudless, the moon paper-bright and high in the sky. The walkways all around were lit by flaming torches. Couples were talking, flirting, snogging. Friends were drinking or sharing a joint. I walked around the lake at the bottom of the hill, where the torches showed a path. After a few hundred yards I passed a clump of bushes where a couple were unmistakably fucking. The branches of the bushes were shaking rhythmically and I could hear the 'hn, hn, hn' grunting of the man, the woman's half-excited, half-pained 'ah, ah, ah'. I walked past as quietly as I could and if they heard me they gave no sign of it.

The lake was fed by a thunderously tumbling weir. An overhanging branch trailed across my face and I remembered that it was in a similar spot, far from people, by a river, that I had injured myself so severely that I had never quite risen again. As I walked, the loud crashing water soon blotted out the noise of the party.

On a wall covered in a soggy sponge of moss, I sat down, stretching my legs in front of me. I found I could not help thinking of Mark. I hadn't seen a great deal of him in the past months. But when I had seen him I'd felt glad to be his friend. Yes, that was it. Glad to hear the little woes and triumphs of the business of the wedding. A wedding is bound to make the bride and groom seem glamorous. Mark and Nicola had been like movie stars today; one could not help wanting to be close to them. That was it, too.

But this thinking could not hold. I began, almost without willing it, to observe my own thoughts. And I laughed. I could not help it. I sat in the roaring silence of the weir and laughed like a madman. What a pathetic thing to realize. What a stupid thing to want. How typical of myself I always was. For it had become suddenly clear to me, horrifically and hilariously clear, that I was in love with Mark.

18

At first, I simply kept on saying no. No, I said, to the mirror in the mornings, no I won't. No, I said, to my mind when its thoughts strayed, and they did stray, and they would not cease from straying. No, I said to Nicola when she called from the country and said would we come for a weekend, it's so beautiful this time of year. And she was a child, just a child really, and could not keep the hurt from her voice when I kept on saying no and no and once again no. No, I said, to Jess when she said wouldn't it be nice, Nic and Mark were in town, wouldn't it be lovely to see them for dinner? No, I said, I don't want to. And I felt like a child, sticking out my lower lip, offering no further explanation but no, and no, and no.

'I don't understand why you won't, that's all.'

Jess was packing. She spoke in her calm and sensible voice.

'I just don't want to.'

I knew it would seem I was being unreasonable.

'If you don't want to tell me I suppose you don't have to, but I do think that you're being unreasonable.'

'There's nothing to tell. I don't want to come. I've got marking to do and I'd rather have a quiet weekend at home. I wish you'd stay with me.'

She folded her cream cardigan over the top of her clothes and closed the case briskly. She took a deep breath, then let it out again. I wondered if she was going to shout at me, but she never did, it was not in her. She said, 'You know I'm not going to do that. I promised them. *You* said you probably would.'

'But I can't,' I said. And that at least was true.

No, and no, and no. It could not hold.

It wasn't a good weekend for me. Jess telephoned to say she had arrived safely and in the background I heard Mark saying, 'Tell him

he's a silly boy for not coming himself. We'll expect him next time.'
And I felt as though I might vomit. My home, our quiet safe home,
had been invaded by something I could not contain or control.

That weekend I had a recurrence of my old problem. It was mid-
December, seven months after the wedding, and the days grew dark
at 3 p.m. I found myself simultaneously terrified and numb, staring
at the lowering sky from the window, unwilling to leave the flat. I
could not control my moods, could not stop fear rising in my throat.
The winter was cold and dark and never-ending. I imagined Jess sitting
by the fire in Mark and Nicola's home, warmed and encircled by
golden light and laughing with her feet up on the sofa and the dogs
leaping up to demand her attention. I did not eat much that weekend,
I barely stirred from bed. It was clear to me that this was my natural
condition; that without Jess I would return to the state in which she
had found me – incapable, bleak, desperate. It was only late on Sunday
night, when I heard her key in the door, when I saw her face, that the
mood lifted, suddenly, all at once, as though it had never been.

I described this to Jess as best I could. I told her I had felt low while
she had been gone. She, because she is good, did not say, 'Well, you
should have come with then.'

She kissed my forehead, ruffled my hair and said, 'I'm home now.
I missed you too. Come and help me unpack.'

Things with her were always as simple as this. She was good for
me, in this way as in so many others. But why do we so often want
the things that are not good for us at all?

There is no safety that does not also restrict us. And many needless
restrictions feel safe and comfortable. It is so hard to know, at any
moment, the distinction between being safe and being caged. It is hard
to know when it is better to choose freedom and fear, and when it is
simply foolhardy. I have often, I think, too often erred on the side of
caution.

Jess said, 'James, I really think you should see Mark.'

I felt a line of fear work through me, like a swallowed needle.

'No,' I said.

She looked at me. We were in bed, she warming her hands on a mug of tea.

'What's he done to you, James? What's this about?'

What could I possibly say? I reached around in my mind for something that was not, 'I am afraid, Jessica. I am afraid that if I see him I will well up with longing so that I cannot bear it.'

'Look, I don't know. He's just not our sort of people, is he?'

She frowned. A thin layer of ice glistened on her surface. This had been the wrong thing to say.

'What do you mean?' she said.

I pushed on. 'Just . . . Look, he's so . . . I mean, I think he wants to be friends with a different kind of person to us. I mean, Emmanuella's more his sort of . . .'

Jess said, 'I think you're totally wrong. In fact, he spent all weekend telling me how much he wanted to see you, how disappointed he was you hadn't come, how he misses your chats.'

At this there was a kind of stirring in me, a detestable hope unfurling.

'If you're just staying away because you think we're not *rich* enough for him . . .'

I gulped unhappily and stared at her. Her frown melted away. She snuggled up to me.

'It's just the silly winter depression, love. Mark loves you, you know he does, and he's never cared about other people having money.'

I nodded.

'Anyway,' she said, 'I'm a bit worried about him. He's restless down there in the country. Edgy. It's not good for him, and it's not good for Nicola. I said he should come to London when your holidays start, to get away for a few days.'

She finished her tea, put the mug on the bedside table and, looking away, said, 'None of us know how long this marriage will last, but he needs a friend, James. Whether they stay together or not. You shouldn't keep away from him. Promise me you won't.'

And I thought of what it would take to say no, again, to this.

'All right,' I said, as she turned off the light.

*

I said the following things to myself. Number one, Mark doesn't know. If Jess doesn't know – and she didn't, of that I was sure – then Mark could not know how I felt. Number two, he doesn't want you. He's got his own ideas about the right way to live, about what he's doing now. You don't figure in them, except as a friend, so pull yourself together. Number three, if he doesn't know and he doesn't want you, then the only thing that can make anything go wrong is you. It's just a matter of willpower, James, just like resisting an extra Yorkshire pudding at Sunday lunch. All you have to do is not act, not say anything, not do anything that would make him think you wanted him. Come on, James, you're good at *not* doing things. This should be easy.

He pulled up at our door around lunchtime on the first day of my holidays in his little red sports car. His hair had grown longer than before, touching his collar and creeping around the sides of his face. In jeans, a white shirt with thin blue stripes and a battered blazer, he looked like the boy in school who was always on the verge of expulsion. He beeped the horn and leapt out of the car, all energy, and hugged me.

That first day, we were like students again. We went to Piccadilly Circus, where Mark declared loudly how much better the lights were in Times Square. He bought a disposable camera and insisted I take pictures of him posing next to Eros, one foot off the ground, as if about to take flight.

'He's supposed,' he shouted, although I was only three feet away from him, 'to be facing the *other way*. He's *supposed* to be firing his arrow down Shaftesbury Avenue. It's a joke, you see – he's supposed to be burying his shaft in Shaftesbury Avenue. Do you see, James? Do you understand?'

I nodded and went red. The tourists sitting on the statue's steps looked at us. I thought, they must think we're lovers.

In the British Museum, walking through the hushed marble halls, he began to talk nonsense at the loudest possible volume.

'I mean, what do you think, James?' he said. 'I think she's making a fuss about nothing. After all, I only gave her a BLACK EYE.'

This directed at full blast towards an elderly couple peering at a Greek fresco.

'What?' I said.

'I mean HONESTLY, if she's going to provoke me, she'll have to expect to get a HOT IRON IN THE FACE FROM TIME TO TIME.'

'What?!' I said.

The elderly couple looked at us in horror and scurried away.

He grinned. 'Go on,' he said, 'you try one. How about the sketchers?'

He motioned with his head towards two young men sitting at the foot of a broken statue, pencilling furiously in their sketchbooks.

We strolled towards them and I searched my mind for something funny to say. As we walked past, I found myself declaring, 'He's making such a bloody fuss, you'd think I'd given him AIDS. After all, it was only CHLAMYDIA.'

And Mark replied, not missing a beat, 'But he did get it in his THROAT, DARLING.'

The adrenalin pumped in my throat and my heart and my brain. I thought, this is exactly what I need. This, exactly this. I cast a glance over my shoulder as we left the room. The sketchers were staring at us, their drawing momentarily forgotten. When we walked into the next room I began to laugh and soon I could not stop, and the frowns and the stares of the serious museum-goers were nothing to me.

On the way out of the museum, we went to the lavatories. Under the eyes of the other men, he pulled me into a cubicle with him and I thought, another tease? I could not tell and I thought, perhaps, James, he does know and perhaps he does want. But he only pulled a tiny plastic bag filled with white powder out of his pocket and said in, at last, a whisper, 'Powder your nose?'

'We're in the British Museum, Mark.' I could not keep the tone of shock out of my voice. 'The *British Museum*. You can't do that in the British Museum.'

We were crammed into the cubicle, almost touching but not quite.

He said, 'You don't imagine I'm the first person to have done this?'

He tipped a little of the powder on to the toilet cistern, pulled a credit card out of his wallet and began to chop at it, scraping it into two orderly lines.

'Someone will catch us,' I hissed.

He leaned in very close to me and whispered, 'Only if you don't stop talking.'

I tried to look through the gap at the hinge of the toilet door to see if anyone was staring at us: two men together in a cubicle, surely doing something offensive to someone. But there was no staring anywhere. I turned back. Mark had rolled a £50 note into a tube. He proffered it to me.

'Go on,' he said.

I thought, I am being offered drugs in the toilets of the British Museum. This is what my life has been missing up to this moment. I shook my head again. Mark shrugged.

'Your loss,' he said, and snorted both lines. As he tipped his head back to stare at the ceiling and his eyes watered and he began to grin I thought, yes, perhaps this is all that I need. Just this is quite sufficient.

The next day, Mark arrived at 2 p.m., beeping his horn and doing a handstand in the streets while he waited for me.

'Do you know,' I said, bending over to talk to his head, 'that there are two parking tickets on your windscreen?'

'Oh, those!' he said. 'I just wait for the letters to come and send them to the banker. Come on. Let's go and see the wizard.'

And I thought of the energy it would take to explain to Mark the workings of the Penalty Charge system and how intensely useless it would be and instead just said, 'The wizard?'

The wizard lived in a grimy basement flat in Clerkenwell. His name was Jee, he had pale skin, dirty blond hair and wore a patterned smock and brightly coloured hat.

He greeted Mark warmly with a hug, looked me up and down through narrowed eyes and said to Mark, 'You sure?'

'Oh, totally. He's never done a thing wrong in his life, have you, James?'

'S'what I mean,' said Jee.

'Nah, he's all right,' Mark said, and we walked through the door.

It was clear to me at once that he was rich, that he had been born rich. My time spent with Mark and his friends had accustomed me to sifting the long-term rich from the nouveau from the purely aspirational. The key is the possession of objects which are clearly tremendously expensive but are treated with disdain and often held in surroundings of squalor. In Jee's case, the kitchen with its broken orange plastic dish rack and dirty cupboards was enlivened by an enormous espresso machine, worth at least £1,000. But the machine had not been cared for: its surface was already pockmarked with kitchen grease and old coffee grounds had been dumped on the top. No one who had had to work to acquire this thing – either to buy it or to steal it – would have treated it in this way.

In Jee's living room, a group of men were hunched over a low mosaic-topped table, examining a collection of small coloured tablets and printed paper squares. From a distance, they looked like schoolboys admiring a selection of marbles and stickers.

I thought I recognized one of them: a tall, thin man wearing drainpipe trousers and with a slicked-back hairstyle. When he looked up I realized with a shock that he was a television presenter; famous for an anarchic programme he hosted on the subject of, in roughly equal parts, pop music, high culture and his genitals. He stared at me for a moment, grunted, then said to Jee, 'Fine, fine, but what if I just want to lose, like, three whole weeks?'

Jee nodded sagely, reached under his kaftan and produced a small bag of white tablets and a sheet of red paper squares.

'Very mellow, my friend, extremely sybaritic.'

The television star grimaced.

'Will it get me off the fucking planet?'

And Jee nodded slowly.

On the other side of the table, next to Mark, was another face I found vaguely familiar. A muscular man in an open-necked shirt and jeans. He, however, recognized me as well.

'Hello,' he said. 'It's Jack, isn't it?'

'James,' I said.

I placed him; he was an acquaintance of Mark's and had attended that first New Year's Eve party at Annulet House.

'Know anything about steel?' he said.

I blinked.

He drew his attention away from the collection of coloured powders and tablets.

'Only I'm thinking of going all in on steel. If they're right and all the planes are going to fall out of the sky, what will we need?'

'Ambulances?' I ventured.

He puffed out his cheeks and shook his head.

'Too late by then. No one survives a plane crash, no one. Safety cards and "brace, brace" are just to stop people panicking. It's true. I've looked into it.' He pursed his lips. 'No, if the planes fall out of the sky, what are we going to need? Steel. To rebuild them, see?'

'*Are* planes made out of steel?'

'What else would they be made of?'

'Ummm,' I said, 'maybe aluminium? Or some kind of composite? Something light like that?'

He thought about this for a long time, while fiddling with a 10-pence piece, turning it over and over, flipping it between his fingers, throwing and catching it.

'Very good point,' he said, 'very good indeed. Yes. Very good. Aluminium. You might have saved me a bundle there, fella, an absolute bundle.' He leaned towards Mark and said, 'Clever chap, your friend. Positively insightful.'

Mark looked at me, smiled and said, 'Yes. Yes, he is.' And a crazy happiness spread warm and liquid in my chest.

Mark made a large and expansive purchase. So large, in fact, and so expansive that Jee thoughtfully provided him with a Marks & Spencer bag to carry it away in.

'Where to now?' I said.

'Home,' said Mark decisively. 'Get some of these babies down me.'

I could not keep the disappointment from my face.

'Oh,' he said, looking at me, 'what a face you have, James! Like a sad little puppy. Do not worry, my darling, there will be treats tomorrow.'

And he kissed me lightly on the cheek, jumped into his car and disappeared in it before I could think of how to persuade him to stay.

We'd arranged to meet the next day at his flat in Islington at 2.30 p.m., but when I arrived he was surprised to see me. He was dressed in only pyjama bottoms, his hair still sleep-muddled.

He said, 'I thought you weren't coming till the afternoon?'

I said, 'This is the afternoon.'

He said, 'Oh.'

And he shook his head sadly and went to get dressed.

We drove to my flat – his windscreen had acquired another two tickets, I noticed. Jess was out rehearsing and wouldn't be back until the evening. Mark lay on his back on our sofa, holding his head in his hands. I made a late lunch and we ate in the kitchen. I realized that I hadn't seen him eat since he arrived in London and this thought filled me with compassion for him. He seemed smaller now than he had been.

Mark poured himself a large whisky and we talked about Oxford people, about what had become of them since we left. Mark had heard that Dr McGowan had finally been arrested for his cottaging activities and that the college had asked him to resign. He had, however, been immediately offered an even more prestigious chair at the Sorbonne so, as Mark said, 'no harm done'. We talked of Franny, who'd coincidentally spent a few weeks of the summer at the Sorbonne. We wondered whether she'd seen Dr McGowan, and whether she'd managed to keep a straight face if so. Mark became more and more animated during this conversation, wildly fantasizing that they *had* met, that they had become great friends, that they were together right now, that if we called her we would find that he was in her rooms.

'I'll call her now!' Mark said. 'She could come down from Cambridge tonight. And *then –*' a wild gleam flared in his eye – 'we could go and see Emmanuella at the weekend! In Madrid! Or she could come here! I could fly her over. Maybe Simon could come from Chile, or Peru, or wherever he is.'

He frowned, acknowledging that this was unlikely, but he had still not given up on the idea entirely. He picked up the phone and dialled Franny's number in Cambridge.

'Hello, my darling. Guess who it is.'

A pause. A grin on his face.

'S'right! And guess who I'm with.'

Another pause, a wider grin.

'No! Wrong! Guess again . . .'

A shorter pause.

'It's James! I'm with James in London, and Jess is going to be home in a few hours, and *we thought* . . .'

Another pause. A slight wrinkling of the brow.

'No, she's not. She's still in Doorbl . . . Doorbi . . . She's in Door-bell.' A giggle from Mark.

A pause. Mark bit his upper lip.

'Well, yes I am, as a matter of fact, but there's nothing wrong with *that*, is there, darling?'

A short pause.

'*No*, listen! Jess will be home soon, and *we thought* you could come down to London tonight and it'll be *just* like old times, do you remember? In the house?'

A longer pause. More lip chewing.

'Oh, but darling Franny, it won't take very long . . .'

Cut off. A short pause.

'I'm sure you can stay here tonight. Can't she, James?'

I nodded.

'He's nodding. Of course you can stay here tonight.'

A long pause.

'Oh, but you'll have a wonderful time. We're all here and we can go out on the town, or stay in and order some food, and I've got some *lovely* stuff, haven't I, James?'

He did not look at me this time to see whether I nodded or not.

'Oh, but Fran . . .'

Pause.

'But you know that you'll . . .'

Pause.

'But it's our last chance in . . .'

Long pause. Frown deepening on Mark's face. A twist of the mouth.

'I really can't persuade you . . .?'

Lines appearing at the sides of his mouth. A slight scrunch to his eyes.

'OK, bye then.'

He put the phone down and looked at the receiver for a moment.

He said, 'Uptight bitch.'

I said nothing.

He sat on the sofa for a while, staring out of the window at the blank grey sky. At last he said, 'We had an argument.'

I did not have to ask who he meant. I didn't know how to reply to him. Instead, I simply waited.

'She said she thinks this all might have been a mistake.'

'She probably didn't mean it.'

He looked at me, a broken smile. He shrugged.

'But it can't be perfect any more, not like it was. Nothing ever stays.'

'It's not . . .' I began, and then did not know how to proceed. I wanted to tell him something about how it was with Jess and me, how I had found that love was a constant cycle of coming together and breaking apart. But I did not want to talk or think about Jess just then. And perhaps I did not at that time have the ability to explain the truth about relationships: that they produce their fruit intermittently, unpredictably. That every relationship has moments when someone says, or thinks, or feels that it might not be worth doing. Every relationship has moments of exasperation and fear. And the work of the thing is to come through it, to learn how to bear it. And even if I could have explained this, Mark would never have understood it. He has always been rich enough that if something breaks he can simply throw it away and buy a new one. He had never used string or glue to bind something together again. He had never been forced to learn how to mend.

Mark poured himself a second whisky, or was it his third now?

'I don't know why things have fallen apart like this.'

'Between you and Nicola?'

His face dropped. He stared into his glass.

'No, between us, all of us. We used to be such good friends, didn't we? I mean, didn't we? You and me and Jess and Franny and Simon and even Emman . . . Emmanuella, although –' he gestured with his glass, sloshing a little of the auburn liquid on to the carpet – 'I never could get to the bottom of her. So to speak.' He giggled. 'So to speak.'

'Yes, we used to be good friends.'

'When we were all together. It was better then, when we were together in the house.'

'It was a good time.'

'No,' he said, sitting forward, suddenly earnest. 'No, it wasn't a good time. It wasn't just that. We were all more ourselves then. We were all who we really are, only we forget because of bills and responsibility and having to go to work and be married and that sort of thing. We've forgotten, but we have to try to remember.'

His voice softened, lowered.

'You, James, you were just so beautiful then. You're still beautiful now. But then, when you were really yourself. God, I remember that just watching you cross the lawn, you know, just seeing you lying in the hammock, made me . . .' He breathed out loudly. 'You should all come back and live in the house again.'

I thought back to that time. It was already brighter now than it had been; I could feel already the days of rain erasing themselves in my mind, the days when I had been lonely or sad. It was beginning to seem utterly golden, although I knew that it had been life, only life, with no mystery to it or redemptive quality or unattainable glories.

Being with Mark I felt I could hear again the sound of rain on the conservatory roof, smell the ham hock cooking in the kitchen, see Franny and Jess arguing over their card game. I heard the shrieks of laughter as Simon pushed Emmanuella around the garden in the old wheelbarrow, or tasted the lip balm Jess used then, something with a hint of vanilla. Being with Mark, I remembered happiness, not as it had been for me, but as I imagined it was for him: rich, unending and enveloping.

'And you and me, James, we were always good friends, weren't we? Very good friends. Better than friends.' He leaned closer. 'You always fancied me, didn't you? Do you remember that day, the day you left Oxford, in the kitchen? Do you remember, James?'

He was quite drunk; I was much less so. I should have called a cab for him, sent him home. But he smiled at me, stretched, and touched my cheek with the back of his hand. I could smell his skin, that faint scent of raspberries still, as though he had taken summer into him, as though high heat and sun were just below the surface of his skin.

I tried to resist. I did try. In so far as I was able. When he put his hand up to my face, I pulled back. He was still for a moment, looked at me. I looked at him. I tried to shake my head, or say something: you should go, I don't want. Something along those lines. But I didn't. Mark smiled his easy, lazy smile and moved forward again.

I kissed him. He kissed me.

He muttered, 'I've been thinking about this for years, you know,' and I wanted to remind him that he'd said that before, he'd said it the last time, but I couldn't. I couldn't say anything at all.

That evening, after Mark left, after I'd showered and shaved and gathered up my clothes and put them through the washing machine, I tried to start an argument with Jess.

Jess and I rarely quarrelled. It's difficult to quarrel with Jess, because she's so essentially self-contained there's no purchase, nowhere to get a handhold, pull her open, make her angry. And, truthfully, I disgusted myself even for wanting to. And I did want to. I wanted to make her cry. I wanted her to tell me to fuck off, or to throw something at me. I wanted her to say, 'How dare you?' or 'I hate you.' I wanted to know what it was would make her do those things, because it wasn't anything I'd been doing up till then.

And if I could have broken her open, what then? If I could have found the right place to direct my hammer-blow, or wedged my chisel into a hairline crack on her shell and smashed or levered her apart, what would I have done next? She would have just been shattered, the parts of herself which fitted together so neatly now suddenly painful, never again as comfortable as they had been. There are enough of us in that condition already, without wanting to create any more.

19

'Hello?'

'Oh, hello, Nicola. It's James. How're you?'

'Mmmm, fine. Leo and Eloise are staying with us for the weekend while my parents are away, did Mark tell you?'

'Oh yes, I think he mentioned it. Does your sister still think she's got glandular fever?'

Nicola laughed. 'Either that or dengue fever, she's not sure. Mark diagnosed her with beriberi. She enjoyed looking up the symptoms to that one.'

'I bet she did. Is he there by any chance?'

As though she had reminded me of his existence.

'Just a moment. Mark!' A pause. 'It's James on the phone for you! He's going to take it in the study. Just a sec.'

And then Mark's drawled 'Jaaaames', and the click, always waiting for the click of her putting down the phone.

'Hi,' I said, 'you rang?'

'Yup,' he said. 'Planning a trip to London next week. Are you free at all? After work? Free to come over to the flat, that is?'

And I said yes. Every time, I said yes. I couldn't not.

I had told myself repeatedly not to expect that we would continue. It wasn't just that he had a wife, but also that he had never been one for revisiting his old grounds. Mark had been maudlin, it meant nothing. But Mark came up to town again two weeks later and it happened again. Wine and conversation, nostalgia and regret, intimacy and sex. And then again. And then again.

And I remember thinking one morning, while attempting to bash the rudiments of differential equations into the heads of twenty-six recalcitrant boys, oh, I am having an affair. It was a thought that occurred between one word and the next, making me stumble in my sentence. I would not have thought myself the kind of person capable of having an affair. But life teaches us who we are.

But then, of course, there had to be visits with Nicola. I was spending so much time with Mark that failing to see Nicola would have been an insult. And there was this too: now that I had dealt her this invisible blow, I wanted to see for myself whether she had guessed yet. To see if I could tell from the tiny turns of her head whether she knew that in the privacy of his flat Mark and I had screwed until I had shouted out all the breath in my lungs, until I thought by my trembling legs that I would never stand up again, until I thought, now I must be sated, now I must, and yet my appetite proved otherwise. I sometimes thought it must be obvious from every look between us that all I wanted, every moment I was near him, was to feel his naked skin on mine and to see him hard and willing and ready.

But apparently I was wrong. It wasn't obvious. Mark always flirted with everyone, of course. So that the first time he slapped my arse as he walked past me from sitting room to kitchen, my stomach turned to meltwater. But Nicola looked on mildly and Jess smiled and I remembered, oh yes, he does this with everyone. And me? Perhaps I had looked at Mark with dog-like yearning for so long that no difference was discernible.

Nicola had become a little tetchy since I last saw her.

'Oh, my God, Mark,' she said, when he wanted to show us his collection of remote-controlled aircraft, newly acquired at considerable expense, 'no one wants to see your toys, all right?'

She was kneeling in the long conservatory, jabbing at the earth around a ficus bush with a trowel.

'They do,' said Mark in a whining tone. 'James wants to see them, don't you, James?'

It was our second or third visit to Mark and Nicola's gargantuan farmhouse-villa in Dorset. Mark and I had been together five or six times by then and I was still full of wonder and desire and excitement; every time we met there were new things to try, new explorations to be made. But this was a difficult situation. I couldn't say, 'Yes, I want to see your planes.' I couldn't say, with Nicola, 'No, I don't want to,' even though it was true: I did not want to see his planes, I did not want to stand next to him in a chilly field, with Nicola and Jess looking on, while each of my joints ached to move closer to him or share some secret word. I found that my knee started to ache with its old sensitivity on these visits; perhaps from the damp, or perhaps from the country walks, or perhaps from the longing that devoured me.

'I, um, I don't know much about planes,' I said.

'See?' said Nicola. 'No one's interested, Mark.'

'That's not what he said,' said Mark. 'He said he doesn't know much about planes, ergo he needs someone to teach him. Like me!'

Nicola stood up and frowned at me, and at Mark. When had she become so constantly angry over trivial things?

'I know,' said Jess. 'Why don't James and Mark go off to fly the planes and you can show me the garden, Nicola?'

And Nicola, red-faced and snorting slightly, let us go.

In the field, damp creeping in through my trainers, I stood with Mark in the concealment of a clump of trees and kissed and groped and wished for more until Mark, perhaps feeling some sudden sense of propriety, broke away.

'Come on,' he said, panting, 'enough of this. Let me do a loop the loop for you.'

On the next visit she became irrationally angry again. It was at dinner on our first night. She was handing plates around and when she came to me she stopped, hand half-outstretched, as though her motor had wound down.

'I'm really sorry,' she said, 'but seeing you makes me angry, James.'

And I thought, God, not now, not yet, for perhaps some part of my brain had already begun to accept that this conversation must happen one day.

'I know it's not really your fault. I know what he's like.' She wiped the back of her hand across her forehead, an angry agitated gesture. 'James, I just –' and she smiled, as though she knew she was being foolish – 'all it is is that I think you're getting what belongs to me. And it makes me angry, OK? That's all.'

I swallowed, a hard lump building in my throat. I thought, God, am I going to cry? I said, 'Well, I . . .'

And Jess stopped me, with a hand over my hand, and said, 'James, let her finish. Go on, Nicola, why don't you tell us what's troubling you?'

And I wondered for a moment if the two of them had planned this together. Could it be, could it possibly be that Jess knew?

Nicola pouted and sat down. 'All the bloody trips to London,' she said, 'the two of you together. It's –' her voice became very small and hushed – 'I want to come too, sometimes. I just wish you'd take me too, Mark.'

'Oh!' said Mark.

The world started to move again. I let out a breath I hadn't realized I was holding. My pulse crashed in my ears.

'I know it's silly,' she said, staring at her plate, 'but I just feel so left out, down here by myself while you're having fun in town.'

Mark smiled, and if he was a little pale Nicola did not seem to notice. 'Why didn't you say so before?'

So our simple pattern became a little more complex. Sometimes Mark would come to town alone, and then I would meet him at his flat. Sometimes he and Nicola would come together, and then he would book a hotel room nearby, somewhere small and discreet. Often, when I arrived at these rendezvous, he was late and I would have to wait for him, flipping through a newspaper, certain that the staff knew exactly what I was here for.

Once, as I sat waiting in the lobby, I thought I saw someone I knew – one of Jess's friends from the orchestra. Had he looked my way? Had he seen me? Was he about to come over and say hello? Would Mark arrive then, at that moment? And would this orchestra friend then speak idly to Jess and would Jess then say, 'Darling, why were you meeting Mark in the Patrum Hotel?' I stood up sharply and walked to the bathroom where I was out of sight. I waited there, trembling, for almost half an hour and when I emerged Mark was waiting at my table, smoking a cigarette, wanting to know if I'd got the runs. 'If so,' he said, 'you should really *go home*. You know?'

On another occasion, Mark had told me to meet him at the flat on a particular afternoon. It was almost five weeks since I'd last seen him and I waited with a sense of mounting excitement. When he arrived though, breezing through the door with an armful of glossy paper carrier bags, Nicola was with him. Her hair was windswept, her cheeks red. She beamed when she saw me.

'It doesn't bother you, does it, James?' She had that earnestness of youth. 'I wanted to tell you I was coming, but Mark said you liked being surprised.'

'Yes,' I said, 'it's a lovely surprise.'

As she bent down to kiss my cheek, I looked at Mark. He opened his eyes very wide and smiled a close-mouthed smile as if to say, 'Who, me?'

We managed to have sex on that visit, a breathless few minutes when Nicola, bemoaning the lack of dogs in the city, went for an afternoon walk. We barely had time to smooth our clothes down before she returned.

Once or twice Nicola asked me, in a half-joking voice, illuminating her interest by pretence of non-interest, what I thought Mark *did* in London.

'Not when he's with you, obviously.'

This was the visit when she had surprised me with her presence. It was a little after her walk and Mark had left on some unexplained errand.

She lit another cigarette – I couldn't remember her smoking before Mark. She was so young, and this thought did give me pause. So young, and trying to pretend to be older. Perhaps that was part of Mark's attraction to her: to feel herself an adult, in the company of adults. But she was still so young, and trusting like a child. She trusted me to tell her the truth. I felt ashamed that I would not.

'I don't mean you,' she continued, 'I know you're old friends. But what do you think he does when he goes off by himself?' She tried laughing. 'He's like *oooooh* –' she waved her hands in the air – 'big mystery, you know? Like he's a spy or something.'

The truth was, I had wondered this myself. I tormented myself with the possibility, the probability that he was with other men. I had no right to feel angry. Nicola had far more right than I and she suspected nothing, it seemed. But late at night, curled in bed around Jess's soft-breathing body, I would find myself imagining over and over again scenes of Mark in a bar, a club, an alley, doing with another man what he did with me but better, of course, more fiercely, with more glory.

It lasted about a year, this interlude. A little more. A year and three or four months before things began to slip, as things do. It was spring, the sky a rich blue. I arrived early at the hotel and flipped through the newspaper, but my mind snagged on an anecdote I'd heard that morning in the staffroom. It was nothing: one of the boys, a lesson, an amusing gaffe, but I thought it might make Mark laugh. I ran over the story several times in my mind, noting the points where I should pause in telling it, where I might emphasize a word and where to trim it slightly to improve its style. Mark could make me laugh easily with his blend of bawdy and archness. I had to work harder.

He arrived late and in high spirits, dancing from foot to foot. Before I could stand up he swiftly looked around the almost-empty lobby and dipped down to kiss me on the mouth. This was not a thing we did in public, not so incautiously. He hauled on my arm.

'Come on,' he said. 'I've got something to tell you.'

I gathered up my newspaper, my backpack full of exercise books. Some of his excitement had caught me too and as we made for the lifts I wished I could break into a run, or jump. His jeans were tight, outlining his bottom. I longed, as ever, to be touching him. As the doors closed in the little wood-panelled cabin he grabbed my belt, pulled me towards him and kissed me hard, his hands reaching around my back and under my shirt.

I pushed him away, frightened that the lift doors might open again or, irrationally, that we had failed to observe someone else standing in the tiny space with us. Mark pouted. He knew behaving like this in public frightened me.

'What's this about, Mark?'

He slouched back against the wood panels.

'Maybe I'm not going to tell you now.' He smiled. 'Oh, all *right* then. But not till we get to the room. Don't want to do anything in public we shouldn't, do we, James?'

By the time we reached the room, though, he was bouncing again. He placed me in a chair, bent across me, kissed me and then stood up again, drawing breath for his announcement. I couldn't imagine what it might be. Perhaps his mother was divorcing again; Mark didn't like her new husband much. Or perhaps Nicola was going away for a while and we could spend more time together.

He stretched out his arms, the right directly above the left, both clutched into fists, as if he were reading a proclamation. He made a noise like a trumpet, then grinned at me, threw away the proclamation and said, 'Nicola's pregnant.'

He stuck his hands in his pockets, bit his lower lip.

'What?'

'Nicola,' he said, 'is expecting a baby.'

I didn't understand at first. I had assumed, but had not realized that I'd assumed, that they didn't sleep together any more, or at least that they used contraception.

'Is it, I mean, do you want it?'

Mark looked at me. And I understood. I could not fathom how it had taken me so long.

In my dreams, this is where it happens. It is here, the fulcrum of my life. When I dream, or daydream, this is where I exert a gentle pressure and move the world. Sometimes, I am the noble one. I say, 'But Mark, we can't carry on *now*. Not now you're going to be a father. It wouldn't be right.' I can't convince myself of that though.

More often I imagine it the other way. I imagine Mark teasing me. That is easier to bring to mind. He says, 'Well, of course, you know what *this* means, James.' I shake my head. He says, 'We can't very well carry on sleeping together, *can we*? Not now I'm going to be a father.' He raises an eyebrow. 'It wouldn't be right, would it? Would it, James?' I think he's mocking me, making fun of some imagined James with moral convictions and high ideals. But he's serious. 'Come now, James,' he says. 'You must have realized I wouldn't want to carry on like this forever. It's been fun, but now it's over.' I lunge for him and he dances out of reach. He leaves the room and I remain.

But it did not happen this way.

Instead, we made love and Mark was so filled with delight that it seeped through his skin and into my body, and when I held him he was radiating warmth like a star. And when he came, he was shouting and panting and telling me in my ear that I was the best, the most wonderful, the sexiest, the most glorious, that I was Christmas and the Fourth of July, and St Patrick's Day and, yes, the Feast of the Holy Virgin all in one, and I saw that, yes, yes, this was a holiday, a celebration of life, and all things that celebrate life should be done upon it.

And later, when we lay in bed with his arm thrown across me, it still seemed that way, a day of rejoicing and celebration.

That evening, after Mark was gone, after Jess was asleep, I remained awake, staring at the ceiling of our bedroom. I found a thought coiled inside me, kept at bay by the hum of daily life but now stronger and louder. I shied away from it even as I recognized it as a true wish, a heart's cry. Can I confess it now? I have never whispered it to Mark, tried never even to think it in his presence. I could never tell him. It is my own particular evil. It is this. I wished for his child to die. Then, before the child was born, when it was only a mixture of blood and water, I wished it dead, flushed, gone.

I think of this sometimes, on the worst days here in San Ceterino, when I wonder why I ever came, or what keeps me here. When I clean up his mess or make his telephone calls or comfort his weeping, I remind myself that I wished his child gone because I saw that our lives could not continue as they had done. I wished it gone so that I could keep him near me. Because of wanting, because of the amount I wanted him, I could not see anyone else.

20

Once, about a year ago, I came upon a picture of Nicola and Daisy unexpectedly. I had been searching through the drawer next to Mark's bed – he was raving by the pool in the moonlight. I wanted to know what he'd taken. I looked in the vitamin-pill bottles, ran my fingertips along the seam of the drawer lining feeling for loose places, flipped open his sunglasses case and there they were. Nicola and Daisy in the sun smiling. The photograph was creased, carefully fitted to the curve of the case lid. Nicola was wearing a blue and white patterned dress, with dangling earrings, three slim squares of porcelain held together by silver rings. She was holding Daisy – who looked to be about eighteen months old in the picture – on her right hip. Daisy's hair was very blonde. In the photograph you could see the sun shining on it. She was reaching out to grab one of Nicola's earrings, and Nicola had caught her arm at an awkward angle to stop her. Nicola was smiling into Daisy's face. Daisy's mouth was set in a determined line, her eyes focused on the earring, oblivious of photographer and surroundings.

This photograph stopped me. In the courtyard, Mark was still shouting at the moon and I thought, I could take this out now, show it to him and it would stop him too. I sat on the corner of his bed and looked at the photograph, feeling as though I could walk straight through it and out into the sunny day, where Nicola was holding Daisy on her hip and her earrings were moving in the sunlight. I wanted to do that. I knew just where this photograph was taken. On Broad Street, by the Sheldonian Theatre. Just out of sight to the left was Blackwell's, then the White Horse, then Trinity College. I could almost hear the sounds of the street – there would be music playing out of some open window, and the air would be a little too thick with exhaust fumes. It was Oxford, on a sunny Saturday afternoon at the start of May. It was the day we graduated.

Oxford, which likes to do things differently, dissociates graduation from the end of the degree course. It's possible to graduate only a few months after finishing a degree but most people do what we did – wait four years and then take both the BA and the honorary MA at the same time. The MA is another piece of antiquity, lovingly carried in cupped hands into the modern day. We didn't have to do any extra work for it, or take another exam. Seven years after joining the university, provided we passed our finals and survived that long, the degree of Master of Arts was awarded us.

So, for a day, we took our place in the Oxford clockwork mechanism again. There was a great business of putting on robes, of learning the correct Latin words and gestures for the occasion. There was something comforting about it. After so long away, we returned and Oxford still had a role for us. People pass from school to school, from job to job, and though a great fuss is made when we leave – parties, cakes, gifts and farewells – a year later we might never have been there. No record is kept. There would be no special welcome if we returned to our old job four or five years after we left. But Oxford, whose speciality is remembrance, remembers. After BA there is MA, and after MA there are gaudies, decade after decade. And at the end of our days, if we have made our college proud, there will be an obituary, sent in the *College Record* to every eager first year, saying, until the end, this one belonged to us.

After the ceremony, we stood in the street with our families, taking photographs of each other in our robes. Emmanuella's family were polite to us, but distant; more interested in talking with her boyfriend. Franny's family and Simon's embraced. My parents and Jess's greeted each other slightly nervously – they had met several times before but not often enough to have become easy in one another's company. Jess's father bent in to kiss my mother, who simultaneously took a step backwards and made an awkward little noise, so he missed her face completely. Eloise, Simon's little sister, tugged on Jess's father's sleeve and asked if he was really a doctor and if so what were the symptoms of rickets. And it was there that the photograph was taken. Nicola was holding Daisy: a little girl, half-baby, half-toddler, babbling and charming in red leather sandals and a white embroidered dress over her nappy-clothed bottom. Mark borrowed Jess's camera, Nicola hoisted Daisy on to one hip, Mark waved, Nicola smiled, Daisy grabbed for her earring and the picture was taken.

And then what happened? Then, I think, Mark grabbed her from Nicola's arms, clasped her to him and then made as if to drop her, catching her before she fell, swinging her into the air as she laughed and gasped. Nicola watched with a frown.

'Mind her arms, Mark. She's too heavy to swing.'

Mark wrapped his arms around Daisy's waist and brought his face close to the place where her neck met her shoulder.

'You're not too heavy, are you, darling?'

Daisy was wriggling, trying to escape down to the ground.

'What's more, you are brilliant. You are my brilliant, beautiful daughter and one day you'll come to Oxford just like your father.'

Daisy chuckled and babbled at him. He lifted up her dress, blew a raspberry on her tummy and she screamed with fear and delight.

She grew tired later, as children do, and we were all surprised, I think, by how tiresome it can be to spend time with a cross child. Mark and Nicola were the first people we knew to have a baby, we had not yet learned of their trials and difficulties. Nicola strapped her into the pushchair and Daisy did not like this at all. We were in the entrance hall of the Randolph – Mark had booked us all rooms there and though our parents had tried to protest, they had not done so strenuously. Mark paid for things in Oxford; it was not worth fighting the inevitable. On arrival, there was a little wait and Daisy became fractious, struggling against the bindings of her chair, desperately trying to push them out of the way so she could escape. Nicola offered her pieces of cut apple or dried apricots in an attempt to distract her, but she rejected these angrily.

Daisy writhed in her chair, whimpering and bellowing, pushing the straps down again and again, fiddling with the buckle over her stomach. She was trying, it was clear, to open it the way she had seen her parents open it so many times in the past. But her coordination wasn't good enough; she twisted and screamed and yelled.

'I'm going to let her out,' said Mark.

'No,' said Nicola, firm as a rap on the hand. 'Look at this place. She'll just spill people's coffees on them, and break things and hurt herself. Leave her there. It'll only be another few minutes. She can have a nice run around outside soon.'

Daisy was working herself into a furious rage, twisting and turning, plucking at the straps. Jess and I, Franny and Simon looked at her mutely. Despite our inexperience it was clear that we couldn't just let someone else's child out.

'I have to find a bathroom,' said Nicola. 'Try her again with the apple?'

Nicola disappeared around the corner. Mark, holding a limp plastic bag containing brown apple chunks, looked at us, then at Daisy. He put one finger to his lips, winked and knelt down in front of the pushchair. Daisy, with red, tear-filled eyes, grew quiet staring at him as he stared at her.

'Look, Daisy,' he said.

He took one of her little pudgy hands and pressed it on to the pushchair buckle. He pressed down himself too, until the buckle sprang open. Daisy wriggled free, hiccuping and stumbling in her haste to get out of the chair.

'You all saw,' said Mark. 'She let herself out, didn't she? There was nothing we could do.' He leaned over to kiss Daisy's head.

She, now calming down, put her hand out for his and led him off to try to eat the bowls of potpourri.

When Nicola returned, Mark shrugged and said, 'She must have learned how to do it herself,' and Nicola was too distracted preventing Daisy from hurling herself into the fireplace to consider this very carefully.

For memory's sake in the late afternoon we visited the old house in Jericho, rather like grandchildren paying a visit to an elderly relative – hoping for treats, dreading to see signs of decrepitude. The house had been shut up for several years now, and the garden was almost as overgrown as when I had first visited it. The base of the sundial was covered by long grass, the brambles had made the pathway to the frog pond impassable. The house itself had that damp smell again, a smell of old rot.

We were charmed to find Franny's elaborate revision timetable still on the wall in her old bedroom, with the days counting down to finals crossed out until the very last one, still left uncrossed. Simon's old room contained piles of his lecture notes – most of which started hopefully at the top of the page, but quickly degenerated into elaborate doodles with the occasional jotted word or book title. Emmanuella had left clothing, books, a shelf full of CDs and video cassettes. When questioned she shrugged and said, 'But these are not my favourites, you know.'

I think, that if Mark had suggested then that we all come back to live in the house we might have agreed. We had been sufficiently bruised by the difficulties of adult life to make this house seem more of a paradise. But he was too busy with Daisy. He walked down to the carp-pond with her, held her so she could see the orange fish circling under the water and sprinkled breadcrumbs on the surface for them to rise, open-mouthed, to feed. Daisy made the same motions with her mouth, opening it into a wide circle of O and closing it again. It occurred to me that if the fish were still alive, someone must have arranged for a gardener to be tending them. But the functioning of Mark's life was still opaque to me then.

Later on, we all lay on our backs in the long grass next to the sundial.

'This is the wonderful thing about loving Oxford,' said Mark. 'She will never change. Our youth will always be here waiting for us if we want it.'

I was expecting him to make the same promises and plans he always did: come back and live with me, stay here, let's be here forever. But he didn't. Daisy had changed something. I suppose he finally had a reason to want to separate from us.

I had been surprised in general by how much Mark doted on Daisy. When they were together he was constantly holding her, tickling her, singing to her, making faces for her. I had expected that he would be uninterested in fatherhood until the baby became an alert toddler – because then she would be able to give him her attention. Instead, he was transfixed from her first puzzled, finger-grasping days, blinking at the world with dark blue eyes.

He sang 'Daisy, Daisy, give me your answer, do' to her when she was a baby and a little later in life she would believe that he'd written the song specifically for her. Jess and I had visited for her christening and I watched him rock her to sleep in the nursery. The room was small, just enough for a cot, a changing table, a child's wardrobe filled with expensive Italian baby clothes sent by Mark's mother and little cardigans knitted by Nicola's grandparents. It smelled of faeces and nappy-rash cream and talcum powder.

Mark laid Daisy down on her back, pulled the blanket halfway over her and beckoned me to stand and look into the cot. As I did so, he put his arm around my waist and thrust his hand into the back pocket of my jeans. He never found such combinations in any way incongruous. I believe that was the visit during which we made love in his father-in-law's corrugated-iron barn, behind a tractor with clumps of mud and horse shit caught in its tyres, while a sudden spring rainstorm clattered on the roof and passed on.

'Are we damned, do you think?' I remember saying to Mark afterwards.

He looked at me and smiled.

'Damned?'

'For this. You and me. According to your God, are we damned?'

He pulled a crumpled packet of cigarettes out of his back jeans pocket and lit one.

'Only if I die unexpectedly between now and my next confession. You're damned anyway, of course. Atheists are.'

'You go to confession?'

Mark grinned.

'When the mood takes me.'

'Do you confess this?'

'This?'

'What we do, all of this. You know.'

'I confess everything. It feels wonderful. I come out and feel that I've never done anything wrong in my life, that God has forgiven all and I am utterly new again.'

'And then what? Start your wickedness all over again?'

Mark flicked his eyes up at me and held my gaze. His eyes looked deep blue, cornflower blue and hooded, more mysterious than ever.

'This isn't wickedness, James.' He leaned forward and planted a kiss lightly on my lips, pulling away when I tried to draw him closer. 'Don't you realize that you are the thing that allows me to be a good husband?'

He jumped to his feet faster than I could manage and was off and out of the barn while I was still struggling to pull myself upright and go after him.

Mark and I did not always have sex when I visited Dorblish. During Daisy's first two years of life, he came to London half a dozen times, and on each occasion we reverted to our usual ways, but the distance between each visit was so great that, each time, I began to wonder whether in fact we had now finished with that episode in our lives, whether the occasional lapse was a mere aberration. I was even able to convince myself that this was what I wanted. After all – I was able to think away from Mark's presence – hadn't our affair run its course?

And then he would call some afternoon and say, 'Oh, James, I thought you might like to know I'm running up to town for a few days next week. It's half-term, isn't it, James? Would you like to meet up? At my flat, on Tuesday afternoon?' And I would say yes. And when we met he would stand above me and gently insist that I admitted the truth, and I might enquire, 'What truth?' and he would explain that I knew quite well what he meant, and prove it to me until I could only shout out that yes, I still desired him, that yes, I wanted him, and this gave him satisfaction.

Daisy grew sturdy and sweet. She learned to say her own name, 'Daidy', and mine. She began to recognize Jess and me, to trust us as she trusted her family. Once, on a walk, she could not quite clamber over a fallen log and held out her little hand to mine with such an expectation of my aid that I felt suddenly heartsick at the charm of her. I wondered then what she might make of me when she was grown. If she knew the truth, what would she think? Dirty old man, corrupter of parents, breaker of sacred trusts. She already knew how to place her hands together to pray with Nicola before bed; she would grow up a Catholic child, and I doubted that her views on morality would be as flexible as Mark's. I took her hand and grabbed her around the waist, lifting her high into the air as she giggled and shrieked. But she'd already grown too old to enjoy being held. As soon as we were past the log, she struggled and wriggled until I put her down.

Did I imagine it, or did Nicola not want me around her child? I began to notice this, or think I noticed it, when Daisy was nearly two. There began to be a little habit. Jess and I would arrive for a weekend and Nicola would say, 'Good news, my parents are taking Daisy for the weekend. You've just got time to say goodnight to her and Mark will drive her round.'

And we'd protest of course, but Nicola would say, 'No, we grown-ups should be allowed to talk. I'm sure that's what Mark wants, isn't it? Grown-up talk like you have in London.'

And there was a little business of bringing Daisy out, beginning to be sleepy in her pyjamas and socks, and a round of kissing and maybe a story or a game, and then Mark would buckle her into the car seat and drive her around to Nicola's family. They were so close that this back and forth was constant; they drove to each other for meals, to watch television in the evening, and to ferry Daisy between all the places she was loved the best. Mark had his wish: to be at the heart of such a family.

And at this point, Mark would say, 'Oh, James, keep me company on the drive?'

And I would say yes of course, certainly I will.

And on the way back there was a place, invisible from both houses, a sharp bend in the road where we would stop the car and allow ourselves to be overtaken by desire. Cars rocketed past us round the bend, faster than I thought safe, but we were parked on the verge and Mark would say, 'It's fine, it's fine, they go faster in the country than we do in the city.' And I thought of making some joke about how fast we were going now, but the moment had passed and his scent was too intoxicating and his hand on the bare skin at the small of my back was too great for thought.

*

And one night, after one of these visits, driving back home to London, Jess said, 'Darling, something awful.'

She was driving. I was lolling in the passenger seat, drifting on the edge of sleep.

'Mmmm?'

'Nicola thinks Mark's having an affair.'

I was cold. Just that. As if I might have been cold for a long time but had only just noticed. I tried to decide what sort of noise an innocent man might make.

'Really?'

'Mmm-hmm.'

A click, a tick-tock. Jess changed lanes.

It seemed plausible to sit up a little, to open my eyes.

'Does she know who with?'

Jess shook her head, keeping her eyes on the road.

'She thinks it's someone he sees in town.'

Cold again. Very cold. Cold and empty.

'Huh,' I said.

'Have you ever seen him with anyone?'

I swallowed, made a noncommittal hmming sound.

'Don't think so. Not that I've noticed.'

Jess nodded.

The traffic thickened a little. The car slowed. I opened the window a crack. To the right and left of us were luminous yellow fields of rape and lanes of traffic, fumes, honking.

I swallowed. 'It'd hardly be surprising, would it? I mean, we know what Mark's like.'

Jess nodded. 'Yes,' she rolled her shoulders, stretching the joints. 'I think Nicola wants us to talk to him for her . . . but there's nothing we can say really, is there? He is how he is. He always has been.'

A pause. The traffic inched to a standstill. An engine revving behind us.

'What's she going to do?'

Jess pursed her lips. 'I tried to explain that maybe it's not about her. And perhaps she should talk to him. Or find a way to let him know she knows. Because it needn't mean the end to a relationship.

220

Not everyone thinks that way. Perhaps Nicola could find a way to accept it.' She sighed. 'But I don't think she understood. I think, if she found out it was true, she would take Daisy and leave.'

The cars ahead started to move again. Jess nudged the car into gear and began to gather speed.

21

Nicola's voice, whispering from behind the hedge, said, 'Yes, I'm sure she does, but you'll have to tell her they aren't suitable.'

Then Mark's voice, angry but restrained: 'I'm not telling her anything of the sort. They're family stones. Daisy can have them set differently when she's older.'

'She's not having them set at all. I don't want any presents from your mother. You *know* how she spoke to me when we . . .'

'She speaks to everyone like that. It's only that you take everything so bloody personally. Look –' now he was wheedling slightly – 'it's not for you or me, it's for Daisy . . .'

'I don't care, I don't bloody care. She doesn't need your family's presents.'

'Oh, for fuck's sake, Nic . . .'

'Don't use that language with me.'

'Oh, what, fucking what?'

A caught-back sob from Nicola, could have been a laugh or a cry of despair.

And then from Mark simply, 'Nic . . .'

And then, 'Don't you touch me.'

At my elbow Nicola's little sister Eloise said, 'Uncle James, I think Daisy's done a poo in her knickers.'

Eloise, who had reached the stage of braces and awkwardness, was holding Daisy at arm's length towards me. From the smell of her, Eloise was right. Daisy's face was screwed up, her body trying to wriggle away.

'Dowwwwwwn,' she wailed, 'want go dowwwwn.'

When we rounded the end of the hedge, Mark and Nicola were gone.

*

And then again, later, in the conservatory. Dark clouds lowering at the horizon, wind whipping up although the day was still bright in our little square of green. Daisy reached out her chubby little arm to her birthday cake and said, 'Cick! Cick!' so Mark cut her another slice and placed it in her reverently open hands. She looked at it with rapt attention – her mother had fed her some earlier with a spoon – then, decisively, buried her face in the cake, came up smothered in chocolate and wiped her hands down her dress.

I was just beginning to laugh when Nicola turned round, looked at her daughter and said, 'For God's sake, Mark, why the hell did you do that? Look at her! Just look at her!'

And it was too sharp, too angry, too loud. It was disproportionate, so that for a moment we were all staring at Nicola. And she felt it too, the heat of inappropriate rage.

'Come here, Daisy,' she said, and pulled the child to her a little too roughly, crouched down and began to scrub at her face with a napkin a little too forcefully.

Daisy, feeling the pressure of so many eyes on her, burst into noisy tears. Nicola sat back on her haunches with a sigh, releasing Daisy's arm, and the little girl ran stumbling to her father, burying her face in his cream trouser leg, covering it in chocolate.

Mark lifted her up, cuddled her to his chest, more chocolate everywhere.

'Shhh,' he said, 'it's all right, Mummy didn't mean to upset you, did you, Mummy?'

And Nicola looked up from her crouch at the circle of her family around her, and at Mark holding Daisy, and at Daisy's smiling complacent face, now that she had attained her father's arms. Nicola made a low noise at the back of her throat, got to her feet and reached for Daisy, but Daisy snuggled closer to her father. Nicola's mouth turned down, her arms still outstretched for her daughter. Her brow darkened, she took a breath to speak but instead turned on her heel and marched back into the house and upstairs.

There was a moment of silence.

Nicola's father said, 'Well then.'

Rebecca said, 'More cake for anyone?'

But soon many of us had to leave.

Nicola did not come down to see us off. We stood in the outer atrium with Mark, next to the piles of presents which had been sent by Simon, who could not come, and Emmanuella, who could not come, and Franny, who also, for some reason, could not come. Daisy was climbing over Mark, as if he were a tree, biting at his neck and ear, pulling on his shirt, popping off buttons as she clambered and dangled.

'I'm sorry about Nic,' he said. 'She's got a headache.'

'It's all right,' said Jess. 'Tell her we send our love. We'll see her next time we're down.'

I leaned in to hug Mark goodbye, and as I did so Daisy detached herself from him and, for a moment, put her arms around my neck. With her softness, she planted a wet kiss on my cheek, unbidden. I have remembered this so often that the memory is worn through and now I wonder if I imagined it entirely.

Mark waved us off as we drove away. I looked back, and saw Daisy still clambering and exploring the contours of her father. And when I think of Daisy now, that is how I remember her still. Slung in Mark's arms like a monkey swinging in a tree. Climbing over him like he was the most solid thing she knew.

About six weeks after that, Mark called me.

He said, 'James?' in a broken voice. 'I'm in London, because Nicola,' but he could not finish the sentence. The tears overran him and he gulped to a wheezing halt.

'Are you at the flat?' I said. 'Do you want me to come over?'

'Yes,' he said. 'Yes please.'

It surprised me, considering the matter as I drove to Mark's flat, that he was so devastated. Perhaps it surprised me that Nicola had managed to accomplish this thing; to pierce the armour and wound him. I have never been able to hurt him myself. I might say I have never wanted to hurt him, but it's not true. I wish he cared enough about me that I could hurt him. I wish I thought that my leaving would cause him pain. I wish I felt I had ever meant more to him than someone convenient to pass a pleasant afternoon or weekend with. I wish that I could break him by telling him I have ceased to love him, but I can't. He will never cry those tears for me. Sometimes contemplating this makes me so angry that I find I want to hurt him. But, of course, that is the one thing I can't do.

When I arrived at the flat, Mark was crumpled in a brown leather sofa by the window. His eyes were bloodshot; the tip of his nose was red. He was wearing a ragged jumper and a pair of old, paint-stained jeans. I let myself in, and he opened his arms wide, like a toddler looking for comfort. I hugged him, his head on my shoulder and the wet of his weeping trickling on to my shirt. After a while, he disentangled himself from me and I poured us both whiskies.

Mark said, 'This is it. She wants a divorce.'

I nodded.

'She thinks I'm seeing someone else. I tried to tell her she was being silly but she's so . . . she's very final, you know?'

I knew.

'And anyway, look. You're not *someone else*, are you?'

Suddenly I was afraid, with a fear louder than my concern for Mark's marriage.

'Did you tell her it was me?'

He shook his head. 'I mean, it's not just . . .' He chewed at his thumbnail. 'You knew that, didn't you, James? You knew that it wasn't just you, didn't you?'

I nodded creakily. I supposed I had known, in a way. He began to sniff again.

'But . . . can't you tell her you'll stop?'

'She won't listen.'

'Do you want her back?' I said. 'Do you still –' I stopped, reflecting on how little I wanted to know the answer to this question – 'love her?'

Mark curled his lip at his empty tumbler. He refilled it.

'No,' he said. Then, 'Maybe I do. Maybe.'

'OK,' I said. 'So it's not . . .'

'It's not that. It's Daisy.' Mark looked past me at the bookshelves behind my head. 'Don't you see? She could take Daisy away from me.'

Ah, I thought. Melodrama. This was the Mark I knew. I spoke gently.

'She can't do that, Mark. It's not legal.' I thought of the thin veneer of gold covering Mark's body, of his touching lack of comprehension of what it could purchase. Children could not simply be taken away from a man with money.

'You'll get good lawyers, Mark. You can afford it and she can't stop you from –

He turned his head to stare out of the window. He was calm now.

'She can though,' he said, 'and she will. I might have the money, but there's enough dirt to be dredged up, and she knows most of it already. The drugs and the boys and the cottaging – there're police records of that. You should know.' He placed the flat of his palm against his forehead and rubbed in a circular motion two or three times, as if trying to ease some sudden pain. 'No judge in the world would choose me over her.'

'It can't happen.' I moved over and sat next to him. 'Fine, maybe she'll get custody and you'll have to visit and . . . it's just life, Mark.'

He said, 'But this isn't . . .' and he stopped and gasped and said finally, 'I didn't want this for Daisy.'

And I thought I could see what the trouble was. Mark had come to a real limit. He would not be able to buy Daisy from Nicola. There was no price. When they divorced, Mark might have to understand that someone else could limit him: like his mother or the word of God.

As if he had pulled the thought from my mind, he sniffed, blew his nose and said, 'Fuck, my mother's going to have a field day. My mother and Nicola, how did I not see that . . .' and he muttered something half into his jersey.

I rubbed his back. 'Love,' I said, 'we'll sort it out, you'll sort it out, it'll be . . .'

But he was talking over me. 'You've seen what my mother's like, you've seen her. Always too close. I know Franny thinks it was Ampleforth that made me go wrong, or Catholicism, but it wasn't. It was my mother, taking me away, wanting me so close to her. She always wanted me too close, never could let me go. And now I'll be right back where she wants me.' He looked at me, the broken veins in his eyes red, face swollen. 'We got much too close, James, when I was a teenager. Much too close.'

'Mark,' I said, 'do you mean that . . .' but he cut me off.

'Don't ask me what I mean, all right? I don't want to talk about any of it any more. That's all.'

He laid his head on my shoulder and kissed me softly – almost pathetically – tugging at my bottom lip. I felt the warmth of his body down my side. I pulled him towards me with a strength I hadn't intended, and our lips mashed together painfully, and I could taste salt, but I did not stop to consider this as I pulled off his shirt.

Later, we lay in bed together, he smoking and I curled up next to him, stroking his chest, his head, his shoulder. I could not help inscribing lines of kisses along his arms and up his neck, writing my worship with my lips.

'I think I should tell her,' he said. 'I think I should just come clean.'

I rolled away on to my back and stared at the spider's web of cracks frosting the ceiling.

'Tell her what?'

He took another pull on his cigarette, exhaled the smoke slowly.

'Tell her about us. I mean –' he leaned up on one elbow and looked at me – 'I don't think she'd mind so much if she knew it was just you. It'd be containable, you know? And then we could give it another go. I think I want that. Another go. I want it for Daisy.'

An icicle of fear.

'You'd tell her it was me? Specifically me?'

'I think it'd make her feel better, you know? I mean, it's only you.'

And I wondered then, with a rush of heat, whether this had always been my purpose. I was always someone Mark could give up if necessary. I could always be thrown out to confuse pursuers.

'And what do you think's going to happen then, Mark? She'll tell Jess and Jess will leave, and then . . .'

Mark sat up in bed and watched me impassively, his cigarette held in calm fingers.

'It's time you two broke up anyway.' He ground out the cigarette in the saucer by the bed and stood up. 'You can't really expect she'll stay with you forever, can you? I'm sorry, James, I have to go.'

He was pulling on his jeans then, and I was sitting in bed, and a madness touched me on the inside of my skull. It was the thought of losing both of them, *both* at one stroke. I thought, and it is only now that I begin to understand that perhaps I was wrong in this, that in losing them I would no longer know where to find myself. There are those who can love without losing themselves: and Jess is one of these and Mark, for all his wild ecstasies, is one of these. And there are those of us who love unboundedly, giving everything, offering up their whole selves as a sacrifice of love. Nothing short of total love was ever enough for me.

I said, 'You can't tell her, Mark.'

He bent down, groped around under the bed for a stray sock and said quite casually, 'I'm sorry, James, honestly. I know it'll be an inconvenience for you, but you can't have expected this to last forever, can you?'

He kissed me on the forehead as if I was a child and I think this was what broke the spine holding me upright. I should emphasize that I loathe myself for what I did next. But desire has very little to do with morality.

I said, 'I'll tell her about the music box. I'll tell your mother.'

And he frowned and half-smiled as he pulled on his socks, because he'd almost forgotten, of course, that I knew things about him he would rather not have revealed.

I spoke slowly. I was working it out as I went.

I said, 'If you tell Nicola about me, about you and me, I'll call your mother in Italy and tell her it was you who smashed the music box that time in Oxford. And I'll tell her about the time you were arrested, and I'll tell her about the drugs, and your other friends in London. I'll tell her you're out of control, mad. Mad like you were before.'

And this pulled the last traces of a smile from him and left him grey, like a man who has seen the open grave before him.

He stopped, one shoe on and one shoe off, and said, with an unconvincing flick of the wrist, 'She won't care. She won't . . . It's all a long time ago. I'm older now.'

'So you won't mind if I tell her. You won't mind if your family know all about the life you've been leading. If Nicola knows, you won't mind.' And, remembering something I had heard long ago, I said, 'You won't mind if they think your *trouble* has come back?'

He stood up suddenly and took a step back, away from the bed.

'Fuck you,' he said. 'Fuck you, James, and fuck your bloody threats. As if you'd even know how to do it . . . as if you'd even know how to make it convincing.'

'I would,' I said. And then, although I knew this was not likely to be true. 'Your mother would take Nicola's side, you know, if it came to it. She would, with all the things I could tell her about how you've been living. And Daisy would be brought up by Nicola and her family and your mother and they'd shut you out forever.'

Mark began to speak but did not speak. He was shaking now, an erupting storm passing through his body. I could see the anger rising up his throat, clenching his jaw, bunching his muscles at the temples, and for the first time I was a little afraid. I thought, I really don't know what he could do.

He looked around the room and grabbed a thick glass ashtray from the bookcase. He glanced at it and then, with a fluid strength, hurled it at my head. I dodged to the side. It hit the wall behind me, shattering into several large pieces, and a shower of glass dust fell over my naked shoulders.

'Fuck!' I said. 'Jesus. Jesus, Mark . . .'

His face was cold and still.

'I'm leaving,' he said. 'I'm not staying in London. I'm going to Nic's family to get my daughter and I'm taking her home with me. Put your clothes on and go.'

He picked up his other shoe and fitted it to his foot. He brushed his hands on his jacket and walked out of the flat, slamming the door behind him.

I sat in the bed for another twenty minutes before I levered myself out, avoiding the chunks of broken glass. I found I'd been nicked; once on the shoulder and once on the ear. I reached over for one of the packets of cigarettes he left everywhere in that flat, pulled one out and lit it. It was years since I'd last smoked; I'd never got much beyond schoolboy experimentation. But the sensation was calming. I opened the window and smoked it slowly. It was November, the day was very cold, an early snow predicted. The cool air was peaceful, bringing up delicious goosebumps over my torso.

I thought, he won't do it. He won't tell her. Not now. I stared at the pieces of broken glass in the bed.

I thought, I'll call him tomorrow, after school. I'll call him then, and he'll be calmer and we'll work something out. I even felt a certain wry satisfaction. I felt sure our argument could be papered over. Nicola and Mark wouldn't last much longer together, that was clear enough. And as long as he didn't go through with his plan of confession, things would be better for us afterwards. Perhaps he would take a house in London; perhaps he would after all have custody of Daisy. Perhaps he'd live around the corner from Jess and me, his great friends, and we'd always be wandering from one house to the other, which would make everything very easy.

I found a dustpan and brush under the sink in the kitchen and swept up the broken glass. I shook out the sheets and remade the bed. He had been angry, of course he had, but that was only to be expected. He would calm down, I thought. He would see that it made sense.

I was lying to myself. Just as I was lying when I decided he had not meant the ashtray to hit me, that it had been an accident it had come so close. And the question I ask myself now, years later, is: would I really have done it? Really? In the moment, would I have poured venom into the ears of Mark's family, revenging myself upon him for all the slights and all the bad grace and all his failure to want me as I wanted him? Or would I have continued to hold his secrets for him, waiting for the moment he might turn back and see me carrying his burdens and feel grateful at last?

It doesn't really matter. He believed that I might speak, and that was enough.

I smoked another cigarette, watching the people walking about the streets. And as the day turned to evening and the cafés and restaurants of Islington began to tinkle and rattle, I let myself out of the flat and went home.

Night, rising from the sea-green depths of a dream I forgot instantly on waking to the insistent sound of a telephone.

Jess, awake fractionally sooner than me, switched on her bedside light. A cloud of yellow and blinking resolved at last into her face looking at mine and the sound of a telephone still. She frowned at me. I attempted to frown back, furrowed with sleep.

She walked into the hall and picked up the telephone.

I heard her say, 'Hello?'

Then, 'It's all right. What is it?'

Then a long pause. Then, 'Oh, God. No.'

She walked back into the bedroom, holding the phone to her ear. Her expression was unreadable.

'Yes,' she said. 'Yes, I'll tell him. Yes, he's here now. Do you want us to come?' A pause. 'All right. We'll see you tomorrow.'

She sat on the end of our bed and took hold of my hand, turning it over to put her palm against mine.

'Oh, James,' she said, and I think I knew then. Nothing other than this would have caused such horror, nothing less would have stretched the skin around her eyes or made her mouth convulse. 'Oh, James, there's been an accident.'

22

There was an inquest, of course. There had to be. A slow judicial uncovering of facts, a piecing together of shattered things, laying out the bones of the matter and noting: first this happened, then this, then this. This is how we make sense of the world, by trapping it in words and sentences, by pinning it like a butterfly to a felt backcloth, killing it to keep it still, so we may trace its lines.

So, there was this: the November night was cold and the road was icy. Slides were shown of the ice on the road, the place where the tyres failed in their grip, the long, dark streaks where Mark's foot had hit the brake but the car had not stopped, and had not stopped, and had not stopped. The depth of the tread had been measured, the length of the skid marks, the distance to the point of impact. The figures were carefully recorded.

And there was Mark's condition. Not drunk, it was ascertained, not over the limit. His blood and urine had been tested, but nothing of note had been discovered. He was lucky in that, if one can call it luck. If he and I had not argued he might have stayed in London for his usual excursions which would have left their traces. But if we had not argued and he had stayed in London everything might have happened differently. At the least, if we had not argued his mood might have been different. Mr Winters, they said, was in an agitated state. He and his wife had argued, the coroner heard. A separation had been discussed. A highly agitated state. It was recorded.

But was he speeding? No. At the point when the brakes were applied, it could be calculated using various models, the car was travelling at between 40 and 45 miles per hour. Perhaps a little fast for an icy country road late at night, with a child fast asleep, he thought, strapped into her car seat. Perhaps a little fast, but not excessive. One would not criticize him, said the police witness, on that score alone. And we who knew how Mark drove when he was in a highly agitated state, we who had seen him take his eyes from the road . . . I who had seen the bead of sweat on his upper lip and known that he himself did not understand why he did what he did . . . We did not speak up, of course we didn't. It was too late for that, too late for it to do any good. No one could know, now, precisely what had happened despite all tests and calculations. The night was cold. The bend was sharp. The speed was not excessive. These were the preliminary conclusions. Mr Winters, approaching a sharp bend, did not perceive the patches of black ice on the road. The front nearside wheel of his car hit the ice, causing the car to skid. Mr Winters wrenched the wheel, an overcorrection. The car hit a second patch of ice and skidded for several yards before colliding first with a fence and then, careening sideways, a tree at the side of the road. On impact, the car was travelling at approximately 20–25 miles per hour.

And the child. Yes, here we came to it. I heard the sigh in the fingers of the coroner as he turned the page to look once more at the photographic evidence. I did not see the photographs, did not wish to see them. I believe that Franny looked, with Simon. I believe that he wanted to see. Mr Winters, they said, naturally thought the child was asleep in the back seat. He had picked her up from her grandparents' house – 'wildly demanded her,' one testimony reported. They did not think it wise to withhold the child from him although the hour was late and the child already asleep. She could in any case be carried to the car, fastened into her seat and taken to her own bed without waking her.

He would have held her close to him, as he always did. The inquest did not go into this point, but it is clear to me. He would have smelled the milky, honeydew-melon scent of her breath and heard the quiet snuffle of her snore. Daisy, asleep, always had a look of tremendous seriousness; a frown between her closed eyes. He would have held her close to him and kissed the side of her neck and placed her, with such care, sleeping into the car seat, and fastened the buckle at her waist.

On this point, a great deal of time was spent. Who had seen him buckle it? Who had heard the harness snap shut? Had they been certain the click was heard? It was a matter of grave importance, not least for the manufacturers of this brand of child's car seat, and for the several thousand other parents who had purchased the same brand in the past three years. It was necessary to apportion blame, if blame there were to be apportioned. For when the car was examined it was clear that the buckle was undone. Could she have done this herself? The evidence was inconclusive. It had been known for children to undo their car seats, although a parent carelessly fastening a seat was more common. Mrs Winters had in the past seen the child trying to undo the buckle, little fingers and thumbs pressing down on the central latch, tongue out in concentration, pressing and pulling. Daisy was always trying to free herself from harness. Mark encouraged her. But there was no way, at this stage, to be certain.

The child had been in a deep sleep when she was placed in the car, it was concluded, but the cold might have woken her. Would Mark not have noticed that she had awoken? Would she not have cried out? Would he not have seen her move? Ah, but he was in a highly agitated state. And she, sleepy and confused, might have made a little noise but been drowned out by the roar of the engine through the cold and frosted night. Perhaps Mr Winters had not, in his agitated state, fastened the buckle correctly. Perhaps it had already been open. Or perhaps Daisy had worked her little fingers down under the tight-fitting straps to the buckle, where she had pushed and wiggled until the webbing holding her in place released. It is so hard, sometimes, to tell the difference between the bindings that trap and those which secure; too hard for a child to know.

It was impossible now to ascertain which of these scenarios had occurred. But certain it was that, at the moment of impact, the child was unsecured. At the first impact, she had been thrown forward, upward and to the side, into the window. She did not, as the expert witness averred, 'exit the vehicle', but the impact was sufficient to crack the window's toughened glass. It was then that the most serious injury was sustained: the fracture of the skull, the unstaunchable cerebral haemorrhage. The second impact had thrown her back against the floor of the car, but the damage this had caused was by comparison minor. If the parents might find a modicum of comfort in it, the coroner said, they could be assured that the child had died without regaining consciousness.

The verdict was accidental death. The coroner expressed his sorrow. The grieving parents could not look at one another as they passed from the court into the brittle winter day without.

For several days, it seemed that no one spoke. There was a rushing sound constantly, like the sound of planes taking off, a blanket of noise which made speech intolerable. For several days, there was nothing in the world but the sound of weeping.

But there was madness, too. A hideous, scrabbling, madness which blew in great choking lungfuls through us so that we cried out suddenly, or woke terrified in the night, or looked at ourselves in the mirror and thought, I do not know who that person is, I do not know at all. There was no reasonable response but madness. There was no reason.

Jess developed again the eczema which had not troubled her since childhood. Long raw streaks appeared on her legs and on her back and on her freckled chest, burning weeping flaking patches as if she had been licked by flame. She could not bear to be touched; even the flick of a bedsheet as she turned in the night could make her cry out.

Mark did not attempt to hide from us the fresh scars, red and raging down his arms. He had come to stay with us because Nicola did not, because she could not, because they were not, there were no words between them. Even the language of glances or of touch had gone, even that. And because she blamed him, yes of course that too. There was no evidence of dangerous driving and yet we knew, we all knew, every one of us knew. It might have happened to anyone, the coroner had said, and yet it had happened to Mark. An icy road, an unfastened buckle, a highly agitated state.

And so there was a taking of sides. Simon, of course, was with Nicola. The family wrapped itself tightly, a nexus of guilt and pain. I did not hear their conversations, but I can imagine how they would have spoken between themselves, each one saying to the other,

'Why didn't I stop him? Why didn't I tell you to stop him? Why did we hand over that sleeping bundle, why? What were we thinking?'

Franny attempted, at first, to go between sides. She loved Mark, she did, and hung on his neck and wept with him, and all her sardonic wit was gone and instead she lit cigarette after cigarette for him, holding two between her lips and lighting them both and passing one to him as if she were giving him oxygen or vital medication. But she loved Simon too, and it was hard for her. She grew pinched and drawn as the days went on, harder and with her grief inside her like a stone.

It came to an end one day while Jess was in the bathroom of our flat dressing the fresh wounds on Mark's arms and Franny and Emmanuella had walked on to the balcony to smoke. We were talking of nothing, as we did, and Franny became silent and then said, with a return of her sardonic smile, 'Has it ever occurred to you that, if Jesus and God are the same person, and God made Jesus suffer on the Cross, then Jesus is a self-harmer?'

There was a shift in the atmosphere. Emmanuella moved her weight from one leg to the other and threw her cigarette over the balcony.

'A self-harmer too, I mean,' Franny persisted, 'like Mark.'

Emmanuella moved suddenly, with a jerky motion unlike her accustomed grace, half hesitating as she acted. She took a pace forward and slapped Franny hard across the cheek.

Franny staggered back, her hand clutching her face.

'Fuck!' she said. 'Fuck, what did you do that for?'

Emmanuella was impassive, her features calm.

'It is not to joke, Franny, not about such things, not now.'

'Fuck,' said Franny, nursing her face.

Emmanuella watched her and said nothing.

And after that Franny did not come to our flat any more.

There were days and days to wait before the funeral. Acres of time to fill. And after the first numbness, the days were long and the nights were terrifying. Mark raved and stamped and wailed in the night, not sleeping or waking from sleep to find the knowledge new and fresh and all horror once more. We put a photograph of Daisy in the living room and it seemed both too much and not enough. Father Hugh visited Mark and sat with him for an hour in silence. Mark's mother telephoned, but he would not speak to her. Jess applied aqueous cream to her red-raw streaks and Mark came home with pills in tiny bags or with folded pieces of paper and we waited for the funeral.

It was for Nicola's family, that responsibility. There was never any argument about that.

Rebecca telephoned to let us know the arrangements. Here the location, here suitable hotels (and here, she told us, the family's hotel, the hotel we were to keep Mark away from). She preferred not to speak to Mark. Once, he leapt up as I was talking to Rebecca and grabbed the phone from my hand.

'Where's Nicola?' he demanded. 'I want to talk to my wife.'

In the silence of his listening we heard Rebecca's crisp tones buzzing through the receiver.

'She doesn't want to talk to you, Mark.'

The old Mark would have wheedled and persuaded. This Mark said nothing; like a broken prisoner, he hung his head and passed the telephone back to me.

Later, I said to Jess, 'I expect they wish they'd never met him.'

Jess said, 'He saved Leo's life. He still did.'

So few things in life permit clear calculations. Unlike the equations of velocity and heat transfer I'd learned at Oxford, the effect of one person's life on another cannot be weighed in micrograms. 'What is truth?' said jesting Pilate, and would not stay for an answer.

Something disturbed me before dawn in the hotel on the morning of the funeral. I awoke quivering, alert. A thump, a series of clanks, a muffled thud from the connecting room; Mark's room.

The door was unlocked and he was not in bed. The bedsheets and duvet were tangled and twisted. The drawers of the dresser had been flung about the room, the table upended. A keening sound came from the bathroom. I opened the door. Mark was leaning over the sink, breathing heavily. In his right hand he held a razor blade, which he was pressing deeply into the surface of his chest, just below the collarbone. Blood was running down his arm and chest, thick like syrup. There was blood in the basin, and on the wooden floor, on the white towels. There was a bloody handprint on the mirror, where he'd been leaning. He looked up, his pupils large and dark.

He said, 'James.'

He said, 'I can't. I mean, it's not. It's not a good time for a party, James.'

I felt my heart thump in my throat.

I caught at his arm, the one with the razor, trying to pull the blade from his grasp.

I said, 'Stop, Mark, stop.'

And he started to scream.

Jess called her father, the GP, staying in a hotel a few miles away. Mark was seeing things. He talked about ghosts and demons, horses and angry avenging angels. I walked him up and down on the balcony. The night air calmed him a little and the screaming stopped but not the muttering, the slow murmur of sibilant syllables.

'Somewhere,' he said, 'somewhere something, I can't I can't stop, stop them, ask, she didn't ask, she says.' He picked at the gushing wound on his chest.

Jess's father was all cool medical professionalism. He shone a light into Mark's eyes and tipped out one tiny white pill from a brown bottle.

'Now,' he said, looking directly at Mark and holding his gaze, 'I'm going to give you something to make you feel better. Do you think you can swallow this little pill?'

Mark nodded abruptly several times.

I washed the blood from my hands, brought him a glass of water and he took the pill.

Jess's father said, 'It'll take about twenty minutes to kick in.'

He took Mark's hand in his and laid Mark's head on his chest. And then Jess, stroking the hair at the nape of Mark's neck, began to sing:

'Au clair de la lune, mon ami Pierrot,
Prête-moi ta plume, pour écrire un mot.
Ma chandelle est morte, je n'ai plus de feu.
Ouvre-moi ta porte, pour l'amour de Dieu.'

I wouldn't have thought she'd remember, but memory is a strange thing and pulls what is necessary from secret crevices at urgent times. It was the tune of the music box, the sound he had loved as a boy, and after a while Mark did begin to calm. His muttering ceased, his fidgeting grew still and, a little later, he yawned.

Jess's father looked over Mark's cuts with professional calm. Seven deep lacerations above the heart; we could see the sickening white of rib at the bottom of some of them.

'I'm going to suture these now,' he said. 'It might sting a bit. We could go to the hospital if you'd prefer.'

Mark shook his head. No, he would not prefer. His eyelids were sagging and then creeping open again, whites of his eyes flashing.

It was a slow and meticulous process, sewing Mark back together. It reminded me of my mother, when I was a child, sewing up an old toy whose stuffing was falling out. The needle went in through the flesh and slowly the thread was pulled after it. And again. And again. Sewing the skin together with even, elegant stitches until all the raw edges were gone. While he worked, Jess's father muttered to Mark, telling him the stitching was going well, that it would soon be over, that he was a good boy. Mark meanwhile lay perfectly still, breathing in and out, his raked chest rising and falling.

When it was over Mark slept, and we changed from our blood-stained clothes and went downstairs to drink coffee.

Jess's father said, 'He was lucky you found him, James. Another few minutes with that razor and he could have done very serious damage. If he'd passed out from the blood loss he . . .'

He paused. We understood what could have happened if Mark had passed out, bleeding heavily, alone in a hotel room in the middle of the night.

He continued, 'You know, when Jess was little, I thought about this constantly. Constantly. How many ways there are to hurt a child.'

He took a gulp of coffee.

'One tries not to let them know, naturally, but one begins to be haunted by these visions the moment they're born.'

He took Jess's hand and pressed the back of it to his lips.

Mark held my hand through the funeral like there was no other thing in the world he knew for certain. He threaded his fingers through mine and gripped so that he could lean into me. His feet did not know how to walk. His toes pointed in. He was lamed.

There were crowds there. They washed around us like the tide, sweeping in and out, impersonal in their scale. Mark clearly did not know a great number of the people who approached and pressed his hand between theirs and told him they were so sorry, so very sorry. And some of them were sincere, of this I am perfectly certain. But one or two were there for quite different reasons. At one point, a man turned from us and said distinctly, 'That's Mark Winters, I know, but where's cousin Tom? I want a word with him; I've some business he'd be interested in.' And a woman, seeing Mark's mother behind her veil, turned to her companion and said, 'Isabella's looking old, do you see?' And I would not have believed, had I not been there, that such crassness was possible. But for some people nothing that happens to someone like Mark can ever be real. It is Mark's money, his shining golden armour. They make his very essence appear unreal. This, too, is Mark's problem: the details of his life are so dazzling that most people cannot see past them. His false exterior is so grand that no one can quite understand, that even I can sometimes scarcely grasp, that he is real, there, behind the trappings.

I don't know who had chosen the priest. He was a little man; not imposing, like Father Hugh. He was small and mostly bald, with wispy tufts of hair at the sides of his head and for all I knew he had never met Daisy and never seen the sweetness of her, never known the delight she took in blowing bubbles into her milk through a straw. He stood before the small coffin, in the full and buzzing church, robed in his authority, and said, 'This life is but a garment that we wear for a little time.' And slowly but insistently silence spread throughout the church. Because we wanted sense, that day.

He said, 'Grief is a journey which, if we undertake it, can bring us closer to God.' And he said, 'The death of little Daisy may cause us to ask if God is really here, if He is indeed real. How could a loving God, a just God, a merciful God allow such a terrible thing to happen?' He paused. 'If there is no God, then these things are truly meaningless. And for some, that meaningless life is enough. But there are those of us who look at this world, and its mystery and beauty – at the beauty of Daisy's life, however brief – and cannot accept that it is all for nothing. There is meaning even here, if we can see it. We trust in the promise of the Cross and know that –' and here he read from the lesson – '"now we see as through a glass, darkly; but then we will see face to face. Now I know only in part, then I will know fully."'

'We cannot know the purposes of God. But if life has any meaning then this too has meaning. And it must. It is simply impossible that it does not. We trust in the resurrection to eternal life. And we know that the living God can speak through the smallest of us, the least of us. He speaks to us now through the short life of Daisy. We know that her precious life was full of joy and significance. We must trust that the best of her continues. God has even now enfolded Daisy in His arms. She has gone home to be with Him who waits for all of us.' And here the man's voice broke. '"While we are at home with the body, we are away from the Lord."'

Mark was sobbing then, silently. And as the tears poured down his face he turned and put his lips close to my ear and he said, quite clearly, 'All I want now is to be with her. Everything in this world is broken. Everything here in this world is wrong. It is not our home.'

I grasped his hand very tightly and I thought, then this is what I am here for. Here, to save him from this. To wed him to the earth. I had not yet thought of what might come next for me, after this cracking open of the ground beneath our feet, but it became clear to me that whatever happened, I could not leave him.

Mark tried to speak to Nicola after the funeral – went up to her, murmured a few words. She listened, stony-faced. He spoke a little more, gesticulating as he always did when he was nervous or unhappy. He reached for her hand. She pulled away, her face suddenly angry.

Or perhaps simply desperate, for I saw tears starting in her eyes. She spoke a few words to him. He blinked and swallowed. She turned her back on him and walked towards the roadside, where Simon and the family were waiting.

Out of the massed ranks of the family, only one figure separated itself and walked towards us. It was Leo, awkward in his black suit. He must have been eleven or twelve by then? He had shot up like a leggy plant, tall and skinny, very unlike the little boy he had been. Mark flinched when he saw him. His hand went up to his forehead, to the little crescent-shaped scar half-hidden at his hairline.

Leo smiled. I think it was the first smile we'd seen that day.

He stuck out his hand and said, 'I'm sorry, Mark, I'm so sorry,' as though the whole thing had been his fault.

I think Mark barely even noticed who was speaking to him. He stared at Nicola until the car drove up and she was taken away from him as surely as if she had sunk to the bottom of the ocean.

Emmanuella came back to London with us, sitting in the back of the car with Mark while Jess and I shared the driving. Jess's father had given Mark a sedative immediately after the funeral. He lolled on the back seat quietly, sometimes falling asleep, waking a little and then dozing off again.

We brought him into the flat and he sat on the sofa next to me, drifting between sleep and wakefulness. We did not talk a great deal. There was nothing to say. Mark was woozy, confused, his eyes focusing and defocusing.

After a little while I said, 'Mark, we should get you to bed.'

And he leaned over and kissed me, hard, on the mouth, pushing his body into mine, rubbing his thumb at the nape of my neck. It was a lover's kiss, not a friend's or even an attempt at seduction. It was a kiss of intimacy. I jumped away, stood up, took a few paces back from the couch. I looked around the room. Emmanuella was smiling slightly, a confused smile as though she hadn't quite understood a joke. Jess's face was unreadable, quietly calm.

Mark smiled at me, wrinkling his nose. 'C'mon then, lover. Let's go to bed.'

Jess said, 'Can I talk to you for a moment, James?'

I followed her out into the hall.

In the darkened passage I said, trying to bring a laugh into my voice, 'I don't know what that was about. It's just, it must be Mark thinking that I'm . . . well, you know Mark.'

Jess nodded slowly. I barrelled on.

'God knows what that cocktail of drugs has done to him. He's so confused he doesn't know where he is.'

Jess nodded again. She pursed her lips. I tried to say something else but she held up a hand.

She said, 'He's in pain, James. You should go to him. Be with him tonight.'

I didn't understand. I said, 'He's confused. He doesn't really want me. Maybe Emmanuella? Or you, maybe you could talk to him.'

An odd expression flickered across her face then – almost amusement, almost affection. I still think of that sometimes, trying, as always, to understand her. In her way, she was always more opaque to me than even Mark.

She said, 'James. You should sleep in the spare bed with Mark tonight. You should be with him. He needs you.'

It's a strange thing to say, but I think I loved her more in that moment than I'd ever done before, and I had loved her a great deal. It wasn't gratitude, or guilt, simply a fleeting understanding of what she was, this short, slight woman standing in a darkened hallway, wearing jogging bottoms and an old jumper, with her hands on her hips and peeling eczema scars on her arms. I couldn't think, then, why I'd ever wanted anyone but her, how she could ever have seemed nothing to me when, so clearly, she was everything.

'Jess,' I said, wanting to express all of these things.

She shook her head.

'Not tonight. I'm tired. You're tired. We can talk about it in the morning.' She looked at me, her eyes unreadable. 'It's all right. I'm OK.'

And she turned and walked down the hall away from me.

SECTION 3

The Lessons

23

I don't believe that Jess ever asked me to stay. A few days after the funeral, I went with Mark to arrange some matters in Dorblish and she did not object. After we returned to London, I stayed at his flat and she did not beg me to come home. The thing was settled before we had discussed it at all. I was reminded of the way we had become a couple, no fuss and no awkwardness. In the same way now our lives were unpicked without mess, simply and cleanly.

I tried to talk to her but she said, 'He needs you more than I do.'

And I could not disagree with this. Over the spring, Mark began to heal physically – the scars on his arms faded, the cuts on his chest knitted together – but mentally he was worse than ever. There was no sign of improvement. He could not bear to be alone. He woke me repeatedly most nights, imagining monsters and spirits come to punish him.

And I? I remembered several things. I remembered how I had longed for Daisy to be washed away before she began. I remembered how Mark and I had argued the night she died. And I remembered, most of all, Mark. He is the thing I have never been able to loose myself from. And now, for the first time, he wanted me as I wanted him – to be always near me, always close, holding one another. I did not think then of the things I have subsequently come to consider. I knew that I loved him and I knew that, at last, he needed me.

Can I confess this too? It is the worst thing yet, in my litany. It is the thing of which I am most ashamed and which has made me learn the lesson that Mark has always known: that we are not, in essence, good. It is this: I was pleased. Not that Daisy was gone, not that. But pleased because at last Mark needed me. At last, I was not to be thrown away or beckoned with a gesture. I had wanted this; there was a triumph to it. My love had never been enough without his pain.

There was a moment, I think, a teetering point when I doubted what I should do. It was just at the end of the school holidays. I was due to return to the school where I worked. I explained this to Mark and he frowned at me, puzzled.

'I don't understand.' He shook his head. 'Just tell them you won't be coming back. I can pay for a supply teacher or whatever.'

It had occurred to me, but only dimly, that such things were possible. Mark took it for granted that I would not work now. He gave me signing power for one of his accounts. I looked at the sum of money sitting in the current account and was astonished.

'There's enough here to buy a house, Mark. A couple of houses. It should be somewhere it can earn interest.'

He shrugged.

'I think that *is* interest. From something else. I'm not sure. There's a man in the City who deals with it. You can talk to him if you like.'

I took the dog-eared card he gave me from a private bank in London but never called the number. It seemed impertinent. I took what was provided and was grateful. The anger of my headmaster at the late notice of my departure flowed over me and fell away. I thought of it for a day or two and then lost it forever. I began to appreciate what money can provide: a waterproof imperviousness to the demands of others.

We stayed in the Islington flat for a while, and left London in the early autumn, just as the days began to be touched with a moist coolness and the smell of rot. At first, we tried to go back to the house in Oxford, but it didn't take. The rooms were empty without the six of us to fill them, and the memory of Daisy was everywhere she'd crawled and toddled and fallen on the day we graduated. Mark's nightmares grew worse there, the dreams of Daisy sometimes infecting his waking hours to such an extent that he thought he saw her at every turn. And Oxford is so full of youth and joy. We could not be at home there.

We went on. The limits of Mark's territory seemed infinite. We spent a few weeks in a *manoir* in Normandy which had been owned by his father's brother but he thought had now passed to him, 'or as good as, anyway'. My French is extremely imperfect, but the housekeeper seemed to be reminiscing about his mother as a young girl. I mentioned this to Mark but he had no explanation.

In January, the fogs fell over the orchards and Mark became restless. He talked of Brazil, of Bangalore and of Sydney. It was then that we hit upon San Ceterino, the villa here in the heel of Italy which he and Nicola had never visited. We had intended it to be just a way point, a stopping place on a journey which at the time we thought might bring us back to England one day. Perhaps two years of recuperation and then a return. But we have stayed, and stayed, and stayed. It is not that the house or the town has won us with its charms. I believe it is partly the squalor which appeals to Mark, the slight degradation of a town whose once-busy port has all but closed and whose major tourist attraction is a crumbling medieval monastery with a mildly picturesque campanile.

We came to it in the most unattractive part of winter, when the sky was mould-grey and the grounds were so sodden with water that our shoes were half sucked off our feet as we walked the grounds. The beds were all mildewed, speckled and stinking. On the first night, we slept wrapped in rugs on the summer-house sofas, lighting our way with the candles we'd found in crates in an outhouse. We made love that night. As we were falling asleep, he clutched at my shoulders convulsively and whispered, I thought, 'I love you.' It was the first time he had said such a thing.

I whispered, in the chill dark, 'What did you say?'

'Hmm?' he said. 'What?'

The next day, his credit card conjured new beds and furniture, television sets, stereos and extravagant quantities of groceries. Money smooths over all possibility of adventure.

It was the cathedral, I think, which sealed it. In our first week here we walked down to the town and explored its cascading hillside of shops and houses and its dead dock, gazed up at its famous bell tower, which neither of us had the heart to climb. The Cattedrale di San Ceterino is too large for the town, which has shrunk in recent years. It is old and dark, furnished and panelled in burnished brown wood.

It holds a relic of San Ceterino, it is said; the bones of one finger, covered by glass, next to a statue of the saint. One portion of the case is open, just enough for the faithful to touch their finger, or their lips, to one knuckle bone. The brass there is smooth and shiny, the bone itself worn to a brown gloss by the centuries of humanity who have approached, asking for favour, for blessing, for release from the various miseries of human life.

Mark touched his lips to the stained bone. I stood back and looked at the figure of Jesus on the Cross that hovered above us. His back was twisted. His mouth gaped in a silent scream. And I thought, oh, I see. At last I see. It's not about the visible suffering. Greater suffering than this can of course be imagined. It is about the celebration. Even the perfect life of God on earth culminates in suffering. We don't have to clothe ourselves in imaginary woe. Each of us, if we live long enough, will have material for our own suit of sorrow. And when we do, it is this God who is waiting for us: who has known all along that life is nothing but pain.

There were a few months, I remember, perhaps as much as a year, when there was some promise here. When spring sent up fragrant air and soft green shoots Mark talked of inviting some friends from London out for a house party. He had the grounds prepared and the bedrooms aired. I believe he even made some telephone calls, but no one came. That summer was the first time Mark brought home some of the teen-agers from the town. The whole place was prepared for visitors, it was gaping for them. So Mark found some visitors for the house.

One July morning he took a cab into town – he does not drive any more, not anywhere, not at any time – and in the late afternoon he returned with a rabble of teenage boys, about four or five of them. They seemed more to me then. It was only later, when I came to know them individually, that I understood how few there had really been. They were shouting, and as they walked they tossed a rugby ball from one to the other. The day was drenchingly hot, absolutely without mercy. I was in the garden, lying on a sun lounger, struggling through an Italian newspaper article with a dictionary. Mark barely acknowledged me as he and the young men walked past. His eyes caught on mine and slid off. One of the boys finished his Coke and tossed the empty bottle into the swimming pool, where it landed with a gentle plash. He laughed. The others, more apprehensive, looked at Mark. Mark looked down at the bottle slowly filling with water, circling and being dragged under. He raised his eyebrows and grinned. The other boys laughed. They went into the house. I watched them go. After a minute or two, I dived into the pool to retrieve the bottle from the tiled floor. I held it in one hand and floated, eyes closed, ears filled with water, weightless.

Later, when the boys were gone, Mark came out to talk to me. He sat on the lounger next to me, wearing only a pair of shorts, his hair tousled.

He said, 'You don't mind, do you? It's only for fun. I need something to take my mind off.'

'Can't I do that?' I said. 'Aren't I enough?'

There was a pause which seemed to last for hours. I could hear the sounds of children playing in the nearby fields, that high-pitched shouting which carries for miles.

He shook his head.

I don't remember feeling anything in particular at that moment. Except, perhaps, a slight sense of recognition, the fulfilment of an old prophecy.

He bit his lip. 'It doesn't mean . . .' he said. 'I mean, it's not that I don't want you. And you could –' he attempted a little smile – 'well, there's nothing to stop you, if you want to. I mean, there's nothing to stop you joining in.'

It was a generous offer. He was more tongue-tied than usual as well. I focused on these things.

After a while I said, 'It won't be every day, will it?'

'Oh no,' he said. 'Not that often. Just. Sometimes. You know.'

The truth was, I did know. I might try to turn this into a moment of betrayal and loss, but it was nothing of the sort. I know perfectly well that sex is sex and love is love and one need not imply the other. And I knew that Mark's adventures with sixteen-year-old boys did not mean that he didn't love me, just as I had known that my liaisons with Mark had not meant that I no longer loved Jess. I knew it then,

I had always known it and I did not begrudge him these pleasures. Mark and I had made no covenant. He and I, and now these boys, were in the business of keeping him alive – a longer and more arduous journey than I could have imagined when I undertook it. And if the price of his life has increased over the years, it has grown so slowly and subtly that I have scarcely noticed.

Eighteen months or so after we arrived in San Ceterino, I found a job. Mark was unhappy about this, uncomprehending and despondent.

'I don't see why you *need* it,' he complained.

I did not see why I needed it either. Nonetheless, I continued. My options were limited – I got the only job for which I was in any way qualified. I became an English tutor to businesspeople and would-be emigrants in San Ceterino. I have, over time, become rather fond of my gently determined pupils, with their ambitions for business expansion, or promotion, or a move to a different country. I find something charming in their dreams. Mark doesn't agree. He calls them my waifs and strays, my hopeless ones. Once, on a particularly bad day, when it really seemed that he should not be left alone, I took him with me to my lessons. This was not a good experiment. Mark's Italian is excellent, much better than mine. I can't always follow what he's saying. After those visits, two of my pupils requested that I should not come and see them again.

It would be ridiculous to attempt to contribute to the upkeep of the house. The housekeeper comes every morning; the fridge is filled with the bounty of the seasons whether I work or not. The wages I earn are meaningless when compared to the unfathomable depths of Mark's money. And yet I do work. I save the money I earn. It has become a tangible record of achievement – a tiny heap of useful things done. And time passes. It seems to me sometimes that I have come to the end of my life. Time passes here in San Ceterino, but it changes very little.

Mark's regret over the swimming-pool soup did not last long. Summer is his favourite season of the year – the town is full of young people with time on their hands. June melted into a blistering July and more young men and women traipsed up the hill to our house, escaping from the insistent irritation of the tourists and the demands of their parents, and hoping for the parties which Mark did not cease to provide. He was starting to look a little old, I thought, compared to these dewy-skinned young people. When he stared into the mirror and demanded my opinion of his faint crow's feet I said I couldn't see any lines at all. I wondered what he might be like in twenty or thirty years' time – fifty or sixty years old and still bribing the young to keep him company? What was it he was looking for in these people? Was it simply that they were beautiful and easily dazzled, with a natural sympathy for those whose lives were as chaotic as their own? Or was he seeking a memory of himself in better times? Or, in some curious twist, a memory of Daisy, who would by now have been approaching her own teenage years?

'Do you know who I miss?' he asked me one evening in late July.

We were sitting in the pergola behind the apple orchard. He was drunk but placid. We had had a visit the previous day from several of his friends – they hadn't made a mess, nor had they left him in an unbearable condition. My sister Anne had telephoned earlier in the evening with the news that Paul had been appointed a Junior Minister while she had risen another rung in the department dealing with the regulation of edible oils. Mark and I had already passed a pleasant half-hour in mocking them.

I knew who he missed, but I hadn't expected him to talk about her so easily.

'Who?' I said.

'Nicola.' He said it looking away from me, towards the trees, with an expression of firm decision on his face.

'Nicola?'

'Yes,' he said. 'My wife.'

This was not strictly an accurate description of their relationship. The divorce papers had arrived a couple of years earlier and he had signed them with all the appearance of disinterest and then spent the next four days insensible with drink.

'Oh,' I said.

'What do you think she's doing now?'

'I really don't know, Mark.'

He nodded sagely.

'I've been thinking,' he said, 'that we should have some more children. Don't you think that's a good idea?'

I noticed myself breathing in and then out. I moved my thoughts around Mark while he sat, cow-eyed, looking at me. It must be the drink. He has these lapses occasionally – not quite a loss of function but more an intensification of certain parts of himself, a voicing of impulses which he normally knows are absurd. Had he only had alcohol or something else as well?

'Mmmm,' I said.

'Yes,' he said, 'I think that would solve everything.' He paused and took a sip of his drink. 'Do you know why I married her? Because the moment I met her I thought, she will make a wonderful mother. And she has done. She was. She ought to be again.'

This was not the first time he had tried to explain to me why he had married Nicola. It is a subject he returns to often, each time proffering a different interpretation of the facts. I wonder if he even remembers his own feelings, after all this time.

'I think,' I began gently, 'that Nicola might have moved on. You know, it's been a long time since you last saw each other. She might not feel the same way any more.'

'Hmmm.' He took another sip of his drink, as though we were having a perfectly reasonable conversation. 'I don't think so. You see,' he said, gesturing with his glass, splashing some of the contents on to the baked earth beneath, 'Nicola has a sort of loyalty to me which can never entirely vanish.'

'Ah,' I said.

Mark took this as permission to continue.

'I can see why you'd think it, of course. After all, you and Jess never had that kind of relationship. In your case, you were the dog and she was the master, while with me and Nicola it was quite the other way around.'

I thought my silence might stop him pursuing this avenue.

'Yes,' he went on, 'it was always like that between you two, wasn't it? I always got the feeling that she didn't love you so much as *tolerate* you. You would have forgiven her anything. But one little slip from you and all your usefulness to her was gone. Dogs have to be faithful, after all.'

'I think that's enough on this topic, Mark.'

But he was warming to his theme.

'Of course you've always been like that, haven't you, James? All you can ever do is follow someone round. Jess, and now me. I wouldn't be surprised if before Jess you used to follow someone round at school. Or your sister! Did you go to Oxford just because your sister did? Honestly, it's surprising Jess put up with you as long as she did.'

'Mark! Stop this now please.'

He turned his face to me, hard and sneering. I was reminded of the way he'd been in Oxford the first time I'd met him, of the way he'd said 'the paramour'.

He said, 'Do you know what, James? All you ever are is a reflection of other people. With Jess you were loyal, with me you're dissolute. What *are* you really? Nothing. You're all shadows and mirrors. All you've got is the power to ingratiate yourself with whoever you're around, to make them like you. But the thing is, James, it doesn't work. We *don't* like you, none of us do – I don't and nor did Jess.'

He must have seen my face turn at that. A colour or a shading of the features. He has always been so good at picking up these little cues.

'She talked about it with us in Oxford. She thought you were *boring*, James. She said so to the rest of us. She thought you were boring, and did you know, did she tell you, that she slept with a violinist in her orchestra the term she was a soloist? When she was playing that Sibelius? Did she tell you that? Because she told *us*.'

'That's not true,' I said.

'It is true. They slept together that term and she almost left you, but she couldn't bear it because you were so *pathetic*. That's the kind of loyalty you inspire.'

I gathered together my towel, my book, my bottle of water. I stood up and said, quite quietly, 'Whether it's true or not, we both know that you are the one who needs my pity, not the other way around.'

I turned to walk back to the house.

*

The first blow caught me sharply on the side of my head, hard enough to make me reel dizzily and half-turn in the direction it had come from. Mark's second punch, to the bone below my eye and catching my nose, sent me sprawling to the floor, a red flare exploding behind my eyes, a sickeningly familiar agony in my right knee, the pain suddenly vivid like a whip crack. I put my hand to my face and there was blood on my fingers, and I think I tried to say something at the same time as noticing that Mark was wearing shoes, not sandals, and although I saw him aim a kick at my stomach I could not process it quickly enough to think how I might defend myself except that I wanted to make myself very small.

The kick, when it came, felt like it had forced the acid out of my stomach as well as the breath out of my body. I felt that I would vomit at any moment, that I was already vomiting. I saw the blood from my nose and my eye on the stones beneath my head and I realized that only one of my eyes was open.

I managed to whisper, 'Stop, please,' and, looking down thoughtfully, he did stop. He tipped his head to one side and after a few moments, saying nothing, he walked back to the house.

When he was gone I was surprised to find my body still breathing. In and out. Without any directions from me. There. In and out. Breathe, my body said to my mind, breathe. And after a short pause it said, come on. This has happened before. It is possible to survive. Stand up now. Walk away. Come on. Breathe.

Mark was in the converted stable block, watching videos – I could tell from the noise. I stood wincingly. I had fallen on my damaged knee and, as I put weight on it, a bright star of pain flared in the joint. I limped to the main house, supporting myself on the wall, and found my stick in the umbrella stand next to the door. I packed a bag quickly – a change of clothes, sunglasses, my wallet – and called a cab, telling it to meet me at the end of the drive, not at the house. Through all of this, I continued to breathe, entirely without my own volition.

24

I went to a hotel in the town. They know me there, and know not to ask about the blood on my face and the blossoming red and purple across my eyes and cheek. Nevertheless, I put my sunglasses on before I went in.

In the room, I called down to reception for ice and rinsed the blood from my face in the basin. I bent my head one way and then the other experimentally. A crunching of gears, grinding of bone, but not too much pain. My nose was unbroken. When the ice arrived, I wrapped some in a cloth napkin and held it to my nose and eye, hoping to stop the worst of the bruising.

It hadn't happened for months, not like this. It doesn't happen above twice a year, if that. And I understand it, although I understand that it can't go on.

I sat on the bed, feeling my knee shriek as it bent. That would have to be dealt with, but in a moment. Outside, it was coming on for dusk, the sky half-visible through the thick dark-red patterned curtains. It is an old hotel in the centre of the town with rooms on two sides with views of the campanile. The rooms are dusty in a way that modern rooms do not become dusty – they have high ceilings and drapes and dark carved wood to hold the dust. I breathed through my mouth – sneezing would be painful at this juncture.

I pulled myself up, holding on to the bedside table for support. I undid my trousers and let them fall to examine my knee. Yes. Some swelling already, a grinding twist as it moved. I prepared another icepack, positioned a chair next to the bed and raised my leg on to it. I sat there, facing the view of the campanile as dusk settled, a napkin full of ice held to my face and another to my knee. The ridiculousness of this situation struck me for the first time and I wanted, briefly but intensely, to call someone to share the joke. I felt that somewhere I had gone wrong, since I found I had no one to call to share a joke as good as this.

Just after sunset a stream of bats began to leave the roof of the campanile. They nest there during the day and come out at night to feed. Against the pink-orange of the sky, they are a steady stream of milling black, pouring from the peaked corners of the roof, smearing dark across the sky before they dissipate into the town and surrounding countryside. Their fluttering noise is loud and uncanny. The event – the evening flight of the bats – is something of a local attraction. Many tourists lie on their backs in the square beneath the campanile, watching the bats pour across the sky. I, sitting in my chair in the hotel, clasping my ice, wearing only a shirt and pants, fell asleep without warning or hesitation.

The next day, I went down to the harbour for lunch. It's a twenty-minute walk and I wanted to test out my knee, feeling it bend and flex awkwardly, but not as painfully as the previous day. I drank coffee and orange juice and had hunks of cheese with bread and fruit. I tried to think of what I should do, but my mind continually slipped off the subject. I wondered again if there was anyone I should telephone. I supposed I could call my parents in England, but the thought was absurd – what would I say? What would they say to me except 'Come home'? There was a thought curling alongside the coffee and the fruit and the view of the ships in the harbour, a simple seductive thought. It said that I would do what I had always done for the same reasons I always had. My debt to Mark was not yet paid, my business with him not yet concluded.

I stared out at the ships, tiny paper triangles on the horizon. A few tourists were meandering along the seafront. An elderly couple had set themselves up with side-by-side easels, painting watercolour views of the sea. A young family dashed past, parents calling the children to heel in clipped Italian phrases. I paid my bill but remained seated, sipping my juice, watching the sea and the harbour.

There was a couple – a man and a woman – a few hundred yards away, at the other end of the curved front of shops and restaurants. They were standing outside a souvenir shop, looking at some postcards on a stand. He was facing in my direction but so far off that I couldn't see his face. Her back was towards me. All I could do was admire her; the long elegant legs in wide, linen trousers, the low-backed halter top, the broad straw hat with a black-and-white scarf tied around the crown. I was looking simply because I thought she was beautiful. And there was something in her bearing as well, a self-control as she stood resting her weight on one hip, searching calmly through her bag. My eyes stung. I shaded them from the sun and looked at her. I found myself thinking, I could love that woman. That one right there, I could love her.

Fantastic, I thought. Just great. Well done, James. As if things weren't confusing enough already. But somehow I couldn't stop looking. She handed her camera to the man at her side, resting her arm lightly on his. She reminded me of something. She slipped off one sandal, shook out a pebble, then replaced it on her foot. She posed, leaning against a bollard on the quayside, and he took a picture of her. She linked her arm into his and they walked away from the quay, towards the centre of town.

I was overwhelmed by a sense of loss – what if, I could not help thinking, what if she were the great love of my life, that woman? I knew it was absurd and yet I could not rid myself of the sensation. Hurriedly, I took up my stick, left a few coins on the table and limped after them.

I knew which way they would go – there's a well-worn tourist route around San Ceterino indicated by the only guidebook to feature the town, and followed faithfully by thousands of tourists each year. First the harbour, then the market, then the campanile and, for the dedicated, the 500-odd steps to the top of the tower. I have never climbed up, though we have lived here for a number of years. I have always feared that my knee might give out halfway, that I might be stranded in the middle of a narrow, worn spiral staircase, people behind and in front of me, stone walls to either side, unable to go either up or down. I felt certain that I would catch up with the couple before they reached the tower, though. Tourists meander, stopping to look at lacework on market stalls or to admire the hand-carved toys. I would reach them quite soon. What I would do then was another matter. Perhaps I would look at her face and find the spell broken. Perhaps I would ask her to marry me. I would have to see when the moment arose. The simple sense of purpose was seductive, after the roiling clouds that had overpowered my brain that morning. I simply needed to catch up with them, there was nothing further.

But they walked surprisingly swiftly. When I reached the corner of the road – a long, straight cobbled street with tiny shops to either side – I was just in time to catch sight of the woman's wide-brimmed hat at the far end, turning left into the market. There were no great crowds, but my stick is awkward on cobbles and I had to go slowly. When I turned into the marketplace, I couldn't see her at all. I looked left and right. My view was blocked by the awnings of the stalls. She could be anywhere. Heading straight through the centre of the market, past stalls selling fish and books and flowers and knitted blankets and wooden painted horses, I made my way uphill. I thought that perhaps, from the far corner of the market, its highest point, I might be able to spot her distinctive hat.

But when I reached the other side I saw that they were not behind me but ahead, already taking the winding path that led up to the campanile. I paid a street vendor for a bottle of water, gulped it down and began the ascent of the hill.

The day was becoming increasingly warm – it was bright and cloudless, the sky a deep and harmonious blue, echoing the colour of the water in the harbour. Sweat began to prickle all over my body as I walked on, slower than the tourist couple, finding myself falling further and further behind. Before long, I caught them only at the corners, at the edges of the winding path, when they were at the furthest end and I at the nearest. They were laughing, walking easily. I was leaning heavily on my stick, pulling my injured leg along with me, the joint becoming stiffer.

With a quarter of a mile to go to the top of the hill, I watched as they bought *gelati* and entered the hall beneath the campanile, where one buys tickets for five euros to make the trip to the top. I said to myself, why am I doing this? I thought, I am trying to escape from my own life by burying myself in someone else's. I am doing what I have always done, following a stranger in the hope of finding a way out of my own maze. The woman is nothing more than a symbol. It is ridiculous. I continued.

I reached the top of the hill and made one brief circuit of the buildings, searching for them. I imagined what her face might look like if she turned and I could see it from beneath her wide-brimmed hat, imagined that it might be a revelation, the kind of revelation that I have always been waiting for. And what would I do if it were? They were not here. They had bought their tickets and were, even now, slowly making their way to the top of the tower. I imagined them urging each other on with gentle camaraderie, relishing the burning in their thighs as they continued the ascent.

And I could have waited. There are two thin staircases, one going up and one coming down. I could have waited by the 'down' staircase as it disgorged the tourists one by one. It might have been an hour or two – people generally like to admire the view once they reach the top – but I could have sat on the bank, bought myself a *gelato* and waited for them to return. My first instinct was to do so, but the thought of sitting waiting, of allowing those clouds to return to my mind, of the aimless hours I might be here filled me with sudden horror. It was very clear to me – up the tower or back to the hotel – nothing else was possible.

I purchased my ticket from the middle-aged woman with dyed black hair behind the counter. She looked at me, flicking her eyes up and down, noting my stick and my bruises. I could hear her thinking, who is this stupid Englishman who thinks he can climb the tower with a stick? She tapped the sign taped to the glass in front of her which said, in several languages, 'Warning: there are 487 steps to the tip of the tower'. I nodded. She gave me a weak, amused smile as if to say, ah, now I understand. The stick is an affectation. You are not crippled but a poseur. She slid a small blue ticket under her window and I took it, rubbing the soft edges of the cardboard along my fingertips. I thought: is this madness? Have I finally succumbed?

The stairwell was cool and dim, a pleasant relief from the wet heat of the day outside. As my eyes adjusted I looked up the staircase, a stone spiral starting broad but becoming rapidly thin, with deep wells worn into the centre of every step by centuries of footfalls. Here, again, were the warning signs in several languages. And what if I heeded the instructions and stepped back? Again, the thought was intolerable. I knew that this was not right, that there must be some other solution, some way that did not involve climbing too many stairs, more than I could reasonably expect to achieve without pain. And yet sometimes, though one knows there must be another solution, one cannot find it. And so we take the only choice we see. Up the stairs.

The stairs were crowded. While I had waited at their foot, another ten or fifteen people had passed me heading upwards: backpacking teenagers and middle-aged couples, families of husband, wife and small children carried on shoulders, even three sprightly women in their seventies, each wearing shorts exposing their various veins, varicose and thread. The good-humoured confidence with which they approached the stairs gave me comfort – the thing surely could not be so difficult? And indeed, the first 100 steps or so (the numbers carefully carved into the walls at intervals) were fairly pleasant, a deep and satisfying form of exercise, causing me to reach down into my lungs for oxygen, past all cotton wool and thought.

At 125 or thereabouts, an awkward step, a deeper than usual dip in its centre, threw me slightly to one side. My knee wrenched and keened, a thrum through my body as of a ligament painfully plucked. I felt the joint misalign and then right itself. I became a little nauseated. I went on a few more steps slowly. The backpackers behind me slowed down too, and I heard a tutting further back, past the bend in the staircase. For a while, I stepped up only with my good leg, keeping the other leg straight to let the knee recover. Some space opened up between me and the middle-aged couple I was following. After ten or twenty steps in this fashion, I went on slowly with both legs. Every time I pushed up with my injured knee the joint gave a lick of pain, dull at first, then sharper and sharper, as if a thread of metal were being worked into the flesh.

By 250, I was counting each step as I trod it. The pain was becoming more intense. I thought, this is absurd. I really should not go on. But the thought of traversing the distance I had already come going down, of pushing past these people, even if such a thing could be done, of squeezing by them, of tripping on their feet or the trailing straps of their rucksacks, of falling again – and here I could feel the sensation of falling in the tendons of my neck and the muscles of my stomach – of injuring myself even more. All these thoughts kept me moving onward, kept me counting the steps.

By 350, I was telling myself at each step that if I just did one more I could turn back. With each step I said it again. One more and I will turn back.

At 400 steps, the pain in my knee was excruciating. Every step was like damp fire, a squelching, wrenching boggy pain. I thought, if I collapse now, they'll carry me to the summit. I wondered how I would be taken down. I imagined a helicopter floating above the roof of the campanile, or teams of abseilers bearing me between them to the ground. I tried to move my attention away from my knee, to focus on my hand instead, or my head, or the bridge of my nose – still aching. But every other step drew me back again to the knee, the bright red pain banging like a fire engine, shouting like a child. With twenty steps to go, I felt something collapse and sag in it, a hollow, desiccated feeling, as though I had put my foot down expecting a step and found none. I knew I could not put any more weight on it. I hauled myself up the last few steps towards daylight with my arms and my one good leg. I thought perhaps I was sweating or groaning, but the pain was so intense it was hard to make anything else out.

As I came out into the sunlight and wind at the top of the bell tower I collapsed with a grunt on the floor in front of the steps. Other tourists gasped and turned to look at me. I crouched on the floor, my injured leg stretched out rigidly. People coming up the stairs behind me stared and walked around me. I heard voices muttering in Italian, asking – when I grabbed a few words from the air and translated them – for a doctor, or what was wrong. And then, mysteriously, I was sure I heard my name. A woman's voice, saying, 'James?' I shook my head. It came again. 'James?'

I looked up. The woman with the broad-brimmed hat was leaning over me, saying my name. She was directly in front of the sun, her face silhouetted. I held my hand over my eyes to look at her.

She said, 'James, are you all right?'

It was Jess.

25

She made all the arrangements smooth, as is so often her way. I said, 'Is it you? Is it really you?' and little else. She arranged for the guide at the top of the tower to radio down to those at the bottom of the tower to stop incoming and outgoing traffic while we gingerly, with stiff legs and braced arms, made our way down. I said, 'But is it you? How are you here?' And she said, 'Yes. Yes, it is. Now concentrate.' Her boyfriend, Seth, a double bass player, an Australian, offered to support me. I refused initially, but when it became obvious I wasn't going to be walking anywhere without help he slipped an arm around my waist and took part of the weight of my body. He appeared fairly good-natured about this enterprise, telling me I hardly weighed more than his instrument. I couldn't think of any appropriate response to this news.

At the bottom of the tower, we collapsed on the grass – I found I could support myself fairly well with my stick on the level – and Seth brought *gelati* and packs of crisps.

'So, James,' he said, 'I've heard a lot about you.'

I nodded and attempted a smile.

'Are you the one who's a quazillionaire?'

Jess touched his arm lightly. Her skin was paler than his, the contrast clear when her fingers rested in the springy blond hair on his forearm.

'No, darling,' she said, 'that's Mark. He also lives in Italy though. Or is that still right?'

I nodded. 'Yes,' I said, 'we live here.'

I looked at Seth, with his disarmingly open features topped by a mass of dirty blond hair. He reminded me in looks of Jess's first boyfriend, Christian, whose picture I had seen in a scrapbook in her bedroom. I tried to remember what the first violin from her orchestra had looked like. I wondered if the memory I came up with, of a ham-faced man with a pug nose, ruddy features but, yes, blond hair, was of the right man. Had I been the only aberration in her collection?

'James?' said Jess.

'Hmmm?' I had evidently missed something while contemplating Seth.

'I said, if we get a cab into town, do you think you could sit comfortably on the ride?'

I could hardly bend my knee. Still, I would have to go back to the town eventually. I nodded.

They looked well together, Jess and Seth, relaxed in one another's company. He was at least twice as broad in the shoulder as she – I imagined what he must look like when performing. Like a gorilla in evening dress, constantly threatening to burst the buttons and beat on his chest like Tarzan. I thought again of what Mark had told me, about Jess's infidelity. It seemed that Jess had sprung directly from my thoughts, like a demon summoned by a magician to answer a particular question.

It was only when we were in the car that I thought to pose the question myself. I was in the front passenger seat. I pulled down the vanity mirror and peered at them in it. His arm was resting casually on her thigh, her hand on top of his.

'Why are you here?' I said.

They glanced at each other, then Jess smiled.

'Sightseeing,' she said.

Seth looked at her.

'We have a couple of weeks' rehearsal break and we thought we'd do churches and cathedrals of southern Italy. How amazing that we should run into you!'

And did you, I wanted to ask, sleep with the first violin of your orchestra, what was his name, something like Rudolph, in Michaelmas term of our third year?

I imagined asking the question. I imagined what she would do in response. Would she blush? Would she deny it? Would her denials be honest? Would I be able to tell?

It occurred to me that she might deny nothing. She might say,

'Yes, I did. What right have you to ask? You slept with Mark.' But it was impossible to ask the question of her.

We found a place in a restaurant on the square. Jess asked me again whether I wanted to find a doctor to look at my knee but I repeated that I did not. Seth looked between us, a mildly interested expression on his clear, broad face. We ordered food, then Jess excused herself for a moment, leaving Seth and me alone.

I looked at him surreptitiously while pretending to peruse the menu. His strength was visible in his broad shoulders and powerful calves. In his T-shirt and shorts he looked as though he might have strolled in from a weightlifting competition. I wondered how he managed to play his instrument without smashing it to matchwood.

'So what do you do then, James?' he asked.

A waiter brought us beers and antipasti.

'I teach,' I said. I speared a prawn with my fork and bit into it.

'Ah, right,' he said. 'In a school?'

'No.' I shook my head. I could feel my mouth becoming tighter. 'I teach English to private pupils.'

'Ah,' said Seth, and took a mouthful of beer, foam just touching his upper lip. 'And you live with the quazillionaire?'

I nodded.

Seth smiled broadly. 'Pay much, does it, teaching?'

'Not a lot, no.'

Seth nodded and took another swig.

'That must be kind of tough for you. Living with someone so rich. When you're not rich yourself, that is.' He popped three olives into his mouth at once.

I found myself wishing, for the first time in twenty-four hours, that Mark was there. His presence always discourages these macho pissing contests. No one wants to compare wallet size with him. Jess precluded further such conversation by returning to the table.

'James,' she said, sitting down and smoothing her trousers with her characteristic, stiff-handed gesture, 'you must tell me all your news.'

News, I thought, *news*. What a curious concept. Of course, other people's lives moved on in this way. There was news – of promotions, of marriages and children, of new purchases longingly saved for, of holidays planned, business ventures undertaken, dreams brought closer or abandoned. So much of 'news' is really about money. The getting of it, the spending of it, the hoarding and increasing of it. Once all possible money has been obtained, what is left of news? Only love affairs, procreation and the passing enthusiasms which substitute for other people's employment.

'We're planning a trip to the mountains,' I said, knowing how little it was to show for several years of my life. 'In the autumn, probably. We'll rent a chalet near the border.'

'Sounds nice,' said Jess, stirring her coffee. 'Do you travel a lot?'

I remembered the time, about three years earlier, when, after watching a late-night National Geographic programme Mark had developed a burning desire to see Peru. For days he was full of excitement about Machu Picchu and the sites of human sacrifice, talking with glee about the marvellous Incas and the wicked Spanish who had forced them to stop their wholly excellent practices. He booked plane tickets within the week, and paid for hotels and excursions from Lima, but the day before we were due to go to Rome to start the first leg of the journey he changed his mind. Sulking, he said that he'd rather stay home after all, and no persuasion of mine could move him from his bed. When the time came the next day for the planes we were supposed to be on to depart I thought of how I would have behaved if I had paid for the tickets with my own money, if I had had to scrimp and save to afford them, to dream for months of the trip. This is a feature of wealth: by allowing one to do more, it prevents one from doing anything.

'No,' I said, 'we don't travel a great deal.'

There was a long silence.

Eventually, realizing it was expected, I said, 'What about you? Do you have news? How are your family? How's Franny?'

Jess smiled. 'Hmmm . . . news.' She put her hand to her lips; her nails were neatly manicured, with pale pink polish, perfect half-moons of white at the tips of her fingers.

'You know Simon asked Franny to marry him?'

I shook my head. It was like hearing about events on Mars. I could hardly believe that lives continued in this sensible, joyful fashion.

'She said no. Well, first she said yes and then she said no, so it was a bit difficult. They got back together after, well, you know –' she looked down – 'after Daisy. She said it was too much, too fast, too intense. I understood what she meant, but Simon obviously didn't take it well. In a way, I can see what he meant too. I mean, they've known each other for more than ten years, so it's hardly *too fast*, is it?'

I shook my head, unsure of how to respond.

'Anyway, it's all done now. Franny's teaching something clever at Harvard: psychology of consumption. Oh, *and* I think she's a lesbian now. Or bisexual. She's in a relationship with a neuroscientist woman anyway. Her name's . . . ummm . . . Rachel something. She wrote a very popular book – *How to Work Your Brain*? Something like that.'

'And Simon?'

She pursed her lips. 'He's back to the usual. Working all hours – I think he's in Rio now. The last time I saw him he brought along a French lawyer called Béatrice – very glamorous, about six feet tall. But I can't see it lasting really.'

I nodded.

'Emmanuella's become rather unexpected. You remember she was seeing that man with fifteen titles and a pedigree back to the thirteenth century?'

'Mmm-hmmm.'

'Well, *she* broke it off. No one quite knows what happened, because he was absolutely the best catch her parents could have envisaged. I think they were pretty cross. She went a bit strange, actually – it was a few months after . . . after you and Mark left the country. She kept sending me bits of cloth blessed by saints, and now she's gone off to volunteer in Africa. With nuns, if you can believe it, working with AIDS patients.'

I blinked. I tried to imagine glamorous Emmanuella working with the terminally ill in Africa.

'Oh!' said Jess suddenly. 'Do you remember Leo? Simon's little brother? The one Mark rescued from drowning?'

How could I possibly not remember Leo? He was Mark's one good deed, his saving grace.

'Can you believe he's off to college next year?'

'God, not Oxford?'

Jess laughed, then stopped and flicked her eyes towards Seth and then back to me again.

'No,' she said. 'Not Oxford. Agricultural college. In Wales. He's turned out rather the healthy outdoors sort.'

'That's great,' I said, and meant it. I found this thought pleasing – of little Leo grown to manhood, healthy and strong.

'And how,' said Jess, 'is Mark? How are you and Mark?'

I looked down at the table, then up at Seth, his smooth face still blandly interested.

'We're fine,' I said brightly. 'Still the same, just fine. Nothing much to report.'

She looked at me and chewed on her upper lip. The clock in the square tolled out the quarter-hour with sonorous slowness.

'Seth, darling,' she said. 'James and I have a few things to talk through. Could you maybe get me some of those soaps we saw in the little shop by the harbour this morning? I want to give some to Granny.'

Seth gave me a thoughtful look, as if he were deciding precisely how quickly he could knock me cold should it prove necessary.

'Right-o,' he said, and leaned over to give her a swift kiss on the mouth. I felt emotions rising in me at this to which I had no right at all. With his water-bottle carrier slung over his shoulder, Seth loped off towards the harbour.

'Don't mind Seth,' she said. 'He's only a bit jealous. He doesn't mean any harm.'

I nodded and made a noncommittal noise.

'He knows we were together for a long time and he's worried you might have gone stalker, that's all.'

Jess poured herself a glass of red wine and held it up to the sun.

'Look,' she said. 'What were you doing climbing that tower today? With your knee? Were you following us?'

'Yes,' I said simply. Then, thinking that this needed some explanation: 'I saw you from a distance. I thought it was you, but I wasn't sure, so I followed. OK?'

She traced the edge of the ashtray with one fingertip.

'Yes, I suppose so.'

'My turn?' I said.

'OK.'

'Why are you here? Why are you in San Ceterino, really?'

She looked up swiftly and then down again.

'We're here on holiday,' she said.

'Here? Of all places?'

'We are,' she said. 'We had holiday, we wanted to do something with it. And Italy's so lovely at this time of year.'

'And that's the only reason you're here?'

She frowned.

'Well, there's also –' she spoke quickly – 'Nicola's getting married again. In the autumn, she's marrying a Yorkshireman, a farmer. We're all invited to the wedding – well, Franny and Emmanuella and me and Simon of course. And it made me think of you both, and how someone should tell you, and I suppose I could have written but you never answer letters, so Seth and I were planning a holiday and I thought if we came here for a couple of days maybe we'd, you know, bump into each other. Which we did. So . . .'

She trailed off and went back to playing with the cocktail sticks on her side plate.

I wondered if her answer contained the same measure of truth as mine.

'And that's all you wanted to tell me? That Nicola's getting married?'

'I thought maybe you'd write to her. I know that Mark wouldn't. But I thought maybe you could just tell her . . . well, that's what I thought, anyway.'

The evening chimed around us. A flock of doves paced the piazza floor, pecking at stones and crumbs. Across the square an accordion player started up a melody with lambent brio. Three children chased over the paving stones.

Jess raised her hand to my face and traced her finger around the outline of the blossoming bruise. The sensation reminded me so strikingly of the first times we had touched in Oxford that it made me hold my breath.

'James, what's this?' she said.

'Oh that,' I said. 'I walked into a door. Stupid of me.'

She looked at me, her eyes very clear and light, and shook her head.

'No,' she said. 'That's not what it is.'

'No, it's not.'

'Is it the marks of love, James?'

'I don't know,' I said. 'Is it?'

She pursed her lips and paused, then spoke very softly. 'No,' she said, 'I don't think so. He's poison for you, James.'

I looked down at my hands and then out across the square.

'That wasn't what you said six years ago.'

'No,' she said, 'it wasn't. But I think I've changed my mind. I think that's what I came here to tell you. Perhaps I didn't know it until now.'

I remained silent.

'And,' she said, 'something else as well. I want to say you don't owe me anything, there's no debt between us. I knew, or thought I knew, about you and Mark for a long time. Maybe even before it started. It was that last day in Oxford, wasn't it?'

I nodded, dumbly.

'I've always thought, well, it was a different sort of thing. It wasn't that you didn't love me, I knew that you did. But I couldn't be that for you. And you were so happy, *we* were so happy when it was happening. You were happier than I'd ever known you.'

'You didn't mind?' I was bewildered.

'I think,' she said, running her finger around the rim of the ashtray again, 'I think that I didn't. I wish it hadn't been Mark, for your sake. And I wish we could have spoken plainly with each other. But that's all.'

Jess took a sip of wine. 'Oh,' she said, 'Seth's coming.'

I looked up and there he was, the gorilla-man, hulking his way through the crowd. He was still a little way off. We had time for a few more sentences before he arrived.

I thought, I could say now what I thought while I was following her. I could say, 'I saw you from a distance and knew that you could be the love of my life.' I could say, 'Take me back. You are all I desire.' I could say, 'I love you. And I know you love me.'

Instead, I said, 'Jess, do you remember the first violin from your orchestra in Oxford? Rudolph something?'

She frowned. 'Randolph,' she said, 'Randolph Black. Yes, why?'

'Did you sleep with him, in Michaelmas term of our third year?'

Seth was approaching rapidly across the square, smiling.

Jess remained silent.

'Did you?'

She looked at me and shook her head.

'Really?'

'James,' she said, 'after all this, why would I lie to you?'

26

Jess and Seth left me the details of their itinerary, where I could find them if I wanted to find them. She did not specify why I might want to find them again. She copied the names of hotels and phone numbers and dates on to a square of card and pressed it into my hand. As she did so she said, 'Remember.' Just that.

In my room at the hotel, I stripped naked and stood in front of the mirror. I observed myself, turning one way and the other. That, I thought, is me. There, that man is me. I could not quite make the connection. That man, I thought more slowly, that man with the pale skin and the gammy knee and the decent arse and the dark arrow of hair pointing towards the genitals. That is me. I lifted my arm and let it flop down, watching how it was me. That face, long, with a sorrowful arrangement of nose and eyes, more like my father with every passing year. That face is me.

I heard once that a puppy raised among kittens will grow up thinking it is a cat, will behave like a cat, will move like a cat, will not recognize dogs as its own kind. I thought of the society in which I'd spent the past fourteen years of my life: the rich and the glamorous, the successful, the driven, the talented. Mark and Emmanuella, Franny, Simon, Jess.

But that man there in the mirror, that man is me. I have done less with these past years than Anne with her edible oils or Paul with his position as a Junior Minister. Even those accomplishments, which once struck me as so crass, now seemed solid to me. More solid than myself, a man made of smoke. They would be something to hold up against my body and say this too is who I am. I had never desired accomplishments, never longed to be a doer of great feats. But, it occurred to me, I should have tried to desire *something*. Or can one try to desire at all?

What is it that one learns from life? I had always supposed that

I would accumulate some wisdom as my life progressed. That, as in my progress through Oxford, some knowledge would inevitably adhere to me. I suppose I hoped that love would teach me.

But the very question is redundant. It is ridiculous to think we can learn anything from so arbitrary an experience as life. It forms no kind of curriculum and its gifts and punishments are bestowed too arbitrarily to constitute a mark scheme. There is only one subject on which the lessons are in any way informative.

That man in the mirror is me, I thought. For good or ill, that's me.

After two nights and three days in the hotel, my bruises had faded from livid purple and red to yellows, greens and browns. I kept my sunglasses on even in the hotel lobby. In the privacy of my own room I examined the bruises in the mirror.

And on the third day I returned to the villa above the city. Mark was waiting for me by the swimming pool. Ricardo, a boy who had been one of Mark's favourites but, at twenty-four, had grown too old, was sitting on the stone wall by the patio, flipping through a magazine. Seeing it was me, Mark leapt to his feet, smiled almost shyly, turned to Ricardo and said, in Italian, 'Get out of here.'

Ricardo grunted, looked between me and Mark, then jumped off the wall and walked sullenly back towards the house.

Mark walked to me slowly, smiling, holding his arms wide in a gesture of welcome, or surrender.

'I'm so glad you came back,' he said softly.

He pulled me close to him, lifted off my sunglasses and examined the side of my face, my eye, my nose. He breathed out a heavy sorrowful sigh.

'I'm so sorry,' he whispered into my neck. 'I'm so so sorry. I didn't mean to do it, you know I didn't mean it. You know how I am.'

I nodded and wrapped my arms around him. I thought about how-he-is. Was that an explanation for anything? I had once thought that I could come to some deeper understanding.

He lifted his face contritely for a kiss and I bent to kiss him, tasting again the taste of Mark: cigarettes and mint chewing gum and black-currant wine gums.

'Listen,' he said after a while, 'I've been thinking, we should get away from here. I hate this place. It's horrible, being cooped up here day after day. What do you think about moving to Rome for a few months? Or out of Italy? How about autumn in New York?'

He was eager and excited. I brushed the hair out of his eyes and he blinked at me.

'No,' I said, 'I don't think so.'

He tipped his head to one side.

'OK,' he said. Then, as if a little aggrieved, 'What do you want to do?'

'I want to go away,' I said. 'Maybe travel, or maybe go back to England. I'm not sure yet. Not be here, anyway.'

He nodded. 'We could go to England. Not . . . well, not . . . But I think we have a place in Kent? Or how about Cornwall?'

I looked at him and then around at the villa. Our villa. My home. Almost everything I could see belonged to us, from the grove of cypress trees on the hills in the north to the shy little river murmuring its way through a deep cut towards the town. It is one of the most beautiful places I have ever been.

'Not we,' I said, 'me.'

He tipped his face up towards mine and observed me quietly, thoughtfully.

'How long for?' Then, before I had a chance to reply: 'Not more than three months? Be back before the winter.'

As if we were beginning negotiations.

'No,' I said, 'forever.'

Can it be true that I felt nothing then? It is true. I was steel and ice. He started against my body and I looked out at the watercolour hills of misty blue and green and brown and the clouds, huge and sunlit in glory, and I felt nothing at all.

He took several steps back from me.

'What happened today?' he said. 'What happened while you were away? Did you meet someone? Who is it? What's happened?'

I was surprised he had understood so quickly. I sat on the stone wall by the swimming pool, my bad leg stretched out stiffly before me.

'Jess,' I said. 'It's not important, though. It's not about her. But yes,

I happened to meet her the other day in town. With her new boyfriend, from the orchestra. They're on holiday. I met Jess and we chatted, that's all.'

I did not tell him about Nicola. He sat very still as I spoke and nodded, running his hand quickly through his hair.

'So,' he said when I had finished, 'you're going back to her.'

'No,' I said. 'Didn't you hear? She has a boyfriend.'

He shook his head, as if to clear the air of buzzing, swarming things.

'It doesn't signify,' he said. 'She'd take you back if you really wanted her. Do you want her?'

I thought about that. Did I want Jess? Did I want anything?

'No,' I said. 'I don't want her.'

He leaned back in his chair, apparently satisfied.

'Aren't you going to ask me anything else?'

He put his feet up on the lounger and looked at me.

'No,' he said. 'I know you're not going to leave.'

I felt suddenly angry.

'I am,' I said. 'I am leaving.'

'No,' he said, 'you're not.' He cocked his head to one side and smiled. 'Or, well, you might leave for a while but you'll come back.'

'I won't,' I said. 'I'm leaving, Mark. Forever. It's over.'

He smiled, wolfish.

'And what,' he said, 'do you think you're going to do?'

'I'm going back to England. Back to my parents. Start again. Teaching. Life.'

He shook his head, slowly.

'But *James*. Who are you going to follow? Who's going to tell you what to do? If you're not going back to Jess, and you're not staying with me, whose dog are you going to be?'

'I'm not,' I said. 'I'm not.' And, to my horror, I felt tears pricking at the corners of my eyes and a pain rising in my throat.

I turned and walked as quickly as I could back to the house. His laughter followed me all the way.

*

I packed my belongings that night. Mark went out, to one of his usual haunts in the town, I supposed. I did not enquire. There were few enough items to pack but I took my time. I wanted to be perfectly sure that I took nothing of his. The only money I would take would be the carefully harvested earnings from my tutoring. I identified, among my clothes, a few T-shirts and jeans I'd had since living with Jess in London. Everything else I left hanging in the wardrobe.

As I packed, I thought of the conversations I'd wished we would have, the conversations I'd imagined in those nights at the hotel. He would tell me he loved me, he would beg me to stay. At least he would understand what he was losing. He would show by some sign that he understood what I had done for him, what I had sacrificed. He would flash from behind the curtain the man I knew must be within him. I would finally understand him and in that understanding all I had done would be justified. I think, even as I packed, I hadn't fully accepted that none of these things would ever occur.

There is a kind of love which is selfless. It is a love which waits through all things, which is patient and hopeful, which does not need to be returned. It is a love which is confident in itself and burns on and on though no fuel is added to the fire. It is the love of the man nailed to the cross saying, here, look, this wound, and that I took for you. It is a perfect love; more perfect than the love between equals. I do not know if it is a love towards which it is proper for human beings to aspire. Perhaps it is the love reserved for angels, and for the Almighty.

For a long time, I thought I loved Mark with this love. But I was wrong.

When I left the house, before dawn, I scribbled a note and taped it to the refrigerator. I told him to contact Franny at Harvard for news of Nicola. I am a coward, I thought, but at least I am free.

That morning I boarded the train from San Ceterino to Rome. It pulled out of the station at 8 a.m. The journey would take most of the day but I was not dismayed by this prospect. I found an empty compartment and hoisted my suitcase on to the rack above the seats. I opened the window. The air was mild and fragrant. In the verge by the side of the track little blue flowers were growing among the grass. I sat facing the direction of travel as the train pulled out, and looked out of the window to see it curve ahead of me around the track. There was something comforting about the sight of the tidy line of carriages like a column of vertebrae bending this way and that. I leaned back and rested my head on the seat. I had purchased a novel and a newspaper but I did not examine them yet. The train was heading along the coast, so that for much of the way I would see the shining sea to my right hand. I looked out at the water curving off into the distance, the shoreline brightly white, flecks of light dancing on the waves. I heard the sound of Italian voices from the next carriage – boisterous, confident teenage voices arguing and laughing. This moment, like all moments, would be lost. I closed my eyes, inhaled. And when I breathed out I felt nothing at all.

ACKNOWLEDGEMENTS

With tremendous gratitude, as ever, to my agent, Veronique Baxter, and my editor, Kate Barker. Thanks also to Katherine Stroud and Mary Mount, and to Lesley Levene and Helen Campbell.

Thanks to the London Jewish Cultural Centre for giving me a place to write the first draft of this novel, and to Detective Inspector Andy Rose, Commander Shabir Hussain, Steve and Toni Hazell, Chris Philp and Adi Bloom for help with research. Special thanks to Jey Biddulph, web wizard, and Guy Parsons, rock god.

For support, pep talks and inspiration, thanks to my parents, Geoffrey and Marion Alderman, my brother, Eliot Alderman, Anna Balinsky, Deborah Cooper, Jeremy Cooper, Esther Donoff, Russell Donoff, Daniella, Benjy and Zara Donoff, Dr Benjamin Ellis, Diana Evans, Natalie Gold, Dena Grabinar, Bob Grahame, Yoz Grahame, Tilly Gregory, Peter Hobbs, O. M. G. Adrian Hon, Dan Hon, Victoria Hoyle, Rivka Isaacson, Rabbi Sammy Jackman, S. W. J., John Kemp, Ewan Kirkland, Rebecca Levene, Joel and Emma McIver, Margaret Maitland, Mariana Nolan, Helen Oyeyemi, Andrew Page, Andrea Phillips, Helena Pickup, Gabriela Pomeroy, Robin Ray, Poppy Sebag-Montefiore, Jennifer Seligman, Miki Shaw, Lord Smith of Clifton, A. C. Ben Todd, David Varela, Perry Wald, Adrienne West and Samuel West.

He just wanted a decent book to read ...

Not too much to ask, is it? It was in 1935 when Allen Lane, Managing Director of Bodley Head Publishers, stood on a platform at Exeter railway station looking for something good to read on his journey back to London. His choice was limited to popular magazines and poor-quality paperbacks – the same choice faced every day by the vast majority of readers, few of whom could afford hardbacks. Lane's disappointment and subsequent anger at the range of books generally available led him to found a company – and change the world.

'We believed in the existence in this country of a vast reading public for intelligent books at a low price, and staked everything on it'
Sir Allen Lane, 1902–1970, founder of Penguin Books

The quality paperback had arrived – and not just in bookshops. Lane was adamant that his Penguins should appear in chain stores and tobacconists, and should cost no more than a packet of cigarettes.

Reading habits (and cigarette prices) have changed since 1935, but Penguin still believes in publishing the best books for everybody to enjoy. We still believe that good design costs no more than bad design, and we still believe that quality books published passionately and responsibly make the world a better place.

So wherever you see the little bird – whether it's on a piece of prize-winning literary fiction or a celebrity autobiography, political tour de force or historical masterpiece, a serial-killer thriller, reference book, world classic or a piece of pure escapism – you can bet that it represents the very best that the genre has to offer.

Whatever you like to read – trust Penguin.